Shaman's Fire

a novel

SANDY CATHCART

with

DIANA SHADLEY

Visit Needle Rock Press at www.needlerockpress.com

Visit Sandy Cathcart's Website at www.sandycathcartauthor.com

Visit Robert Kruse's Website at www.rmkruseart.com

Visit Ghostdancer Shadley's Website at www.ghostdancershadley.com

Visit Bill Miller's Website at www.billmiller.co (not a typo. Leave off "m")

All of the above can be found on Facebook.

Shaman's Fire

Copyright © 2015 Sandy Cathcart

Cover art by Robert Kruse. Copyright © by Robert Kruse (Photos for cover art by Sandy Cathcart)

All rights reserved. No portion of this book may be reproduced, stored in a retrieval system, or transmitted in any form or by any means-- electronic, mechanical, photocopy, recording, scanning, or other--except for brief quotations in critical reviews or articles, without the prior written permission of the publisher.

Scripture quotations (unless otherwise specified) and quotes by Creator Yahweh are taken from the HOLY BIBLE: NEW INTERNATIONAL VERSION © 173, 1978, 1984 by International Bible Society. All rights reserved.

Words of Bill Miller's song, "Ghostdance," used by permission.

Shaman's Fire is a work of fiction. The events and characters portrayed are imaginary. Their resemblance, if any, to real-life counterparts is entirely coincidental, except in the character quotes by "Ghostdancer." Those quotes are by the "real-life" Ghostdancer Shadley and used by permission from his widow, Diana Shadley.

Published by Needle Rock Press.

Needle Rock Press books may be purchased in bulk for ministry purposes. For information, please email sandycathcart@gmail.com

ISBN-10: 1943500029
ISBN-13: 978-1943500024 (Needle Rock Press)

For—

Grandma Bessie

For sharing stories of our Cherokee Grandmother who was a healer in the Red Rock, Arkansas area. Thanks for keeping our heritage of visions and healing practices alive.

Richard and Katherine Twiss

For sparking the desire in my heart to find out more about my Native heritage and to discover what it means to walk the Jesus Way, fully Native and fully Christian.

GLOSSARY OF KLAMATH WORDS & PHRASES

Blaydal'knii!	God above all
Bonwa	Drink
Cha aat	That's it for now
Cheelaqsdi	Sacred Mountain of vision quests
Dici stinta	One with one another/Good love
Dic li	Good
Giiwas	Crater Lake
Goos	Ponderosa pines)
Hahas? Iwgiss	Teacher
Heyhey	Silver fox
?os ?ams	So, so.
Moo ?am ni stinta	I love you very much.
Moo dic	Very good
Pleya gi	Go with blessings or Be blessed
Qenqan	Grey squirrel
Sat'waaYi?is	Come help me
Waqlis?i	How are you? (Hello)
Saayoogalla	Imitate/Mimic/Apprentice
Sawalineeas	Best friend
Sepk'eec'a	Thank you.
Taamtgi	Be still (Isn't used)
Wach	Horse
Yaks dwa!	Common exclamation, like "Goodness!"
Bustle	Feathers worn on the back of a traditional male dancer
Roach	Male headdress of Porcupine

Chapter 1

*If one lives long enough,
as this old man has,
they will see the shifting shadows
that darken Creator Yahweh's smile.
But they may also see the light of life
that sprouts from those dark places.*
Ghostdancer

Charlie Whitewater
Above the Guano Desert
Southern Oregon, May 17, 2013

SOMETHING OMINOUS twitched in the shadows beyond the headlights of Charlie Whitewater's GMC flatbed, or at least that's the way it seemed to Charlie. For the past thirty minutes he had been catching glimpses of white fragments flashing through the black night. The first flash had appeared as the rear end of an antelope just beyond the left fender. He had pulled the wheel to the right trying to avoid some animal that never fully appeared before he realized he was running from his imagination, mere shadows and sighs.

Foolish old Indian, he told himself.

Next the white patch flashed on the right, impossibly near the open passenger window where Nate slept the sleep of the dead. Charlie's daughter-in-law Melissa slept just as soundly with her head tucked into Nate's shoulder. The hum of the GMC had lulled them both into dreamland.

Charlie had almost called out when he saw what appeared to be a laughing face on the other side of the door, but soon his brain registered the fact that no person could keep up the sixty-mile-per-hour pace he had been pulling across the high plateau, and a face without a body could be nothing more than imagination. Perhaps the long day chasing wild horses across Sheldon Wildlife Refuge had damaged his brain as much as his worn body.

He straightened his back against the bench seat and felt a shudder cross his upper arms. The smell of horse sweat filled the cab. Most men would have slowed when nearing their seventy-fifth birthday, but not Charlie. The day he slowed would be the day they lowered his body into an oven and scattered his ashes to the wind. Even in death he would be moving. Life held too much promise to be sitting around.

Another flash of white flew across the windshield and lifted into the sky. Most certainly an owl, a bad omen for sure. And where did an owl come from way out here on top of the world, where gale force winds kept trees from growing and stunted sage brush to no more than knee high?

A chill rippled across his forehead. If he didn't know better, he would say magic rode the night wind—the work of a shaman. But Jacob was the only shaman in these parts and he had fled long ago. Tribal Council members had suggested it would be in Jacob's best interest to get out of town after Charlie's friend Ghostdancer had discovered the man had been receiving money to cast evil spells on innocent people.

Thinking of innocent people took Charlie's thoughts to his granddaughter Sayla. Nate and Melissa had meant well, but they hadn't done right by the girl, taking her off to Southern California, away from the reservation, away from the horses and land she loved so well. Her songs could not touch the heart of her people while she lived far from the land of the Klamath tribes.

Charlie's mother was full-blooded Klamath. His father was Cherokee and Irish, a mixture that shouted of the changes taking place in the last two centuries. Charlie's family had endured the changes that took their land away from them, and then he and his tribe had battled bureaucracy until their land, including the Sacred Mountain Ranch, was finally restored.

"Bring Sayla back," Charlie whispered to Creator. "Let her fall in love with you all over again."

His mind was in overdrive, sorting out Sayla's problems while another part kept the truck and trailer on the winding road dropping into Guano Valley. He had just passed the hang glider launching area when a white shadow appeared on the left. He registered the outline of a goat and lined up his wheels to hit it straight on. Any other action would send the truck plunging the full six hundred feet to the valley floor beyond; not even so much as a guardrail broke the edge of the road. But then, Charlie registered a man's face in the beam of the right headlight and instinctively pulled to the left. With a screech of rubber, the front tires left pavement and plunged into blackness.

Charlie thought of Loretta and Sayla and prayed Creator would be with them. A knowing washed over him, the sure knowledge his death was no accident but a perfect answer to the prayers he had been praying. It was strange he thought nothing of his own loss. Indeed, he felt no loss at all, simply a wonderful knowing that soon he would be in the arms of his Creator.

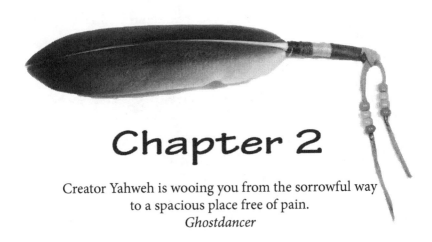

Chapter 2

> Creator Yahweh is wooing you from the sorrowful way
> to a spacious place free of pain.
> *Ghostdancer*

Sayla

    A SINGER, A DEATH, A SHAMAN . . . what have I gotten myself into? I'll tell you my story, though I'm not proud of it. My feet now touch the land of the Klamath Tribes where wild horses run free and eagles soar above sweeping vistas of open meadows and tree-covered mountains along the banks of the singing Sprague River. Spiritual worlds collide here below *Cheelaqsdi,* the mountain where our young men do vision quests in Southern Oregon.

    I lived my entire life here until I decided that living on a Rez wasn't good enough and I finally accepted my parent's plea to move to Oceanside, California where many of our tribe now call home. They told me I had a good chance of making a name for myself and our people down there in the land of white celebrities, and they were right. My plaintive songs caught the white people's imaginations. "Haunting," they said of my voice, and they awarded me with a Grammy, which made my tribe proud.

    I'm not sorry I won the Grammy, but living in a white man's world took something from my soul. How could I have left the lifeblood of this great land where my people have long been in touch with Creator? I just wish it hadn't taken the deaths of my parents and Grandfather to make me return. Now, Gran and I are the only ones to care for the horses and carry on our traditions at the family ranch below *Cheelaqsdi,* Mountain. Of course, Kadai ThunderHorse helps us. He's as much a part of our family as if he actually had Whitewater blood flowing through his veins.

Kadai is another story. I'm still wrestling with my feelings for him. I had always thought of him as a brother until he returned from Iraq. Something dark happened to him there, and I heard stories of how he walked the alcohol way for a while, but he won't talk of it. Now my heart melts whenever he turns his amber eyes on me. He is a man of few words, unless he is talking over the back of a horse, and oh, how he can dance. I fall in love with Kadai every time I see him dance, then I fall out of love as soon as his dark eyes cloud over and he turns back into his shell. That happens every time the old ways clash with his idea of how to worship Creator. He's very clear on his beliefs, more clear than I care to know.

Gran is also clear on her beliefs in Creator as being the same God of the white man's Bible, though she does not see it as white. I always thought I believed the same as her, but after discovering the Shadow Warrior in the shamans fire, I'm not so sure. The old ways seem to hold much more power than her worn out Bible. But then, I'm getting ahead of my story and all good stories have a starting point best seen from afar.

Sayla
Chiloquin, Oregon, August 24, 2014
Sunday afternoon

Modoc drummers beat a tune as old as the earth. My mind groans along, caught up in the tradition of my people, but my voice remains silent. The source of my songs has flown away on eagle's wings far beyond this land of the Modoc, Klamath, and Yahooskin band of the Snake Indians. I fear I will never sing again.

Uncle Cobby taps my shoulder causing the elk teeth and beads on my dress to jangle. "After this you will sing."

I shake my head and stare out over the ceremonial circle. In normal life it is the Chiloquin High School football field, a place where I've held many concerts and have danced in even more powwows. But there's nothing normal about today.

Though it is August and the sun hangs high in the sky, its golden circle is hidden behind a thick blue haze drifting from nearly a hundred wildfires burning throughout southern Oregon. Dancers on the other side of the field look like ghosts drifting between worlds. Filling the bleachers beyond the dancers are the people who have come to hear me sing. I have not promised a song, but they expect it, because today marks the end of our mourning, and we are getting ready for our Coming-out of Grief Ceremony.

First, we will give away gifts, including items belonging to our dead relatives. This is unusual but Gran insisted we honor others first. Then we are expected to dance our way into a new life. After that, I'm expected to sing, even though not one song has touched my heart for over a year.

A clap of thunder shouts from the sky, making its voice heard over the beating drums. Curious and frightened eyes look upward. Weather forecasters call it an inversion. Gran says we must trust Creator for whatever he gives this day, including the weather, but it doesn't surprise me Creator has chosen to hide on the very day we could use the light of his smile. He did the same a year ago when he took away my parents and grandfather in a mysterious accident.

But I still have Gran.

I shoot a glance at Gran, making sure the lightning didn't strike her dead on the spot. It would be just like Creator to take her away too. The basket hat sitting atop her gray braids reassures me she is okay. A breath escapes my throat in one long swoosh.

"Look at the people," Uncle Cobby says. "See how they honor your parent's memory."

Tears flood Uncle's wrinkled eyes. They remind me how much he loved his father and brother, and I am shamed at thinking only of my own loss. I open my mouth to answer, but the taste of wood smoke clogs it. I turn instead to examine the sea of people either taking part in or watching the Grand Entry.

Tribal members from Warm Springs and great distances have shown up in their finest and most colorful regalia trimmed with singing bells. Interspersed among the tribal members are Grandfather's white friends. There are many of them, for Grandfather Charlie was generous in both his hospitality and wisdom. Patches of red and gold painted buckskin mingle among cowboy hats and blue denim. Enough eagle feathers adorn heads and bustles to cover the small town of Chiloquin. Grandfather would have loved to see such a turnout. So would my parents, but none of them are here to enjoy it.

"You must sing, Sayla. Do it for Grandfather." Uncle's rumble of a voice is now demanding. He expects me to do as I'm told; as well he should, because I've always done exactly what I've been told in the presence of my elders, like a good Native girl.

Now, for the first time, I shake my head.

A strange gust of wind whips across the field, knocking bustles askew and tumbling shade tents that had been standing like sentinels around the dance circle. In one powerful swoop the wind takes the smoke away and the sun appears. A shiver runs down my arms in spite of the blazing August sun suddenly beating down on us. I am cocooned in a heavy deerskin dress trimmed with rows of elk teeth and beads that make their own music when I move. The dress alone is usually enough to make me swelter, and the leggings above my moccasins stretch to my knees, adding to the heat. Two wide beaver fur extensions hang from my dark hair. These are not the thin hair extensions white girls weave. These lie heavy on my narrow shoulders and extend past my waist. The single eagle feather atop my head lets the world know I am a single woman.

Yet, in spite of all the layers, a feeling of doom sends cold shivers into my bones. It is not the storm racing through the sky I fear, it is a tempest from another world, the kind that wreaks havoc in the physical realm. I try to shake off the feeling, but it will not leave. It started this morning when we first stepped through the gate to enter the ceremonial field and discovered one of my former classmates was stabbed in the back four times last night, right there on the street. Choking sorrow gripped me so hard I stopped and gasped for air. It was as if I had hit an invisible force shield. When I finally regained strength enough to move forward, I did so cautiously. This may be the twenty-first century, but some things never change among tribal people. We have always walked with one foot in the unseen realm.

Last night the unseen realm opened to give me a glimpse of my parents and grandfather crashing into the Guano Desert. Did they feel the tongues of flame that took their lives? Or did they, as Gran says, fly straight into Creator's arms?

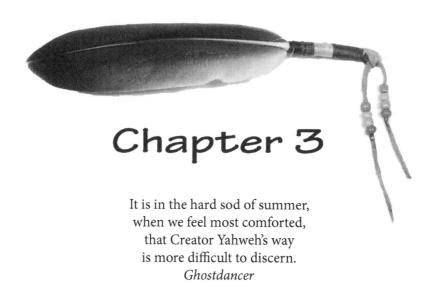

Chapter 3

*It is in the hard sod of summer,
when we feel most comforted,
that Creator Yahweh's way
is more difficult to discern.*
Ghostdancer

Loretta Whitewater

LORETTA STOOD IN HER DESIGNATED PLACE wishing she could take away the obvious pain breaking Sayla's heart. It was a sad thing to see her granddaughter taking a wrong path and walking away from all the things Loretta held most dear. She had tried to warn Sayla. She had prayed for her. She had talked until the words ran cold, but young people seldom listened to their elders these days. And who could blame them? Loretta certainly hadn't been the best example.

I'm a silly old woman, she thought, *who lost my mind for a time and walked a very dark path.* She couldn't bear the thought of her granddaughter following in her dark footsteps. Sayla believed Creator had taken away her songs, but Loretta knew it was Sayla's heart grown cold toward Creator that had deceived the girl. Sayla had turned her back on the Giver of Songs, plain and simple.

And Kadai ThunderHorse. Oh, that dear boy. After all he had been through in Iraq and finally coming back into himself at Sacred

Mountain Ranch. It was easy to see Sayla would soon break his heart. How could Loretta stand by and do nothing?

Yaks dwa! Listen to this silly old woman! Do nothing? Prayer was the first and best thing she could do.

Ghostdancer was always reminding her of that, and he was right. He was the only one who remembered the sins of her youth, the sins that left Kadai without a mother and father, the sins that finally caused Loretta to leave many, but not all, of the ancient ways. Sayla was not aware of such things. Loretta simply could not find the courage to tell her granddaughter that she, too, had once turned away from walking in beauty.

She straightened her eagle fan and put on a bright smile. This Coming-Out of Grief Ceremony was much harder than she had imagined.

Chapter 4

*If you make Creator Yahweh your dwelling place
HE will cover you with his feathers.*
Ghostdancer

Sayla

A PINCH ON MY ELBOW reminds me Uncle will not be ignored. "Don't be so selfish," he says.

He still sees me as his young niece, though I'm twenty-three years old. It could be because of my small stature. I barely reach five-foot-two and weigh 110 pounds. But I suspect it is because he sees himself as wise. I guess being forty-five and living off the reservation makes him a man of the world. It's hard to believe I used to be part of that world. For a year now, since Grandfather's death, I've been living with Gran. I'm all she has, other than Kadai, who refuses to leave her.

Looking over the field, I am glad this year has brought me back to my roots. How could I have ever allowed my parents to drag me from the land and the horses—all that is sacred among my people? How could they have chosen traffic noise over the singing Sprague River that borders our Sacred Mountain Ranch? I will never know the answer to that question, now they are dead, and it seems wrong I still blame them for so much sorrow. The Sprague runs behind me now, on the other side of the fence. It travels from our Sacred

Mountain Ranch and joins the lazy Williamson River dividing the town of Chiloquin. Both rivers give life and song to our daily existence although their song is lost today in the beat of drums.

I know these borders well. To the west are the High Cascade Mountains hugging the Siskiyou Range on the south with snowcapped Mount Shasta rising above them like a great chief in full headdress. On the north is the rim of *Giiwas,* or Crater Lake, as whites call it, which has always been a sacred place for our people. Between the mountains is the Wood Valley, crisscrossed with marshes and teaming with wildlife. Great flocks of geese and ducks live there, often painting the sky white. To the east, on the other side of the hills surrounding Chiloquin are the great grasslands making up our home at the base of *Cheelaqsdi,* the Sacred Mountain of vision quests. Wild antelope graze with our horses on those grasslands and there is no other place in the world quite like it.

As the Grand Entry circles the field, Uncle nudges me again. I throw him my most determined scowl, but the sight of his mournful face undoes me. His is a rugged face, round and full of laugh lines, but today his full lips are squeezed into a hard line and his eyes, shining through the black paint surrounding them, hold the fire of determined courage.

"I am sorry Uncle," I whisper, "I have no song."

Strength goes out of my shoulders as I look at the little huddle of what is left of our family—Gran, dressed in a blue and red cloth dress trimmed with elk teeth. She carries an eagle fan in her right hand, and a beaded purse hangs from her left arm. Gran's two brothers, Cobby and Henry are dressed in colorful regalia trimmed with bone breastplates. Both wear porcupine headdresses we call roaches on their heads, with two eagle feathers sticking out of the top and beaded rosettes and headbands on their foreheads. Their dark eyes peer through paint and beaded webbing. Uncle Cobby carries an eagle-head staff and rawhide shield. Uncle Henry carries an eagle fan. Both men look as if they are ready for battle. My sister Moriah should be here, but of course she's not. She's standing on the other side of the field, shaking her head every time Uncle Cobby waves for her to join us. The sight of her turns my stomach. I've never seen one tear fall from her eyes over the death of our loved ones.

I turn my attention back to Gran. A long line of extended family, cousins I have not seen for years, stand on her other side. A grass dancer stands at the end of the line with his long streams of colorful ribbons flowing behind. Tradition calls for the grass dancer's feet to clear an invisible path across the field before we dance or set up our booths. Earlier today their feet stomped out any evil that might dwell there and made a safe way for us to follow. I wish this grass dancer would stomp across the fields of my heart and crush the demons hiding there.

Uncle Cobby pinches my elbow again, this time harder. "Sing an old song, one of our traditions."

Nausea grips my stomach. He's asking too much of me, and we both know it. I cannot sing over the fallen lives of the people I loved most in the world, especially when there was so much left unsaid. Grandfather should be standing next to me, dressed in white deer hide as a dog soldier with his impressive headdress of over five hundred eagle feathers. I can almost smell the heady scent of his regalia. How I used to love burying my face against his chest as he pulled me into a tight embrace of soft leather.

"You must sing." Uncle Cobby's voice is softer, pleading.

The pungent scent of burning sage comes to my rescue.

Kadai ThunderHorse waves a smoldering bundle of sage up and down inches from my body as he speaks comfort and blessing. "I, too, have known loss," he says, "and the pain that clenches the heart until it can no longer feel."

I know Kadai's words are true, it is the only reason a young man like himself has been chosen to speak the blessing. I cup my hands and pull the cleansing smoke and aroma over my face and hair. Kadai's voice drops to a whisper.

"Seek comfort in Creator, Sayla. I pray you do not allow your heart to grow bitter, that no anger finds fertile soil there, that you will cling to the good things Grandfather taught you." Kadai switches to our Native language as he circles me, until the smoke curls and covers every part of my body from head to beaded moccasins. "*Pleya gi*," he says, but the blessing is lost on me as one without faith. My faith flew away on the same eagle wings that took my songs, the same wind that stole my parents and grandfather.

When I look up, Kadai towers over me. At six-foot-two, he is taller than most of our people. He wears his dark hair in long braids over his wide shoulders. He looks a little like Adam Beach, the Native American movie star all us girls are crazy about. A year ago, part of our family cut our hair in respect of the dead, but Kadai and I gave up dancing instead. The ceremonial roach, with its crown of red fringe and three eagle feathers, sits atop his head and makes him look as wild as the grass blowing in the wind.

"I-I'm sorry," I try to say, but the words catch in my throat.

Kadai nods. He will be the last person to condemn me for not singing. He is my self-appointed protector, and has been since I was a young girl.

Warm liquid slides across my palms. When I look down, I see I've clenched my fists until my painted fingernails cut into flesh. When I look back up, the sight of Kadai's amber eyes takes my breath away. His eyes do that, switching from dark brown to light amber. Now they shine like deep, hidden pools; a secret place that offers safety.

I want to dive into the depths of those pools, to lose myself in that hidden place, to be anywhere but in this stadium.

His dark eyes seem to pierce into the deepest part of me, a place I want no one to see. His raised eyebrows testify he has sensed the foreboding storm that sickens my heart. He has always been spiritually sensitive.

I drop my gaze and take a step back.

A startling cry makes me jump and gasp, but it does not come from the black storm as I expect. It is the shout of a drummer whose voice rises in cadence with the escalating beat. The Grand Entry is nearly finished and our coming-out of grief ceremony will begin. Kadai takes my hand and leads me to help Gran with the gift giving.

For a while I perform the duties of a good granddaughter, helping Gran give colorful Pendleton blankets to our closest family and friends. As usual, Gran has gone far beyond the expected and has also brought special gifts for all the widows. Even in the midst of her own sorrow, she thinks of others. My cousins help spread gifts across the parade grounds in succession, first for elders, then adults, then teens. My heart takes another hit when the children circle anxiously to run out and get their gifts. The tradition is similar to an Easter egg hunt. Grandfather always loved this part. His laughter would ring out loud and long as the peewees filled their arms with candy and trinkets.

When the field empties, I take a step back, causing the shells and beads on my dress to rustle. It is a new dress with special leggings made by Gran for this Coming-Out. The beadwork alone must have taken her a hundred hours. I suspect she sewed each bead with a prayer and a tear that was seen only by her and her Creator.

I'm not as tough as Gran, and my faith in her Creator is wavering, but I know how to hide my tears, and my eyes remain as dry as the well source of my songs.

Kadai's dark eyes catch mine as Gran finishes the gift giving. Worry lines his face as a hushed silence falls over the ceremonial field. Uncle Henry rises to his feet holding the enlarged photo of my parents and grandfather. He steps out with Gran to lead the dance.

When the drum begins to beat and Kadai starts to dance for the first time in over a year, I see Moriah walking across the field. At first I think she is finally joining us, but then I see she is carrying my Martin guitar in her hands with every intention of making me sing. And if that isn't bad enough, I see Grandpa's beautiful bustle hanging on a pole behind Gran. The sight of it undoes me. I turn and run.

Chapter 5

> Do you have an arm like Creator Yahweh's,
> and can your voice thunder like his?
> *Ghostdancer*

Kadai ThunderHorse
(Note to reader: Kadai refers to himself in the second person)

YOUR HEART KNOWS the exact moment the one you love runs. Like a frightened rabbit she runs. And you, who are bound by tradition and honor, cannot follow. There is still much for you to do here this day. You must dance as you are meant to do and then be available to help Grandmother in the receiving line. Yet the muscles in your legs quiver with anticipation as your eyes mark the path of your love's retreat. She soon disappears in the crowd. All you can register is that Sayla is headed for the river.

"Creator!" Your heart cries out. "Be with her!"

You think of the many suicides that have happened in this land, of the sadness and sorrow that chokes out breath. It was no different in the back streets of Iraq where brother fought against brother, a world gone crazy with hate. There too, young ones chose the easy way out, drinking themselves senseless or stepping in front of a tank. You hope Sayla will not take the easy way.

Your heart cannot bear such thoughts of Iraq this day, so you push them aside, but thoughts of Sayla remain. This family you love has lost much, and there is little you can do to heal the pain. You know of such wounds that fester and sicken the heart. Grandmother has healed well, her scars are smooth and shining; she is ready to come out of her time of grief. But Sayla's wounds are deep, and her scars merely hide the sickness that festers beneath.

Though your thoughts are on the one you love, the bells on your feet instinctively match the rhythm of the drum. The drummer's yell is as ancient as *Cheelaqsdi,* the Sacred Mountain where you meet with Creator. You wish you were there now where you could fight for Sayla with flaming arrows whose fire cannot be quenched—arrows lifted high to the heavens. But you do not need *Cheelaqsdi* to wield your weapon of choice. Creator is with you wherever you are, and he hears your every thought.

Prayer is your weapon and its carrier a bird in flight.

"Soar high!" Your heart commands, as you twirl and stomp, each movement as much a part of you as blinking your eye.

You are a trained warrior. You know how to set aside your own pain, yet you find yourself jumping high, looking over the heads of the crowd. There! She has passed through the gate where blood was spilled last night. Now, she stands transfixed in the field, a hand shielding her eyes as she stares at the sky. You see it then, a flash of light, and then an eagle, flying straight for Sayla.

Your heart rests.

This eagle will not harm her. It is sent as a sign.

Chapter 6

> Be careful, child, that no one entices you
> with the object of your dreams.
> *Ghostdancer*

Sayla

KADAI CANNOT FOLLOW ME, for to leave Gran would be breaking high tradition, an error a seasoned warrior like him would never commit. Grandfather's friend, Ghostdancer, trained him well. My teeth clench like stone mallets grinding hard corn as my moccasined feet crunch across the pavement and head into tall grass. My sister, Moriah, and I have never gotten along, but setting me up in such a way during one of our most heartbreaking moments is beyond comprehension. How can a relative be so devious?

I haven't gone far when a sharp cry from overhead pulls me out of my wayward procession.

Halting, I look up, but sunlight reflects off the steeple of the white man's church in the distance striking me momentarily blind. When I raise my hand to shield against the light, an enormous bald eagle appears with its wings spread wide. It's flying straight at me!

Too stunned to drop, I brace myself for the expected pummeling.

A breath of warm wind washes over my face as eagle wings swoop inches from my head. The wind is alive with energy, sending prisms of small rainbows in front of my eyes. Heat rises in my chest in a swell that threatens to burst my lungs. Then the eagle soars back into the heavens and becomes a speck in the distance.

It is a sign.

Of what?

I am not sure.

Gran believes eagles carry our prayers to the sky, that they represent Holy Spirit and Creator's work in our lives. If she is right, the eagle will have to fly far and high, because from my view, Creator is very far away. As if to prove the point, thick darkness falls back over the sun. The wood smoke returns, making me choke and cough. I head to the river and drop down the steep bank, surprised at what I find. It is as if I have been dropped into a bubble of clear air. The Sprague River sings beside me.

The smell of hickory and sage draws my attention to a bonfire, certainly illegal during this season of extreme fire danger. Fascinating that it burns within a circle of rocks on the wet grass next to the river. Seems too wet for a fire. A bronzed skeleton of a man with long gray braids stands on the other side of the flames. A single eagle feather hangs from his hair and he wears nothing but a loincloth. Slashes of red and black markings cover his body. Part of me wants to look away, but a greater part of me cannot.

I've heard of the shaman's old ways, of how he has refused to accept anything considered modern or white, but this is the first time I've been close to him. Gran does not approve of his ways. She claims he has soiled the office of healer and that the title of shaman is a sham. "There are no shamans in our tribe," she always insists whenever the subject is brought up. "There are only medicine men and healers, and this man is neither." Gran is sorry the shaman returned to our tribe a year ago, right after Grandfather died, but others of our tribe disagree. They say he is bringing back the powerful magic of the old ways. They claim he is a great healer.

Perhaps he can heal my wounded heart.

Looking at him now, his wrinkled skin looks as ancient as *Cheelaqsdi*. He seems to care nothing of material possessions or of what people think about him. His gray braids lack adornment, except for that single feather, and he wears no headdress or regalia. Transfixed, I watch as the shaman lifts one clenched fist straight into the flames. He holds it there for what seems an eternity, as if the heat is nothing. His lips move in what I am sure is a forbidden chant. It is both frightening and thrilling. The shaman's dark eyes hold mine and, for a startling moment, I see a storm brewing there. But when his fingers open, magic falls into the fire.

Bright sparkles of light crackle and send heat waves rippling across my bare forearms. I smell the scent of rich earth and spicy manzanita mingled with wood smoke and something else I cannot name. Gold and blue flames dance dangerously close, heat burns my face, but I cannot look away.

Then, impossibly, in the center of the flames, stands a warrior with a headdress made of hundreds of eagle feathers. His hair, dark as raven wings, flows unbound over his glowing breastplate. A ghostly wind blows through the hornpipes of his breastplate creating impossible harmonies. I think of the song of the mythical sirens from my school days. Their enchanting beauty caused sea captains to turn into shore where their ships were tossed and broken by waves. This heartrending song captures me in the same way, and I wonder for a moment if I, too, will be tossed and broken upon those rocky shores.

Untouched by fire, the shining warrior lifts an arm of invitation toward me. His lips mouth one word, stretching my name.

Saaaaaaylaaaaaa.

His voice is the sound of wind whispering through trees, of songs long held secret, of melodies that charm the soul. My heart leaps and I feel strangely comforted, as if Grandfather is standing next to me. I take one step, then two, drawing closer, ignoring the tribal elder's teaching to stand still in the face of a predator.

I don't know why the word *predator* comes to mind, for surely, no predator is as beautiful as this.

The warrior's golden eyes bore straight into my soul.

"Ohhhh." A groan escapes my lips, but this time it is not from sadness. This flaming warrior knows me as no one else ever has. And, oh how I want him, I, a virgin, who has never given my body to anyone.

His arm is still stretched out to me, an invitation to another world where the pain of loss does not exist. Bronzed muscles strain at the band worn high on his arm. The red slashes on his band are familiar, yet strange, something known yet forbidden. I cannot place the significance.

I lift my arm toward his outstretched hand and take one more step. Flames heat my moccasins. I am too close, but I do not care.

Saaaaaaylaaaaaa.

The warrior's voice captures my heart. The pain I have lived with for the last year falls away, lost in his immersing love song. Waves of ecstasy wash over my body and the well source of my songs opens in a rush of joy. I take one more step toward the shining warrior, a song lifting from my lips, but before my foot hits the earth, the stink of burning leather clogs my nose and my outstretched arm drops to my side.

I cannot breathe. Pain shoots up my legs and black smoke fills my lungs, but the call of music is stronger than my pain. The warrior reaches out, his fingers nearly touching my throat.

Saaaaaaylaaaaaa.

Smoke suddenly swirls in the other direction, revealing a vision of raven claws reaching out to dig deep into my neck. I stretch out my arms and cry, "No!"

In that instant, strong hands grab my shoulders and pull me away from the fire. "NO!" I cry again, this time to the one who would save me. The same strong hands beat at the flames rising from the hem of my regalia. The jangling beads and shells on my skirt ring an alarm.

Though the physical pain is excruciating, it is nothing compared to the loss of my beautiful warrior. I struggle and push against the helping hands, knowing they belong to Kadai ThunderHorse, but I am still caught by the shaman's spell.

I push against Kadai and look over his shoulder, yearning for another glimpse of my Shadow Warrior. The last notes of the siren's song rings in my ears. Then all air leaves my lungs.

Instead of my beautiful warrior, I see a solid black shadow hovering above the smoldering embers of fire. Even as I reach out, the shadow form thumps to the ground. A swoosh of black smoke covers me and Kadai, leaving darkness and the stink of wet ashes where once had been glorious light. Pain hits me in one blinding jolt. With one last cry, I am lost to this world.

Chapter 7

*Creator Yahweh loads the clouds with water
and weeps upon the earth.*
Ghostdancer

Sayla
Chiloquin, Oregon, August 25, 2014
Monday evening

"IT'S A MIRACLE, PLAIN AND SIMPLE," Gran says for about the hundredth time.

I'm not sure which is the greater miracle—the fact the skin on my ankles is smooth and unscarred or the fact Kadai was able to convince the hospital personnel I was sane enough to go home this morning. Either way, if my unburned hands are a miracle, then why didn't Gran's Creator heal Kadai? His blistered palms look as if someone took a meat chopper to them. I don't ask the question aloud, because to do so would be disrespectful of my elders.

Kadai sits tall and still with his arms outstretched on the table. Gran applies another fresh aloe treatment. It is the third time today she has done this. The glaze in Kadai's expression signals he is off in that place where strong warriors go when they must bear the impossible.

I look away unable to watch the pain I have caused my friend. I stare, instead, at my Martin guitar leaning against the far wall, a reminder of my sister's deceitfulness.

Red Dog, Gran's faithful mutt, whimpers. The golden retriever in him sympathizes with us humans while the red heeler in him obeys the command to sit at Gran's feet. His skin quivers with the urge to run to Kadai. I reach out and run my fingers through his warm fur.

Earlier today Gran sent me to gather leaves from a healing plant growing along the Sprague River on the north side of our ranch. Now she lays the leaves over Kadai's palms.

The voices of Paul Revere and the Raiders singing Cherokee Nation suddenly blast through the kitchen, alerting me to a call on my cell phone. My bare feet slap across the linoleum as I grab my phone and head to the front porch. Kenny Liparulo, my Italian agent, who lives in San Diego, is on the other end. When my father was alive, they ran a recording studio together. He still acts as my agent.

"Sayla," he says. "Tell me what happened."

I didn't have time to call earlier. I was too busy helping relatives pack up and leave and cleaning up all the pallet beds spread throughout our house. Natives don't often head off to fancy motels; they are content to plop wherever as long as they can be with family. The entire town of Chiloquin has traipsed through Gran's kitchen today offering food gifts. Our refrigerator is bursting with deer and elk roast, salmon, watermelon and boiled potatoes. I plop onto an overstuffed chair with my head on one arm and my legs dangling over the other.

When I finish my story about the warrior in the fire, Kenny says, "Sounds like some kind of demon from one of Steven King's novels."

I straighten in the chair. Speech fails me. White people always think anything from the supernatural world is a demon. But then, Gran probably agrees with him. Coyotes howl in the distance, a barn owl hoots nearby, warm rain weeps on the roof—a fact we are extremely grateful for. It's just a sprinkle, but we're all hoping it will stop the fires. Kenny is not aware of any of this in his San Diego apartment, twenty stories up, overlooking the harbor.

Kenny says, "Or you've been popping some weird drugs."

"No drugs," I assure him. "You know I don't use them."

"Then what was it?"

I remain mute. Kenny does not understand our Native culture. To us the spiritual realm collides with the material world every day. I am torn between a terrible sense of loss and an overwhelming fear. I yearn for the Shadow Warrior, but there's something about him that frightens me. I certainly won't admit this to Kenny, though. It will just give fuel to his argument the warrior is a demon, which in Kenny-talk, means he thinks the warrior is something I conjured from my imagination.

Rising to my feet, I say, "I'm telling you, Kenny, there was a real warrior in the flames, more beautiful than any man I've ever seen, and I think he might be my path back to writing songs."

I hear an intake of breath. Kenny is puffing on one of his ever-present cigars. A flash memory of raven talons fills my mind, and I hesitate for a moment before saying, "Aren't my untouched ankles proof the warrior was good?"

"Don't know about that," Kenny says. "Sounds weird to me, and what about Kadai ThunderHorse's hands? Didn't you tell me they're a mess?"

Silence fills the line. Kenny and my father worked together for many years. He's more friend than agent to me and has been boldly trying to fill the empty space of my father's death.

"AP picked up the story," Kenny says. "Want me to read you the headlines?"

"Probably not. Are they bad?"

"Bad enough, but I can turn this around, make it look as if you're adding a spiritual element to your songs instead of going nuts."

My year sabbatical is just about up and it won't be long before Kenny thinks of a marketing angle regarding the Shadow Warrior. Gran will not approve, and I'm not sure I do either, but Kenny is a powerful force, impossible to stop once he gets moving.

"Do what you have to do," I say. "Gotta go."

I end the call before Kenny can respond. It's a short reprieve. He'll be climbing down my neck soon, demanding a new song. First Uncle Cobby and now Kenny. Seems the world is short on songs these days.

Moonlight breaks through the intermittent clouds making the summer rain look like shining tears; a warm breeze caresses my face. I wish Grandfather were here. He was the one person in the world who understood my needs, the one person who never tried to change me. I could have talked with him about what happened at the shaman's fire. But now Grandfather is gone—crossed over, Gran says, to a much better place. Maybe better for him but not better for me. And not better for Gran. How on earth is she going to run a two-thousand-acre ranch without Grandfather? Kadai has helped her keep it up for a year now, but will he stay forever? *Will I?*

The thought brings me full circle. What if the warrior was sent from Creator? What if the warrior's songs are wrapped up in my destiny? I must talk with the shaman soon. I slip back into the kitchen and sit at the table where I watch Gran wrap thin strips of white gauze around Kadai's palms. "You'll be good as new in no time," she says.

Kadai nods, his usual form of communication unless he is talking over the back of a horse. Gran's earlier words haunt me as I stare at his wrapped hands. *Others can be hurt by your mistakes.*

When Kadai's dark eyes catch mine, I shudder. He saw what I saw in the shaman's fire, but like a good Native, he remains quiet. There will be questions later, though, when we are alone and he feels the time is right.

His eyes soften, and I realize he is staring at the tears running down my cheeks. Red Dog is at my feet and lays his head on my knees.

Gran looks up. "Oh, honey."

She throws her arms around my neck, and just like that, I am a little girl again sobbing in my Gran's arms, only this time she is sobbing right along with me while Red Dog howls like a sick coyote. Our wails join the sound of rain misting on the tin roof. The entire world seems to be mourning. So much for coming-out of grief.

"God is weeping," Gran whispers.

From somewhere deep inside I pull enough strength to guide Gran to her bedroom where I help her dress for bed. Then I lay with her wrapped in my arms until she stills and her soft snores fill the silence. Much later I leave her in Red Dog's trustworthy care while I slip out of bed and back into the darkened kitchen. I fill a teapot with water and place it on the gas burner to boil.

Kadai must have returned to his worker's cabin. I can see his lighted window across the field. At least I won't have to answer his questions tonight. The rain has stopped and his flute music drifts across the yard drawing me into memories of moonlit nights where I felt completely safe and loved. It seems a very long time ago.

Chapter 8

*Where were you when
Creator Yahweh laid the earth's foundation?*
Ghostdancer

Kadai ThunderHorse

STANDING OVER A SMALL FIRE PIT in the open meadow below Sacred Mountain, you watch moonlight spill over the majestic peak, covering it with a shimmering silver blanket. It is not the mountain that gives answer to your visions, but Creator, the One who made the mountain. It is his voice you wait for now while you contemplate the coming battle.

You know a man, whether in the body or out, you cannot tell; only Creator knows, but such a man is often caught up to the heights of heaven, to the shadowland where spiritual battles are fought. Such a man hears inexpressible words, which a human is not permitted to speak, and sees beauty no human eye can bear to behold. Such a man also sees terrible things in that world, beautiful dark beasts that strike in a flash of light too quick to avoid. Such a man does battle in that world, whether in the body or out, you do not know, but such a man fights as the warriors of old, with quiver and bow, and fearless as a panther on a night prowl.

SHAMAN'S FIRE

You will boast about such a man; but about yourself you will not boast, except in regard to your humiliations and your one great weakness—a traitorous tongue that cost a boy his life.

You think of that weakness now. You are a warrior dressed in eagle feathers, ready to cross to the shadowlands. You do not rely on your own strength. Human strength is nothing but dust blowing in the wind. You rely on Creator's strength. His grace is extravagant! His power is made perfect in your weakness.

As you breathe in the warm smell of burning sage beneath a night sky you think of how the sweet aroma contrasts the raging battle that has already begun in the unseen world. You offer prayers to Creator, petitioning him to help and protect the one you love. The evil one is after her. You know this to be true. You saw it in the way he lured Sayla into the fire, in the way the fire licked hungrily at your hands and filled the air with the stink of smoke not of this world.

While stoking the small bonfire, you consider the shaman is not your real enemy. Your true enemies are never of this world; they are from the shadowland, the world between worlds. White people have other names for it, calling it a dimension or a figment of the imagination. Yet to you, who have been caught up to the far heavens, it is more real than the flesh covering your bones; it is the place where spiritual battles rage strong.

You lift your voice and shout, "Creator! Redeemer! You alone are worthy! Holy is your name!"

Your prayers are powerful, reaching to the heavens. Moonlight disappears. Shapes break apart and fall into shifting shadows. You lose yourself in the unseen realm.

Chapter 9

*No darkness is dark enough to hide you
from Creator Yahweh.*
Ghostdancer

Jacob Wiseman (the shaman)

MY TEEPEE IS READY, set up close to the cemetery where I can talk with the spirits of our ancestors. A full moon stands above it, inviting my soul to travel. Ghostdancer and Loretta do not realize I have surpassed them both in power and knowledge of the unseen world. Perhaps if they had not sold out to the white man's god they would recognize the worth of my power.

There is too much talk of this so-called Jesus Way. Have they forgotten all the things Christians did to our people? What blasphemy to say Creator and Jesus are one and the same. That's like saying Hitler helped the Jews. They have been paying for their error, but there is more to come.

Sometimes a warrior must experience darkness before they can realize true freedom. Sacred Mountain has two sides—dark and light—and they are there for a reason. I will soon introduce Sayla to the dark side.

Chapter 10

> Where is Creator Yahweh,
> who gives sweet songs in the night?
> *Ghostdancer*

Sayla

A SINGING VOICE awakens me, and I lift my head from the kitchen table.

When your hope is all gone, and you don't know where to run...

The voice is the same one calling my name at the shaman's fire, the sound of rivers flowing and wind blowing, a sound as pure as nature. Though I see no flaming warrior, the words are as clear as if he is standing next to me. I begin to hum along.

When your hope is all gone. Lay it all down. Lay it all down.

The words spill over me in a cascade of fresh vision.

Lay it all down, down down. Lay it all down, down, down.

For the first time in months I want to sing. My journal is open on the table before me, a pen in my hand; my guitar is leaning against the wall. I don't remember retrieving them.

I begin to write, not creating the words as I go, but simply transcribing what I hear. The words drift around me like treasured snail shells washing in from windy Klamath Lake. Wave after wave, word after word, I write them down.

When the song ends, the teapot begins to hiss. I rise and pull the pot off the fire, but instead of making tea, I grab my guitar. For an entire year my Martin refused to give me any songs, but tonight it returns to my hands as if it wants the song as much as I do. I can almost forgive my sister for getting it out. I wail out my pain with each rise and fall of the cadence until all my grief is spent.

Lay it all down, down, down. Lay it all down.

When the last chord rings out, Gran enters the kitchen in her bare feet. A blue-flowered nightdress covers her from neck to toe. She lifts the teapot and pours water through a sieve, filling a porcelain cup with spicy tea. Then she sits at the table across from me. Her brown eyes are strangely clear for someone who cried herself to sleep just hours before. She sips from her cup and smiles, the laugh lines crinkling her face.

"So, you have a new song?"

"Yes." I prop my guitar against the wall.

"Tell me about it."

I shrug. "There's nothing to talk about. It's just a song."

"Hmm. Is there such a thing as just a song?"

We've been through this before. I refrain from rolling my eyes, knowing the rude gesture will just egg her on. "Of course, there's such a thing as just a song."

"Like there's just art?"

"Gran." I shake my head. "You must realize not everyone is as serious about their art as you are."

Gran examines me above her glasses. "Really? Give me an example."

"Okay." I stop and think a minute. "How about Andy Warhol and his soup can? You think he took his art seriously?"

"Humph. He took it seriously enough to rake in the bucks."

I laugh. "That's the point, Gran. Sometimes it's not about meaning at all. It is simply art. Or music."

Gran leans forward. "I'm glad you're singing again, Sayla, but the words worry me."

Gran's faith in Creator gives her no room for doubt, and hope is always within her sight. Unfortunately, I no longer share her faith, and hope is as elusive as the pot of gold white people claim sits at each rainbow's end.

Gran's wrinkled face is twisted with concern, her eyebrows raised in a question.

I shake my head. "At least I'm making a start. It's more than I can say for you and your painting."

Her eyebrows drop as she shoots a glance at the blank canvas sitting on her easel in the kitchen nook. She hasn't created a single painting since Grandfather's death and, as if that isn't enough, she has removed all her paintings from the house and stored them away. It's as if seeing them is too painful for her. What does that say about hope?

Gran straightens. "When your hope is all gone?"

"They're good lyrics."

"For who?"

"It's relatable." I lean forward. "I bet even *you* can relate."

Gran stretches a hand across the scarred, wood table and places her wrinkled fingers on my arm. Though her voice is no louder than a whisper, she enunciates each word with firm conviction. "For those who hope in Creator. Hope. Is. Never. Gone."

I swallow. I've heard the words before, but right now they hold no meaning. Pulling my arm from her hand, I stand. "It's just a song Gran. I need some sleep."

Leaving Gran sitting there alone without a soul to help her, I pass into the darkened hall leading to my bedroom and think I am beginning to walk down a path Gran will never follow. The thought takes my breath away. *It's just a song. No one has ever been cursed because of a song have they?*

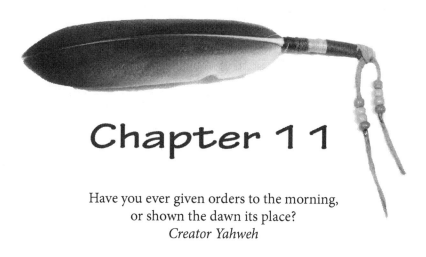

Chapter 11

*Have you ever given orders to the morning,
or shown the dawn its place?*
Creator Yahweh

Kadai ThunderHorse

CROSSING THROUGH THE SHADOWLAND, you recognize the faces of the gray-haired ones who have stood beside you and mentored you in Creator's ways. These gray-haired ones have passed from this world, yet they dance beside you. They sing their prayers along with yours, your voices melding into one mantra. They will be your witnesses. Their courage and faith strengthens your heart.

You lift your voice and shout, "Creator! Redeemer! Worthy are you! Give me strength to overcome the evil one!"

You dance your prayers with a fervor welling from somewhere outside yourself, somewhere outside earth and time.

Suddenly the evil one stands before you. His form is not horrid or ugly as many have pictured him. Brilliant rainbows of color spill over his magnificent wings and across his muscled chest. Yet his taunting eyes reveal nothing but deep pits of darkness. You lower your gaze, catching sideways glances instead, because peering long into those black pupils will cause utter despair.

The beast is enormous.

His golden hair swirls in the moonlight, sending cascades of stars across the meadow. Hornpipes fill his breastplate. The dangerous song of the ancient sirens blows with each heave of his mighty chest. It reverberates through the night nearly overpowering the sacred drum song.

You stop and pull a flaming arrow from your quiver. The flames are unquenchable. Your burned palms are still bound but painless in this shadowland. You aim for the sky. The arrow flies true, arching high then dropping before it pierces the evil one's chest.

An angry roar shrieks through the night. The siren song grows louder. You can barely hear the music of heaven.

Your arrow passes between the hornpipes and through the beast's chest as if he contains no heart, but you know Creator's fire has seared yet another hole in the beast's soul. The arrow drops and sticks straight up out of the earth where its endless flame becomes a torch.

While the beast continues to roar, you step to the side and aim again, sending another arrow through his heart and into the ground.

Flashing light illuminates the night leaving you momentarily blind. Talons as long and sharp as knives slash across the right side of your face. Reeling, you pull back but recover long enough to send another arrow straight through the beast.

Thunder rumbles through the ground as the beast steps forward. The quake of his footfall lodges in your thighs. Fear suddenly tastes like iron on your tongue and sits like molten lava in your gut. The stink of death clogs your nostrils. Singing sirens drop to a whisper more alluring than before.

"Be strong!" your Chief and Captain commands. "Do not be afraid!"

Warm blood drips down your face. The beast has struck a wound. His nostrils flare with excited hunger, and another swipe of his death-filled claws slashes across your right thigh.

"Aaaugh!" Your cry breaks through the battle, like that of an old warrior growling a charge.

A tongue lashes out, rough and forked like a serpent. It laps your flowing blood. The beast does not realize your blood and Creator's is mingled together. Creator has set His Spirit within you. Poison drips from the beast's tongue, but you do not fear it, for it has no power over you, you who are covered with Creator's invisible shield. On your knees now, you send another flaming arrow through the heart of the beast.

Drunk with Creator's blood, the beast does not realize his mistake.

You stand and send another arrow to its mark, knowing the beast's thirst will soon undo him.

The end comes suddenly. The beast's painful screech echoes through the night. He holds his face in his hands and writhes in agony. The taste of Creator's blood accomplishes what flames do not.

You stand and continue your circle, shooting arrows you wish were ten times bigger. Like twigs they stick out of the ground while the beast moans, yet in spite of their smallness they accomplish their task. A circle of flaming arrows now surrounds the beast. He can go thus far and no farther. He is hemmed in by light. Golden hair turns to shadow as he lets out one last roar and melts into the night.

The siren song is at last silenced, sent back to the netherworld where it belongs. Heaven's music washes over you in cleansing waves of healing. You will carry no wound from this battle.

Victory runs strong in your blood as you return to the natural world. You are back beside the small bonfire, offering sweet smelling tobacco and incense cedar as a thank offering to your Chief and Captain, and to the gray-haired ones, the great cloud of witnesses, who have walked beside you in this battle. The sweet tobacco is moist and soft in your fingers as you break it across the fire. As is always the case, you feel a strange mixture of weakness and power. Muscles and tendons flex weakly, but your spirit soars.

You pick up your flute and play, sending peace through the night. Though your people were not aware when they first fashioned the flute, it is patterned after the same instrument the psalmist David and his musicians used to touch the heart of Creator. You play for Sayla, the one who knows not how much you love her.

You lift your heart on the wings of the wind.

Chapter 12

*Creator Yahweh is mightier
than the thunder of the great waters.*
Ghostdancer

Sayla

RED DOG SITS IN GRAN'S bedroom doorway. Instead of his usual friendly greeting he slinks back and whimpers. Shudders ripple across the back of his neck making his hair stand straight up. The only other time I've seen such a reaction is when a bear came too close to the house.

Leaning down on one knee I call to him. "It's okay, Red Dog. It's just me."

Red Dog sticks his tail between his legs and backs up. His frightened eyes dart past me, staring at something above my shoulder.

Thinking about my classmate who was stabbed this weekend and expecting to see some enormous monster, I spin around. But nothing more than flickering shadows fill the hallway, no ghosts or predators to cause such fear. I turn and reach out to Red Dog, but he backs farther into Gran's room.

Outside of Gran, I have always been Red Dog's favorite. It would be impossible to number the hours I have wept into his warm fur. His strange behavior unsettles me. I think about it as I return to my room and dress for bed. Gran believes animals are more in touch with the unseen world than most humans. She recites many Bible stories like the one about a donkey who saw a ferocious angel blocking the way long before his rider Balaam saw it, and the story about animals entering Noah's ark, hearing and obeying Creator's call without a single hesitation. One of her favorite stories is of Jesus saying the very rocks will cry out if humans refuse to give him praise. Natives have long believed all things carry life, even stone, so the story holds more weight for us than it does for most white people.

Red Dog's behavior seems to prove Gran's theory of animals having spiritual sight. He clearly saw something other than the physical realm back in the hallway, something I did not see. A shiver sweeps over my shoulders. I pull back the Pendleton blankets that cover my bed and discover an odd piece of tanned leather on my pillow. A crude painting of my shining warrior stares up at me. It is more a stick figure than a true rendering, like a totem my ancestors would have drawn over a century ago, but the likeness is unmistakable. The warrior is dressed in eagle feathers and dancing in the flames of a bonfire. Beneath the drawing is a painted phrase written in our Klamath language. It takes me a while to transcribe the meaning but when I do all air leaves my lungs.

It was not an accident . . .

My mind begins to spin. Someone wanted my parents dead? Or perhaps they wanted grandfather dead and my parent just happened to be in the way. But who? For a moment I consider showing the note to Gran, but she has enough on her plate without this worry.

I scan my room, looking for sign of anything missing. My regalia still hangs on the hook by the door; my jewelry is still hanging from a moose antler rack Grandpa made for me; and my smart phone sits on my dresser. Except for the note, nothing seems out of place.

When I turn back to the bed, I discover a sealed envelope sticking out from under my pillow. I tear it open to find a note from James. James is the son of Gran's best friend, Mary, and one of my biggest fans. Like my sister Moriah, he's two years older than me, and because his mother's ranch is not far from ours he drove us to high school. I remember being squished next to the passenger door of his pickup and thinking if I fell out on one of the many curves, neither he nor Moriah would notice. James had a huge crush on my sister in those days.

The note simply says the shaman asked him to give me the leather message when no one else was around and with all the visitors in our house he thought it best to slip it on my pillow. The breaths I've been holding come out in one swoosh as I read the final paragraph.

"The shaman wants you to be his *saayoogalla*. It is a great honor."

Saayoogalla is to mimic, more akin to being an apprentice. It is indeed a great honor to have the shaman take me on as his apprentice, and it appears as if he intends to help bring justice to the death of my family. Relief washes over me, and then a deep sadness clutches my heart.

Gran will not approve.

I crawl into bed and stare at the ceiling. Gran is probably still sitting at the table worried about her poor granddaughter who has lost her way. I wish I could tell her about the shaman's offer and about the warrior I saw in the bonfire, but I cannot. This will be the first secret I have withheld from her. Sadness fills my heart, but I try to shake it off. After all, by following the shaman I'll be helping to bring justice; it's more than I can say her Creator is doing.

Unable to sleep, I pull the packet of journals Grandfather gave me from beneath my mattress. These are not journals Grandfather wrote himself. They are nearly as old as the river and have been passed down from generations for so long no one knows their beginning. No words adorn the leather pages. Simple markings of a tribe long forgotten tell story after story. The markings are similar to the petroglyphs at Tulelake. Grandfather gave the journals to me long ago and I've spent hours poring over the colorful markings, trying to figure out the stories they are telling—a horse ride gone bad, a message given by eagle wings, a story of gold being stolen and hidden.

I turn to the story of fire, straining to see if my Shadow Warrior is somehow pictured there. There might be a face on the other side of the flames, but it's difficult to tell. The paint is fading and the leather cracked, but then I see one arm raised high and my breath catches. Red and gold slashes clearly mark the armband, the same slashes I saw on the Shadow Warrior. I shove the journals beneath my bed, planning to hide them beneath my mattress again in the morning.

I lie on my bed and stare at the ceiling. What could it possibly mean that the Shadow Warrior may be the same one pictured in the old journals? Is Grandfather trying to send me a message from the other side?

My eyes grow heavy as far-off flute music overtakes my dreams. The last thing I remember is it wouldn't take much tweaking to put the words and flute music together.

When you're all alone . . . and your hope is all gone . . . lay it all down, down, down.

Chapter 13

*Creator Yahweh scatters his lightning about him,
bathing the depths of the sea in light.*
Ghostdancer

Sayla
August 26, 2014
Tuesday morning

IT IS LATE MORNING when I crawl out of bed, but the music is still with me. Sinking my toes into the sheepskin throw rug, I stare at the bare walls. Three lighter squares on the green painted walls mark the places Gran's paintings used to hang. One was of Grandfather breaking a horse in the corral. One hand flew high over his head and his legs stood nearly straight in the stirrups. He was a young man at the time, and his black braids hung suspended in that moment just before the horse dropped back to the ground. I always loved that painting and the feeling of belonging it gave me to know I had inherited part of his connection with horses. There wasn't a horse alive Grandfather couldn't tame. I'm not as good as him at breaking horses but, as a teen, I could outride any other woman west of the Rockies. Trophies line a high shelf on one side of my room as proof. I'm sad Gran removed the paintings, but I certainly understand her need to do so.

Still barefoot and dressed in cotton pajamas, I search the house for Gran, intending to make up for last night's rude behavior, but she is nowhere in sight. Neither is Red Dog.

Sacred Mountain captures my gaze as I stare out the kitchen window and across the fields stretching to the tree line. It's the first time in weeks the sky has cleared enough of smoke to see that distance. Enormous puffy clouds dot the horizon, piling on top of one another and signaling an imminent thunderstorm, not unusual east of the High Cascade Mountains, but certainly not something we need at the height of fire season. I catch sight of Kadai riding hard across the open fields, probably rounding up cattle to weather the storm.

I stick a pop tart in the toaster and grab a cup of cold black coffee. Soon the sweet raspberry smell makes the morning seem almost normal, but it's not. The storm is building, sending wind in all directions. I eat at the counter, watching the wind whipping trees every which way. It spins the top of the hundred-year-old, *goos* (ponderosa pine) in the front yard as if the giant tree is nothing more than a child's toy. Several limbs we call widowmakers have already fallen off. They stick straight up out of the ground. Something clatters on the slanted roof above me. The sound alerts me of danger.

Grandfather is no longer here to "batten down the hatches," as Gran would say, so I run to my room and change from my pajamas to jeans and a tee shirt and then twist my black hair into a French braid. After lacing my feet into a pair of Ryder boots I hurry outside. When the screen door slams shut behind me, I brace against the wind to look for Gran. There are only a couple of choices. She's either in the garage, which I very much doubt, since it's full of junk we never use, or she's in the barn with the horses, which I also doubt, since Kadai and I take care of them, or she's in the chicken shed, either gathering eggs or on some secret mission. I head for the low red shed and find her inside nailing up boards against the weakened walls, her thick white ponytail bobbing behind her.

"Should you be doing that?" I ask.

"Whyonearthnot?"

I can barely understand her muttering through a mouth full of nails.

"At least let me help," I say.

"Surething." She points to a board. "Grabtheotherend."

I do as she asks and wince when she brings the hammer down squarely on her thumb.

"OwOwOw." She shakes her wounded hand, but doesn't let go of the board or the nails in her mouth.

Typical for Gran. Most people say she's full of it, meaning she's full of passion and attacks everything in full power, but sometimes, as in the case with the hammer, she uses a little too much power.

My cousins say I'm like Gran, but I've never seen the resemblance. She's as transparent as a mountain spring and believes in Creator with all her heart. She talks with Creator, often without closing her eyes. Half the time I don't even know she's praying until she's halfway through it.

In fact, she's at it right now, doing that prayer thing, talking to Creator as if he's here in the chicken shed of all places. She's asking Creator for healing and for safety for Kadai and me. At least she's gotten rid of the nails. I don't know whether to close my eyes or bow my head, so I do neither. When she's finished praying, I offer to help.

"Good idea." She mumbles the words while sucking her wounded thumb.

Howling wind shakes the little shed as I hammer, and I can't help but notice the building needs more than a little bracing against the storm. "Sheesh, Gran. This shed is about to fall down."

"Yeah, well, your Grandfather wasn't much of one for replacing broken buildings or repair work. Spent most of his time on the back of a horse."

At the mention of Grandfather, we both fall silent. Though I know it's true Grandfather didn't get around to repairing things, I somehow feel as if I need to stick up for him.

"He had a lot on his plate," I say.

Gran stops and stares at me. "I'm sorry, Sayla. You know I love Grandfather more than anyone in the world, but fixing stuff just wasn't his thing."

I don't bother to correct her on the love part. It should be in the past tense now that Grandfather is in heaven. I look at her. "You still love Grandfather?"

"Of course I do. Don't you?"

I think about it and realize I do—nothing has changed regarding my feelings for him other than the fact I can't talk to him or reach out and touch him, yet my love for him is just as strong as ever.

I nod, afraid to say anything over the lump in my throat. If I start crying, we will both turn into bawl babies again, and that won't help anything at all.

"And I still love your mom and dad too," Gran says.

"Ohhhhhhh," a keening wail escapes my throat. I drop the hammer and run from the shed. Wild wind whips my face, but I do not care; in fact, I am glad for it. How can I possibly think of my parents? Both gone? And before I made things right with them? What kind of Creator would allow such tragedy?

Our Coming-Out of Grief Ceremony didn't work at all. In fact, it seems to have brought all the pain back. Tears blur my eyes as I run toward the barn; then suddenly a dark shape looms in front of me.

I freeze, forcing my breathing to slow.

War Paint, Grandfather's famous bucking horse, stares at me with demon eyes.

He's an enormous horse, known for his unpredictability and fiery temper. He snorts and stamps his right leg, his rust-colored coat quivering. The only thing that can save me now is if I can sprout wings and fly, which of course I cannot do.

Uncle Cobby has always described War Paint as an outlaw and swears the horse is too treacherous to keep on Sacred Mountain Ranch. Kadai agrees but knows we will never get rid of him, because he's the grandson of Grandfather's favorite rodeo horse of the same name. Kadai says the animal has a belly full of bedsprings. He should know, he's the only one who's ever tried to tame War Paint, and he's one of the few who can get near enough to care for the crazed horse.

Kadai has warned that if I ever encounter War Paint, in the way I am now, I must either slowly back off or remain completely still and hope for the best. My mind registers the fact, but I'm so distraught with thoughts of the unfairness of life, I end my stillness far too soon and do the unthinkable.

I raise my arms and shout. "Out of my way!"

To my surprise, War Paint kicks up his heels and runs, not through me, as expected, but away to the far side of the yard. I hurry to the safety of the barn where I find my favorite paint, Duchess, tucked in her stall. I bury my head in her mane. No tears come, but it seems as if all air has left my lungs.

Duchess stands still, turning her head into mine and making little whimpering noises. Then she folds her legs and the two of us drop to the straw. I sprawl across her back, rubbing her soft neck and feeling strangely comforted.

Creator seems far away, yet his creation is close. I wonder what Gran would have to say about that. Breathing in the familiar scent of horse and hay while the storm rumbles against the barn, I lean into the warmth of Duchess and think if Creator ever wants to reach me, he'll have to do it through a horse.

Chapter 14

> Brace yourself like a man.
> *Creator Yahweh*

Kadai

FROM YOUR POSITION on a ladder leaning against the barn, you watch as Sayla challenges War Paint. Sorrow rides on the wind, casting dark shadows over the one you love. It is not the wind of the building storm striking fear to your heart, but the winds of doubt that often attack a weakened soul so soon returned from the shadowland. You petition Creator for Sayla while nailing a board across the last of the barn's open windows.

The animals will be safe from the coming storm, but what of the people?

Grandmother is a mountain of faith that cannot be moved. Oh, she will grieve and shed tears for her loss, but she will not fall so far that Creator cannot lift her up. He will raise her to high places where her feet will run like that of a deer. She will yet praise her Maker.

But Sayla is weak, though she does not know it. Her mistake with War Paint is proof enough. Though she thinks she has won the battle, War Paint will now be her enemy, and nowhere his feet trod will be safe ground for her. Sayla has other enemies she underestimates as well, proving her need of a great warrior who will fight for her. If you are around, you can protect her from War Paint, but your memories of Iraq remind you of the terrible consequences of promising to always be there for a person. Only Creator is able to always prove true on such a promise.

Thoughts of Iraq darken your soul and, before you realize what is happening, you have crossed over to the shadowland.

You feel strength rising inside, but fear rises as well. You, who have failed in the past, cannot lose this battle. The stakes are far too high.

"Be strong!" your Chief and Captain calls. "Be of good courage."

Gritting your teeth, you steady your heart, slowing it to the beat of a sleeping man. Seeing more than a barn window, you stare into darkness where you must soon tread. There is no light to illuminate the path, nothing to mark the treacherous boundaries you know exist. One wrong step and all is lost. Discouragement slashes its sharp edge into your heart.

"Have I not commanded you?" the voice calls out. "Be strong!"

The shadowland disappears as sunlight pours through a break in the clouds. It is as if you can still hear the echo of *His* voice as your fingers cling to the ladder for support. This is the first time the crossing over and back has been so abrupt, a vision of its own making, creating havoc in the light of day. Perhaps the battle is more imminent than you first thought.

You pound in the last of the nails and climb down the ladder on trembling legs. By the time your feet hit ground, you're as shaky as an old woman. A hot wind falls over your back, breathing courage into your soul. You close your eyes and allow the strengthening quivers to flow through muscle and tendon. With each pulse you feel stronger, until at last you stand as determined and full of faith as the shepherd boy, David, who was armed with nothing more than a slingshot and five small stones.

Though you are armed with nothing more than a quiver full of flaming arrows, you know full well the beast will fall. You hold that assurance until the sun falls behind another cloud; then doubt shadows your affirmation. Losing this battle will mean more than the death of a body.

Sayla's soul is at stake.

You must stand strong. You must take courage. Yet both fall through your fingers like melting ice in the heat of a summer storm.

Chapter 15

Creator Yahweh longs to deliver those who suffer.
Ghostdancer

Loretta (Gran)

LORETTA RAN INTO KADAI as he exited the barn. He placed a bandaged hand on her shoulder. His wounds must have hurt, but like the true warrior he was, he gave no sign of pain. "She's okay," he said. "Resting with Duchess. I threw a blanket over her."

"But the storm—"

"The barn has outlasted more storms than we've witnessed. She'll be fine where she is. Just needs some time."

Loretta started for the barn, but Kadai turned her back. "Trust me," he said.

She stared hard into his eyes. They were as dark as the clouds above his head. When had he grown into such a courageous young man? She had known him from the day of his birth, his father being her husband Charlie's best friend. He had grown up on Sacred Mountain Ranch, and of course there was talk about him eventually wooing Sayla, but nothing had ever seemed to come of it. Yet, as she looked into his eyes, she saw strength of courage seldom seen in youth. "Just how old are you, son?"

Kadai laughed. "Twenty-seven. Do I need to be older for you to listen to me Grandmother?"

Loretta shook her head. "No, you have well proved your spiritual maturity, the entire Tribal Council agrees; but I think I missed a few years when you turned into a man."

He gently, but firmly, pushed her toward the house. "If we don't get out of this wind, you'll be missing a few more years. The cattle are safe under the eaves and the horses bedded down. Let's get you safe inside."

"But—"

"Trust me. I'll come back to check on Sayla."

As if to prove his words, the clouds over *Cheelaqsdi* rumbled. Kadai sheltered Loretta beneath his arm as they plowed against the wind. Before they reached the porch, a shower of hail dumped from the sky.

"*Yaks dwa!*" Loretta shouted. "We're in for a big one."

When they were tucked safely beneath the cover of the porch, Loretta turned to look at the angry sky. "Haven't seen it this bad since the flood of '64."

Kadai said nothing. He never was a boy to waste words. Seemed he hadn't changed much since becoming a man. He put his hand on the door as if getting ready to head back outside.

"Don't go," Loretta said.

He stopped and turned toward her.

"Let me make some tea. You can take some to Sayla after we talk a bit."

Afraid to give him time to argue, she hurried into her kitchen, wet boots and all, dripping on her clean linoleum and not minding the mess one bit. Red Dog followed her with a whimper. He hated storms, usually choosing to hide beneath the bed until the weather changed. She patted his head, poured water into the teapot and had it warming on the stove by the time Kadai ducked beneath the doorframe. He was tall for a Modoc, but then she remembered he had some Lakota Sioux blood as well. He must have gotten his regal stature from his mother's side. Modocs were usually built lower to the ground and tended toward a stocky frame, like herself.

She grabbed Charlie's mug, resisting the urge to hold it to her chest. Her dear husband would want her to share his mug with this capable young man. She placed some freshly picked chamomile inside a small wire basket and poured boiling water over it. Kadai remained standing until she set the mug on the table. Then he sat and stared at the steaming brew as if she had offered him poison.

Loretta reached into the fridge and pulled out a cellophane-covered plate containing a piece of huckleberry pie. That had always worked to loosen Charlie's tongue. He hadn't been a man of many words either, unless you primed the pump with something sweet.

She removed the cellophane wrapper and placed the pie and a fork in front of Kadai. He looked at the pie and then at her. "Grandmother?"

"Huckleberry. It was Charlie's favorite."

Kadai blinked. Then he lifted the fork with his bandaged hand and took a bite. After one bite, he took another before offering his declaration. "Good."

Loretta laughed. The strange sound echoed around the kitchen until she caught it on a near sob. She had always known that tears and laughter were close kin. She swallowed and got down to business.

"What happened at the Coming-Out?"

Kadai took another bite, obviously in no hurry to answer her question. Never much one for patience, she pressed further. "You saw Sayla go to the shaman's fire?"

"She was cold."

"While the rest of us were sweltering in the heat?"

"Wasn't that kind of cold."

Kadai looked straight into Loretta's eyes. Was the young man challenging an elder? She stiffened and held her ground, but on close inspection she saw no guile in the young man's face. Stabbing pain pierced her heart as she realized the truth. The cold Sayla felt was from the spiritual realm, not the physical.

Loretta shook her head. "But I've warned her of the consequences."

"Warnings aren't always heeded, Grandmother."

"But she knows how we believe."

"Doesn't mean she believes the same."

Loretta caught her breath. Was it possible Sayla didn't believe in Creator? "W-what are you saying?"

Kadai pushed the half-eaten pie away, and then he straightened. "This is a battle of the soul, Grandmother. It will not be won with words."

Loretta leaned forward. "That's good for you to say. Words would never be your weapon choice in the first place. But words are all I have."

"I don't mean to be disrespectful, Grandmother. But you are wrong."

Loretta drew back. "What?"

"You have pictures."

"Pictures?"

"Your paintings."

Loretta shook her head. "What good are pictures in bringing someone to belief in Creator?"

Kadai smiled. "Someone I respect highly told me a picture is worth a thousand words."

Loretta swallowed. "So say my Chinese friends."

"So they say."

She stared at the blank canvas on her easel that stood lonely and lost in the kitchen nook. That nook had been her most special place for many years, yet not one brush stroke had touched the canvas since the death of her loved ones.

The blank canvas was always a terror, but more so now.

Though she agreed with Kadai that she should be painting, she had no idea how to begin. He was probably right about the uselessness of words and about her rushing things, trying to make events happen before it was time. It was like pulling dirt away from a seed just to have the seedling wilt in the sun, but darn it all, she had just lost a son and a husband, not to mention a dear daughter-in-law. She couldn't stand to think of losing her granddaughter to Jacob, the self-appointed shaman.

If even a tenth of the rumors were true, Jacob was deep into the black arts and taking money to cast spells, both good and bad. A chill seeped into Loretta's heart. Sayla had come close to being seriously burned in the fire. Loretta didn't for a minute believe Sayla had tried to take her own life, though the white doctor believed that very thing. Was the shaman responsible for Sayla's reckless actions?

Suddenly Loretta remembered the words to Sayla's song. *When all hope is gone.*

"Oh, dear," she said. "There's more truth in her words than I first thought."

Kadai stood. "I should be checking the horses."

Loretta rose and grabbed a thermos. "Let me fix some tea for Sayla. It may warm her later."

Kadai made no objections, but neither did he offer any information. Loretta hoped he would find more words for Sayla. Perhaps being with the horses would loosen his tongue. She certainly hoped so. Huckleberry pie hadn't quite done the trick.

Chapter 16

*Who is this that darkens my counsel
with words without knowledge?*
Creator Yahweh

Sayla
August 27, 2014
Wednesday morning

I WAKE TO THE SOUND of horses munching on grain and wind whispering against wood. At first I have no idea where I am or how I got here, but then I remember the argument with Gran and how I had fled to the barn. Jerking up, I cause trembles to scatter across Duchess's body. A blanket falls off my shoulders. Though shadows engulf the barn, I can make out enough markings to know the Pendleton blanket belongs to Kadai. No surprise there, but I wonder when he discovered me asleep and what he made of it.

The barn door flies open sending a shower of light pouring over the stalls. Sunlight fills the barnyard, backlighting Kadai's muscled body; a breeze carries the scent of fresh, wet grass. I can't believe I slept through the entire storm.

Nickering, Duchess begins to rise. I scramble to get out of her way and find myself face-to-face with Kadai. He's dressed in blue jeans and a black cowboy hat, no shirt—pure Klamath style. It's always unsettling to see him dressed in such a way. I much prefer his regalia; he's easier to keep at a distance when he appears as a warrior from another time and place. Staring at his bronzed skin and thick muscles, I wonder when Kadai turned into such a hunk.

Hunk?

I want to slap myself for such a thought. Kadai is my *sawalineeas*, my best friend—the guy I grew up with, the one who taught me how to fish and swim and who introduced me to riding bareback beneath a full moon.

Angry at myself, I turn on Kadai. "Why?"

Ignoring my question, he hands me a thermos with his bandaged hands. Strangely, seeing those bandaged hands makes me even angrier. Who appointed Kadai as my guardian?

I grab the thermos and unscrew the attached cup. A sweet cinnamon aroma wafts into the air. After filling my cup with lukewarm tea I lean against the barn wall. I don't bother to offer any to Kadai. He won't accept it. He probably dines on rabbit and venison he kills with his bare hands. At least, that's the way it seems to me after watching his wild ways my entire life. He's much more at home in the woods than he ever is with people, unless you bring out the drum; then he turns into a regular party animal, dancing in ways that appear impossible.

Kadai is brushing Bronze Healer, his magnificent brown-and-white paint. It's the most beautiful gelding in the Klamath Basin, with intelligent eyes that always melt my heart. The horse has never felt the weight of a saddle. For that matter, Kadai has never felt the need of a saddle. It's always mesmerizing to watch the duo fly like the wind across open fields as free as if man and horse are one unit.

I envy him that. Like Kadai, I am a born rider, but I have never learned to sit bareback good enough to fly like he does. He's one of the best Indian relay riders alive.

The warm tea makes me feel a bit more alive and more than a little sorry for having been such a pain to Gran. When Kadai opens his jar of gray paint made from ash and animal fat, I narrow my focus. It is his habit to paint his horse with symbols, each one carrying a meaning that stems from long ago traditions. I watch as he brushes a circle of white around each of Bronze Healer's eyes. It is an easy symbol I can well remember. The circle serves to give the horse better vision.

Kadai is big about vision.

What he does next takes me by surprise.

Kadai runs seven white stripes across Bronze Healer's flank. Then he dips his finger into black paint and stares straight into my eyes while he runs a thick black stripe from his own forehead to his chin, dividing his right eye in half.

A shiver runs across my neck.

"Before I answer you, Little Fire, let me ask you a question."

As usual, he's waited so long to answer I nearly forgot my question. And I hate it when he calls me Little Fire. It is his way of pulling rank on me. He started calling me Little Fire after finding me twirling in the field at midnight when I was a scrawny kid. Moonlight spread like fire across the meadow and I was so enthralled I couldn't stay in bed. That was the beginning of our midnight rides and dances—another of the things that could make me fall in love with him if he wasn't so darn religious.

Staring at the black stripe, I wonder what it means.

It's probably a warrior symbol that has something to do with counting coup. If I am right, the seven symbols on the horse's flank mean Kadai has come in contact with his enemy seven times, seven being the number of completion. That means he has received a full amount of courage, strength and energy from his enemy. But the black line broken over his eyelid, signals the battle is not yet won. I shudder, hoping the mark has nothing to do with my recent contact with the Shadow Warrior, but fearing it does. I hold my tongue. Two can play this silent game.

Kadai speaks into the neck of his horse. "Who plays with fire and doesn't get burned?"

I look at my feet. Not even a hint of scar remains. Bristling, my answer comes instinctively. "She who plays no games, but who mourns the death of her loved ones."

"Death cannot hold those who worship Creator."

"Then why are their ashes thrown to the wind?"

"They can kill the body, but not the soul."

Clenching my hands into fists, I shout, "They're gone, Kadai. Gone!"

Bronze Healer whimpers. Kadai raises his head. A soundless tear slips from his blackened right eye. Wind still whistles against the barn.

I wrap my arms around my shoulders. My voice comes out as small as a young child's. "Why? Just tell me why?"

Kadai's voice drops to a whisper. "I cannot say why, Little Fire, but I know Creator is always good."

"This doesn't *feel* good." Anger burns in my chest, but Kadai continues his relentless questioning.

"Who owns the sun?"

My voice rises in volume. "The same one who stole the light!"

"Who told the ocean, 'You may come this far and no farther'?"

Past help now, my voice comes out in choking sobs. "The same one who took away my parents."

"Who gives the wild horse his strength?"

Several choking moments pass before I can answer, but finally the fight leaves me along with the sobs. "The same one who leaves me weak as an old woman."

"In weakness Creator's strength is made perfect."

I stand mute, shaking my head. Wind pounds against the barn door. If Kadai only knew. *Perfection* is not a word for me. All night I have been thinking about the Shadow Warrior and how I can make contact with the shaman without Gran's knowledge. Perhaps all our problems are caused because we have left the old ways and embraced the white man's God.

My hands fall limp to my sides. Kadai moves in close and lifts my chin. The rich smell of him is intoxicating. "Who counts the months till the doe bears her fawn?"

This is a new one to me. How can the same one who cares enough about his creation to count off birth months be the same one who stole my parents and grandfather? It makes no sense.

Kadai stares into my eyes and answers his own question in the soft low voice that always sends shivers through my heart. "The same one who understands your pain, Little Fire. The same one who rises to show you compassion."

Stepping back I shake my head. The loss of Kadai's touch makes me feel strangely alone and a huge chasm stretches between us. I see nothing of what he says Creator is offering. Creator is the taker, not the giver. He took my parents. He took Grandfather. He took my songs. He allowed white people to take our lands, our way of life, our language, our heritage, our identification. He allowed Gran to be raised in a boarding school without a mother's hugs or spiritual influence. He allowed her to be treated as less than something human. Creator allowed Grandmother to be beaten nearly to death by her first husband. Memories of all the sorrow ways fuel my anger, and my words dart out like poisoned arrows aimed straight at Kadai's heart. "How do you know you haven't sold out to the white man's God?"

Kadai jerks as if I have slapped him, but he quickly recovers. "We are all one tribe in Creator's eyes."

"Tell that to our ancestors who gave up land and families in the name of Christianity."

"Little Fire. You know that much of what is done in the name of Christianity has nothing to do with Christ."

"And who is *this* Christ, but another white man?"

"He was no white man." Kadai's voice rises. "He was born in the Middle East. He's a tribal person like us."

That's news to me, but it makes no difference. It was white men who came with the message of this Christ, and it was the same white men who annihilated my heritage. At any rate I'm not ready for this Christianity stuff.

I turn and march out of the barn, leaving Kadai and his Creator behind. Though I hate the thought of hurting Gran and Kadai, I will make contact with the shaman and let him know I am more than willing to be his next *saayoogalla*. For Gran's sake, I will keep my dealings with the shaman a secret, but my decision is firm. Gran's God has done nothing to bring about either justice or peace. I suspect walking in the way of my ancestors will bring both.

Chapter 17

> Who shut up the sea behind doors
> when it burst forth from the womb?
> *Ghostdancer*

Kadai

YOU MOUNT YOUR HORSE and ride as hard and fast as Bronze Healer will go. You are a worm of a man, not the warrior you hoped. How foolish to dream big dreams. Who were you to think you could fight the powers of darkness that dwell where no human should tread? Did you truly believe Creator had called you for such a lofty task?

What a foolish thought . . . you, who were born of flesh and blood, causing death even as you took your first breath and your mother took her last.

Swallowing the bile in your throat you become aware of horse sweat beneath your legs. The smell of plowed earth rises from beneath Bronze Healer's hooves. Leaning into his neck, you push him higher, aiming for the top of the mountain. He knows the way. The two of you have traveled this path many times. You and the horse have become one, both animals, both answering a call of the wild, born to run, born to hunt, not fit for the world below.

Stopping at last on the rocky face that forms an overlook, the two of you breathe hard. You have time to think now, to ask yourself why you chose the weapon of words when silence would have been the better way. Had you thought to reach out to your love through a more human form, something she would understand? How foolish. You knew your words held the power of life and death.

Death reigns on this day.

You have lost her. She will go. And there is nothing you can do about it.

Chapter 18

*Creator Yahweh endowed the heart with wisdom
and gave understanding to the mind.*
Ghostdancer

Loretta

LORETTA WATCHED AS KADAI flew across the field on the back of his gelding. She picked up the phone and punched in the familiar number.

"It has begun," she said. "Tell Ghostdancer to come." She disconnected the phone and hurried back to the kitchen table just as Sayla reached the porch.

Chapter 19

> Creator Yahweh does speak
> —now one way, now another—
> in dreams in visions of the night,
> though you may not perceive it.
> *Ghostdancer*

Sayla

MY PHONE BEEPS on my way back to the house. Checking the reading, I see Kenny, my agent, has left a message. My throat tightens as I read it. He plans to arrive in a couple of days. After a year of silence and talk of demons he's worried about me. It's time to see if I can turn my new song into a winner.

Gran is at the kitchen table stitching my burned regalia when I enter the house. It is amazing how she can work such miracles with beads and material. I lean down and hug her. "Thanks Gran. You're the best."

She pats my arm. "It will be better than new in no time, but I can't say the same for your moccasins. We'll have to start fresh on those."

Globs of melted beads form an unrecognizable mass. The leather is burned clear through in places. Looking at my feet, I wonder how my ankles can be completely free of burns.

"I wondered the same thing," Gran says. "Kadai's hands took most of the burn. His palms will never be the same again."

The thought sickens my stomach. I had no intention of causing pain to Kadai.

Thankfully, a knock at the front door keeps me from dwelling on the thought. I open it to find Mary Summers with her arms full of towel-covered fry bread.

"Hi Auntie," I say, offering to take the fry bread.

Mary is well acquainted with our kitchen. She ignores my offer and rushes ahead with her usual cheerful gusto, hollering at Gran and setting the fry bread on the stove. I follow and lift the towel and pull out a piece. The sweet honey smell fills our kitchen as I take a bite. "Oh Mary, this is so good."

Red Dog sniffs Mary's feet and looks up for the expected pat on the head, but before she can oblige, the dog darts for the door in a fury of mad barking.

Mary's son, James, stands in the doorway holding an enormous cardboard box. He laughs and scolds Red Dog, but the silly mutt continues barking like crazy.

"Red Dog, what's the matter with you?" I offer him a bite of fry bread, effectively rescuing James from any further dog scolding.

After setting the box on the counter, James throws me a shrug and a smile. Thinking of the shaman's note James slipped beneath my pillow, my face warms. I want to ask him about the note, but not in front of Gran.

"*Yaks dwa!*" Mary exclaims after opening the refrigerator. Both she and Gran use the Native term in the same way a white person would exclaim, "Goodness!" or "Sheesh," which is one of the terms I picked up in California.

"You've enough food here to feed a small army," Mary says.

Gran is already chewing on a piece of warm fry bread and pouring iced tea into tall glasses. "Never too much food. You never know when company might show up."

James takes two tea glasses and starts adding sugar to one and sweet leaf stevia to the other.

"None for me," I say. "I'm working on a new song."

"Hey! That's great!" He turns to me and winks. "I'd say that calls for a celebration." He hands me the tea sweetened with stevia, and I take it in spite of my denial. We clink our glasses together and drink in celebration. Feels good to have someone interested in something other than death. The tea is cold and sweet, just the way I like it. While Gran and Mary fuss over food, James and I move into the living room where he sits on the couch. I remain standing.

"So, are you ready for the community concert and relay race?" James asks.

The thought of a new song has given him hope, so I play along. "Perhaps."

"You realize it's less than two weeks away?"

"Yeah."

James swallows his tea in one long gulp and plunks his glass on the coffee table. "I don't blame you for leaving the powwow. Some restoration."

We've been over this before. James is full-blooded Klamath, but after his grandfather died, his grandmother married a white man who owned a large ranch near the town of Dorris on the Oregon-California border, effectively cutting herself off from the rest of the tribe. Ranchers and Natives have long been arguing over water rights. Natives want the waterways returned to the promise written in an 1864 treaty, a promise that would have the waters teeming with Native fish.

White farmers call our Native fish suckers on a good day and much worse on a bad day. They are angry at having their farms dry up in order to save what they see as a useless specimen, but we Natives see the fish as a connection to our spiritual roots, a connection that promises healing. There's a lot more to the argument. A lot of whites misunderstand that we were made to sell our land at a much cheaper price than what it was worth, that none of us had a choice other than *when* to take the money.

Not wanting to rehash old arguments, I finish my tea and grab my guitar. When Gran and Mary appear, I say. "I'm heading out to the sound room."

When I step through the back door I think I see something darting through the forest behind our house. The air is heavy with warning, and the cold dread I felt at the powwow returns. I hurry to my sound room on the other side of the garage. My hand is shaking as I unlock the door and flip the light switch. A single bulb illuminates the entire room. I drop my guitar case and lean against the closed door, catching my breath.

I haven't been out here since the crash. Directly across from the door, cabinets and speakers line the wall. A soundboard and computer stand on the left beneath one of two large monitors. An electronic piano sits in the middle with a microphone stand above and a low stool below. A framed, eight-by-ten photo stares at me from the shelf on the right, depicting the opening night of my first national tour. I cross the room and pick it up. Floodlights sparkle in my eyes, and I look as if I am ready to fly. The frame feels cool in my hands. Kadai is in the background, dressed in Army fatigues, on special leave to join me. That was back before he turned so religious, back when I considered him my *sawalineeas*.

My eyes refuse to move to the image of my parents. Every line of their laughing faces is already burned into my memory. Even though it seems as if I could never please them, they were always involved in my life. Life is now empty without them. I move to replace the photo on the shelf, but what I see there causes my hand to shoot to my mouth.

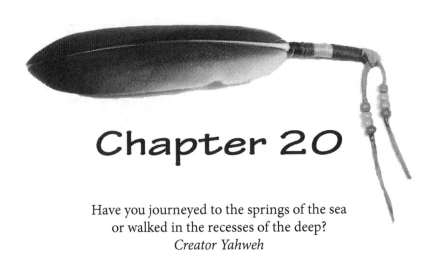

Chapter 20

> Have you journeyed to the springs of the sea
> or walked in the recesses of the deep?
> *Creator Yahweh*

Kadai

SHADOWS STRETCH LONG as you leave the overlook and drop over the back saddle of Sacred Mountain. You are now on foot, leading Bronze Healer, ducking through thick groves of manzanita brush and crossing small patches of shadowed meadow. No sound breaks the silence. Not even as much as a frog croaks out a song. A chill fills the air as you remember the elders warning regarding this land of evil spirits—only those who long for dark power should visit here. You do not long for dark power, but you have discovered the secret of light shining brightest in the midst of deep darkness.

Moccasins and hooves dig deep, sending a crackle of breaking kinnikinnick echoing through the woods. The first time you came here you were on the back of your gelding, recently returned from Iraq, not caring whether you lived or died, riding your horse with the wind, when suddenly hooves met air. Land dropped away, and your body hit the hard earth with a jolt that stole air from your lungs. Pain exploded through your bones. You choked on your own blood until you felt yourself drowning. You thought it was over then, that death would finally put an end to all pain, but you were wrong.

Instead, you woke floating on a clear pond surrounded by a prairie filled with stunning light. The light blinded you until all you could see was a glimpse of Creator's face. At first you were convinced you had died, that this must be the place Creator called heaven. Then you realized Creator was riding on the wings of the wind, coming from that far-off place to meet with you. His voice thundered as He drew you out of the water. His hot breath dried your body and clothes. He delivered you from death and set you on your feet. Earth became solid and strong beneath you until you borrowed its strength and it became your own.

Your Creator and Redeemer talked with you then and called you by name—a name no one had ever called you before, a name you will never repeat, a name that spoke of courage and strength.

You long for that name now, to hear it upon Creator's lips. If he would talk with you now, you would gain the courage necessary to face the coming battle.

He has told you to be strong; he has commanded you to not be terrified, to not be discouraged, but your mind has forgotten how it is you can walk in such a way. So you lead Bronze Healer through thick forest surrounding the meadow called Skookum, so named because you named it, Skookum—large and powerful, strong and courageous, magnificent and awesome—all the things that elude you in your quest for courage.

Standing on the edge of the meadow, you muster enough strength to step into glorious light. Immediately, a man stands before you with a sword drawn in his hand.

"Are you for us or against us?"

Several moments of silence pass before you realize you are the one who speaks the question. A shudder crosses your chest and your bow is at ready.

"Neither." The man's voice rumbles like the sound of many hooves on hard ground. "As Commander of the host of Yahweh I have now come."

Yahweh . . . this is the word that has been in your Native tongue for centuries, atonal, often sung in song but whose meaning has long been forgotten. Yet you have heard this word from the tongue of a Native called Ghostdancer who claims to have discovered the true meaning in the Sacred Scripture called the Bible.

"Who is this Yahweh?" you ask.

The man stands firm, feet apart, a terrifying opponent but worthy Captain.

His expression softens. "Yahweh is the one you call Creator. He is your Redeemer and Restorer."

Dropping to the ground in reverence, you smell the scent of earth and feel the sense of crossing worlds.

"What message does Yahweh have for his servant?" The words come out strong, belying the weakness you feel inside.

The man unsheathes his shining sword and touches its tip to the ground. "The ground on which you are standing is holy."

In response to his flaming sword the ground shimmers with light. You tear off your moccasins and fall flat on your face and immediately hear the voice of the One for whom you have longed. He is calling you by your special name. Strength seeps into your bones. Courage lifts your face. Laughter erupts from your belly in joyous waves. Your Chief and Captain is with you, no battle is too difficult, no opponent too strong. The prize is worthy of the ultimate cost.

Chapter 21

Look for the Blessing Way.
Ghostdancer

Sayla

MY EAGLE FEATHER sits in the exact spot where the picture frame was. Impossible! My eagle feather is safely packed away with the rest of my regalia. But there is no mistaking the beautiful beaded design on the quill and the three small silver circles making it truly mine and a part of Grandfather's Klamath heritage. "Let this feather be a reminder of Creator's care for you," he had said. "Never let your voice go silent in sending up prayers of thankfulness."

Nausea turns my stomach as I remember Grandfather's words. How can I be thankful when Creator has taken so much? And why shouldn't I be silent? Creator is anything but talkative with me.

I place the frame back on the counter behind the eagle feather and search the rest of the room. It has been closed for a year and holds the musty smell of disuse, like a tomb newly opened, but nothing else seems to be out of place. Perhaps the shaman used his powers of transformation in sending the feather to me. I have heard talk he can do such things. That thought brings me back to my reason for being here.

I open my guitar case. The snap is softened in the sound buffered room, but when I pull out my guitar, another leather note falls to the floor. I pick it up and translate the words that are destined to change my life.

Bigger magic is soon to come.

I hold the note to my chest. The shaman knew I would return to my guitar. How the note got in my guitar case and how the eagle feather appeared on the counter, no longer seems an issue. If the shaman's magic can make a warrior appear in the flames, then it is nothing for him to transport a note to my guitar case and send one of Grandfather's feathers to me. I suspect the shaman moves in the unseen realm as much as he does the known.

My sister, Moriah, used to sneak away and visit the shaman in the dead of night. I once followed her until she turned on me like a mountain lion screaming in her fury. I don't remember her words, but I do know they signified a deep jealousy of my singing talent and Grandfather's favoritism toward me. It didn't help that I pointed out her rebellion is what kept Grandfather from being able to show more affection. Her constant lies and thievery got in the way. But she claimed to never see any wrong on her part and was quick to point the finger at others.

Moriah hasn't changed much today, and I'm not sorry she's gone. She lived with us most of her life until marrying a successful white man. Now, she is completely wrapped up in the lives of her ready-made family, not to mention her own two-year-old identical twin girls. It is as if the rest of us do not exist. Her exceptional dark beauty has gotten her everything she has ever wanted, which is mainly a life away from the Rez. She didn't even bring her husband and daughters to the Coming-Out. Although she only lives on the other side of Klamath Falls, she might as well be at the other end of the earth for all she has to do with us. Her one exception is working at the Klamoya Casino. She certainly doesn't mind being part of us when it comes to money.

I stuff the note into the pocket of my blue jeans and open my Apple laptop. The sound of its welcome fills the room. I insert my thumb drive into a USB port and plug my guitar into the system. All the settings on the soundboard are already in place from my last recording a year ago. I'm not looking for perfection here, just something to give my agent.

I sit on the stool and begin to play. After only two run-throughs I'm ready to record. That too seems like a miracle after a year's absence.

When your hope is all gone, and you don't know where to run—

I give it my best voice, sliding in all the right places, emphasizing the feeling of hopelessness, which isn't that difficult considering the circumstances. Singing the chorus makes me wonder just what I am supposed to be laying down. Is it my dreams? Is it my life? I hope it's the striving, because I am not ready to lay down either my dreams or my life.

You've tried it all before, nothing ever works—

The music performs its magic on me. It is a bittersweet song that will remind people of all the things they have lost—innocence, love, freedom. I hope the reminder will make my fans appreciate what they have, so they will work harder to keep those things instead of taking them for granted. And I hope they will realize it is wrong to rip these things from others.

Lay it all down when you've completely run out of grace, when you fall on the floor, when darkness covers the moon. Lay it all down. Lay it all down, down, down.

Exhaustion falls heavy on me. I place my guitar in its stand and perform the computer steps that will copy the song onto my thumb drive. While waiting for the computer to do its work, I feel strangely out of sorts. I plop into my beanbag chair in the opposite corner, meaning to rest for a few moments.

Time drifts away as I dive into a strange dark world where my body takes flight like an exhausted bird above a sea of anguished faces. They stretch in every direction below me, miles and miles of shadowy crowds. I feel as if I should know their names, but everyone looks the same, no one with any identity. My arms grow heavier as I spread them out and push the air in flight. I desperately try to stay aloft, finding purchase on the wind, knowing if I touch those faces below, their anguish will completely overtake my soul.

It seems as if the struggle lasts for hours. I fall and float, soar and drop, using every ounce of energy to stay above the sea of anguish, until finally I can struggle no more. My body plunges toward earth, and like in all my falling dreams, I wake moments before landing.

The room is completely dark.

Chapter 22

> Creator Yahweh has been our dwelling place
> throughout all generations.
> *Ghostdancer*

Loretta

THE SUN STOOD HIGH over the meadow as Loretta and Ghostdancer sat in their rockers on the porch, a cliché if ever there was one, two old people rocking their lives away. Yet things weren't always as they appeared. Though Ghostdancer's eyes were closed, Loretta knew the white-haired elder was deep in thought. After Mary and James had left, she had certainly given him enough information to keep his mind busy.

Looking past Ghostdancer, Loretta could see her blank canvas. It stared back in all its white starkness. She had brought her easel out to the porch thinking a new location might inspire her, but as yet she hadn't picked up a brush. She wanted to paint a portrait of Sayla, but the aura of turmoil surrounding the girl stopped her. Desiring to paint something beautiful, instead of a muddy mess, she decided it wasn't a good thing to throw paint on a canvas in such a mood.

She forced her vision back to Ghostdancer. His white hair hung in a single braid down his back. He wore black sweat pants and a red tee shirt, looking very much like her Charlie, minus the beard. As a young man, he had been named for the way he lived and danced between two worlds—the seen and unseen. When he began to walk the Jesus Way, he felt his name was more fitting than ever.

Many Christian elders disagreed. They thought his name was too closely associated with the ghost dance brought about by what they considered a false prophecy during the nineteenth century. Over one hundred fifty Native men, women, children, and babies, bordering on starvation, had been murdered at Wounded Knee partly because of their belief Jesus was going to give them back their fields of buffalo and provide abundant food for their families. He argued that any of the Natives who had truly believed in Creator had found the greatest object of their desire when they crossed into eternity.

Loretta was divided on the issue, as were other tribal members, but she would always look to Ghostdancer as a mentor, because he thoroughly walked the Jesus Way. And though she and Kadai had never talked about it, she knew Ghostdancer had helped bring Kadai out of his dark night of the soul following his return from Iraq.

Ghostdancer claimed to be thoroughly Native and thoroughly Christian. He still danced in flowing regalia, as a Dog Soldier with a full headdress of eagle feathers, but did so only in honor of Creator Yahweh. He had turned eighty-three in February, making him six years older than Loretta. He lived alone, somewhere in the High Cascade Mountains, and could only be reached through a secret messaging system set up by Karen Forbes, a strong-willed white woman who lived alone in a cabin she had built with her own hands. Looking at Ghostdancer's wrinkled but handsome face and strong hands, Loretta wondered if there was more to the relationship than either he or Karen would admit. Yet, it wasn't Karen who had so quickly delivered Loretta's message. Ghostdancer had come because he had seen a vision.

Ghostdancer's eyes shot open. For a moment, Loretta thought she might have inadvertently voiced her thoughts aloud, but just as she was about to apologize, Ghostdancer pointed past her. "Look at that dog of yours down in the creek."

Loretta chuckled as she watched Red Dog turn and bound up the bank and across the meadow, his tongue lolling in ecstasy. All she could see of Red Dog at times was his head as he leaped like a deer to see his way above the wild wheat. When he crossed the green grass of the yard and reached the porch, he drenched Loretta and Ghostdancer with a shaker dance that had nothing to do with religion. Loretta hollered and leapt to her feet, but the harm had already been done. Now they both carried the smell of mustard weed growing along the creek. Red Dog must have rolled in it before taking a dip.

"No harm," said Ghostdancer. "It's a good way to cool off on a hot day. Besides, I'd like to move out to the ground where we're more in touch."

It was Native tradition that to be closer to the earth was to be connected with nature and with one another. The more things you placed between yourself and the earth, the more distant you became from true reality.

They moved to a grassy area beneath a towering madrone tree. Loretta, dressed in a long skirt and blouse, settled in a squatting position that would soon hurt her knees. Barefooted, Ghostdancer sprawled on his back while Red Dog settled beside him and leaned his wet head on Ghostdancer's chest. Man and dog shared a smile. It made Loretta's heart ache.

Charlie and Ghostdancer had served together in the Vietnam War along with Luke Cathcart, a white rancher on the north side of Sacred Mountain. None of the men ever called the Vietnam War a conflict as the government did. All three had earned medals. All three had been machine gunners on the front line. All three had left home as young boys and had come home as men because there had originally been a circle of four friends, but the fourth had not come home alive. Now two of the four had passed on.

At the memory of her dead husband, Loretta swallowed a sob. Ghostdancer laid a hand on her knee and started singing in their Native tongue. The song and the sound of her Native language soothed Loretta as nothing else could do. It was a song of Yahweh, of Creator being very much in touch with his creation. It lifted her to heights far beyond that of Sacred Mountain. By the time the song was finished, the cicada's melody took over in high fervor. Peace finally settled over her like a warm Pendleton blanket.

"These young ones must walk their own walk," Ghostdancer said.

Loretta opened her eyes. Finally, her *sawalineeas* was ready to give needed advice.

Chapter 23

Do not long for the night.
Ghostdancer

Sayla

IT TAKES ME A MOMENT to figure out where I am.

Nothing makes sense. I remember turning on the light, and the computer screen should be giving some illumination, yet I can see nothing. I crawl toward the door, swimming through thick fog that steals air from the room. Standing takes a lot of effort. If I didn't know better, I would think I had been drugged.

Running my hands along the wall, I reach for the light switch, finding it strangely in the off position. I turn it on and a sudden burst of light pops the single bulb in the center of the room, sending a shower of sparks to the floor before plunging the room back into darkness.

In the middle of the light show, I catch a glimpse of the Shadow Warrior, reaching his arms out to me.

"Saaaaaaaaylaaaaaaaaaaaa."

I grab for him, but in my hurry, I stumble and fall. Something sharp, like claws, scrapes against the inside of my left wrist as I slip to the floor.

I cry out and grab my wounded arm where warm liquid oozes from what feels like a deep gash. Unlike before, soft computer light illuminates the room.

Of course, the Shadow Warrior has disappeared.

Everything moves in slow motion as I rise to my feet. I pull the thumb drive from its holder and stuff it in my pocket; then I reach for the doorknob. When the door finally opens I stumble from the room and fall against the wall. Warm sunlight washes over me.

Blood drips from my arm to the dry earth, which was damp before. How long have I been asleep? The sun stands straight overhead. The gash in my arm is bleeding profusely now, and I feel myself growing faint. My brain wills myself to move, but my legs refuse.

"Gran," I call. "Kadai." But my voice comes out in no more than a whisper. The back door to Gran's house seems a hundred miles away.

Chapter 24

> Before the mountains were born,
> from everlasting to everlasting,
> Creator Yahweh alone is God.
> *Ghostdancer*

Loretta

"OUR YOUNG ONES can walk their own walk," Loretta said, "but we can help strengthen weak arms and feeble knees."

"True."

Silence dropped its mantle over the yard. Though Loretta was comfortable with it, she couldn't outlast Ghostdancer. She took note of the thin haze of smoke forming between them and the base of *Cheelaqsdi*. The rain hadn't put out all the fires, but it had certainly dampened them. Eventually she asked, "What about the shaman?"

"Hmmph. Are we in Africa? We have no such thing as a shaman."

"Maybe not," Loretta agreed, "but that's what Jacob has been calling himself for some time now. If rumor proves true, he's left our medicine and picked up the old ways."

"Many of the old ways are good," Ghostdancer said.

"True again, but Jacob now leans toward the dark side. Several folks have seen owls cross their paths and a couple even saw wolves.

They paid Jacob to break the curse, knowing he was the one who probably set the curse in the first place."

"So I've been told."

Pain shot through Loretta's knees. She left her squatting position and sat on the ground, legs straight out. Instead of feeling more connected with her Creator, her mind was focused on her abused body. Her legs were numb from the knees down. She wondered how Ghostdancer could be so comfortable with the hard earth. Rubbing numbness from her legs she said, "Jacob has grown very powerful."

Ghostdancer shook his head. "He has no power other than Creator Yahweh allows."

"The dark forces are real."

"Of course, but don't give them too much credit."

"Jacob led Sayla into the fire!"

"He may have led, but it was her choice to go."

"I hate to think what would have happened if it wasn't for Kadai's quick action."

Ghostdancer turned his light blue eyes on her. The color was unusual for a Native American, and few could take such a straight-on piercing. Loretta tried to hold her ground but failed. She looked down at her hands, the wrinkled fingers fiddling with her skirt.

"You say you have faith," Ghostdancer said, "and that is good. But don't forget the object and giver of your faith is Creator. If you believe he is who he says he is, the creator of all things seen and unseen, then you must also believe there is nothing that can come against him or his followers and win."

Loretta watched a red hawk leave a tree beside the creek. It began sailing in circles, eyeing something in the grass below. "What about the battle between good and evil?"

Laughter erupted from Ghostdancer's throat making Red Dog's head come up. "This battle you talk of is something we made for ourselves."

The hawk left his circling and dove hard toward the field, grabbing a ground squirrel and heading back to the creek.

"I don't remember choosing this battle," Loretta said.

Ghostdancer pointed toward the creek. "The first time we chose to do wrong, we voted with the first man, Adam. We gave the evil one his power."

The hawk lost his purchase on the squirrel and it dropped to the ground, scurrying to a hole before the hawk could reclaim it. The hawk circled twice and flew back to his tree, waiting for new opportunity.

Ghostdancer continued. "Don't forget that evil's power is limited to this time and age and is nothing compared to Creator Yahweh's power. Creator's power will last for eternity. Evil has an end in sight."

Loretta shook her head. "I don't know—"

"Think about it. The evil one is like a bug beneath Creator's feet. Creator isn't even the one who puts Satan down in his final hour. While Creator Yahweh sits on his throne, he sends Michael, the archangel, to do the job, and he does it very well."

"But all the evil in the world—"

"Life apart from Creator. One day we will be with him forever. Creator Yahweh is only good. He rescues and saves, but in his time. His battle is not one of good and evil, but one between his perfect justice and his perfect love. You know as well as I do that justice and love met in the most perfect way at the cross."

Loretta threw her hands in the air. "Okay. We have no problem."

Ghostdancer chuckled. "Of course we have a problem."

"But I thought you said—"

"Listen carefully Shining Arrow, Creator has work for us to do. That is our privilege, but he is not depending on us."

To hear her name, Shining Arrow, spoken on Ghostdancer's lips, did more to encourage her than any admonition. As a new mantle of silence fell over them, Loretta felt a strengthening beginning in the pit of her stomach and working its way to her extremities. The old excitement of being needed washed over her as if she were standing in a clean waterfall. Perhaps she and Ghostdancer were still green trees. Perhaps they would still bear good fruit.

Ghostdancer was right, of course. There was evil in the world, yet even as she closed her eyes and listened to the warble of a mountain bluebird, she realized victory was reachable. Creator was still writing their stories of life and loss, death and hope. And Creator was still in the business of turning what the enemy meant for bad into something wonderful. She basked in the feeling of purpose until Red Dog's whimpers alerted her to trouble. She opened her eyes and stared into Red Dog's pleading face.

"Something's wrong," Loretta said. "Where's Sayla?"

Ghostdancer was up in a flash, moving like a man half his age. Loretta took longer to rise, and then she followed as Red Dog led Ghostdancer toward the back of the house. A cry escaped her lips when she spotted Sayla lying in a pool of blood. Dark crimson made rivulets in the hard earth. Ghostdancer ripped off his shirt and tied it high around Sayla's arm, promptly stopping the flow of blood. Loretta hoped he wasn't too late, but there was so much blood. She stared at the red pool and wondered if anyone could survive such a loss.

"Open the door!"

Loretta shook herself back to reality. Ghostdancer had already lifted Sayla into his arms and was moving toward her Jeep Wrangler. Loretta ran ahead and opened the door, crawling into the backseat to hold her granddaughter. A clean cut ran down the length of Sayla's forearm, starting just below the elbow and ending at her wrist. Perhaps the hospital personnel had been right about Sayla being suicidal. Had Loretta missed the warning signs? The clinic was over thirty minutes away. She prayed they would make it in time.

Chapter 25

> If I rise on the wings of the dawn
> and touch Creator Yahweh with my prayer.
> HE is there.
> *Ghostdancer*

Sayla

I WAKE TO A WORLD of white—white sheets, white walls, and white light pouring through the window. I can't come up with a reason for being in this white world. My brain feels drugged. It seems the only nonwhite thing in the room is Kadai. He stands in front of the window with his hands raised to the sky, singing in our Native tongue. I'm glad for all the hours Gran spent teaching her language to me. Sinking into white sheets, I translate the words.

I cry out to you, O Creator Most High. In you I take refuge. Let your glory be over all the earth. For great is your love, reaching to the heavens; your faithfulness reaches to the skies.

Beautiful words. I grab them from the air and wrap them around my heart.

Kadai picks up a flute and begins playing a tune as old as the earth and as familiar as Gran's face. Yearning clenches my heart. I swallow a sob, longing for that love that reaches to the heavens, yearning for faithfulness that lasts more than a day.

As the setting sun paints a golden glow over the room, Kadai's music wraps its arms around me, drawing me back to a place of sanity, back to connection with the *sawalineeas* of my youth. Closing my eyes, I let the music wash over me in healing waves of grace.

Grace? I used to believe in the grace Grandfather talked about.

The music stops. "Little Fire," Kadai says. "You are back."

His fingers caress my hair, and I look up into his worried face.

He leans close. "Tell me what happened."

"I-I'm not sure. My brain feels all foggy."

"Ah. It is the drugs. Grandmother tried to talk the doctor out of it, but she was concerned about your depression."

"Depression?"

A nurse chooses that moment to enter the room, marching to the side of my bed.

"So, our patient is awake." She lifts my right arm. "And how are *we* this evening?" Looking at her watch, she counts off my heartbeats.

Kadai removes his hand from my hair and takes a step back. An inexplicable feeling of loss washes over me, making me strangely angry. "I don't know how *we* are, but I'm fighting some kind of drug reaction and would like to know why?"

The nurse straightens and her lips tighten. She flashes Kadai a disapproving look. "You'll have to speak with the doctor about that."

"Okay," I say. "I would like to speak to him, right now."

"He is a she, and I'm afraid that's impossible. Dr. Rosenbrock is in surgery."

Dr. Rosenbrock? I've never heard of the woman. "Fine," I say. "Then I'll just leave. She can talk with me later."

I start to push up from the bed, but Kadai moves closer and places a firm hand on my shoulder. "Careful, Little Fire," he whispers.

"I think there's too much careful going on around here," I say.

Kadai removes his hand and I sit up. Nausea and dizziness threaten to topple me, but I fight them off, determined to escape this white prison cell.

The nurse grabs a rope hanging near my bed and gives it a pull. Before I can rise to my feet, a male nurse enters the room. He forces me back to the bed. The first nurse jams a needle in my thigh.

"What's going on here?" I cry.

The male nurse commands Kadai to leave.

"Please!" I plead. "Let him stay."

"Out!" The man demands, pointing a finger toward the door. "Now!"

As the drugs pull me into darkness I hear Kadai say, "I'm staying with my sister."

But when I awake, Kadai is gone, and I am in another room. This room is not white, but everything is the same muted color as the carpet. The walls and the bench I lie on are padded.

I can't imagine what happened to place me here as a prisoner.

I move to sit up and discover nausea is still with me. I hunch over and reach for the door, intending to find a bathroom. The door is only one step away. But when I try the handle, it will not turn. Spewing vomit across the floor sickens me further. Cramps take over and continue long after the food has left my stomach. The room stinks.

I pound on the door and ask for help. Finally the door opens, but instead of the relief I seek, three men surround me and another needle is plunged deep into my thigh. As I sink into darkness I realize the nightmare has only begun.

Chapter 26

*If I make my bed with the enemy,
that evil trickster,
Creator Yahweh is still there.*
Ghostdancer

Loretta
August 28, 2014
Thursday morning

SPICY SMELLING SAGE smoke still clung to Loretta's clothing as she exited the teepee. She felt anything but relieved as she thought about the fact she had just made a liaison of sorts with the shaman. Ghostdancer would certainly disapprove, but she couldn't just stand back and do nothing while Sayla needed help. Of course, she had been praying, which Ghostdancer said was the most important part, but praying had also left her feeling helpless. She just had to *do* something.

Now, having *done* the thing she had set out to do, she felt worse than ever, suspecting she would soon be sorry had jumped the gun once again and taken matters into her own hands. After all these years, she should have known better.

Five young men stood in the parking lot of Whatchawant Market and watched as she made her way from the cemetery at the top of the hill to her Jeep Wrangler. She hoped they didn't recognize her. Earlier in the day, she had parked at the white people's church not far from the market. It was an easy thing to slip to the shaman's teepee up the hill afterward. She thought she had covered her tracks well enough so no one would know where she had been, but the streets were now deserted as she walked alone down the hill. She felt as exposed as a black ant in a sea of white sugar.

Each of the five men held a beer, typical for many Chiloquin youth, even though the sun was still high in the sky. Alcohol was another of the white people's gifts that had led to the downfall of the Indian way of walking in beauty. The thought hit her hard in the stomach. She stared at her feet as she made her way along the gravel road, willing herself to be invisible.

White people had taken so much from her people. First, they had said her Native religion was false and everything they had believed in up to that time was from the evil one. All of her mother's family heirlooms were destroyed because the white men mistook them for some kind of demonic artifacts. Yet Loretta knew not everything they had believed in was evil. What was evil about believing in a Great Spirit who had created their world and watched over them? Didn't Christian white people believe the same thing? According to Ghostdancer, Native Americans should have been the first to recognize Jesus as Creator, because they had already been in touch with him without knowing his name. They had felt his presence in all of creation. They may have gotten a few things wrong, but so had the white people.

Charlie had told Loretta often enough that the Gospel was not about keeping rules or getting everything right, it was about receiving an unearned, priceless treasure and spending the rest of your life captured by grace.

And what was evil about protecting your loved ones and desiring to wipe out your enemies? Didn't the white man do the same thing? And what about this so-called civilized people? White people were only half civilized at best. Hadn't the white people's government proved well they were unable to order their lives into a way of peace?

Loretta was surprised at the fierceness of her thoughts. She had long ago dropped such nonsensical thinking that led to a no good end, or at least she thought she had dropped it, and she thought she had forgiven the white people. Now, as the hot sun beat down on her through a smoky haze, she had little control over her mind. She wondered if today's thoughts reflected the real truth of her heart attitude.

Perhaps the shaman had already cast a spell upon her, but even such a thought made her angry. Who were these white people who had taken away Native healers? A healer would never have placed Sayla in a cell of a room and kept her there. It was crazy making to think confining people in tiny rooms would lift their spirits. The white people weren't truly interested in lifting Sayla's spirit; they were out to break it, and breaking a person's spirit was serious business. Sayla needed fresh air and wide, open spaces, a place where she could feel the breath of Creator.

Loretta was determined to do whatever it took to get Sayla out of that cell.

"Grandmother," one of the youths called.

She ignored him, keeping her steady pace down the hill as she continued her one-sided argument. Whites had left the Indian's way of life in shambles. She recalled the train ride when she was eight years old, that had taken her and her siblings away from this land and off to Nevada. At first she thought it was going to be a fun vacation, but then she was separated from her brother and sister and placed with other young Indian girls in a big white house. She felt like crying when the scissors chopped off her prided long hair, but she was able to hold her tears. She continued to hold her tears when they commanded all the young girls to never speak a word of their Native tongue, but then the tears fell like rain after she inadvertently called out to a girl she recognized from Chiloquin. *"Sawalineenas"* had fallen from her mouth before she could stop it. The other girl had responded in kind, with a flow of Native words that sent them both to solitary confinement. But the worst was the baptism. Just thinking about it sent shivers up her legs.

Yaks dwa! Loretta's thoughts were certainly out of control. She picked up her pace.

The youth called out again, this time closer. The next time he called, he was walking beside her. She looked up into the laughing brown eyes of Mary's son, James.

"*Yaks dwa!*" Loretta cried. "You about scared the life out of this old woman."

James laughed. "Seems like someone must have already scared the life out of your ears. I've called you several times."

"Really?"

Now she had added lying to her list of sins. Maybe it wasn't an out-in-the-open sort of lie, but it was certainly withholding the truth. "I'm in kind of a hurry, James."

"That's what I wanted to talk with you about."

Loretta stopped.

"Heard Sayla was taken to hospital."

Loretta stared up into James' face. Were all these young men built like strong trees? He towered above her, waiting for an answer. She shook her head. "I don't know exactly what to say. Sayla fell and hurt herself. We're hoping for a quick recovery."

"Must have been some fall to end up in the hospital. How bad's the cut?"

James raised a hand to shade his face from the sun that was now sinking through the red horizon, reminding Loretta of how long she had been away from the hospital. She started moving toward the Wrangler.

"Come on, Grandmother. Surely you can give us some news. Must be bad if you darkened the shaman's teepee."

Stopping abruptly next to the Wrangler, Loretta realized the enormity of her sin. Everyone would soon know of her visit to the shaman. Would they think Creator wasn't good enough or strong enough to answer her prayers? What had she done? Her legs felt weighed down with boulders as she pulled herself into the driver's seat.

"Grandmother?"

Ignoring James' call, she turned the key and drove away from the white people's church, not in the direction of the hospital, but back toward Sacred Mountain Ranch where Ghostdancer kept his steady pace of prayer. She had no right to return to the hospital after what she had done. Everyone would think she had sold out to the dark forces. Tears slid down her cheeks as she thought of her husband Charlie. If he had been here, this would never have happened. He always knew exactly how to take care of things. Oh, how she missed Charlie's arms about her.

Miles passed slowly beneath the Wrangler's tires. This was one trip Loretta was in no hurry to complete.

Chapter 27

> If I forget you, O Creator Yahweh,
> may my right hand forget its skill.
> *Ghostdancer*

Sayla

EARLY SUNDAY AFTERNOON, my non-talkative lawyer wheels me out of the Sky Lakes Medical Center as a free woman in an obligatory wheelchair. I feel anything but free. Dr. Rosenbrock reluctantly allowed me to leave only after my lawyer promised I would take the prescribed drugs until my next doctor visit. I argued that as an adult I should be able to leave any time. Dr. Rosenbrock pointed out that Gran had brought me in for attempted suicide, so I had lost all those rights. The revelation caused my brain to explode.

Why would anyone think I wanted to take my life?

Dr. Rosenbrock claimed she had my best interest in mind. She had also been kind enough to let me call a trusted friend. That offer bothered me even more. Kadai is not at the hospital and not answering his phone. I tried calling Gran, and then my white friend Bailey, but when no one answered, my agent seemed the next best choice. Kenny was able to get hold of a lawyer friend in Klamath Falls, and the rest is history. No more confinement for me, but I have lost more than a little confidence, and I'm worried about Gran and Kadai. The worst part is that I am still stuck on prescribed drugs. I have no memory of what happened to land me in the hospital, and I suspect the medication has something to do with that.

Dr. Rosenbrock said Ghostdancer and Gran had come to the suicide conclusion because of the deep slash on my wrist and the fact I was alone when it happened.

I insisted just as strongly they had to be wrong.

The doctor pointed out I may be experiencing repressed depression over the deaths of my parents. She said the Coming-Out of Grief Ceremony probably triggered emotions I didn't even know existed.

She is wrong, but I didn't bother to point it out. I am well aware of the emotions warring in my soul, but I played along with the white people's game and kept calm in order to leave. But I still don't understand what happened to cause such a deep slash in my wrist. The frustrating brain fog refuses to lift.

When my wheelchair reaches the curb, Mr. Lawyer leaves to get his car. He's a balding white man, draped into a suit a size too big and looks to be in his late thirties. He smells of Irish Spring soap and has probably never seen the back of a horse. I can't imagine why my agent thought we would make a good team, but at least the man was able to free me, for that I am grateful. He has a name, but my drugged condition keeps me from retaining it.

Mr. Lawyer drives up to the landing in a four-door, black Lexus. I can see the hospital's reflection in the shine of his car. It is clearer than a calm pool. I resist a whistle as Mr. Lawyer opens the door. "Hey," I say. "Nice wheels."

He gives me his first smile but says nothing. I drop into the low seat that smells of fresh leather and think about how my people in Chiloquin will get a kick out of seeing me drive up in the fancy car. It will also give me the opportunity to see if anyone knows what happened. "Can we stop at the Watchawant Market in Chiloquin?"

Mr. Lawyer peers at me over his rimless glasses that remind me of John Lennon, one of Gran's favorite singers from her hippie days when she travelled the art circuit.

"Just need a few things," I say.

"Why not stop at a market around here?"

By around here, he means somewhere in Klamath Falls. I don't want to tell him my real reason for stopping is to see what's going around the rumor mill, so I tell him Watchawant has what I need. He punches in some numbers on his GPS and his car begins talking to him in a soft female voice, telling him how far he has to go and which way to turn. I settle back to enjoy the fancy ride.

No sun reflects off Klamath Lake as we pull onto the highway. Instead eerie smog-like puffs of smoke have settled over its surface. The lake boasts one hundred forty-one square miles of open water and has earned a reputation as one of the top ten sailing destinations in North America. Long ago, it was the place where my people harvested wocus seeds and tule reeds. There are no sails on the lake today, probably because not even a whisper of wind touches its surface, but there are plenty of birds. Literally thousands of migratory birds stop by the lake and its surrounding marshlands on their way to wherever. Today, I see a group of pelicans lazing on the shore while geese fly overhead.

Mr. Lawyer and I ride in silence while I take in the beauty and bask in my freedom. Once or twice I look over at the speedometer and notice Mr. Lawyer likes his freedom too. He's running well over the speed limit, though the Lexus is as smooth as if we are meandering through a school zone. I wonder for a minute, why the GPS isn't telling him to slow down.

Soon we enter the forestlands and pass the Klamoya Casino where my sister Moriah works. I peer across the parking lot to see if I can get a glimpse of her, knowing full well she is tucked deep inside making sure everything is running smoothly. Gran hates the casino; says it makes a mockery of our Native ways. Others disagree. They say the casino brings in needed money to make our lives better.

Gran's counter argument is always the same. "Too many of our own people are dropping their money in there, not to mention how many of them fill up on booze while they're at it."

As if to prove Gran's point, I see James' father stumbling from the entrance. He reminds me of my father before he went to work with Kenny. My father's drinking problem was the main reason he left Chiloquin. The only way he could give up his homeboys was to put a thousand miles between them.

Three minutes later, Mr. Lawyer turns off Highway 97 into Chiloquin. It's hard to believe it was once a rowdy boomtown referred to as "Little Chicago." At least, that's what Gran tells me. Today, the lumber mills that brought in the rowdy crowd are all gone, and our tiny community has gained a quiet respect. Several children are swimming in the river as the Lexus crosses the bridge. They wave and shout when they see the shiny car, and I wave back through the open window. When we near the railroad tracks, the car tells Mr. Lawyer to slow down. I chuckle at the thought Mr. Lawyer's car talks more than he does. He hasn't said one word since we left Klamath Falls.

When we pull into the parking lot of Watchawant Market, every eye in the place is trained on the car. Loud whoops greet me as I step out of the passenger side. I smile. James and his crew are at their usual task of getting drunk before nightfall.

"What's up?" I ask.

James places an arm around my shoulders and walks me toward the market. "Got some juicy news for you. Bet you've got some for me as well."

"Juicy?"

James' smile doesn't reach his eyes, which are a dark chocolate. His long hair hangs loose past his bare shoulders. He looks as if he stepped out of some cowboy movie, but he smells of whiskey and sweat. I wrinkle my nose.

"Heard you went to hospital," he says.

News travels fast in Chiloquin. I hope he doesn't know about me being stuck in the mental ward. James takes my left arm and looks at the white gauze covering my eight stitches; then he gives a long whistle. "When you decide to do a thing, girl, you decide to do it up right. Why not slash sideways?"

"I didn't slash."

"Could have fooled me."

"I fell." Even as I say the words, memories come flooding back. I remember the darkened room and the Shadow Warrior, the eagle feather that appeared out of nowhere, and my earlier talk with James. I slip from his arm and run a hand through my wind-blown hair. "Need to speak to the shaman."

James stops mid stride and leans down to whisper. "Not a good time."

"Why not?"

James straightens, his smile still wide. "Your grandmother was here earlier. Left the shaman's teepee not more than half an hour ago."

So that was why I hadn't been able to reach Gran by phone. I feel my mouth drop open just like in a slapstick comedy, but this isn't slapstick, and it sure isn't comedy. "Gran?"

"Broad daylight. We all saw her. Even talked with her."

My eyes stray to the cemetery above the white man's church. The shaman's teepee is as near as it can get to the cemetery; he claims he's watching over the souls of the ones who've crossed over. The church's steeple and top of the teepee both point skyward as if saying there is more than one way of reaching heaven, or perhaps there are two heavens available—one for white people and another for Natives. In my way of thinking, the two simply carry the age-old war into another dimension—the battle between a clean white steeple versus painted canvas. If given a choice, I will take canvas every time, because it speaks of heritage and hope. The white people's steeple speaks of death to me, as sharp and deadly as any spear.

Focusing my eyes back on James, I say, "So Gran entered the shaman's teepee?" I try to sound like it's just an everyday, normal occurrence.

"Broad daylight."

I scowl. "Gran probably had a thing or two to say to the shaman."

James loops his thumbs around two belt loops of his jeans. I try not to look at his hairless chest glistening in the sun. When James isn't drunk, he falls trees for a living. Lately, he's been fighting fires, but he's back now because of some misunderstanding, or so he says. His muscles are hard and tight. I turn away.

"Grandmother paid the price."

I spin around. "What?"

"Paid the price." His eyes turn into dark slits. "Question is . . . what for? Looking at your arm, could be healing. Or—" His voice trails off.

"Or what?" His immature needling is beginning to nag.

"Or perhaps . . . to break a curse."

"Break a curse?"

James looks at my arm again. "Maybe not everyone's a fan."

Thinking of my dead parents and the fact someone was not a fan of them, there suddenly isn't enough air to fill my lungs. I bend over, gasping for breath.

James grabs my shoulders. "Whoa. Easy there, Sayla. Didn't mean to scare you."

"Get away from her young man!"

I look up to see Mr. Lawyer crossing the lot, waving his cell phone like some kind of weapon. "I've already dialed 9-1-1."

James curses and runs to his pickup truck. All five guys pile into the single bench seat before he peals out on the street. He probably has a kilo of marijuana in his truck and can't afford to get caught.

I straighten, feeling less dizzy. "You didn't need to do that," I say to Mr. Lawyer. "He's a friend."

"Sorry miss, but he didn't look like much of a friend from the way you doubled over. You need to consider you were just released from the hospital. If you'll clue me in on what's so important in the market, I'll get it for you while you rest in the car."

"Girl stuff."

"What?"

"Girl stuff," I repeat. "Gotta get it myself."

"Oh." Crimson flushes the lawyer's face, and his voice drops to a timid whisper. "I could go with you?"

I nearly laugh at Mr. Lawyer's old-fashioned embarrassment, but Gran taught me better. Though the man is white, he's still older, which makes him an elder and worthy of respect. Besides, it was kind of sweet how he stood up for me.

"That's okay," I say. "I'm feeling stronger now. By the way, did you really call 9-1-1?"

A wispy smile crosses his face. "No. But I would have if those hoodlums didn't leave."

"Good job," I say, meaning it. I rush into the store, slinking through the narrow aisles and grabbing several items to satisfy Mr. Lawyer's curiosity. The market isn't much bigger than Gran's living room, but it holds a surprising array of items. Gran's friend, Diana, is the checkout lady. She doesn't say anything about seeing Gran at the shaman's teepee, so I figure she must not have noticed. Seeing my bandaged arm, she says, "What happened there?"

"Fell," I say. "It'll be good as new in no time."

She accepts my answer with a nod and proceeds to tell me about a neighbor who fell and was stuck on the floor overnight. She's still talking when I exit the market surprising Mr. Lawyer, as well as myself, with my newfound strength. When he isn't looking I drop Dr. Rosenbrock's pills into a trashcan on the other side of the Lexus. Mr. Lawyer doesn't need to know every detail of my life. I need a clear mind.

As emotionally painful as it is, I sit back in the leather seat and think this might be a good time to consider how my parents and grandfather died. All three were returning from a trip to Sheldon Wildlife Refuge on the Oregon-Nevada border. They were pulling a loaded horse trailer behind, just as they had done a hundred times before, but this time they lost control of the flatbed and dropped six hundred feet into the Guano Desert. A single set of goat tracks crossing the road was the only explanation the investigating State Trooper found.

Now, after ending up in a mysterious accident of my own, I can't help but wonder about the cause of the crash. Especially after what James said about a curse. In our Native way of thinking, curses are real. They are not superstition. They are the result of someone calling upon an evil spirit to go into an animal and do harm to someone. The question is, who would want to do us harm?

As Mr. Lawyer pulls out of the parking lot, I consider the shaman can probably conjure some kind of supernatural power to figure out what's going on. Who knows? Maybe that was why Gran sought him out. Perhaps deep down Gran believes more in the shaman's power than she does in the power of Creator.

For some reason that thought gives me little comfort. Gran is like a rock in my life, the one force that never changes. If her faith in Creator is wavering, then what hope is there for ever seeing my parents and Grandfather again?

Depression sinks me deeper into the seat. If Mr. Lawyer could read my thoughts he would turn his fancy Lexus around and rush right back to the hospital.

Chapter 28

I will sing of the love of Creator Yahweh forever.
Ghostdancer

Kadai

EVERYTHING YOU WORKED so hard to attain in the last two years is shot down the tube like so much toilet water. You failed the one you love, and you failed yourself. Yet before you travel far down the self-pity way, heavy footsteps and rattling keys signal the guard's arrival. He stops at your holding cell and opens the door.

"Visitor."

He motions with his head for you to lead the way. It's an easy thing to do. You've been here before. Same jail. Same cell. Same concrete walls.

As you pass the pod, you think of the Medal of Honor stashed away in your cabin. So this is how America treats her heroes. You've had no trial, no lawyer consultation, not even one phone call. You did hear your Miranda rights. At least they got that right.

The guard opens the door to a row of visitor stations. It is no surprise to see Ghostdancer sitting on the free side of the petition about halfway down. You are surprised, however, to see the two of you are alone. The last time you were here, every booth was filled on each side of the partition with each prisoner and visitor trying to yell over the top of the others. At least this time, you will be able to hear what Ghostdancer has to say.

You pull out a chair and sit, picking up the phone in one motion. With a glass wall between the two of you, the phone is the only way to communicate. Ghostdancer nods and you nod back. His strange blue eyes tell the story, pain and anger mixed in one bath, yet no bitterness finds his tongue.

He leans into his phone and says. "You are sane and sober."

You dip your head in acknowledgement. It is a good reminder. Sane and sober. Two things you had not experienced on your last trip here. Yet, watching Ghostdancer through the glass, you also acknowledge little has changed for Natives in the last hundred years, other than giving you a name that makes the white people feel better about their not-so-hidden prejudices.

"Sayla?" The word falls off your tongue like a song. Some defender you've been, leaving her behind to defend herself.

"We're working on it." Ghostdancer raises a hand to stop the curse that nearly falls from your mouth.

"Bitterness is not the way." Ghostdancer's voice is soft, yet firm, as it crackles over the phone. "Creator will be faithful to Sayla.

You shake your head, but Ghostdancer continues, undaunted by your bitterness.

"Don't get confused about the battle," he says. "It is not confined to open places. You can fight here as well as there. Make ready. Your time has come. You must be strong."

Yet you do not feel strong. Nor do you feel ready.

You tried to stand your ground back in the hospital, and you ended up in handcuffs and carried to this place where you have been before and, because of your past record, you will not get out of here anytime soon.

You shake your head. "It's easy to think the enemy has gained ground."

"*Cha aat!*" Ghostdancer's voice is strong with passion. "Let the evil one think what he wants."

Ghostdancer's command takes you by surprise. As a trained soldier, the man seldom allows anyone to hear such passion in his voice. The command, "*Cha aat!* That's it for now!" is not meant for you but for your mutual enemy.

Ghostdancer pauses, and his fingers loosen their grip on the phone. When he speaks again, his voice is a near whisper. "Creator is with you. His Spirit fills you with strength and wisdom."

Though the cold smell of hard concrete fills your lungs, you suddenly remember the smell of warm grain and rich earth. You pull up the feel of horseflesh beneath your legs. As you close your eyes, it's almost as if you're flying free across the fields below Sacred Mountain to the music of thundering hooves.

But then you remember John the Baptist, that great man of faith, who prophesied the coming of Christ. He, too, was stuck in a jail cell, and his faith was weakened until he sent others to ask Jesus, "Are you the One?"

"I Am," came the answer.

You have always wondered if the answer was enough. Where was John's faith when his neck felt the cold blade bite into his throat?

But you believe and trust "I Am" was the one who met John when he stepped through the veil to the other side. "I Am" rings out through time, through eternity, through past and future, forever. "I Am"—the Great Spirit of whom your forefathers caught a glimpse. "I Am." Creator. Yahweh. Messiah. Redeemer.

"In the beginning was the Word—" Ghostdancer quotes.

Not for the first time, you are amazed at your mentor's gift of understanding. Creator has allowed him to know some of your thinking. It is enough to let you know that Creator understands, that he is aware of your every thought.

"And the Word was *with* Yahweh," you answer.

"And the Word *was* Yahweh."

"He was with Yahweh in the beginning."

"Through him all things were made."

"Without him nothing was made that has been made."

You continue your singsong, the back and forth responses that kept you from going crazy when you were here the first time.

Someone in another room hollers obscenities. Ghostdancer's voice rises in strength and volume. "In him was life."

"And that life was the light of men."

Your heart jumps at the realization that Creator Yahweh, your Chief and Captain, is your life and light. No darkness can hide his light; no walls are strong enough to keep him away. It is a good reminder because footsteps echo from the hall.

"Time's up!" the deputy says.

"The light shines in the darkness." Ghostdancer's words are soft as he hangs up the phone, but the meaning stays with you long after the guard leads you back to your cell and closes the door, long after the words, "Lights out!" plunges the cell into darkness. Ghostdancer's quotes from the *Sacred Writings* give you strength where once you were weak. Wisdom from your own people weaves itself through the words. You think of the time your people walked in the true way. The way of walking in beauty. The way of Creator. Long before the white people brought fences and walls to this land.

This is the true strength of the warrior, not with shield and sword, though the time may come for that, but with a heart bursting with strong medicine and filled with the Spirit of Creator. You feel his presence here in this dark place, the place that could rob you of your soul if you allow it.

The choice is yours—walk in beauty—or walk in darkness.

You choose beauty and begin to dance, without feathers or music, in a cell with hard stone for a floor. You dance your prayers to Creator, knowing he accepts them for what they are—a true praise offering for the one who has given you life. The old ones join you, the ones who have passed from this life; their praise reaches fervor unlike any you've heard before.

Stone walls slip away as the vision transports you to open fields where you dance beneath moonlight. The smell of ripe grain and sweet tobacco wraps itself around you, replacing despair with hope and strengthening your body with courage. When at last you close your eyes and lay on the hard cot, your thoughts turn to wonder.

If you had not been thrown into this white man's pit, if you had not tasted such bitterness, you may have missed the sweetness of a soul set free. You are ready for whatever battle the white man's agenda may throw at you. Ultimately, that agenda is in Creator's hands, and he is forever faithful. Such knowledge carries you into a peaceful sleep.

Chapter 29

> With my songs I will make known
> Creator Yahweh's faithfulness.
> *Ghostdancer*

Sayla

    WHEN MR. LAWYER pulls up at Sacred Mountain Ranch, I wonder what he thinks of our home. Open fields—some green, most yellow grass and sagebrush—stretch from the Sprague River to the base of Sacred Mountain. The smoke is much thinner here than back at Klamath Lake. Horses graze in the distance along with a herd of elk. An elk will be hanging in the shelter by nightfall if Kadai sees it. Mr. Lawyer turns off the engine and rolls down his window, taking in the scene. The chirping of cicadas fills the car. Still he says nothing. A bald eagle circles high in the sky surveying the field below. Our entire herd of cattle is lying in the shade beneath two lone oak trees.

    Finally, Mr. Lawyer reaches into his wallet pulling out a card for me.

    "Justice Lincoln, Attorney," I read aloud, and then I look up. "You've got to be kidding."

    The blush across his face is red enough to decorate a warrior's shield. "Natives aren't the only ones who believe in the power of a name. My parents had big hopes for me."

"Wow. I guess. No wonder my agent picked you."

He waves a hand in the air, as if swishing a pesky fly. "Please, call me Link. That's much easier to live up to. And speaking of your agent, Kenny wants you to call as soon as possible. I didn't tell you before, because you seemed to need a breather."

"A breather?"

He peers at me through those John Lennon glasses, and I think for a minute he's rather good looking. His eyes are green with laugh lines on the outside edges. I get the impression there's a lot more to this guy than I first thought.

"Kenny and I go way back," he says. "He was married to my sister for a time. I know just how much of a bulldog he can be when he's on a roll. He said something about coming to check things out for himself."

Before I can protest Gran comes to the rescue wearing one of her ever-present, flower-printed shirts over a denim skirt hanging below her knees. Her toes are thrown into bright pink flipflops. I open the door and stand to meet her embrace.

"Sayla!" She wraps her arms around me.

Leaning into the strength of her, I breathe in the scent of sweet pea lotion that makes me feel like a child again.

"I'm so glad to see you." Gran's voice is warm and sincere. "I was so worried."

Yeah. Worried enough to visit the shaman. I pull away.

Red Dog sits at my feet, his tail pounding the earth as he gives me a dog smile. I pat his head.

"Are you okay?" Gran asks.

"Sure. Fine." We both know I'm lying.

Gran grimaces and turns to Link who is now standing beside me.

"I'm Loretta," she says, "Sayla's grandmother."

While they exchange greetings, I lean down to hug Red Dog. First, I want to know what happened to Kadai. Why wasn't he at the hospital? And where is he now? But I don't want to talk about our personal problems in front of Link.

Second, I want to know what happened in the sound room, but Gran will protest. So that will have to wait, but the thought of entering the sound room after dark gives me the creeps.

I stand. "I'm going inside Gran. Thanks Link."

I take two steps and Link and Gran shoot to each side of me, offering support as if I am some sort of invalid. Shaking them both off, I step back. "Come off it. I know how to walk already."

Link's arms fall away as if he's been shot.

Gran laughs. "Now that sounds like my Sayla. Perhaps you're well after all. Come on in for a drink, Mr. Lincoln. I have some fresh squeezed lemonade with your name on it."

"Call me Link, please." He looks at his watch. "I really should be getting back."

Gran waves him off. "Tomorrow's another day. Come on in for some true Native hospitality."

I'm glad for the diversion. There's been too much attention on me. Gran pours lemonade into frosted glasses and takes Link to the living room. Already, he is asking questions about the rodeo pictures on the wall. Seems the guy has a voice after all.

I make a cup of tea and stir Stevia into it before heading to my room. I set the tea on a nightstand and lift the mattress to retrieve Grandfather's journals, but nothing meets my fingers. I lift it higher, and then remember I left them on my nightstand where my tea now sits alone.

A thorough search proves fruitless. The journals are gone, either stolen or borrowed. Not really a surprise, since everyone in my family knows I have them. I'll ask Gran about them later. Avoiding squeaking hinges, I sneak out the back door and head to the sound room. Blood still stains the ground. Crows have picked it over, but I am familiar enough with ranch life to recognize the smell of dried blood. I gasp and duck as a crow flies from nearby trees and misses me by mere inches. It's just plain weird to realize crows have been feasting on my blood. My fingers are shaking as I turn the knob and push open the door.

A river of shadows sweeps across the room. More than shadows. This darkness has the feel of something living. I fight against the darkness that claimed me the day before, but it holds me fast. I hear a thousand whispering voices, but the only word I can understand is my name being called over and over. The door slams with a bang, and the dark room falls silent.

The silence is more eerie than the whispered words. I close my eyes.

"Saaaaaaaaylaaaaaaa."

My eyes shoot open.

The Shadow Warrior's heartbeat joins mine, two hearts throbbing as one, and then I hear a distant drumbeat. The Shadow Warrior is so close his breath falls like warm wind upon my face. Desire rises within me.

He sings my name in an erotic tune of water falling over rocks, "Saaaaaaaaylaaaaaaa."

The drumbeat continues. It is the sound of our hearts beating out a cadence from a long ago time, a time when Native men and women walked in beauty, together, as one. I long for that beauty, long for oneness, long for passion that will sweep away the emptiness I've felt since the death of my parents and grandfather.

"Saaaaaaaaaaylaaaaaaa."

The Shadow Warrior sings my name as a song of purest love. Surely there can be no harm in accepting such love. I raise my arms, planning to take a step forward, but then I remember my stitched wrist and Kadai's burned hands. Was the Shadow Warrior responsible?

I take a step back.

"Saaaaaaaaaaylaaaaaaaa."

The Shadow Warrior's hot breath caresses my face with a soft kiss. Fingers of fire explode through my neck and arms. My legs feel cold in comparison. I long for more, for the warmth to stretch throughout my entire body. I take a step forward as he calls my name again, and I feel the warmth of his kiss upon my cheek. But I want more, much more. I want all he has to offer. Turning my lips to his, I sense my life will completely change once our lips meet, but it is not to be, for suddenly the door bangs open and light replaces darkness. The transformation is immediate and complete.

Ghostdancer stands in the light. "You have no right to be here!" he commands.

At first, I think he's talking to me, but his eyes are focused on something above and behind. Hearing a low growl, I turn. A hulking wolf crouches behind me, ready to spring. His eyes are blood red and shining like fire.

Ghostdancer's strong hands push me down as the wolf springs. I hear the sound of its teeth ripping flesh, but I feel no pain.

"Out!" Ghostdancer commands again. "You have no right."

His voice is growing weak, and I realize the ripping flesh was his.

Sobs break from my throat.

The wolf springs again, bounding through the air to land on Ghostdancer's kneeling form. "In the name of Yeshua, The Christ," Ghostdancer says, "you have no power over me."

In mid-air, the wolf shimmers and breaks apart disappearing into the light rays pulsating above Ghostdancer's head. After the wolf leaps through, the portal closes. Ghostdancer doubles over, falling to the ground. I crawl to him, telling myself I have just witnessed the impossible.

Blood oozes from Ghostdancer's neck and shoulder where the wolf ripped flesh. Those teeth would have ripped into my heart if Ghostdancer hadn't pushed me down.

I pull off my outer shirt that covers my thin-strapped tee, expecting to use it to stop the blood flow. But by the time I smooth it out enough to lay pressure on Ghostdancer's wound nothing but a jagged pink scar remains where the teeth ripped through flesh. All signs of blood have disappeared.

I sit on my knees, holding the shirt, stunned into silence.

Ghostdancer works his way to a sitting position, leaning his back against the open door, looking as tired as an over-ridden horse.

"What have you gotten yourself into, Little Fire?"

His eyes bore into my soul. My hands are frozen upon the shirt.

"What deep darkness are you courting?"

Even while shaking my head in denial, I know the truth. Back at the Coming-Out of Grief Ceremony, the Shadow Warrior called me. Though desire had risen in me at that time, I hadn't yet given myself to him.

Then the gift of a song had been his wooing. My acceptance had given the Shadow Warrior certain rights. My heartbeat quickens, as I stand poised between two worlds. Gran and Ghostdancer's world offers stability, while the world of the Shadow Warrior offers a powerful journey into my Native heritage.

Pulling the gauze off my arm, I stare at the stitches on my wrist. The dark warrior has already placed his mark upon me. Strangely, I don't mind the scar. Like Kadai, marking his horse with paint, the Shadow Warrior has marked me with blood. I am already his.

"None of us live alone, Little Fire. Our choices affect more than ourselves."

My eyes move to Ghostdancer's wound. A wave of doubt washes over me. "Tell me what to do, Ghostdancer. This is beyond anything I've ever known."

His answer is quick. "Run Sayla! Get away from this thing."

Remembering the hot fire of desire travelling through my veins just moments ago, I shake my head. Ghostdancer is old; it's a natural thing for him to be afraid, but I'm young and strong.

"You are not as strong as you think."

Ghostdancer's words startle me. The man is an uncanny mind reader.

"There is no lie this enemy will tell you that you won't believe. He twists everything into a lie."

For a moment, I wonder if his words are true. His gray hair reminds me he is an elder and I should respect his wishes, but the shaman is also an elder and the two men hold completely different beliefs. What if Creator is leading me through the shaman? Yet, I keep going back to the question of whether the shaman's fire would have consumed me if Kadai hadn't been there. And what about the wolf?

"You cannot fight this battle in your own strength," Ghostdancer warns. "Return to Creator Yahweh, the God of your grandmother."

The God of Gran? The same one who stole my parents and grandfather? Hugging my arms to my chest I stare at the floor. I don't think the fire or the wolf would have really hurt me. After all, my feet are free of burns, and Ghostdancer's shoulder looks none the worse except for a scar. I try to push out the thought of Kadai's palms.

Ghostdancer moans, his voice not much louder than a whisper. I reach out to touch him. "Are you in pain?"

His eyes lock on mine. "No pain is as great as that of the soul. You must walk your own path, Little Fire. You have the information needed to make the right choice. I cannot do that for you."

But Ghostdancer is wrong. He's talking about choices made with the intellect. My heart has already made the choice, no matter how much information my brain gives it. I hear the door slamming on my old way of life. Part of me is frightened beyond belief; the other part is exhilarated and ready to begin a new adventure.

Turning from Ghostdancer, I rise to my feet and step over his outstretched legs.

Ghostdancer's hand shoots up and catches mine. His grip is surprisingly strong for an old man. "Promise me one thing, Little Fire."

I hold my lips tight, not willing to promise anything. Avoiding his piercing eyes, I stare at the door above his head.

"Are you so far gone, Little Fire? Can you not honor your grandfather by making one promise to his most trusted *sawalineeas?*"

I close my eyes, but Ghostdancer's grip remains strong. His words cover me like a blessing . . . or a curse . . . depending on how you look at it, but the mention of Grandfather keeps me listening. Ghostdancer was Grandfather's most trusted mentor. His voice washes over me in a low rumble like far-off thunder.

"No matter how far you go, Little Fire, no matter how deep the wrong. Whether the sun hangs high in the sky or deep blackness hides the light. Whether your heart is hard as cold winter ice or soft as a newborn lamb. Whether you run with horses or walk with shadows. No matter who you hurt, or who has been hurt because of you, remember . . . not one drop of Creator's blood will ever be lessened. He spilled his life for you and his arms are always open. One word from you and he will make the shadows fly away."

I yank my hand from Ghostdancer's grip and run.

Chapter 30

> Walk all your paths placing your feet
> in Creator Yeshua's footsteps.
> *Ghostdancer*

Sayla

GRAN AND LINK are still seated at the kitchen table. It seems impossible life is going on as if nothing momentous just happened. Gran's laughter fills the house with cheer, and Link is smiling over an enormous glass of iced lemonade. Red Dog sits at Gran's feet, pulling his ears back in a whimper as I approach.

Gran shakes her head. "Something's got Red Dog in a dither. He's been acting quite peculiar ever since the Coming-Out."

She rises and goes through the motions of making me a glass of iced lemonade similar to Link's.

"Just half a glass for me," I beg.

I slide into an overstuffed chair and raise my eyebrows at Link. He's loosened his tie, and the top two buttons of his shirt are undone. He couldn't have surprised me more if he had struck up a dance on the table. The man is at home, plain and simple, a white city boy as comfortable as you please in the home of an Indian. When Gran sits back at the table, her face is alight with joy. It's the first time since receiving news of the crash I've seen her so radiant. Studying her and the lawyer, I can't figure it out. These two are as different as day and night, yet they have already struck up a friendship.

Link is in the middle of a story; he continues as if I'm not here. "That's when I stood in front of the courtroom and turned as red as a turnip on Sunday. The judge peered at me over his glasses and asked if I needed a translator."

Gran leans forward over the table. "And what did you say?"

A slow smile flits over Link's face. "I said, 'No sir, I don't, especially not after that explanation.'"

"You didn't!" Gran's brown eyes are wide with merriment.

"I did." Link smiles at Gran as if she is the most important person on earth.

"What are you talking about?" I feel strangely left out.

Gran removes her eyeglasses and wipes her eyes. "You wouldn't believe it if we told you."

"Try me."

Gran slips on her eyeglasses. "Link was representing a woman accused of assault and battery against a police officer." Gran stops and chuckles. "And she turned out to be a prostitute."

Again Link's face smolders with embarrassment as Gran continues. "But the police officer had failed to leave the required payment, so she took it out of his hide."

"Uh-oh. I don't think I want to know this one."

Gran is laughing so hard now she again removes her glasses and wipes them on her blouse. Her words come out stuttered. "Sh-she used his own billy club to get even."

"Sap," Link says. "It's not a billy club. It's a sap."

Gran rocks back and forth. "Sh-she used his own sap to sap him one."

Link shakes his head, the smile stretching across his face.

If I weren't so shook over the preceding events with Ghostdancer, I would laugh too.

Red Dog saves the moment by rising to his feet and growling. The hair on his neck is as stiff as a porcupine's quills as he stares at the door. The laughter stops. Red Dog only acts like this when a predator is on the prowl. For a moment I wonder if the wolf has reappeared, but before I can react, Gran stands at the closed door with a shotgun raised to her shoulder.

"Whoa!" Link cries. "Isn't this a bit extreme?"

Spoken like a true city boy, and just when I was beginning to like the guy. I turn to set him straight but am caught up short when I see he is holding a pistol with two hands in a bad boy stance that leaves me gaping.

Gran sees it too. She lowers her shotgun, holding the muzzle with her right hand while she cracks the door open with her left. Link is ready for whatever is revealed.

Nothing.

Gran opens the door wider.

Still nothing.

She flings it completely open and peers out. Red Dog sticks his tail between his legs and runs for the bedroom.

"*Yaks dwa!*" Gran cries. "That dog has gone bananas."

The three of us venture outside. Being the only one without a weapon, I have a fleeting thought of being captured and held hostage. For the first time since reentering the house, I wonder where Ghostdancer has gone and hope he's nearby. Surely he wouldn't have left without saying goodbye to Gran. Yet Ghostdancer is known for disappearing at the oddest times. This could be one of them.

Turning the corner toward the backyard, I freeze.

The shaman stands three feet from Ghostdancer. His jutting chin stretches upward, his mouth pulled back in a grimace, his lips moving as if talking to himself, his pupils rolled back so only the whites of his eyes show. Clenched fists hang from his stiffened arms. I would think him grotesque except for the fact his feet are at least ten inches off the ground.

The shaman is levitating in broad daylight!

In contrast, Ghostdancer's arms hang completely relaxed at his sides. His eyes are open and head lifted to the sky. He looks like a poster child for patience. A slow smile crosses his lips as he raises his arms upward, palms open.

The shaman drops, falling into a quivering heap.

To my surprise, Ghostdancer kneels beside the shaman and lays a hand on his head. I spot a circle drawn in the hard earth. It's about an inch thick and stretches around the shaman like a protective shield. It smells of blood.

Gran's lips move in prayer while Link bends down to help Ghostdancer. The shaman's chest rises and falls so I know he's still alive. I hurry around the side of the house to the front porch. No one follows. Sitting on the second step I hold my face in my hands. What did I just witness?

Saaaaaaaaaaylaaaaaaaaaaa.

I welcome the sweet sound, remembering the levitating shaman and wondering if I can someday know the freedom of flight and levitation. Shamans often leave their bodies and travel the world. Others go into animals and travel the highlands. Being an apprentice to the shaman opens endless possibilities.

When love is high—

It is the voice of my Shadow Warrior, but he does not appear.

When love is deep. When love is a river. When love stands still—

The words draw me. Ecstasy replaces fear.

You'll open yourself to my caress. The caress of one who knows—

I hug myself and rock to the music. It's a lilting melody born in the heart of Native land, the perfect gift of a song. By the time Link and Gran return with Ghostdancer, I've memorized every note and every word.

"Is the shaman okay?" I ask.

Gran's face crumples, and for a moment I think the shaman may have died. She looks up at Ghostdancer with tears in her eyes.

"Already on his way home," Ghostdancer says. "He only came to deliver a message."

"Really?" I'm hoping the message was for me regarding the deaths of my parents. "What's the message?"

Ghostdancer's eyes bore into mine. I have no strength to hold that piercing power, so I turn away.

"It was private," Ghostdancer says. "A message meant for my ears only."

Gran breaks into sobs and hurries into the house.

The news baffles me. Why are all these Jesus followers making deals with the shaman? I think about following Gran. Perhaps I can help her, but the dark cloud on Ghostdancer's face warns against it. This is something beyond my power to heal. For the first time, I feel resentment toward Ghostdancer.

"Well—" Link begins. "Guess I'll be heading back to town." Link's thumb and forefinger fidgets with his chin, rubbing the facial hair that is beginning to form. Then he nods at Ghostdancer and starts for his Lexus. When he turns away, I spot the holstered pistol at his back. "Hey!" I call. "Think you forgot something."

He turns back to me and runs a hand across his lower back. "Yeah." He looks toward the house.

Rising from the steps I feel strangely at ease in spite of the day's surreal events. As I retrieve Link's jacket from the back of a kitchen chair, Gran's sobs drift from the bedroom. Too bad I can't give her some of my newfound peace, but she will have none of it. She's set in her ways and will follow Creator to her dying day, no matter how much she suffers. Just like my parents and grandfather.

Chapter 31

> Creator Yahweh does not allow the wicked
> to go on forever.
> *Ghostdancer*

Jacob Wiseman

GHOSTDANCER THINKS he has gotten the upper hand with me, but he will soon learn differently. Sister wolf has taken strength from the old man. He is not yet aware of it. But with each battle, his body will begin to fail. I cannot yet touch his soul, but his body is quite vulnerable. The old man will have nothing to do with darkness. Such foolishness! If we do not know how to curse, then how will we know how to cure? He will be much in need of a cure by the time I finish with him.

I discovered much when I gave my flesh to the Sundance five years ago. Little can harm me, and material possessions mean nothing. There is not one single human connection that makes me vulnerable. Though Ghostdancer still lives an isolated life on that mountain of his, he has allowed many humans into his heart. They will be the death of him.

Loretta is a lost cause. Why even bother with the foolish woman? The very roosters she brought to me in a weak attempt to buy off the curse were the very things I used to protect my soul in its travels. Ha!

The blood was perfect for my levitation circle. At least she was smart enough to realize her feeble prayers are nothing against my power.

Through my soul travels I have learned Sayla recognizes the power running through my blood. My spell on her is strong. Nothing Loretta and Ghostdancer have done has even made a dent in it. Sayla is like a budding flower ready to be plucked. Very soon I will pluck it and use its quickly fading beauty to gain access to the Sacred Mountain. For now, only one side of the mountain is beneficial for my purposes, but soon, I will own the entire mountain. Then nothing will be able to stop me.

Chapter 32

The eagle soars at Creator Yahweh's command.
Ghostdancer

Kadai

YOU ARE NO LONGER ALONE. The deputy has moved you to a cell within a pod. Times have improved enough that your country has elected a black man president, yet prejudice still runs deep in many hearts. You suspect someone has paid this deputy. Who would benefit from you being here?

Standing near the door of your cell, you survey the situation. There's about eight feet of flat concrete floor between you and the opposite glass wall. A television screen is mounted on the far left where a group of white men sit at a table staring back at you. Breathing is difficult with the stink of sweat. You nod at three Natives you've known your entire life—James, Billy, and Tubs. All three are battered. Billy's head wound is wrapped with bandages but his nose is beginning to bleed again. He's sitting on the floor leaning against the concrete wall. You wonder how many regulations are being broken here and why. You tear off your shirt and push it toward Billy.

"Hey bro," you say.

Billy nods back, but he doesn't take the shirt. His eyes dart toward the other occupants at the table beneath the television, five white men who've spent plenty of time at the gym. Three sit and two are now standing. Before you realize it, you have met the eyes of the biggest. He sneers.

"Got us a pretty boy here."

The others crack their knuckles, letting you know their intent.

Though the cops had you remove your roach when they checked you in, the cut of your hair is clearly Native. Your skin color would have shouted that fact on its own, but the long hair is an offense to these men. While keeping your eyes on the big man, your senses become fully alert. You hand your shirt to Billy and start pulling the bandages from your hands. A door slams somewhere in the distance. You look up to see the guard station is empty.

James and Tubs move close, letting you know they're with you in this battle, which means they will stay out of the way, because they've seen you fight. Billy tries to rise from the floor but dizziness overcomes him and he topples back down, moaning and holding his head.

"Sorry." Billy's nasal voice shoots fire into your veins. What right did these men have to break his nose?

Things haven't changed much in the two years you've been holing up at Sacred Mountain Ranch. Though you've stayed away from alcohol, you still ended up in the same place. An Indian is still an Indian in this town, something a little less than human for white animals to beat on. The thought surprises you. You had believed you had left it all behind—the anger, the hatred, the violence—but it seems to have built inside you like an explosion that cannot be held down.

One white man charges, four others on his heels.

Before you realize what is happening, your Special Forces' training has kicked in. Shouts and screams fill the pod. It's impossible to tell who is making the most noise—the ones who connect with your flying hands and feet, your friends who duck to get out of the way, or your own primal voice behind the movement. It's all over in a matter of minutes. You, alone, stand bloodless and coherent.

Staring down at your handiwork, you command your breathing to slow. The pod looks like a battlefield. All five white men are sprawled on the floor. You hope they are all still breathing, or you will face a murder charge. The country you fought to maintain freedom could be the same one who takes away your freedom. Looking down at Billy, still sitting on the floor, there's no mistaking the hardness in your friend's eyes.

"Big trouble now," James says. "They won't let an Indian get away with this."

The door at the end of the pod bangs open, and you hear the slap of running feet, but remorse has already kicked in. You acted in your own strength, not in the strength and courage of your Supreme Chief and Commander. This brutality you dished out is not of Yahweh's bidding.

"Stand back!" a deputy yells.

You do as he commands, moving to join your friends along the wall, but before you can do so, the deputy shackles your hands while two more start pummeling your body with their saps. You don't even try to fight back and neither do your friends. This battle was lost over a hundred years ago. Besides, you deserve whatever they want to give. Was obedience too much for your Chief and Commander to ask? You have failed him, the ONE who fills your lungs with air.

Chapter 33

*Watch yourselves closely and do not forget
the things your eyes have seen.*
Creator Yahweh

Loretta
August 29, 2014
Early Friday morning

THE CALL CAME at three in the morning. Loretta was half expecting it. Though she had crawled into bed at her usual time, she hadn't been able to sleep. After giving up the battle, she had pulled on her fleece robe and sat at the kitchen table praying and reading her Bible. There were so many things to pray about—her own actions with the shaman, Sayla's strange behavior, Kadai's being jailed for trying to protect Sayla, the shaman's threats to Ghostdancer—the list went on and on.

"They gave me one phone call," Kadai said. His voice sounded scratchy and weak. "I hope you have your prayer warriors in place, because it's going to take a miracle to get me out of this one."

Loretta stood and put a hand to her chest. Sayla's worried face appeared in the kitchen doorway. She didn't look as if she had slept much either.

"What's wrong Gran?"

"It's Kadai."

Sayla's eyebrows scrunched together as she moved near and placed an arm around Loretta. They both leaned toward the phone to hear what Kadai had to say. His voice was growing weaker.

"I'm in the hospital."

Sayla gasped.

"What on earth?" Gran said. "I thought you were in jail."

Sayla's eyes widened and she stared at Loretta. It was about time the girl discovered what Kadai had done for her. Loretta had been meaning to tell her about Kadai's selfless act, but there had been little room for conversation.

"A deputy stands guard twenty-four seven." Kadai's voice was no louder than a whisper. "No matter what happens. Remember. Creator is with me."

Silence filled the line until Sayla found her voice. "Kadai," she said.

"Are you alright?" Kadai's voice was anxious.

"She's fine," Loretta said, "But she doesn't know—"

Kadai's next words were barely decipherable. "Tell Sayla . . . don't go near War Paint. Keep away—"

Sayla grabbed the phone from Loretta and held it to her ear. "I don't know what happened, Kadai, but I've got a lawyer. I'll send him up." Her clenched fingers turned white against the phone. "What? Who am I speaking to?"

Either Kadai's allowed time must have been up or he had grown too weak to talk. Gran sat hard on the chair.

"Well I don't care if you're the king of rock 'n' roll," Sayla said, "you better take care of Kadai, you hear? I've got a lawyer and I see prejudice written all over this one."

Sayla slammed down the phone before the man could have possibly answered.

She was shaking. Her words came out clipped and hard. "Tell me. What happened?"

"It's a long story. You better sit down."

"I'm fine standing."

Loretta couldn't keep the pain from her voice. "Sayla, I'm not your enemy."

Suddenly Sayla was in her arms, whispering words of apology and comfort. They had both suffered great loss and both had made mistakes through their grief. Loretta had visited the shaman. Sayla had stood at his fire. Yet Loretta had put her mistake behind, choosing to walk in the Jesus Way while Sayla was still courting death.

Loretta could think of no words that would change her granddaughter's mind, even though Loretta had gone through something quite similar when she was about the same age. No one had been able to talk her out of her bad choices either, but the persistent prayer of those who loved her eventually saw her through to the other side.

She prayed now, silently asking Creator to help her to continue in prayer, to wake the Spirit within her during Sayla's greatest time of need.

"And for Kadai, too" she said aloud. "Do a miracle for him."

Chapter 34

*Once Creator Yahweh spoke in a vision
to his faithful people.*
Ghostdancer

Sayla

GRAN HAS A LIGHTBULB THEORY, and she reminds me of it often. I think of it now, as I sip lukewarm tea and wait for the first sunrays to break over Sacred Mountain. Gran insisted I wait for sunrise before calling Link. She believes Kadai is safe in the hospital and Link can do nothing to help him in the middle of the night. I told her that in this computer age, a person can work all night. Perhaps there is some research Link can do in preparation. Yet I honor her request, because it's one of the few things I can give her.

"When one lightbulb goes, brace yourself, because the others are soon to follow."

It's a classic Gran line and so very true. I feel as if a black cloud hangs over me wherever I go. I don't dare ask what else can happen. Gran made me watch the movie *Schindler's List* a couple of years ago, and I've never forgotten the scene where an entire Jewish family was moved from their beautiful mansion to a single room without kitchen or bathroom facilities. The head of the family dropped his suitcase and said something like, "Surely nothing else can go wrong."

But it did.

Mere minutes passed before another family showed up, and the man soon realized two families would share his tiny room. And of course we all knew what was coming. The holocaust. There was no way the man could have foreseen that horrific event.

I twirl my empty teacup and hope something like the holocaust isn't in my future. But after learning Kadai went to jail while trying to protect me, I'm thinking things *can* get worse. Kadai tried to keep his promise to not leave me, tried to keep the doctors from detaining me in the mental ward, and though he never used fists or feet, as he is well known to use, he was charged with obstructing justice. To make matters worse, he already has a criminal record.

Though I don't know all the details, the rumor mill went crazy after Kadai returned from Iraq. Something terrible happened to him while he was over there. I was living in Southern California at the time, but according to reports, Kadai turned to alcohol and used his Special Forces' training for all the wrong things. Natives recognized it as PTSD, Post Traumatic Stress Syndrome, and cops knew him well. He received a special discharge from the Army. None of us knew why, except for Grandfather. Now Grandfather is gone, pleasing God in heaven somewhere where we can't reach him.

I place my cup on the table and look at Gran slumped asleep in her chair. Her soft snores fill the kitchen. The sound should soothe me, but it doesn't. I'm going crazy wondering why Kadai is in the hospital.

The eastern sky brightens, and a rooster begins to crow. Carrying the cordless phone to the living room, a curse leaves my mouth when Link's answering machine picks up. I rarely curse, but I'm glad Gran is asleep and doesn't hear.

"Call me. Soon as possible," I say into the receiver. "It's urgent."

A clattering noise sounds on the other end. It appears Link is trying to answer. Then the phone goes dead.

In a few moments, Link returns my call. "Sorry about that. I dropped the phone."

"Kadai has been arrested," I say. We need your help."

"The young man who works on your ranch?"

"Yes."

The sound of rattling paper comes through the phone. "What's his Christian name?"

"Excuse me?"

"His Christian name. What is it?"

"I don't know what you're talking about."

The rattling stops. Link's patience outlasts mine as he asks a third time. "What is the name written on Kadai's birth certificate?"

"He has no birth certificate."

"None?"

"None."

Silence fills the line, and again I realize how different our Native world must appear to this white man. Whites like everything tidy and neat. Native lives seldom work out that way.

"I don't understand." Link's voice softens to a drawl. "Hospitals issue everyone a birth certificate."

"Kadai wasn't born in a hospital. His mother gave birth in one of our cabins and died soon after."

"Your grandmother told me he served time in the Special Forces."

"That's right."

"They would have demanded a birth certificate."

"Gran delivered Kadai," I say. "His mother named him before she died and Gran recorded it in her journal. They have a copy at the Rez office. It was good enough for the Army."

Silence fills the line, and I think of how Kadai's mother had seen a vision of how her son would be a man who loved horses and how he would be strong and mighty. Kadai means "rock" in Klamath and ThunderHorse is a mighty horse. It gives me shivers to think about it.

"Well then," Link says, "if it's good enough for the Army, it's good enough for me. Is that one word or two?"

"What?"

"Thunder Horse. Is that one word or two?"

I can't help it. Laughter starts bubbling out of me. The thought that this man, who can't even spell our names, is all we've got to save the day makes me near hysterical. Wisely, Link ignores my laugh as I tell him how to spell ThunderHorse.

He promises to call back as soon as he has more information. After changing clothes and tucking sleepwalking Gran into bed, I head for the barn. Fingers of light spill over Sacred Mountain, and the sweetness of fresh rain dances in the breeze, clearing the sky of smoke. A pair of nighthawks plays above the pasture. It's a perfect soft morning. The land seems unaware that so much is happening to our family.

The barn door is open, and I am surprised to find the horses all fed and brushed. Heading back outside to free the cows, I discover that chore is done as well. The reason is soon apparent. Ghostdancer stands on the other side of the rodeo arena, dressed in his dog soldier regalia with his arms raised to the heavens. From the amount of chores that have been completed, he must have stayed up all night, and then dressed in his regalia for this moment with his Creator.

A hush falls around me as if I am standing on holy ground. Perhaps I am. It's hard to believe Ghostdancer is an old man, though his white hair glistens in the morning sun. The ivory hornpipes of his breastplate stretch from beneath his chin to his knees, a hundred altogether, fifty on each side. I know this, because Grandfather made the breastplate. Yards of white fringe trimmed with blue, black and yellow, swirl about him, making him look like the ghost of his namesake. Bits of red beading make a splash throughout. But the most amazing part of his regalia is the headdress. It's made of over five hundred eagle feathers, one for each surviving Native tribe in North America. When he dances, he dances for the nations.

A smile stretches below Ghostdancer's closed eyes and a light breeze carries his voice across the corral and back to me. There was a time he was the main singer of our tribe. The cadence and words of his song mesmerize me, as his feet lift to a beat only he can hear.

"Yahwey, ya hey ya hey.
You, oh Creator Yahweh, are the Great Chief.
You have made all things.
By a word you spread out the heavens,
While the morning stars sang together
And the angels shouted joy.
Yahwey, ya hey ya hey."

Before I realize it, I am caught in a vision where I see a great shining Creator with his arms outstretched. Thousands of brilliant angels dressed in regalia and singing impossible notes surround him. The vision holds me until I finally must close my eyes and Ghostdancer's voice becomes a recitation.

"You shut up the sea behind doors when it burst forth from the womb. You said, 'This far you may come and no farther; here is where your proud waves halt.' You journeyed to the springs of the sea and you walked in the recesses of the deep. You bound the beautiful Pleiades and loosed the cords of Orion. You brought forth the constellations in their seasons and led out the bear with its cubs. Who am I, oh Creator Yahweh, that you would pay mind of me?"

Ghostdancer's words spark a fire. He doesn't just talk of love; he expresses it in beautiful words that expose his heart's passion.

Backing away, sadness envelops me. I know little of love that focuses on others. What kind of love have I given Gran by turning away from everything she deems true? What kind of love did I give Grandfather by leaving Sacred Mountain Ranch and moving to Southern California? What kind of love have I given Kadai when he offers the supreme love of laying down his life in my place?

I try to swallow, but my mouth is as dry as summer sod. Imagining Kadai contained in a room with four walls makes me stumble. Leaning against the barn, I try to catch my breath.

And what of receiving love? Shouldn't the receiver give some kind of thanks? What kind of thanks have I given Gran for allowing me to be like a daughter to her? What kind of thanks did I give Grandfather for showing up at every one of my concerts? What kind of thanks have I given Kadai for his endless patience beneath the moon when he abandoned sleep for my whims?

What have I ever given up?

Music comes to mind. For a year, I've given up music, but it wasn't of my own choice so it's not a real sacrifice. Ghostdancer once said I make a god of my music, but without it I would be just another Indian.

Sunlight bursts over Sacred Mountain painting the fields a glorious gold hue and reminding me I have a job to do. It's time to return thanks to the ones who have given me love. Light shimmers through the oak tree above me and a soft breeze caresses my cheeks. I think of Ghostdancer's words from yesterday and wonder if Creator still has love for me or if he is sorry I was born.

A breeze kicks up the green and gold leaves beneath my feet and twirls them around my legs and arms. I stand transfixed, caught in a dust devil that feels more like the caress of angel wings. The wind blows around me, not in one direction as it should. Gran would say it is the breath of God. The leaves lift above my head and twirl in a shimmering mass of beauty.

An impossible love washes over me, stronger than the erotic love of my Shadow Warrior—stronger, because it stays with me as I feed the chickens and complete the rest of Gran's chores. Is Creator offering me love?

But I have done nothing to deserve it.

By the time I return to the house, my brain is a muddle. Stopping in the mudroom, I wash my hands before entering the kitchen. Red Dog meets me with a wagging tail and a smiling face, an interesting welcome after turning tail for the last two days. I bend down and lean into him. He leans back, making little whimpering noises as if I have just returned from a long trip. Perhaps I have.

I rise and reach for the teapot, but my hand freezes midair. There, on the counter, is my eagle feather.

Chapter 35

*Never let your voice go silent
in sending up prayers of thankfulness.*
Ghostdancer

Loretta

"YOU DON'T UNDERSTAND," Sayla said for the umpteenth time.

Loretta found it difficult to decipher her words. The silly girl kept pacing back and forth, wearing a hole in the living room carpet.

"The eagle feather was in plain sight on the counter. Someone had to have placed it there."

"But there was no eagle feather," Loretta said. "Perhaps you imagined it."

"No!"

The force of Sayla's denunciation shocked them both. They stood on opposite sides of the room staring at each other. A photo of Loretta's father riding a bucking bronco hung above Sayla's head. Loretta wondered if her father could have imagined such happenings on Sacred Mountain Ranch. Gone were the carefree days of high-flying rodeos when Natives came for miles to show off their talents, and when their worst worries were about horses and cows.

"I didn't imagine it Gran." Sayla shook her head. "Something strange is happening."

Loretta moved to the couch. Perhaps sitting would calm the girl's nerves. But Sayla refused to sit, choosing to keep up her incessant pacing instead.

"Someone's been in our house, not once, not twice, but at least three times. And Red Dog let them in. It has to be someone who's been here before."

Laying her head in her hands, Loretta sighed. "Nothing's been taken, Sayla."

"Grandfather's journals are gone."

Loretta raised her head. "Not gone. I have them. Been meaning to tell you but things have been a bit hectic."

Sayla stopped pacing and turned her brown eyes on her. "Are you reading them?"

"I didn't think you would mind."

Sayla paced the room again and Loretta swallowed. A partial truth could be considered a lie. "So, you see? Nothing taken. Besides, if someone broke in, they would at least go for my grandmother's jewelry. The turquoise alone is worth several thousand dollars."

Sayla stopped. "Have you checked?"

"What?"

"Have you checked to see if anything else is missing? I'm telling you, Gran, someone's been here."

There was nothing for it. Loretta would have to help Sayla search. Her granddaughter wouldn't rest otherwise. Remaining seated, Loretta looked around the room. Rows of regalia hung on one wall next to Sayla's piano. A new-fangled, flat screen television hung on the wall between the open doorways to the kitchen and nook on the left and the dining room on the right. End tables and chairs took up the rest of the space, except for where Loretta sat on the couch. Everything seemed to be in order, but it was hard to tell. Loretta had never been the most organized person. Books and memorabilia flowed from a mismatch of bookshelves. Sayla had crammed an assortment of drums and flutes into one corner of the room; and large lidded baskets held Loretta's sewing and needlework. Her eyes fell to the low table in front of her. It would take one of those fancy forensic scientists to figure out the mysteries of that jumbled mess.

Halfheartedly she began sorting through unfinished paperwork and piles of tribal newsletters, not expecting to find anything missing and wondering how she would know if it was. She shook her head. Her granddaughter had been acting quite strange lately. It was possible Sayla needed professional help.

Thinking of the hospital she shuddered; she wasn't about to send Sayla back there. Neither would she return to the shaman for help, especially after the message he had delivered to Ghostdancer. He had some nerve to appear on her land after her visit to him. And she had paid the price of two live chickens for his services. How could she have known he would use the chickens' blood to make his levitation circle?

It served her right, taking matters into her own hands instead of trusting Creator. Even now, she should be on her knees instead of this infernal searching.

Screeching hinges caught her attention.

"Sheesh Gran," Sayla said. "When was the last time you oiled this door?"

Loretta rolled her shoulders. "I don't think you'll find anything missing in the broom closet. I moved all that stuff out to the porch."

"Then what are all these boxes?"

"Material and odds and ends for making regalia. I completely forgot they were there."

Scrunching her face in disgust Sayla said, "From the amount of dust, I'd say it might be a good thing if someone did take something out of here."

Loretta couldn't argue that one. She probably needed to get rid of a few things, but every time she did, she ended up needing the missing item a week later.

After closing the broom closet, Sayla opened the sideboard in the dining room that held Loretta's best dishes. It was a family joke the dishes held more junk than they had ever held food. Every little thing got tossed there—loose guitar picks, single earrings, thank-you cards. Sayla picked up a cream pitcher that held loose keys.

"*Yaks dwa!*" The exclamation left Loretta's mouth before she knew what was happening.

Sayla looked up.

"Keys!"

Excitement filled Loretta with renewed energy. In five steps, she crossed the room and grabbed the pitcher from Sayla's hands. Two gold keys rattled in the bottom. "The silver one is missing!"

"The extra house key?"

Loretta nodded, thinking Sayla might not be crazy after all. On the other hand, Sayla could have removed the key and forgotten to put it back. It wouldn't be the first time.

Realizing the obvious Sayla said, "Haven't misplaced it since getting my fancy key ring." To prove her point, she clapped twice. An alarm went off on the kitchen counter. Sayla flashed Loretta a smile and a thumbs up before retrieving her keys and deactivating the alarm. Setting them back on the counter, her smile fled and her eyes grew wide.

Loretta stared at the counter, her throat beginning to constrict. A single eagle feather lay by itself, too far from the door for someone to have snuck in while she and Sayla searched for missing items. It showcased the quilling and beading she had created for her beloved husband.

The honking of a car horn startled them both. Red Dog started barking. Loretta and Sayla held each other's eyes before looking back on the eagle feather. Neither could find the strength to move.

Chapter 36

*At the roar of Creator Yahweh's voice
my heart pounds and leaps from its place!*
Ghostdancer

Kadai

THE CLATTER OF SHUFFLING feet competes with rustling material and muted voices while a beeping monitor taps a slow, even rhythm. You hear it as a Native drumbeat, but you do not rise and dance. Prone and still, you close your eyes and work the healing process, offering every part of your body to the One who breathed life into your lungs.

You feel the life beat now as you breathe in and out, a rhythm so slow the doctor is worried. He talks of how impossible it is for you to still be alive. His voice penetrates your dark realm, but you do not acknowledge it, for to do so, would halt the flow of energy running through your veins. You feel its life-giving breath trickling into your fingers and toes, then back out again, running up your arms and legs, crossing through your loins and chest and coming to rest in your bruised kidney and battered heart.

No drug can match the wonder of this healing caress. No heat can match its soothing breath.

The wild smell of sage fills your nostrils. At first you think it is for your nose only, but the doctor gives orders for someone to search out its source. You try to explain but they cannot hear, because you are caught between two worlds, ready to cross over to the place where all things are made right.

The urge to connect with that perfect world nearly breaks your concentration. "The source of the wild aroma is not of this world," you want to tell the team of doctors. "It comes from the One who made the world. The One in whose essence all life draws its being. Creator. The One who gives orders to the morning. The One who gives the wild horse his strength. The One who sends the lightning bolts on their way."

None will discover the wild aroma's source until they acknowledge Creator, the incarnate God Man whose love is better than life. *Jesus. Yeshua.*

Soft breath blows upon your face sending sage incense deep into your lungs. You pull it in with one slow breath and send it out as a prayer in the same way. Sweet prayers to the One who guards the number of your days on this earth.

The beeping machine quiets.

Weightless and free you fly, looking down on the scene below as doctors and nurses rush to your aid. Watching in fascination, you feel none of their administrations as they hover and work on your body.

Then HIS voice calls. Your secret name falls like summer rain, and nothing else matters.

Comforting wings reach around you and fly you away. You are immediately in another place not of this earth. You turn and begin your journey through the tunnel where endless light prisms spin in a circle. Impossible hues dance upon your skin. You stop and inspect. Yes. Your body is every bit as real as the one below. Laughter bubbles up, exploding in joyous release. Other laughter echoes through the tunnel. Upon inspection, you see faces of the ones who have gone before, dancing across vast green fields in welcome.

Then suddenly HIS voice reaches out, an unmistakable command in his warning to stop.

"Cha aat!"

The next minute you are in his arms, two brothers long separated, now united. Strong arms cling to your back. *"Waqlisi sawalineeas,* hello friend," HE says, and you weep. You, who thought tears would not exist in this place. You weep for joy. His embrace lasts forever, soothing away every vestige of pain and memory. You know, even as he knows. Understanding becomes as common as your breath.

Then as suddenly as HE appeared, HE is gone. One whispered command fills your ears. "Stand firm. I AM with you."

Pain erupts in one mad flash. It seems as if hundreds of hands turn you over and pound on your chest. Your body jerks and jumps without control, and you long to demand the doctors to stop.

"Let me go!" Your heart cries, but they do not hear.

"He's back!"

The room becomes suddenly still, and then a cheer rings out as the monitor beats out a steady rhythm, even and strong.

But you do not feel like cheering, you who touched the embrace of heaven. Hot salt burns your eyes. You were so close—

Chapter 37

*Creator Yahweh cuts a channel for the torrents of rain,
to water a land where no man lives.*
Ghostdancer

Sayla

KENNY HAS ARRIVED as promised. It's a shock to see the Italian standing below Gran's porch smoking one of his illegal Cuban cigars and remarking about the fresh country air. The irony is lost on the man.

I give Kenny a quick hug, introduce him to Gran and then turn to Link. "Kadai is in the hospital."

"I know." He sets his briefcase on the top step.

"You know? But—"

"Let the man breathe a bit," Gran interrupts. "Come on up to the porch and I'll get us some iced tea." Turning to me she says. *"Sat'waa Yi?is."* She's telling me to come help her, but we both know it's so we can check the feather.

Leaving the men to settle themselves, Gran and I enter the kitchen side by side, barely fitting through the door. It's funny how the mind can play tricks. Both of us are so sure the eagle feather will be gone that at first we don't see it.

"Let's touch it at the same time," Gran says.

Hysterical giggles fly from my throat.

"Just in case," Gran says.

"In case what?"

Gran purses her lips and pushes my shoulder, giggling like a young girl. It looks as if she intends on picking up the eagle feather by herself. My hand shoots out and we grab it at the same time. Straight-armed we hold it out in front of us. It might as well be a poisonous snake. After a bit, I realize I'm holding my breath. Gran must have been too, because she lets out a long sigh. Then we both laugh. The feather feels like any other.

Gran lets go.

I gasp.

As soon as Gran's hand leaves the feather, a vision of Kadai fills my mind. He's in a hospital bed with what looks like a hundred white uniformed people surrounding him. I feel a powerful urge to have Gran pray.

"What's wrong?" Gran asks.

"It's Kadai."

Without me asking, Gran starts her prayer, at first with her eyes closed and a hand on my shoulder and then continuing with her eyes open as we pull glasses from the cupboard and make iced tea. She opens a box of lemon cookies someone left for us and places them on a tray. Then we head back out to the porch. Though I am still worried about Kadai, her prayer gives me assurance. I'm about to ask Link what he's found out, but then I notice Ghostdancer has joined our little party. Groaning, I head back to the kitchen to make him some tea. Better to get it out of the way than to argue with Gran.

Half expecting the feather to have disappeared again, I'm pleasantly surprised to find it still lying on the counter. Picking it up, I wait to see if any further visions appear.

Nothing happens.

Still a little spooked, I take the eagle feather into the living room and hang it in the corner behind one of my drums. Now I'm the only one who knows where it is. If it disappears again I will know something other than a burglar is behind it. I don't spend a lot of time thinking about what that might mean. Satisfied I've taken a step in the right direction, I make Ghostdancer's tea and rejoin the party.

Chapter 38

*Receive Creator Yahweh's unearned, priceless treasure
and spend the rest of your life captured by grace.*
Ghostdancer

Sayla

I'M IN FOR A BIG SURPRISE out on the porch. Gran is smoking a cigar.

Kenny opens his portable humidor. "Might as well join us," he says.

I shake my head.

Gran says, "Don't be so surprised. It's not that different from a peace pipe. Kenny wanted to start out on the right foot."

Kenny winks at me. "Gotta love those peace pipes."

"Especially when they come from Cuba," agrees Ghostdancer.

"Via Switzerland," adds Link. "These babies have been around."

Gran laughs. "A bit of international peace-making going on here."

My attention shifts to Kenny. I have never seen him quite this relaxed before. He's a big man with shoulder length dark hair, somewhere in his late fifties, and every part of his face is a smile. He spends his days and nights in the rat race between Los Angeles and San Diego, yet he seems right at home on Gran's porch. He's even won Red Dog's affection. The silly mutt is sprawled at his feet with his head on one of Kenny's expensive leather shoes.

The air smells of hickory. Though I've never smoked a thing in my life, the smokers' camaraderie draws me. "Let me try yours," I say to Gran.

She passes the torpedo shaped wand to me. "Eooow," I say. "How do you hold this thing?"

Kenny gives me a demonstration. "Don't take the smoke into your lungs," he says. "Taste it like a fine chocolate and let the smoke come up through the sinuses and drift out the nose."

Taking his advice, I draw in the smoke. "Not too bad," I say, "but I won't be making it a habit."

Link stands and offers me his rocker.

"I'll let you old folks have the rockers," I say. "The bench is fine for me."

"Old folks?" Link puts on his best sad face. It isn't too bad for a lawyer dressed in a suit, and the suit fits him well this time, a nice charcoal gray with a bow tie and red suspenders. His jacket hangs over the porch rail. He looks ready for a poker party.

"Tell me the news," I say.

"Kadai is still under arrest," Link says. "No visitors. Believe me, I tried. Even told them I was his lawyer, but they rightly pointed out my client hadn't mentioned anything about a lawyer."

"So you didn't see him?"

"No, but I did get things moving."

Ghostdancer interrupts. "By moving, you mean you filled out a lot of paperwork."

"Exactly," says Link.

Heat burns my cheeks. "Paperwork is not what I had in mind when I asked for help."

"More like demanded," Link says. "And paperwork *is* a necessary evil. Doing it properly can insure Kadai's release without any lingering difficulties."

"Difficulties?" The thought sits heavy on my heart.

"Relax," Kenny says. "We're all here to work out this little problem."

"By sitting on Gran's porch smoking cigars?" I stand.

"Exactly." Kenny holds his cigar as if admiring the craftsmanship. "I do my best thinking in just such a position. When your mind is full of anxiety, it twists your reason. He turns to Link. "Are you ready to take notes?"

"At your service." Link opens his briefcase and pulls out a yellow legal pad and pen; the John Lennon eyeglasses are back on his nose.

"Tell us what you have." Kenny says.

Link lists off the items like reading a shopping list. "One. Kadai was arrested for obstructing justice, but I've got that one covered. Technically, he wasn't obstructing justice, so I'm pretty sure I can get him off on that one. Two. He pulverized five white men in the county jail."

"Huh." There's no mistaking the look of pride flashing in Ghostdancer's eyes. When he discovers me looking, he apologizes. "I'm still human, Little Fire. Gotta love it when the Indian wins."

"He's a long way from winning this one," Link reminds us. "Though I will give him credit. He was certainly outnumbered. Several deputies claim Kadai's injuries came from the fight, but a signed doctor's report states a blunt instrument, quite similar to a policeman's sap, caused Kadai's injuries. That will go a long way in court, but it will go a lot further if I can prove he was set up."

Hot fingers of fire burn my neck. Did Kadai fall into a trap because of me? "I thought you said Kadai can't have any visitors?"

Link peers at me over his glasses. "Never got to see Kadai, but I did see the doctor. He told me quite a bit before the deputy stepped in. It wasn't that difficult to get a secretary to type up a memo. Wasn't any trouble at all getting the doctor to sign it when the deputy was looking the other way. Seems something rather miraculous happened in that hospital and Kadai has won himself a good-sized army of nurses. They won't even let the deputy in the room."

"Miracle?" Gran asks.

"One of those out-of-body, through-the-tunnel experiences," Link says. "Guess Kadai actually gave up the ghost. They all witnessed it. One nurse told me the most wonderful sage aroma filled the room, and they never did find its source. She's convinced Kadai saw heaven."

Link's voice drifts away and we sit in silence. Tears burn my eyes as I think of how close we came to losing Kadai. Telling myself the sorrow is because he's like a brother is not very convincing. Remembering his hands caressing Bronze Healer sends shivers across my chest.

Ghostdancer stands. Raising his hands to the sky, he begins a song that gives thanks to Creator Yahweh. None of our guests can understand his Native words, so Gran rises to her feet and translates. Kenny and Link both close their eyes. I remain standing, in respect of hearing our language.

"Yahwey, ya hey ya hey. You alone stretched out the heavens, spread out the earth with just a word, while the morning stars were singing and angels shouted joy."

I try to force the words away. If Creator could save Kadai, why didn't he save Grandfather and my parents? Does he enjoy playing with human emotions? Sounds more like a trickster coyote to me. I want nothing to do with a god like that. But Ghostdancer's words talk of ONE whose love extends through generations, to thousands upon thousands of believers, forgiving wickedness, rebellion and sin.

Watching Ghostdancer with his hands raised to Creator, it's difficult for me to correlate his God of love with the same God who finds it necessary to forgive sin. What terrible wrong has Ghostdancer ever done that needs forgiveness? And look at Gran. Her entire face is bathed in joy as she translates Ghostdancer's praise of Creator. What sin has she ever committed?

"Creator, shining above all morning stars. Creator Yahweh, I feel your presence in the wind. Creator, who am I that you should care? Yahwey, ya hey ya hey."

Ghostdancer calls God, Creator Yahweh. Gran calls him, Jesus. They both say God is available at all times and that nothing is either too big or small for him. Yet my problems seem too big, my heart too small. Hanging my head, I stare at the porch floor. Then all breath leaves my lungs.

An eagle feather is at my feet gently rocking in the breeze.

Chapter 39

*Creator Yahweh is mighty,
and firm in his purpose.*
Ghostdancer

Loretta

IT TICKLED LORETTA to no end seeing her beading room turned into a command station. They had pushed all her plastic tubs of material and beads to one corner and set up an Apple laptop computer in place of her sewing machine. Kenny sprawled piles of paper across the bed. The man himself was chewing on an unlit cigar and reading through page after page of printed documents. Link paced back and forth between Kenny and Loretta, furiously writing on his legal pad and talking into a phone snapped to his ear.

Delighted to surprise the newcomers with her exceptional computer skills she had learned at the Community Center, Loretta set her fingers flying across the keyboard.

"Look up Amnesty International," Kenny said.

She did as he asked and received nearly eight million hits. Clicking on the main US site, she chose the best three and sent them to print within minutes. Next she found a site in San Francisco and printed the contact information.

Sayla was off helping Ghostdancer build a sweat lodge down by the river. She had taken her guitar with her. Loretta hoped she would return with a song, possibly something about eagle feathers from heaven. It was a mystery to beat all.

Another mystery unfolded when Kenny announced he had a film crew flying in to record Sayla live at the community concert a week from Friday. That had set Sayla into a dither and surprised Loretta as well. Kenny had already called the TV and radio stations, not just in the Klamath area, but also as far north as Salem and as far south as Sacramento.

"We'll fill Sacred Mountain Ranch with people," he had said.

Yaks dwa! The man was a dynamo. Loretta could hardly type for thinking of all the food they would have to prepare and of how many easy-ups they would need to provide shade. She'd have to get on the phone and call everyone she knew. And tables and chairs, and—

Handing Link the printouts of Amnesty International, she felt a wave of thankfulness. The man refused to take any money for his services. "Just keep the iced tea coming," he had said. He spent most of his time on his laptop and phone, calling people across the country. Having a cause sent a wash of pleasure over Loretta's tired bones.

"We need to work on getting you a family connection with Kadai," Link said. "Any other witnesses of his birth?"

Loretta turned to face him. "I was the only one. His mother probably wouldn't have died if someone else had been there." She felt a pain jab her stomach.

"So his father raised him?"

"If you can call it that."

"Meaning?"

"Meaning the man drowned himself in alcohol. After his wife died, he hardly knew Kadai existed. But he did make me the boy's godmother."

Link straightened. "Do you have proof?"

"Plenty. He did it in front of a tribal meeting."

"Can you get one of the people in attendance to sign as witness?"

"They already have."

Link's face appeared over the laptop. "They did?"

"We held a Coming-Out ceremony. It's recorded at the Rez office."

Link clapped his hands together. "Then it's official. You're family. If we can get a copy of those records, we should be able to get you and Sayla in to see Kadai.

"The tribal office is open till four thirty," Loretta said. "It's a forty-five minute drive."

Link looked at his watch. "Then we'll need to leave here by three. That gives us four hours."

Stinging shock ran through Loretta's fingers. Seemed like too little time to accomplish so much. And what if the deputies moved Kadai back to jail before they got there? "How long do you think Kadai will be in the hospital?"

Chuckling, Link read through the printout while answering Loretta. "He should be out by now."

Loretta's head dropped.

Link put a hand on her shoulder. "Not to worry. He *should* be out, but he isn't. Those nurses are like bulldogs. Dr. Dan put them straight about what really happened in the jail, and besides, they think Kadai's some kind of angel come back from heaven. He's absolutely healed. Not a thing wrong with him. Not even so much as a bruise. Can't say the same for the other guys."

Loretta's mouth fell open. What on earth? Well, it wasn't on earth. Something otherworldly was going on here. Between Kadai's healing and Sayla's eagle feathers, the shaman's threat seemed like a small problem. But even as the thought hit her, she knew better than to underestimate the enemy. The shaman's visit proved the battle was not yet finished. The cause of the battle still eluded Loretta, unless it had something to do with those old journals, which is exactly why she had hidden them where they would never be found again.

"We'll have to spring him before the cops get him," Kenny said.

Spring him. That's exactly what the man said. They would have to spring him from jail. Loretta felt as if she had been dropped into the pages of a Tony Hillerman mystery. The men were having too much fun with this. Didn't they know how serious it was? Kadai was like a son to her; always had been, right from his birth. She remembered holding him in her arms and thanking Jesus the boy had not died along with his mother.

Thinking of Lily's death saddened Loretta. If she had only listened to Ghostdancer, perhaps Kadai's mother would have lived and Loretta would have been like a grandmother to him. That would have been the more natural way. But she was self-wise back then and thought she knew best. How wrong she had been.

"Earth to Loretta," Kenny said.

She looked up.

"You did a good thing in spite of your mistakes. You ought to be dang proud of the boy."

The byword made Loretta smile. She knew Kenny would use tougher language elsewhere. Respect was something she seldom witnessed from white folks. And as far as being proud of Kadai? She was right proud of him. He had served his country well and continued to help Loretta long after everyone else had left.

Kenny waved a hand in front of her face. "You back yet? You didn't hear a word I said."

Loretta straightened. "Of course I did. You told me I should be dang proud of Kadai, and you're exactly right. I should be. And I am."

Throaty laughter rolled out of Kenny's belly. "You're a feisty one. First you surprise me by joining us for a smoke. Then you turn out to be a whiz on the computer. You certainly blew the Indian stereotype out of the water for me."

Loretta knew most white people thought of Indians as the noble warriors of old. They knew little of the contemporary challenges facing modern Indians. But Kenny was trying and she appreciated that.

He rose to his feet and pushed forward on his lower back. "Let's take a break!"

Loretta shoved back her chair. "I'll make lunch."

"Nothing doing," Kenny said. "I'll call out for something."

Link objected. "Good try. All of the somethings are too far away."

Flummoxed, Kenny turned to Loretta. "Is that true? There's no delivery service?"

"There's delivery service, all right, and you're about to see it." Loretta had been looking for some way to share some of the food gifts.

"I'll help," Kenny said, and to her surprise, he followed her into the kitchen. *Yaks dwa!* This city man sure made a mess of her white stereotypes.

Chapter 40

> How great is Yahweh—
> beyond our understanding!
> *Ghostdancer*

Sayla

RIVER MUSIC MINGLES with the beat of my guitar, so fitting for my newest song.

When love is deep. When love is a river.

Perfectly matching the song's rhythm with the flow of falling water, I sit on a rock and marry Native and folk chords. The music will whirl my audience to the place I now sit beneath white fir and quaking birch. Ghostdancer is several hundred yards down the river. He shooed me away when I tried to help him cut willow branches for the sweat lodge frame, telling me to do what I do best, which is write a song. He believes my eagle feathers are from Creator Yahweh and that Creator will give me more songs.

Rustling leaves scatter across a carpet of rye grass, and forest ferns send up the spicy scent of late summer. A red hawk soars overhead as I sing, lending its screech to the lilting melody.

When love stands still.

Though the sun is high and the day hot, cool shadows cover Summers Glen where I strum my guitar beside the Sprague River.

I don't know whether Ghostdancer is right about the feather or not. The songs are coming, and for that I'm grateful. Thinking about Grandfather's mentor causes the words of Ghostdancer's earlier prayer to enter my song.

You alone stretched out the heavens.

I marry chords and words, a simple tune that blends with running water and soaring wings.

Creator Yahweh. Yah Hey. Shining above all morning stars. Yahweh Ya Hey. Your presence moves upon the wind. Who am I that you should care?

The song won't make the charts. Probably won't make any money at all. But the tune is simple enough to stick in a person's mind, so all things are possible. I sing it again, imagining Kadai dancing beneath the moon.

"*Waqlis?i.*"

The greeting startles me. I drop my guitar and open my eyes.

The shaman is standing in front of me, dressed in moccasins and leather breeches. Markings of red and yellow paint cover his bare chest and arms making a sharp contrast to the white paint and windblown hair hiding most of his face.

"*Mo dic,*" I answer automatically, returning the ancient greeting asking how a person is doing.

He holds a spear whose shaft is pointed upward; two eagle feathers hang from it, blowing in the breeze.

"*?os ?ams*" The words slip from his lips, and then he falls silent. "So, so," he has said, as his dark eyes search my face. There is something of disapproval in the shaman's gaze upon me, and I immediately want to change that.

The shaman bends down and lifts a cup of steaming liquid from a small smoldering fire that was not there just a few moments ago. He hands the cup to me. "*Bonwa,*" he says, commanding me to drink.

I lean my guitar against a rock. The shaman seems like an elusive animal that may leave at any sudden movement.

"I've been wanting to talk with you," I say, reaching out to take the liquid. The first sip is unbelievably bitter and I cannot stop the grimace. "Needs sugar," I sputter.

The shaman continues to stare. Silence is his close companion. I force myself to empty the cup in one swig. Then I hand the cup back. He ties it with a strip of sinew to his loincloth and continues his stare. My ears tune to rustling leaves. I'm aware of the swoosh of a crow's wings overhead.

"About the powwow," I say. "I saw something and was wondering—"

The shaman responds before I can complete my sentence. "For your eyes alone."

"But Kadai saw him."

The shaman gives a brief nod. Then he lifts his spear straight up and sets the shaft down hard upon a flat rock. The sound is that of a warrior's drum. He lifts the spear again and again until drumming echoes throughout the forest. His lips move along with the drumming, but I hear no words. Then he stops.

Saaaaaaaaaaaaylaaaaaaaaaa.

My name vibrates around the small glen. I scan the now darkened forest searching for the Shadow Warrior. I could swear I see a wolf padding beneath the trees, yet every time my eyes nearly bring it into focus, the black form melds into shadow. When my gaze falls back on the shaman, I find it difficult to swallow. His face is contorted as it was yesterday when he levitated. His chin juts upward, lips silently moving, skin stretching tight in a grimace, eyes closed.

Saaaaaaaaaaaaylaaaaaaaaaa.

The Shadow Warrior appears between us, his arms held open in greeting. His features aren't as indecipherable as the last time I saw him but neither are they as bright as our first encounter. Pale color washes his face and feathers. His eyes are a shining black, startling in their intensity.

It is as if my feet have taken root in the ground; they refuse to move. The Shadow Warrior takes a step forward. His form is the same as he first appeared to me, except his beautiful face is quickly fading into gray fog.

Open yourself to my caress. His sweet words come out as a song. *The caress of one who knows you.*

The shaman continues his thump, thump, thumping until the rhythm and beat of the Shadow Warrior's heart becomes one with mine. The cold caress of his arms wraps around me. Yet, strangely, his icy touch warms my heart and makes me yearn for more. A moan leaves my throat. This is the kind of cold that burns. It reaches deep and strong, setting fire to my heart the same as ice sets fire to fingers that touch it.

I know all about you.

His words send a thrill into my heart. This is the forever love I have been waiting for.

He blows into my ear, sending a thrill straight to my heart, but then fingers of ice clench my throat and my heart. The air in my lungs turns to ice, and I fall to the earth in a heap of trembling shivers.

When I open my eyes, the Shadow Warrior is gone.

Struggling to my feet, I feel strangely disoriented. Was it a vision? Or is something else going on here?

The shaman's eyes are as piercing as before. "Tomorrow at midnight, *saayoogalla,* meet me on the prairie called Skookum."

My heart beats like a grasshopper's wings in flight. What an honor to have the shaman choose me as his apprentice. This is not something I can take lightly. Seeing the shaman turning to leave, I blurt, *"Hahas? Iwgis,* I know nothing of such a prairie."

The shaman turns back, making no reference to me calling him teacher ... more than a teacher, really; *Hahas? Iwgis* is more akin to someone who gives an apprenticeship to someone else. My response means I have accepted his offer. His eyes hold mine, and I try to wait him out. I hope being an apprentice will not mean having to practice such stillness, but if it does, I am willing to learn.

"So be it." He continues his stare until I end up looking away. "Meet me here," he says.

He starts to leave but then turns back to me. "I leave you with one gift, a token of more to come."

I blink. And then he is gone.

I search for tracks in the soft earth but find nothing but goat tracks. That isn't incredibly surprising, considering the shaman was wearing moccasins, and a herd of goats comes down here periodically to drink, but it still gives me the creeps. I run my hand above the blackened embers of the shaman's fire and feel no heat at all, yet the tea he gave me just moments ago was quite warm.

Wondering about the shaman's gift, I pick up my guitar and strum a few chords. Fingers of ice crawl across my body. When I begin to sing, a fantastic display of colors drifts from my mouth with every word. Strange triangles of iridescent red and orange float in front of my face.

I drop my guitar and wave my hands through the triangles. They scatter and multiply until I'm lost in a cloud of swarming colorful shapes. It's as if they are alive. Raising my arms, I watch the glowing swarm cover my skin. Then a scream of terror erupts through the forest.

Too late, I realize the scream is mine.

Chapter 41

*The hawk takes flight
by the wisdom of Creator Yahweh.*
Ghostdancer

Kadai

MANY HOURS HAVE PASSED since you first entered this place of healing. You stand at the window and look over a white man's world of gray asphalt and concrete, a parking lot where people come and go without notice of the green scent on the wind. Neither do they take heed of the gift of warmth from the sun piercing through lifting smoke.

Death and illness have a way of halting a human's purpose. Few on that vast surface below walk with a haughty step, sorrow bends the shoulders of many, faces look vacant and lost. For what purpose were these people set here in this time and place? Was there a reason beyond their understanding? Suffering reminds them time is short, what they hold dear will soon be gone.

You understand, you who have flown to the heavens and back. Your life is but a vapor, and yet there is something more. Much more. Creator knows your name. You will leave this hospital a much different person than when you first arrived.

Nurses no longer hover but they remain close, whispering in hushed tones and darting nervous glances your way. Hearing the word *miracle,* you swallow. As yet, you have been unable to utter a sound. Wanting to explain, you struggle for phrases, but they stick in your throat like cold fry bread. The miracle, you want to tell them, is not that you, who were once dead, have returned alive to this earth, but that you have seen HIS face.

Waqlisi sawalineeas.

Creator called you friend. Such knowledge is too fantastic, beyond your understanding.

Tears run down your face. You feel as helpless as a deer caught in the headlamps of a road hunter. Tears are foreign. You are completely at HIS mercy. HE can do with you what HE wants.

The strength of which you were once so proud now seems but a small thing. You thought it was great you could talk with horses, but HE knows the language of trees. You ride bareback across open fields while HE rides the wings of wind. You tame wild horses while He commands the storm.

Surely you spoke of things you did not understand, things too wonderful for you to know. Creator is above and beyond and exalted in power. In HIS justice and great righteousness, HE does not oppress.

Your ears pick up the sound of a gasp as you fall facedown on the floor. You are in the presence of The Almighty. How dare you stand on your feet?

HIS presence falls over you as real as in the other world. But this isn't the other world, neither is it a private world where you are free to worship in solitude. Anxious shouts and heavy footfalls cross the tiled floor to your side. You should have known you could not worship here in this white man's realm. Fingers feel for your pulse and find it; then a hush falls over the room. Sweet warm sage fills your nostrils. Again, HE has given this gift, an awareness of who HE is.

"What's going on here?" A voice shouts. Stomping feet follow. It is the guard who stands by the door making sure you do not break free from your cage. Ignoring the doctor's protests, the guard reaches down and grabs your shoulder. A cry escapes his lips and you look to see what has caused such alarm. Eyes wide; pain registers in the contortions of his face. A nurse looks at his hand and then down at you, her expression a mixture of fear and awe. The guard's hand is burned and raw, as if he had thrust it into a flaming fire.

Inspecting your shoulder you see the flame, small tongues of fire, glowing and hot, enveloping your shoulders and head. But you feel no alarm. You know this flame; it comes from the ONE who made all things.

"It's God!" one of the nurses says. "I've read about this in the Bible. Tongues of flame came down on the people at Pentecost, yet no one was burned."

At the mention of burning, all attention turns back to the guard whose hand is now restored and whole. "What the—" He cuts the curse short, his eyes darting around the room as if some unseen angel is waiting to strike him dead.

Warmth enters your body as the flames disappear. It is HIS Spirit that has settled within you, the same Spirit that's been with you all along. Feeling a tingling in the palms of your hands you discover your burns have been completely healed. Though the scars remain, they carry the look of age. This one physical reminder of HIS presence will stay with you for the rest of your days on this earth. You rise to your feet and take station at the window, wishing you could say something . . . anything . . . that would help these people understand. But they've had Creator's words for centuries, most often knowing but seldom understanding. Like a windblown lake they talk too much and listen too little.

Across the parking lot you can see a line of mountains stretching from north to south. You wish with everything in you that you were out there on those mountains protecting the one you love, because you know full well she is in trouble. Then suddenly you hear HIS voice and nothing else matters.

Taamtgi. Be still. My righteousness covers you.

The whispered voice washes through your mind and sinks deep into your heart, birthing hope where despair had taken hold. This battle you face is not an Indian battle, not one that was lost over five hundred years ago. This battle began back in Eden, back in the beginning of time, when brother Adam made the first wrong choice. This battle has already been won, two thousand years ago when Creator took on flesh.

Peace falls over you and you enter a world where all is made right. You ride beside your Chief and Captain, both mounted on warhorses, flying on the wind. The battle cry is called, but your scabbard is empty.

The Sword is in the Captain's hand.

Chapter 42

Creator Yahweh sees our every footstep.
Ghostdancer

Loretta

LORETTA AND KENNY heard it at the same time, though Kenny was quicker on his feet. He flew across the meadow like a fleeting deer, certainly not like a city man. Loretta, on the other hand, was winded straight-out and had to slow her pace to that of a meandering donkey. *Yaks dwa!* She must be turning into a couch potato. Link was soon at her side.

"What's up?" he asked.

Loretta couldn't believe he had to ask. Sayla's piercing scream had sent heat flashing through her veins. "Didn't you hear?"

"Not a thing. Just saw you and Kenny drop your plates and run like a couple of banshees let out of hell. Thought I should follow."

Any other time, Loretta would have made a comment about the banshee thing, but for now she was too busy trying to pick up her pace. She threw up silent prayers to Jesus, asking for safety for Sayla and clarity for herself. If Sayla needed her, she wanted to be ready, not be some whimpering fool. Yet, even as the thought came to her, a moan left her mouth.

Ghostdancer appeared over the ridge of the riverbank waving his arms.

Kenny had almost reached him. Link stopped. "Is he asking us to stay back or be quiet?"

"Not sure," Loretta said, "but let's keep it slow and quiet just in case." She was wondering if she should have grabbed her shotgun. "You still have your pistol?"

Link glanced at her but didn't answer.

When they neared the berm, Ghostdancer pinned Loretta with his eyes. His grave expression sent a sharp pain across her chest and her hand went to her heart.

"Don't look." Ghostdancer placed his body in front of hers.

He might as well have told her not to breathe. After that crack, she *had* to look. She pushed by him and felt all air leave her lungs.

"Jumping frogs on Easter Sunday," whispered Link.

"God," said Kenny.

Loretta hoped it was meant to be a prayer, because that was exactly what the scene below called for. Vice grips cinched across her heart. Sayla stood laughing below, twirling in slow circles with her arms thrust outward. Her entire body was covered with bees.

"She's allergic," Loretta said. "Oh Lord, oh Lord, oh Lord."

Trying to form words into a prayer proved impossible. She had heard it said once that even a sigh directed at God was a prayer. She hoped so. She certainly hoped so.

Chapter 43

*Gaze long at the clouds so high above you.
If you sin, how does that affect Creator Yahweh?*
Ghostdancer

Sayla

FEAR SHOULD HAVE CONTINUED to grip me. Just one bee sting can bring my death, but I am so sure this is the shaman's gift that after my first fearful scream, I feel nothing but delight. Bees swarm around me like shattered prisms in colors so vivid it's hard to keep my eyes on them. They tickle my skin, but none of them bite or sting. Swinging my arms with all those fluttering wings attached makes me feel as if I can fly. We are *dici stinta*, one with one another.

Talking with coyotes as a child made me think animals could understand me; fearlessly meeting bears face-to-face led me to believe animals accepted me as one of their own; lying next to my horse on a bed of straw let me know the two of us shared a compassionate moment, but never have I felt so *dici stinta* with anything as I do with this swarming hoard of bees—bees who spell danger at any other time.

To be so *dici stinta* is like the eagle with the wind, a fact which Kadai explained well to me when I was a teen. We were riding horses along the fence line when a pair of bald eagles took flight. We stopped to watch.

"Eagles soar *in* the wind," Kadai had said. "They are not merely moved along by it. Their wings beat the wind into currents and every shift of air affects the eagle." I remember the look of awe on Kadai's face as he said, "The eagle is *dici stinta* with the wind."

Dici stinta . . . good love. I like the words. Like all other Klamath words, they carry music in their cadence.

Color shimmers everywhere, through the stream, up and down tree trunks, and in the bees still covering my body. Everything is alive with impossible hues. The bees may stay with me forever. I will become the bee singer drawing crowds far and near. Laughter floats out in blues and yellows, like bubbles from a child's wand. The sight makes me laugh all the more. I am drunk with wonder. Then Ghostdancer steps into my vision and the colors change.

The cool blues and yellows turn to angry red and black as they turn from me in one swoop and head toward Ghostdancer.

"Run!" Ghostdancer shouts.

Mesmerized, I watch as the buzzing hoard bears down on my grandfather's *sawalineeas*. Red and black arrows shoot from the hoard, aiming for Ghostdancer's head. I begin to run toward Ghostdancer, not away as he commanded. I'm hoping the shaman's gift will allow me to retrieve the bees before they harm Ghostdancer.

"No!"

Gran's frantic voice stops me. She is standing on the ridge clutching her chest. Dear God. Is she having a heart attack? I look from her to Ghostdancer, torn as to what to do.

"Back in the name of Christ!"

Ghostdancer's voice echoes through the glen, sending out flaming crimson and gold arrows. I stare at their beauty, wondering how words can be so colorful.

"Run, Sayla!"

Gran's words pour out in a colorful rainbow, exploding before my eyes. I move toward her until finally I am by her side. She pulls me into her arms and we watch the scene below.

"Jumping Saint Christophers on Saturday night," says Link.

"Well said," agrees Kenny.

A glowing blue shield completely surrounds Ghostdancer. It stops the angry swarm. Except for his arms, which are raised toward Creator, Ghostdancer stands relaxed and at peace.

No fear.

I've seen the saying on tee shirts, but it takes on new meaning now. One by one the bees fall away from the shield, changing color as they do. Gran stiffens beside me.

"Never seen anything like it," says Kenny.

Link remains silent. I look to see if he's all right. His face is a question mark. Can't blame him for that. I have unanswered questions too. Like what are all the colors about? And how did Ghostdancer put up a shield? Was it from his Creator? If so, where does the shaman's power come from?

"You alright Sayla?" Gran asks.

I hold out my arms for her to inspect. "Not a single sting."

"That was some show," Kenny says. "Too bad we didn't get it on video.

"I got it," Link says. His voice is surprisingly quiet. I see a soft yellow glow making a puff in front of his face.

"What?" Kenny says.

Link holds up his cell phone. "It's only a three-minute video, but it's enough."

Kenny laughs and pats Link on the back. "Way to go brother. Don't see how you could think of a thing like that when Sayla's life was in danger."

Flashing me a look bordering on awe, Link says, "She was never in any danger."

"How's that?" Kenny asks.

"My grandfather raised bees. Many times I watched him reach into a hive and bring out the queen. It looked very much like Sayla here with her bees, except my grandfather never did the dance."

"Yeah," Kenny says. He reaches in his shirt pocket and draws out a cigar. "Don't ever do it again."

"I agree," says Gran.

Weakness overtake me as we watch the bees swarm together and leave Summer's Glen. It's as if they are taking a part of me with them. Worry lines crease Ghostdancer's face as he makes his way back to us.

"My heart can't take another show like that," says Gran. Her skin is still ashen and she holds one hand over her chest. Is it possible the shaman's gift placed my relatives in danger? I shudder as a strong hand grips my shoulder.

"You alright, Little Fire?"

My pet name falls off Ghostdancer's tongue exactly as it did from Grandfather, and for the first time since Grandfather's death, I feel he is near.

"I'm fine," I say. "Just a little tired." My feet feel as if they each weigh a hundred pounds as I start back toward the river to retrieve my guitar.

"Whoa," Link says.

"Guitar," I manage to croak.

"I see it," says Link. "You go on up to the house."

My legs give out before we are halfway across the field. Ghostdancer lifts me in his arms. I only weigh 110 pounds, but that seems like a heavy load for an old man to carry. I want to tell him to put me down, but the words are too heavy and darkness is taking over.

When at last he lays me on the bed, dreams overtake me, wild and stormy, yellow eyes piercing through fog. The padding of wolves' feet grows louder and stronger until it thrums in my head like a drum. I scream and thrash but no one hears. Long fingers of night hold me tight.

"A little sleep," I hear Gran say as though from very far away, "will do her good."

But this sleep will do no good. It holds the taste of raw evil.

Chapter 44

*The promise of power may turn you aside
from walking in beauty.*
Ghostdancer

Jacob Wiseman

THE SPIRIT REALM offers many treasures, one of which is being able to soar unseen without the burden of a physical body. This ability has proved useful for me in noting the habits of those who oppose my power. I have seen Sayla's reaction and Ghostdancer's stance.

Sayla has enjoyed my gift, and now she will enter the shadowland where she can embrace her dark side. It has been repressed far too long. She has fooled herself into believing she is good.

Many have opposed me for my love of the dark side. But they have not been given the gift of understanding, or perhaps, they do not want to admit the dark side dwells within each of us.

How can we heal others if we cannot heal ourselves? And how can we heal ourselves unless we recognize our need?

It is an age-old question that can be answered simply enough. We are all flawed. It is part of the human condition. We must first embrace that dark side and forgive ourselves that we are flawed. Then we can forgive others for the wrongs they do.

That is why I bring the dark side into the light of acceptance, not to bring harm to others, though sometimes harm will be done, but to gain acceptance of the repressed parts. It has been my experience that those desires we repress and keep in darkness cause more problems than when they are exposed. Sometimes it is a matter of feeding the ravenous beast. Knowing who we are, both the light and the dark sides, makes life easier to deal with.

It remains to be seen how Sayla will deal with her dark side. Ghostdancer thinks he has power over me, but he has lost more strength though I doubt if he realizes this. When the final battle comes, he will be little help to Sayla. Kadai, too, will be of little use. The jail fight was a marvelous plan and James performed his part well. He has received new power because of his allegiance. Loretta is no threat at all. She gave up the battle when she stopped painting and proved the point by trying to buy off my curse. Her faith in her god is too small to be of much use.

Soon, all the pieces will be in place, and my long-awaited goal will be realized.

Chapter 45

> There is no dark place, no deep shadow,
> where Creator Yahweh does not see.
> *Ghostdancer*

Loretta

NOTHING IN ALL of Loretta's days could have prepared her for the speed of Link's Lexus. Seat belts seemed of little use while flying across the pavement like a low flying jet. Gripping the seat with one hand and the dashboard with the other, she felt as if she was being hurtled from a cannon. Kenny sat in back, barking commands into his cell phone. Dozens of typed papers lined the seat around his laptop and open briefcase. It looked like a regular office back there, though it would have been an office in one of those fancy private jets at the speed they were traveling. At least it took her mind off leaving Sayla behind.

Ghostdancer said it was unlikely the girl would wake before morning. She was sleeping the sleep of the dead.

Loretta hated that line, in fact she hated thinking about death at all, but at this rate she would be joining the dead soon enough if Link didn't slow for the curves ahead.

"Amnesty's on board," Kenny hollered from the back. "Isabel's one feisty lady." Kenny's words rolled around his unlit cigar. It made Loretta think of a baby with a pacifier.

"Wants a fax number so she can send paperwork for Kadai's release. Says to heck with bail. The man's clearly been set up. She's already talked with the doctor. Good work there, Link, another one for the good guys."

The curves were dead ahead. Loretta tightened her grip and tried to break into the conversation, but Kenny kept rambling.

"Got a good thing going on the custody angle as well, if you can get us to the tribal office in time."

Link hit the first curve with a screech, slowing to fifty on the second. The sign said 35 miles an hour. Loretta's stomach was flipping. Papers were flying from the back seat to the front. Loretta caught one on reflex and felt herself being slammed into the door. Kenny grabbed papers and kept talking as if this was his usual form of travel.

"Fifteen minutes and counting." Link said. He turned to Loretta. "How much further?"

"An eternity the way you're driving."

Link looked at her a second too long and tires hit gravel as they rounded the last curve. A speed sign said Chiloquin, 25 mph. The Lexus passed as if the sign didn't exist. Relieved they made it through all those curves without dying, Loretta pointed straight ahead. "Turn right, cross the river and then turn left, but take care at the intersection."

The words had barely left her lips when Link dashed through the intersection, nearly hitting a dust-covered Chevy sedan. Two minutes later they came to a screeching halt in front of the office. All four door locks clicked and lifted in unison. Feeling more than a bit dizzy, Loretta pushed open the door and stood.

Link was already by her side, offering an arm and a smile. "We made it," he said, "but just barely. You ready?"

Just barely was a good way of putting it, but Loretta suspected Link was talking about time while she was thinking of life and death. In spite of everything, she felt rejuvenating energy sweep across her legs. "I'm ready," she said and meant it; she hadn't felt this young in years.

Chapter 46

Have you seen the gates of the shadow of death?
Creator Yahweh

Ghostdancer

BEATING HIMSELF UP didn't help matters any Ghostdancer knew that, but the knowledge did little to ease his mind as he sat in the padded chair next to Sayla's bedside. The girl twisted and turned, probably in the throes of a nightmare, and his prayers didn't seem to be helping.

There was a lot he would like to talk over with the girl for Charlie's sake, but he would have to wait for the right time. If he gave her too much information too soon she might abuse it, and if he gave her too little she might end up a victim or, worse yet, she might end up on the dark side. The dark world had its appeal in the beginning, he knew, but he also knew about the cost it would eventually ask of her.

No. For Charlie's sake, he couldn't sit back and watch his friend's granddaughter fall under the shaman's spell, but yesterday's warning had been clear. "If you interfere," Jacob had said, "Vietnam will seem like a piece of cake compared to the battle I'll give you."

Ghostdancer didn't fear facing a battle with the shaman. What he feared was seeing Sayla caught between them. Supernatural gifts were a heady thing, captivating the innocent with promises of power. He'd seen it all before and had even experienced it himself. First came the healings and grateful people offering praise. Then came the temptations, one by one, they passed through the young healer's mind—notoriety, love, happiness, power, control—yet most were short-lived and all of them life-consuming. Most tribal healers made it through the dark night of the soul, choosing the supreme privilege of using their gift to help others over the notoriety of the dark world, but some, like Jacob, did not.

Ghostdancer had to find a way to warn the girl. Ah, but words failed him. He was sure to come off as an old-fashioned fool.

Leaning forward, he folded his hands and laid his elbows on his knees. Then he opened his mouth and began speaking words to Sayla. Words she could not hear.

"Spells and chants are no good, Little Fire. It is better to rely on the *Sacred Writings* found in the Bible. I know you think it is a white man's Bible, but it is not. It is a book of life-giving words given by Creator Yahweh, passed down from one generation to another, kept alive by prophesies fulfilled hundreds of years after they were first given, and fueled by the hope of a Messiah to come. A Messiah, a Great Chief, the Grassdancer of all grassdancers. He made a Way for His people by stomping out evil and preparing the ground for us to walk on. One great new tribe that includes all of us who put our trust in Him."

Bowing his head, Ghostdancer called upon Yahweh, the ONE who sees, the great counselor, the faithful great *Hahas? Iwgis* Teacher above all *Hahas? Iwgiss.* "Sat'waa Yi?is. Come help me," he said. Then he stood and raised his hands toward the ceiling, offering prayer in his Native tongue and moving his feet to a silent drum. "You know every word before it is on my tongue. You search my every thought. You know when I sit and when I rise. You perceive my thoughts from afar. Oh, Creator Yahweh, help me not get in the way of what you are doing. Shine light in this dark place."

After making his petition, Ghostdancer sang on, lifting praise to Creator. He received much more than he gave out. It was always that way. When he felt weakest, when strength was far from him, instead of taking to his bed, he had discovered that praise of Creator gave him renewal. The old tree could still bear fruit.

Red Dog's frantic barking put an end to Ghostdancer's prayer. Instead of hurrying to see who was at the door, he bent over Sayla. A dream catcher hung above her bed. He no longer put stock in such things, but he lifted petition to Creator, asking him to catch the bad dreams and let the good ones slip through. He hoped Creator Yahweh was talking with her through her dreams.

It was best to trust Creator Yahweh.

Chapter 47

*Creator Yahweh's plans for you
are for good and not evil.
Ghostdancer*

Sayla

RUNNING. RUNNING. RUNNING. Forest and trees, hills and mountains, I run them all—heavy panting follows behind, the padding of wolves' feet strong in my ears. Crossing streams and fording rivers, I run. Down gullies and across high meadows, my feet are like those of a deer, running, leaping, but not for joy, for the terror of being ripped apart by enormous teeth. I run through forests deep and dark, shadows dogging my every step. A whisper here, a growl there, mad laughter directly behind, pushing me ever forward.

Why do the wolves come after me? What have I done to earn their hatred?

Otherworldly, their eyes glow, yellow slits of hunger, yet playing with their food like lazy cats with a mouse . . . and I am their food.

As we run, the wolves grow larger, the ground rumbles beneath their weight. One swipe of a behemoth paw and I will be gone, lost to this world forever.

Will my Shadow Warrior fight for me? I look for him through the darkened forest and while skimming the edge of open meadows, catching no glimpse of him but often seeing the glint of strange yellow eyes.

The wolves' stench is strong—rotting flesh, decomposed life, stinking of alcohol. Gasping for air, I choke, then swallow and block my nostrils, always running, moving forward through darkness as thick as water. Clawing a path up ridges, skating my way through mountain scree, the wolves always behind, their breath as cold as ice.

No wind breaks over the forest, no breeze to break the stench. Frigid fog rises from the ground and quickly covers the path, climbing up trees and closing my world. Do I think I can outrun those manic feet, those eyes that can peer through inky black and see as good as if in daylight? I run on, bumping into trees and scraping against nettle. Terror grips my throat and fear becomes my mantle, and all the while the thrumming drum keeps echoing long and far. Grasping, clutching, I grope in the darkness, straining my eyes to see the impossible, stumbling through brush and sliding over rocks.

Any minute and I will feel those horrid teeth sinking into my neck. Goosebumps travel up and down my back and still I run on, through the shimmering fog, like a deer on the loose after being blinded by a hunter's light. Everything in me wants to look back, but instinct demands I keep my eyes dead ahead. Don't give the enemy a moment's chance.

I run, plowing the fog like a swimmer through water, splitting darkness from light.

Excited howling rings through the forest. Is that a victory cry? Or is it simply delight in the chase? Or perhaps confidence in the final win? My body groans from its mad exertion, pain rips through my legs, but still I run. I run through brush that scratches my arms and leaves a trail of blood. Demonic wails grow louder at the metallic scent.

My beating heart matches the thrumming drums, fear becomes a mask contorting my face muscles, stretching skin over bone. Gasping now, I clutch my throat as my weakened legs begin to fail.

Drumming shakes the ground beneath my feet. Then suddenly, a horrible scream fills the forest and everything grows quiet.

The quietness is worse now than the drumming before. I stop, straining to hear every sound. No cicada song, no croaking frogs, no padding wolves' feet. Arctic ice grips my chest. I've experienced this stillness before when a mountain lion roams through the forest, but this is no mountain lion. Something otherworldly roams this night.

Forcing myself to remain motionless, I listen for a footfall. My ears betray me, causing me to think I hear sounds I do not. Then I hear the music of the Shadow Warrior's voice calling my name.

"*Saaaaaaaaylaaaaaaaa.*"

Turning my head toward his voice I strain to see him, my heart beating hard in my chest.

"*Saaaaaaaaylaaaaaaaa.*"

I see him now, directly before me with arms open wide in greeting.

"*Saaaaaaaaylaaaaaaaa.*"

"You came," I say. "I knew you would."

Then I fall into his arms, spent and done.

But instead of a warm embrace, the wind snatches me up and carries me heavenward, above trees and rocks and mountains. This is the kind of wind that tears mountains apart and shatters rocks, and I know it will soon rip me asunder.

Chapter 48

Be strong and very courageous.
Creator Yahweh

Kadai

PADDING FEET and hot panting breath send you running through the forest. Whether wolves or something worse you do not know, but the stench is like nothing you have smelled before. It stinks of death and rotting flesh, sickening sweet as it contaminates the night air. Moonlight brightens the path, so you run as though your life depends on it. You must reach the one you love before this dark monster has its way.

There! Between the trees you see it darting. Yellow eyes set wide and translucent. It's as if you are looking into the face of hell. Calling upon strength beyond mere muscles and bone, you raise your spear. Planting your feet wide and solid, you pull back with all your might and throw. The spear breaks through the forest straight for its target, splitting the dark night with glinting light, but the wolf leaps out and the spear rips earth instead of flesh. Snarling, the creature dashes beyond your sight.

Drawing your knife you wait, breathing shadows and sighs, hearing nothing but your own heartbeat. Retrieving the spear, you see another flash of gray dart through the moonlight and disappear among shadows. You peer into the abyss and lift the spear. Those yellow eyes won't wait long.

Too close.

His claws rip the flesh of your thigh. Swallowing a cry, you struggle, grabbing fur that should be warm but is not. Fingers of ice crawl across your body, while frigid fangs find the flesh of your neck. Instinctively you thrust a fist down the creature's throat before those enormous teeth can draw blood. Unable to breathe, the creature pulls back, but you grab on and hold, one fist down its throat, the other clinging to its ear. Still, the cold sinks into your body, freezing your blood and numbing your mind. Much more and death will overtake you.

Claws sink deep into your chest as the creature shakes his head back and forth. Finally, you lose your grip and fly through the air, landing with a terrible thump that takes your breath away. You cannot move further. Lifting your head you see, beyond the forest, a monstrous wolf runs free.

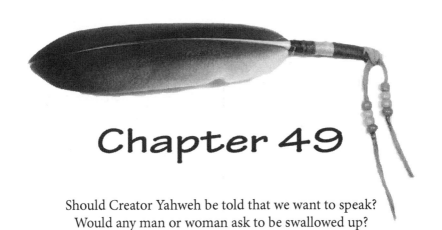

Chapter 49

*Should Creator Yahweh be told that we want to speak?
Would any man or woman ask to be swallowed up?*
Ghostdancer

Loretta

AS SOON AS THEY SIGNED IN at the Tribal offices' airy reception area, Kenny started asking questions. Pointing to the four enlarged photos hanging above the tall windows he said, "Who are these people?"

"Our ancestors, all Klamath, Modoc and Yahoosken women." Loretta pointed out the woven Tule hats and leather dresses trimmed with elk teeth and pebblesnail shells from Klamath Lake. Then she led him to the showcase containing basket and weaving materials. Seeing he was still impressed, she moved to the other cases. "Look closely," she said, "and you'll see how the baskets are woven tightly enough to hold water. They're strong enough to carry heavy loads and make wonderful quivers as well."

"Quivers?" Link asked.

"To hold arrows."

"And Loretta's quiver is full of many arrows of faith." Mary's voice came from over Loretta's shoulder.

"*Yaks dwa!*" Loretta chirped. "Don't sneak up like that." She turned to receive Mary's hug and then introduced her to Kenny. "Mary's our program director," Loretta said, "and her husband is our Council Chairman. They should be able to get something done for us."

Mary pointed toward the large clock clicking away the minutes on the wall. "Grandmother, it would help if you could force yourself to get here a little earlier. Most everyone is getting ready to head home."

"Yes, but—"

"No problem, I have everything you need." Mary started down the wide hall, her high heals clicking on the tile floor, then stopped abruptly and asked, "Would you like coffee or water?"

"Coffee would be great," Kenny said, "if it's not too much trouble."

"Water for me," said Link, loosening his tie.

"Nothing for me," said Loretta.

Mary entered her office and gave instructions over the phone while the unlikely trio squeezed into three chairs across her desk.

"You sure?" Mary asked Loretta.

"Positive. I'm still suffering from motion sickness. This white man drives like a maniac!"

Mary turned off the intercom and chuckled. "Can't be any worse than your youngest son. I've seen him fly by more than a few—" A hand shot up to her mouth. "Oh, Grandmother, I am so sorry."

Loretta felt stinging tears. Why was it a visit to the tribal offices always brought back the pain of loss more severely? "It's okay," she said.

A secretary brought in a tray with the requested drinks. Loretta scanned the room while chitchat passed back and forth. Memorabilia lined every wall and spilled over to the workspace. Photos of Mary's family brought a smile to Loretta's lips: A teen with a graduation diploma, a toddler taking his first steps, a daughter dressed in colorful regalia.

When the secretary left the room, Loretta straightened.

Link carefully arranged his legal pad over a small cleared space on Mary's desk in front of him. A pen was already in his hand.

Mary watched Link's actions but made no reference to the reason they were in her office. She was on Native time, which meant they could be there for a while. Other office people were leaving for the day, throwing curious glances through Mary's open door. Loretta leaned back and tried to still her queasy stomach. She knew what was coming next.

"I hear you're from Southern California," Mary said to Kenny.

Kenny leaned forward in the chair, the bulk of his frame filling the small wooden platform. "San Diego."

"We have two Native communities in your area. A migration of sorts that was forced upon us. One is in Riverside up by Los Angeles and the other is in Oceanside, closer to you. We have many cousins there."

Kenny pulled out a cigar.

Mary raised a hand in protest. "Sorry, Mr. Liparulo. This is a smoke-free environment."

"Uh, sure," He poked the offending torpedo back into his container and stuffed it in his pocket.

"Has Grandmother told you her story?"

Loretta had been dreading this moment. It was Native tradition that a person had to tell her own story. No one else could tell it for them.

"The truth needs to be heard," Mary said.

Loretta looked up and saw both Kenny and Link leaning toward her. Would knowing her story make a difference for them? Would they still appreciate her computer skills and hospitality? Or would they fear her Native ways and distain her as white people did not so long ago? There was only one way to find out.

"I was bussed from the reservation when I was nine years old," Loretta began. "At first my siblings and I were excited about a fun trip on a train, like it was some sort of vacation."

In the best words she could find, she told Kenny and Link how she and her older sister and younger brother were all removed from their family and the land they called home. A train took them to Carson, Nevada, a place none of them had ever been before. There, they were separated into three different buildings—one for young girls, one for young boys, and one for older girls. They were unable to reach one another, and Loretta wondered what she had done wrong to end up there. The white people cut the children's long dark locks. Instead of hanging down in beautiful braids, it stuck out like eagle feathers in a strong wind. They were told not to use their language and were punished severely if they did, either solitary confinement or hanging by their thumbs. They were dressed in white people's clothes of strange cloth.

"Wait a minute," Link interrupted. "Wasn't that like a century ago or something? Are you talking about yourself, or your grandmother?"

"It was 1954," Mary's voice rang out. "And you didn't hear that wrong. Nineteen. Not eighteen. Nineteen fifty-four. It happened to Loretta and to many others of our people, and you haven't heard the worst of it." Mary's voice held anger, but it wasn't directed at Kenny and Link. Loretta knew she wanted these white men to know the story so history would not repeat itself as it so often did.

Loretta continued the story, telling Link and Kenny about the time she and several other children were dressed and eager for an exciting journey to the city of Reno. Giggling as they boarded the bus, they watched in wide-eyed wonder at the stark scenery passing by, wondering what adventures awaited them in the city, but the planned adventure was something none of them could have ever dreamed.

The leaders took the children to a church where they lined them up and, one-by-one, they were each dunked into a tank of water. A white man spoke strange words over them. Loretta had no idea what was happening, why they were dressed up to be soiled in such a way, and in front of people. They were given no towels and, following the dunking, Loretta had to sit in the pew in wet, ruined clothes, still wondering what she had done wrong.

Loretta shivered. It was as if she was back there, a young girl again, missing her mother and grandmother and siblings and the land where she had run free.

"And *that* isn't the worst of it," Mary continued. "The worst is when a federal agency ripped Loretta's firstborn daughter from her arms, and they never saw each other again. All because they didn't think an Indian would be a fitting mother."

"What?" Link's eyes were enormous behind his spectacles, and she saw tears welling up that she knew matched her own. He scooted forward with his arms pushing on the chair, as if he would jump up and bolt from the room.

Kenny's fingers reached into his pocket and Loretta knew he wanted that cigar. What good did her little story do for this meeting other than make everyone uncomfortable? "Things are better now," she said. "We have restoration."

"Some restoration," Kenny mumbled. "What about Kadai? Where's his restoration?"

Mary held up a large white envelope. "I have the paperwork you need. That's your first step. I suspect your journey will be much shorter than what our tribe went through, and we're here to help if you need." She proceeded to tell them how the Klamath Tribe was the second richest in the nation at the time of termination. "The entire nation," Mary emphasized. She also told Kenny how most white people believed tribal members had a choice in selling their land.

"In truth, we had no choice," she said, waving an arm as if wiping the past away. "Our choice was *when* we would receive the money, not *if* we would sell. In 1954 we were terminated from federal funding." She began twirling her arm as if waving a whip with each proclamation. "We lost our land. Whip. We lost our lifestyle. Whip. We lost our language. Whip. We lost our jobs. Whip. We lost our ability to identify with our tribe! Whip. Termination was an Act of Congress; it was not anything we did. We did not vote to be terminated."

"Mary," Loretta said quietly. "It is enough."

The fire behind Mary's eyes was still burning, but she granted Loretta the respect their tribal customs demanded. She fell back in her chair, exhausted from her emotional journey.

Loretta rose and stood behind Mary, rubbing her sister-in-law's arm that must now be sore from all the twirling. "Forgive our emotions," Loretta said to Link and Kenny. "Mary spent many years helping fight this legal battle to restoration. Every time we would figure out the strange wording of the convoluted laws, the government would change them."

"I understand," Link said. "I've spent my life trying to figure them out myself."

But what Link didn't understand was that from 1954 to 1965 Loretta's people left in massive numbers, some forced by the government, some forced by lack of employment, and the tribe was just now beginning to rise from the ashes. Kadai's fight was not a new one.

Chapter 50

None of us will get it right all the time.
Charlie Whitewater

Ghostdancer

"GHOSTDANCER?" a voice called.

He had almost forgotten about the commotion in the other room. Recognizing the voice coming from the front porch, he hollered for Red Dog to stop his infernal barking, then he hurried to answer the door.

Karen Forbes, the woman who held his secrets, along with a part of his heart, had cracked open the door. She smiled hugely upon seeing him. "Does this mongrel bite? Or is he all bark?"

Wearing a red and yellow flannel shirt and a denim skirt above Ryder boots, Karen looked the picture of a modern-day cowgirl. A red Stetson with a beaded hatband sat atop her flyaway curls. Her hair was as white as goose down and thick as a berry patch. Ah, but it was good to see her, perhaps too good. He reached down and grabbed Red Dog's collar, commanding the dog to be still. Surprisingly, the mutt obeyed while Ghostdancer fully opened the door. Karen stepped in and laughed, sending Red Dog into another barking fit. Her green eyes sparkled. "Don't worry," she said. "I don't think he'll eat me."

Ghostdancer wasn't so sure. He grabbed Red Dog's collar with a jerk that made the dog yelp.

Karen bent down to one knee. "Let him go." Her throaty voice was calm but demanding.

Women. If Ghostdancer lived to be a hundred, he would never understand them. A good reason to remain single. He had been married once, and it was a delightful season, but that was another lifetime. Any thoughts of romance seemed betrayal to the memory of his wife. They would share eternity together. That was enough to keep him straight. He let go of Red Dog.

Not expecting such a quick release, the mutt fell forward into Karen's arms. She stroked his neck. The silly dog moaned with delight, licking her face to show his gratitude. How the woman could stand the dog's tongue was another mystery. Her laughs indicated she was as delighted with the dog as the dog was with her.

"Thought I better come and see how things are going," she said.

"You'll see better if you come in all the way. And close the door while you're at it." His voice came out more clipped than he meant, but he didn't have time for these shenanigans. Kadai was in jail, or would be once he got out of the hospital; Loretta was traipsing the countryside with two strange white men; and Sayla was in the other room facing who knew what.

"That well, eh?" Karen stood and moved to the kitchen table, leaving the closing of the door to Ghostdancer.

He shook his head and gave it a push. The door slammed with a bang.

"Feel better now?"

He felt close to cursing is what he felt, but he wasn't about to let her know. She had already found the teapot and was filling it with water. Next she would be asking for scones.

"Got any fry bread or cookies? Chocolate would be even better."

The woman was rummaging through the shelves. He waved a hand, "Help yourself. It's not my house."

He hurried down the hall to Sayla's room. He enjoyed about five peaceful minutes before Karen carried a tray into the room and set it on the dresser. The smell of peppermint mingled with her expensive perfume. Ghostdancer never could figure out what the smell reminded him of—not sweet enough for roses, too sweet for musk—dang it all if the woman didn't drive him crazy. The tray was filled with not one, but two cups of steaming tea, not mugs, mind you, but fancy teacups. She offered one to Ghostdancer.

He took it. Perhaps he was single, but he knew how to pick his battles.

She stirred sweet leaf Stevia into her cup, just like Sayla usually did. The two could be twins, full of sweetness yet stubborn as a calf on branding day. Looks could certainly be deceiving.

Pulling up the rocker, Karen remarked, "Nice heirloom." Sadness filled her eyes as realization washed across her features. "It was her mother's wasn't it?"

Ghostdancer nodded. "And her grandmother's before that."

Karen crossed the room and bent over the bed, running her slender fingers through the dark hair covering Sayla's forehead. "How long has she been this way?"

Ghostdancer shrugged. "Hours. Not sure how many." He couldn't move his eyes from watching those slender fingers caressing Sayla's hair.

"Has she seen a doctor?"

"Isn't a doctor thing."

Karen leveled her green gaze on Ghostdancer and held it for several heartbeats. When she was satisfied with what she saw there, she turned back to Sayla. "Such a pretty girl. If her voice is half as pretty as her face, she'll go far."

She rose and retrieved her teacup. Then she sat in the rocker, holding the saucer with one hand and sipping with the other. A long night just got longer. Ghostdancer leaned forward and closed his eyes. Perhaps she would think he was in prayer and leave him alone.

But no, she was already talking. It wouldn't be long before she would worm the entire story from him. Then what would she think? Ah well, it was time for her to know the truth. He'd been skirting it far too long.

Chapter 51

> Creator Yahweh does great things
> beyond our understanding.
> *Ghostdancer*

Sayla

THE HOWLING WIND does not do me the harm I expect. Instead, it calms me and I rise as if on eagle's wings, soaring through the sky. I know no sense of time; I could be floating for years or centuries, basking in the awareness of purpose being fulfilled. Then, just as unexpectedly, I spiral back toward earth in an endless mad plummet. It is as if some strange god has grabbed me like a skipping stone and sent me hurtling toward earth.

I open my mouth to scream, but no sound leaves my throat. The earth turns into a fiery ball, and I barrel through the flames at impossible speeds. I'm not sure which is worse—the knowledge that my death is imminent or the understanding that my Shadow Warrior cannot save me. I see faces beyond the flames—Kadai, Gran, Ghostdancer—all dancing their prayers to Creator. Their dancing becomes more fervent, causing an earthquake that sends water rushing over the fire, and then the silence is back, more terrifying in its intensity than before.

Chapter 52

*The horse laughs at fear, afraid of nothing;
he does not shy away from the sword.
The quiver rattles against his side,
along with the flashing spear and lance.*
Creator Yahweh

Kadai

THOUGH YOU ARE WOUNDED the battle is not yet finished. Whistling a call to your faithful mount, you suddenly feel his warm flesh beneath your legs. Magically the two of you lift on eagle wings and soar through the sky. This time your spear aims true and makes its mark. A terrible scream rips through the night, but this is not a monster's scream, it is the terror-stricken cry of the one you love.

Realization hits you then, there is more than one monster in this night. You raise your voice and shout. "Ride!"

Thundering hooves break through the heavens in answer to your charge. The herd is strong and ready for battle, each steed with a shining warrior upon its back. Glistening steel slashes through the night. The wolves are outnumbered by far. Yellow eyes grow thin with pain. Whimpering yelps soon fade in the distance while you and your steed remain behind, guarding the path of least resistance. At last the sound of battle ceases.

You strain your ears to hear the call of the one you love. You hear the sound of water falling over rocks but nothing more. An eerie silence has crept over the forest, an alert to a predator on the loose. For now your love is safe, but the wolves will soon return.

Chapter 53

*Creator Yahweh knows
the thoughts of man are futile.*
  Ghostdancer

Loretta

LEAVING THE TRIBAL OFFICES with the necessary paperwork tucked safely away in Link's briefcase, Loretta thought their little entourage must look rather strange—a tribal elder, a wiry lawyer in a fancy suit, and an Italian that looked as if he had come straight out of the movie *The Godfather*. Kenny was still chewing on an unlit cigar. Several locals milled around, clearly wanting to get a better look at whoever was driving the fancy car. When they saw Loretta, their voices dropped to a whisper. She wondered if they were talking about the car or about her earlier visit to the shaman. She really should have used her brain before making that unfortunate little trip.

Forcing a smile, she waved at a group of young people hanging out on the other side of the parking lot. Three of the girls giggled and waved back. James stepped from the middle and came toward her. "Grandmother."

She acknowledged his greeting with a nod, noticing a bruise covering his right eye. Remembering that he had been locked up with Kadai, she realized how impertinent it had been to think people were talking about her. Of course, the talk would be about Kadai. He was the newsmaker now.

"Thought you would still be in jail," she said.

"Out on good behavior." James pointed to the car. "See you and Sayla got some rich white friends. Gonna take more than that to free Kadai. Those white boys weren't doing nothin' wrong."

From the way James slurred his words he was either very drunk or very high. Perhaps both.

Link stepped between them. "Listen young man, Kadai didn't start that fight. Three other witnesses will attest to that."

"Anything to keep Kadai on their good side."

Kadai's name came out in a slanderous slur. Loretta wondered what had caused such obvious animosity. James seemed to realize he had gone too far. He smiled at Loretta and offered an apology. "Sorry Grandmother. Don't have nothin' against the guy, but he really should learn to control himself."

James was one to talk. He was barely able to stand on his feet. "Kadai has more self-control in his little finger than you have in your entire body," she said.

James laughed. An evil laugh that held no mirth; then he turned to Link. "How much you pay those witnesses?"

Kenny grabbed Loretta's elbow and motioned toward the car, handing her off to Link in one movement. When Loretta turned her head to see if he was following, she was surprised to see James on the ground with a crushed cigar sticking out of his mouth. He was sputtering and wiping at his face. The three girls were already on their way to assist him while throwing curses at Kenny. She didn't know which surprised her more, to see James sputtering on the ground like a dog, or to see Kenny nonchalantly coming toward her as if nothing had happened.

Kenny soon caught up with her. "Guess he doesn't like Opus X. Next time I'll offer him a Cuban."

He was nearly pushing Loretta now as she strained to see behind her. She couldn't believe Kenny had actually used force.

"He'll be okay. Mom used to wash my mouth out with soap when I told a lie, figured tobacco might work in this case."

Yaks dwa! These white men had no idea the trouble they were causing. It wasn't their place to get in the middle of an Indian battle. Natives took care of things their own way. As she buckled her seatbelt, she wondered how she had gotten herself into such a mess, first the shaman, now bringing white men into the mix. She was glad of the car's speed on the way home. It was time for a confession with Ghostdancer.

Kenny took up office again in the backseat and let out a whoop before they even got out of town. "Amnesty's sending Isabela. She'll be here in the morning, arriving at the train station in Klamath Falls."

"What time?" Link asked.

"Seven. That work for you?"

"Perfect. But expect later, the trains are never on time."

"Righto. How much you wanna bet she'll spring Kadai before noon?"

Link shook his head. "My mother raised smarter kids than that. I know better than to bet against a sure thing."

Kenny chuckled and the car fell silent. Both men looked at Loretta. "Cat got your tongue?" Link asked.

Blinking back tears, Loretta tried to explain. "All you white people getting involved. It just doesn't seem right."

"If it makes you feel any better," Kenny said, "the Amnesty representative is not white."

"She's Native?"

"No—" Kenny hesitated. "She's black."

"Black? And she's going to help us with a Native problem?"

"That's correct."

The car fell silent again, each of them lost in their own thoughts. Loretta figured she would be on the hot seat in the next tribal meeting.

Truth be told, she should probably have already called a meeting, but things were moving too fast. If Charlie had been here, he would have helped, but now she felt very alone.

"Mrs. Whitewater?"

Kenny's voice sounded strangely quiet. She turned to acknowledge him. For once the silly cigar wasn't sticking out of his mouth.

"Sorry," he said. "Was only trying to help in the best way I know how. Sometimes I get overexcited, but truly, I don't want to offend you."

Loretta nodded, not so much in affirmation, but so Link, who was staring at them both, would turn his eyes back to the road. It was the way of white people to think a few words would fix things.

"Will you forgive me?" Kenny asked.

"I don't think it is a question of forgiveness."

"Even so, will you forgive me?"

The man's face was so serious Loretta couldn't refuse. "Of course I'll forgive you."

"Me too?" Link asked.

"You?" The question startled Loretta. Whatever could Link think he had done wrong? "*Yaks dwa!* You white men are hard to figure. Perhaps it's time for another cigar meeting. We need more thinking and less talking."

Kenny laughed. "I'll go along with that one. I could use a good cigar about now."

"And make sure it's lit," Loretta said. "No pacifiers for me."

That did it. Kenny leaned back and laughed. By the time Link pulled the Lexus into the yard, all three were in a better mood. When Loretta saw the battered roofless Jeep, she knew immediately it belonged to Karen, the woman friend of Ghostdancer who took his messages and kept him informed; the woman Loretta suspected had more than a little feelings for the man. She hoped Karen hadn't distracted Ghostdancer from his job of watching Sayla.

As soon as the car slowed Loretta was out and rushing into the house. Kenny and Link hadn't even opened their doors yet. So much for chivalry. Loretta could make her own way; she had certainly done so many times before.

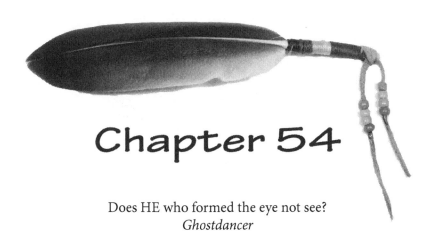

Chapter 54

Does HE who formed the eye not see?
Ghostdancer

Ghostdancer

WORDS POURED FROM GHOSTDANCER like water from a spring. Karen held her teacup in her hands, lifting it now and then for a sip. She sat still and relaxed, allowing Ghostdancer to spill the entire story. He told her how he and Loretta had been schooled alongside Jacob who now called himself a shaman.

Their teacher was Vincent Wildwalker, a renowned healer. Because Ghostdancer was the oldest of the trio, he was given the charge to continue the training sessions after Vincent joined his ancestors. Loretta and Jacob had been young enoughthey had often gone off on their own, dabbling in things that were foolish and dangerous. After Kadai's mother died, Loretta had changed her tactics, but Jacob had continued, getting involved with New Age practices that some tribes had even outlawed. Jacob fancied himself the most powerful shaman in existence.

"I should have seen it before," Ghostdancer said, "but I missed it until I saw the wolf."

"A skinwalker," Karen said.

"Or shape-shifter. However you want to look at it. Neither is good."

"And you're sure it's the shaman?"

Ghostdancer stopped his pacing. "Only a healer of great power could become a shape-shifter."

Karen set her cup on the bedside table. "I wouldn't be so sure. He could have students, and I've read of entire tribes who became shape-shifters."

"Lore."

"Perhaps. Perhaps not. And shape-shifters aren't always bad."

Ghostdancer raised his hands palms upward. "How can you believe such a thing and call yourself a follower of Creator Yahweh?"

Karen remained maddingly calm. "Don't get yourself in a ruffle. A donkey talked to Balaam in the Old Testament. How do you know he wasn't a shape-shifter?"

His mouth must have been hanging open, because Karen stood and placed a hand on his shoulder. A jolt of electricity shot through his veins and he stepped back. Dropping her hand, she sighed. Her voice was no more than a whisper. "There's more capacity for love in heaven than you give credit."

Ah. A woman's mind. Who could understand it? He waited for her to continue, having no idea where she was headed.

"I know you felt something when I touched you," she said. "That's why you stepped back. And before you get yourself in a dither, I also know it's important for you to be true to your dead wife. So don't worry, I don't plan to cross those lines."

Her eyes flashed, as green as stagnant water on a late summer morning. She placed a hand on his shoulder again, daring him to move. He forced himself to stay rigid.

"I'm your friend," Karen said. "I'm here to help, but things aren't always what they seem. Perhaps what you see as bad might be good, and what is good might be bad. It happens."

Grabbing her hand and holding it in both of his, he looked straight into her emerald eyes. "Enough of this nonsense. Holy Spirit reveals what is right and what is wrong. We hold that discernment in our hearts."

"Yes," Karen agreed, "but we are still human, and we often err in our own judgment. Don't be too quick to form opinions. It could lead to underestimating your enemy."

Sadness clinched Ghostdancer's heart. He knew Karen was right, or at least partly right. He let go of her hand, which left him feeling strangely empty.

She had a point about things not always being as they appeared. Old Testament battles proved that. Often Yahweh made havoc of man's wisdom, having the priests and fighting men march around the city till the walls fell. No. Things weren't always what they appeared. When Creator saw fit to save a prostitute and her family and even included her in his own family line—that certainly wasn't a human decision—and the cross, the Father sending his Son, the Son giving himself willingly, one life for many.

Ghostdancer shook himself. Too many words had muddled his mind. Perhaps he had forgotten how to listen. Fine. He would change that now. "Talk," he said, and Karen did, pouring out her heart in strong words that didn't mince truth.

"The shaman might be bad," she said, "I'm not saying he isn't. But I am saying he might not be as bad as you think. Being mistaken is not the same thing as being rebellious."

"In the end they are both just as lost."

"Not necessarily." Karen shook her head. "There may be hope for him yet, if given the right understanding."

"But he won't listen—"

"Maybe not to you."

Her words hung in the air between them. The truth hit Ghostdancer hard in the chest. Had he thought he was the only tool Creator Yahweh could use? How foolish. Or worse yet, had he thought he was the one who could lead Jacob to Yahweh? Only Holy Spirit could perform that task. In repentance and trust, Jacob would find salvation. The fact his heart was still beating proved hope still remained. Meanwhile, what about the people who could be hurt along the way—people like Sayla?

Ghostdancer sat in his chair and leaned forward, trying to keep the tremble from his voice. "Jacob warned me to not interfere with his working with Sayla. Said he had a gift for her that would benefit the tribe. The wolf attacked. How could it not be him?"

"I'm not saying it isn't him, but what if it isn't? Does he have an apprentice?"

The thought jolted Ghostdancer to his feet. "An apprentice? Of course. I knew there had to be more than one." Before he could explain, Red Dog started barking and the house erupted in a flurry of activity.

Loretta appeared in the bedroom doorway. "I've got to talk with you, Ghostdancer. She looked at Karen. "I don't mean to be rude, but this is a Native matter."

In four steps Karen crossed the room and pushed by Loretta. "I'll make more tea."

Closing the door behind her, Loretta turned to Ghostdancer, and then she burst into tears.

Understanding a woman's mind was one thing, but understanding a woman's tears was completely beyond Ghostdancer's realm. He bowed his head and prayed for wisdom. Creator Yahweh in heaven, how he needed patience.

Chapter 55

Creator Yahweh's love stands firm forever.
Ghostdancer

Loretta

LORETTA LAID A HAND on Sayla's forehead. Her granddaughter was hot, but shivers had overtaken her body. Ghostdancer brought a pan of cold water and a wet cloth at Loretta's request. Wringing the water from the cloth, she avoided Ghostdancer's eyes. "Perhaps we should take her to the hospital."

"This is not a physical battle, Loretta. No medicine will heal this wound."

Awareness of the truth gave Loretta no peace. She would have welcomed a bottle of magic pills. How could she fight in the spiritual realm, she who had resorted to her own means with the shaman? A sob left her throat.

"Tell me about it." Ghostdancer said.

He was so perfect; how could Ghostdancer understand? He had never gone down the dark path like she and Jacob had. Shuddering, she threw off the memory of such long ago foolishness. Never again she had promised . . . and yet . . . she had thought she could sway the shaman by paying for a blessing to combat the curse. She shook her head.

"Nothing is so bad that Creator Yahweh cannot fix it."

Ghostdancer's words did little to help. She didn't deserve any kind of fixing from Creator, she who had betrayed his great love. She lifted the cloth and put it to her face, sobbing into its wetness.

After a while, she heard rustling pages. Memories of Charlie opening his Bible spilled into her mind, long evenings with his low voice speaking ancient truths. Ghostdancer spoke those words now, reading from the *Sacred Scripture*. Like warm honey truth washed across her soul.

"Let us fix our eyes on Jesus the author and perfecter of our faith, who for the joy set before him endured the cross—"

Loretta waited, expecting Ghostdancer to talk about the need to endure discipline and of how she should, "Buck up." That's how Charlie would have said it. She knew the passage from Hebrews well. It spoke of how she should consider Jesus and the opposition he endured so she would not grow weary and lose heart, but she was already weary, and her heart felt like crumbled stone.

When no sound but the ticking clock filled the room, she looked up. Ghostdancer's Bible was sitting on his lap, and he was looking at her. "Think about that, Shining Star, for the joy set before him. What causes that kind of joy? The kind of joy that encourages your heart and strengthens your weak knees?"

Loretta said nothing. Joy had fled when Charlie and Nate died.

"Understand what I say," Ghostdancer said. "Jesus endured the cross. Because of joy. It was because he saw something no one else could perceive. Back in the beginning of time, he saw it, when the morning stars sang together and all the angels shouted for joy. He saw *you*, Shining Star. You were worth it. You were the cause of that joy."

Loretta let out a breath in one long swoosh.

"Think of the cross," Ghostdancer continued. "The pain of it, the humility, the betrayal. Think of how the only perfect human to have ever lived took on our guilt, all of it, so we could be free. Think of how that guilt separated him from his own Father. Think of how their relationship was special, a blending of personalities so strong, they call themselves ONE. How that feeling of separation must have ripped out his very heart. But he *knew*. And he endured it. Because of joy."

Loretta saw it all, every aspect that every passion play had portrayed and much more.

Ghostdancer's voice lowered. "Back in the beginning of time, he knew everything and he allowed it. All the pain throughout earth's measured days. Every evil, every bad choice, broken hearts, faithless followers, the full cup of pain . . . and he allowed it, because of joy. He saw treasure in the middle worth salvaging. You are part of that treasure, Shining Star. How can you do anything but praise Him? You have no guilt. He took it all."

The thought should have freed her, but somehow it made her feel even more guilty.

Ghostdancer shook his head. "Creator stands in the gap, Shining Star. He is our mediator. Confess to him. Let his love heal your soul."

Loretta began praying, first with her head bowed and eyes closed. Then she and Ghostdancer both stood with their arms raised to Creator until they could no longer contain the joy, and both began dancing and singing their prayers. Loretta barely moving her feet in the graceful war dance and Ghostdancer ducking and diving in the old style war dance. Something happened in the dance; it was as if they were fighting a spiritual battle, one they were sure to lose. Then the most awesome peace flooded the room, and they both fell to the floor.

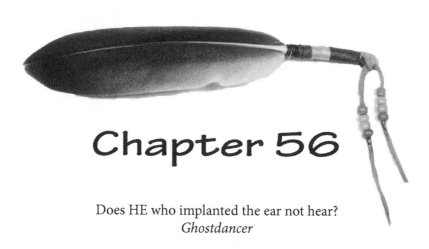

Chapter 56

Does HE who implanted the ear not hear?
Ghostdancer

Sayla

SILENCE STRETCHES LONG and eerie. Burning fire has disappeared but so has the light from its flames. My body continues its speeding descent through darkness thick as blood.

"Enough."

The word is no more than a whisper, yet the strength behind it is like nothing I've experienced before. Light bursts forth and my feet touch ground as gentle as a feather dropping from the sky.

Singing voices surround me, joyful voices praising the ONE whose command stopped my hurtling descent, the voices of my beloved Gran and Ghostdancer. The beauty of their song floods over me and I feel as clean as the day I was born.

At last the nightmare is gone.

Chapter 57

*Creator Yahweh is the river in which I swim,
my delight, my desire.*
Ghostdancer

Loretta

FOLLOWING THE DANCE Loretta and Ghostdancer rose.

"I've something to tell you," Loretta blurted. "I lied to Sayla about Charlie's journals. I've been meaning to give them to you, but I told her I already had. They're in the trunk in the barn loft." She shook her head. "With all the things going on I was afraid the wrong people might discover them. Wasn't even sure it was safe for Sayla to read them after seeing the picture of a flaming warrior."

Ghostdancer nodded once. "You did right. I will hide them." He gave her shoulders a squeeze and left the room.

Loretta sighed. At last, she no longer had to worry about the journals. She would explain to Sayla once the girl was ready, but for now Ghostdancer would make them disappear so they wouldn't fall into the wrong hands. Loretta picked up the water basin and checked on Sayla. She was sleeping peacefully now and her forehead felt cool. Taking advantage of the opportunity, Loretta set the basin and cloth aside and knelt beside the bed. There she confessed her betrayal— her visit to the shaman and not speaking the whole truth to Sayla—

confessing to the ONE who already knew it all. Expecting rightfully earned condemnation, she received love instead. A washing of Holy Spirit, quickening her body's deadest members and rebirthing hope. It swelled inside her until it bubbled over in laughter. There on her knees, she laughed like a young girl.

Of course Creator knew she didn't really trust the shaman. He also understood her weak faith. Yet even a mustard seed, that nearly impossible-to-see grain, was enough, and that she had.

"Gran?"

At the sound of Sayla's voice, Loretta's head shot up. She raised from her knees and pulled a chair next to the bed. Nearly falling into the chair, she asked, "Are you okay?"

Sayla closed her eyes, rubbed them with her fingers, then opened them again. "I'm not sure, but I'm seeing strange colors."

"Colors?"

Sayla's eyes grew wide as she stared at Loretta. "Colors are pouring from your mouth. Don't you see them? Little red and gold triangles." She waved a hand in the air as if trying to catch them.

Loretta didn't see them, but she was afraid she understood. Before she could question Sayla, the girl's head sank into the pillow. She was immediately asleep. Loretta fell back to her knees, this time not praying for herself, but praying for Sayla and for wisdom on how to deal with this latest problem. Never in all her days would she have thought Sayla would turn to drugs, but she knew this one. Back in her experimenting days with the shaman, peyote had painted their world in magnificent impossible hues. The realization Sayla must have used peyote caused her more pain than the guilt had caused her just moments before.

Chapter 58

*Creator Yahweh's voice thunders
in marvelous ways.*
Ghostdancer

Ghostdancer

NO ONE WAS IN THE KITCHEN when Ghostdancer left Sayla's room. Crimson light spilled through the windows and set the darkened house into an eerie glow. After stepping outside he paused. Billowing thunderheads rose high over Sacred Mountain, the setting sun painting them with iridescent beauty. But this beauty held fire in its teeth and could destroy a hundred acres in a short time.

Shouts from the barnyard drew him. Though his body was achy and stiff from sitting so long, he picked up his pace.

"Back you brute!"

It was Kenny's voice. Ghostdancer broke into a run, stopping only when he reached the corral. Breathing hard, he held up a hand. "Be still," he commanded.

War Paint stood not five feet from Kenny. The proud steed dipped his head and pawed the ground with his right hoof.

"Don't move, brother," Ghostdancer said.

Shell-shocked, Kenny obeyed. His body was as stiff as the weathered planks on the barn, yet he looked as if he would spring and run any moment.

"Running is the worst thing you can do," Ghostdancer said.

"How about telling me the best thing I can do?" Kenny's voice warbled like an old woman's.

"You're doing it. Keep your voice low, be still."

War Paint faked a charge. "God," Kenny said.

"That better be a prayer. Otherwise it does you no good and much harm."

"It's a prayer all right," Kenny croaked.

Ghostdancer inched forward. Keeping his voice low, he said, "Some tribes have a custom called the talking stick. We pass it around and only the person holding the stick is allowed to talk. No one else."

War Paint dug his hoof into the ground and snorted.

Kenny stiffened. "This isn't exactly the best time for a story."

"War Paint has the talking stick. We need to listen. Your part is to focus. What is he telling you?"

"Obviously, he's telling me I've invaded his space and he doesn't like it." Kenny's voice was barely loud enough for Ghostdancer to decipher.

"Good," Ghostdancer said. "You're beginning to understand. Now, try to relax."

"Don't suppose I can get a cigar out?"

"Such a movement could get you killed. Think about something pleasant and let your body slowly relax. No jerky movements."

Carefully lowering his shoulders, Kenny remained quiet, even when War Paint roared another warning.

"Now, take one slow step back, slower than you've ever moved before."

Tremors shook Kenny's legs so badly Ghostdancer feared the man would fall to the ground. He felt his own body stiffen until Kenny had both feet planted. "Good. Now keep making your way back to me."

The two men were nearly shoulder to shoulder when lightning shot through the sky. An immediate roar of thunder followed. War

Paint reared, his eyes wide with fright, his hooves coming down toward Kenny's head. Ghostdancer pushed Kenny hard to the side putting his own back in harm's way. He braced himself for the expected pummeling, but it never came. Pounding hooves landed three feet away.

"Get up!" Karen called. "Don't know how long we can hold him."

Feeling every bit his age, Ghostdancer rose to his knees before struggling to his feet. Kenny was already up and helping him. Both men scurried toward the other side of the corral's fence. Karen and Link were pulling hard at the business end of a lariat. The other end was looped around War Paint's neck. The horse was wild with fury, fierce rage burning in his eyes. Rearing and kicking, he pulled until at last the rope swung free.

Karen and Link fell back, Link's body softening Karen's plunge. Ghostdancer was proud of the way the lawyer took it like a man. Kenny helped Karen to her feet, and with no complaints and no cursing, Link stood. The well-polished lawyer was covered in mud, his eyeglasses hung askew, and sweat poured down his neck. Karen swung on the poor man with a hug that nearly toppled him back down. "We did it!" she yelled. "You were great."

Link's face turned red but not from the glow of sunset. The man was obviously not used to receiving compliments from women. Ghostdancer felt a sudden pang of jealousy and silently lectured himself before anyone could see it. What power did this woman have over him? He turned from the yard and stood at the gate, gauging how far War Paint would run. The storm was beginning to howl. It was all the more reason to bring Kadai home. He was the only one who could get near that wild steed.

Kenny clapped an arm around Ghostdancer's shoulders, a cigar already smoldering in his lips. "I owe you one. That was some thrill."

"What were you doing out here?"

Raised eyebrows indicated Kenny hadn't missed Ghostdancer's irritation. "Karen saw the storm heading our way and said we better shelter the horses. Didn't know this horse was different from the rest."

They wouldn't know, Ghostdancer conceded. War Paint's beauty was often deceiving. When Karen and Link joined them, he turned to Kenny. "You're a quick study. Not many men could have remained as calm as you under such circumstances, especially with so little horse knowledge."

Taking his arm off Ghostdancer's shoulder Kenny turned a full circle, surveying the yard. "You have any more like him hidden around here?"

Ghostdancer chuckled. "He's the only one. Charlie found War Paint's grandfather running free on The Sheldon Wildlife Refuge on the Oregon-Nevada border. It was love at first sight."

"Some love." Kenny puffed on his cigar. "I think I've had a woman or two like that. Didn't keep em though."

"That's one amazing animal," Karen said.

"Yeah," Link agreed.

All four stood looking into the distance, watching the horse kicking and bucking against the rope. Ghostdancer and Karen exchanged a glance. Both knew the horse could die out there, fighting against the trailing rope. If the rope caught on something, the terrified horse would fight against it until its dying breath.

"I could go after him," Karen said doubtfully.

"Nothing doing," said Ghostdancer. "Leave it to Kadai."

"He could be back by noon tomorrow," Kenny said.

Ghostdancer turned to Link. "Better come in and get a shower. Take off a layer of that grime."

Link's expression would have been comical in better circumstances. Perhaps the thought of bathing on Sacred Mountain Ranch was not on his list of top ten things to do.

"It's alright," Ghostdancer said. "You can stay in the cabin with me. There's plenty of room for both you and Kenny, and you can get an early start in the morning."

"Sounds great!" said Kenny around his cigar. "Can't get enough of this country air."

"Thanks, I'll pass," said Link, "but if you don't mind I'd like to borrow a towel."

Kenny slapped an arm over Link's shoulder. "That's right. Gotta keep the fancy Lexus shining and clean."

Clearing her throat, Karen started for the barn, all three men turned and watched.

"Where you going?" Kenny asked.

Karen waved and kept walking. When she was safe beneath the barn's eaves, the sky dumped a flood on the unsuspecting trio. They could hear her laughter ringing across the corral.

"Well if that don't beat all," Kenny said. He wrinkled his nose and sniffed the air. "What is that smell?"

It was dark enough Link's face was hidden, but Ghostdancer was willing to bet it was as crimson as the sun falling over the horizon. Link turned to Kenny. "This is a barnyard, not a city street. This isn't exactly beauty mud pasted to our clothes."

Kenny looked down and sniffed again. "Horse manure. Well, if that don't beat all."

Ghostdancer figured if they stood out in the rain much longer, the smelly problem would take care of itself, but as they headed toward the house, a car's headlights rounded the bend and pulled straight toward them. Just when he thought things couldn't get any worse, Sayla's sister Moriah pulled up in her Lincoln Continental, splashing mud over the trio. Cracking her window she looked at them in disgust. "I see things haven't changed around here." She opened the door and stepped out, unfolding her umbrella in one movement. Then she swung it over her head and hurried toward the porch.

Kenny's cigar was missing from his mouth, which was a good thing since his mouth hung agog. "Sayla never told me she had a twin."

"They're two years apart," Ghostdancer said, "but everyone makes that mistake." The likeness would be short lived. Five minutes in Moriah's presence and they would realize the two girls couldn't be any more different. Moriah was a woman of fine clothes, spoiled and self-serving, while Sayla enjoyed the sweetness of earth and cared about her people. He wondered what trouble Moriah had come to stir up this time.

Chapter 59

> When I am poor and needy
> I call on Creator Yahweh.
> *Ghostdancer*

Loretta

RED DOG RAN INTO Sayla's room with his tail between his legs. Moriah's voice entered behind him nearly a full minute before the girl. Loretta stood and hurried to the door, but not soon enough to stop the storm from entering.

Sweeping past Loretta, Moriah headed to Sayla's bed. "Heard my sister's in trouble." She stood over Sayla like a prowling cat inspecting its prey.

Red Dog slithered from the room and dashed down the hall. Loretta wished she could follow the cowering dog but knew it would be a mistake. It was always a mistake to let Moriah out of her sight. No telling what the girl would do if she was left alone with Sayla.

"And where did you hear that?" Loretta asked.

"I have my sources." Moriah bent over Sayla and pried open an eyelid.

Loretta reached out for her hand. "What are you doing?"

"Checking for drugs. Something I'm sure you wouldn't think of doing."

Loretta pulled Moriah away from Sayla. "I don't know what you think you're doing, young lady, but this is my house. You're welcome to sleep in the room down the hall, but this one is off-limits."

Moriah's beautiful face morphed into ugly contortions of rage. It always surprised Loretta how such a beautiful refined woman could change in an instant. Her words fell out in a near hiss. "Perhaps you can't handle the truth about sweet little Sayla, but reliable sources tell me they've seen her hanging out with the drug crowd. My guess is mescaline."

"Mescaline?"

"That's right. It's the closest thing the young people around here can get to having a good time. I wouldn't be surprised if she's swallowed worse things as well. Heaven knows there's nothing else to do in this god-forsaken place."

Looking down at Sayla, Loretta gasped. The girl was staring at Moriah as if she had just spotted the most fascinating creature in the world.

Moriah followed Loretta's gaze with her own, her arm still locked in Loretta's grip.

"Are you my angel?" Sayla asked.

A sickening chuckle rose from Moriah's throat. "Point proven." She looked at Loretta.

Sayla waved an arm in the air, catching unseen treasures.

"If you don't do something about this, I will." Moriah's voice was triumphant.

"Like what?"

"Like committing her to rehab."

"Rehab?"

"I'm sure you've heard of it. It's a place people go when they need help recovering from addictions."

"Addictions?"

Moriah shook her head. "Still in denial are we? Or perhaps senility is moving in. I noticed things aren't quite up to par around here."

A clap of thunder directly overhead seemed to seal Moriah's words. Lamplight flickered and Moriah pulled from Loretta's grip. Loretta was still in shock from such obvious hatred, especially from a grandchild, and talk of rehab and senility made her feel as old and useless as an overrun horse. She was glad when the lights went out and plunged the room into sudden darkness.

Chapter 60

What is the way to the abode of light?
Creator Yahweh

Kadai
August 30, 2014
Saturday morning

YOU WAKE ON THE DARK SIDE of morning.

A nurse sits by your bedside, her red curls hanging wildly beneath a doo rag; her hazel eyes are bright with excitement. "You were dreamin'," she says. "Your heart nearly beat itself out. One hundred and eighty beats per minute. Can you believe that? We tried to wake you, but you were sleepin' the sleep of the dead." A nervous chuckle falls from her mouth. "Except the dead don't dream. From the way your pupils were moving back and forth, and your fingers were clenchin' and unclenchin'... must have been some nightmare."

Taking your blood pressure, she falls silent. Her nametag reads, "River." You remember her as the one who made the reference to Pentecost when flames of fire kissed your shoulders. She's a tiny woman, not much older than yourself and not a full-blown nurse, but some kind of aide. She wears a smock covered in bright peace symbols and stares at you as she counts. After logging your blood pressure she looks up. "It's okay, you know. Lots of folks are affected like that." She looks at you over the top of her notebook, her green eyes wild with excitement. "Of course, lots of folks ain't been through what you have, but out of those who have, most find it difficult to talk when they return."

She loosens the blood pressure cuff around your arm and lets it drop against the bed. "And when they do find words, it's usually to get after us for having brought 'em back. Of course, I ain't had a whole lot of experience at this, but I've done a lot of readin'." She drops her shoulders and sighs. "I'd give anythin' to see what you saw."

Watching her rise you know her heart is true. "It was beyond words." Your voice comes out in a whisper.

She stops and turns, surprise making her pale face glow. "Did you see HIM?"

A nod is all you can muster. You wish you could tell her HE called you *sawalineeas* and that she is Creator's friend too, but your constricted throat fails. Nothing more than a grunt comes forth. Yet it is enough. Glistening tears fill her eyes, and you know the encouragement found its mark. Her faith will grow because of what has happened to you. What marvelous wonder—from soldier betrayer to trusted friend. You could sob for the joy of such knowledge. Such reward is better than the Purple Heart you received from the government.

When she reaches out a hand to wipe your face, you realize tears have fallen from your eyes like a boy who lost his best friend. Strange for a man who lost nothing at all but gained a treasure far beyond imagination. Who could know? Who could fathom? The unspeakable riches of Creator's grace.

River breaks your concentration, pulling you back to the real world. "Had us a terrible storm last night. Thunder, lightnin', the whole show. Between the pourin' rain and your tears there ain't no shortage of water." She chuckles at her joke; then she leans close. "And I have good news. Amnesty International called. Well, not actually the organization, but a woman representative, and guess what?"

You stare at her. Does she really want you to guess?

"You're free. As free as an uncaged songbird. As soon as the doctor gives you a clean bill of health, you're free to fly home."

Searching the open door, you see her words are true. The guard is gone.

Home. The word holds a different meaning to you now. Your real home is far away in a different world, or perhaps very close, because the time it took you to step into that world was nothing at all. You think of Sayla and your horses and of your duties that have long been neglected. Throwing back the stark white sheet, you swing your legs over the side of the bed.

"Whoa," River says. "Not so fast. The doctor ain't been by yet."

"What time does your shift end?"

Startled, River looks at her watch. "Shift changes in thirty minutes."

You find your jeans hanging in a closet and start pulling them on. An exclamation of surprise falls from River's mouth as she turns her head. Throwing off the silly hospital-issued half robe, you realize you have no shirt. River turns back around as you search for your moccasins.

Understanding your need before you state it, she says, "They be in a drawer 'neath the closet. Boy howdy, I'm gonna get in a lot of trouble for this one."

"No need," you assure her. "I'm an adult, doing this on my own. What you do on your own time is up to you. If you pick up a hitchhiker on your way home, who's to know?"

"Yeaaaah?" She stretches the word as her eyebrows rise. "And where will this hitchhiker be wantin' to go?"

"Back to Sacred Mountain Ranch. I'll pay for your gas and Grandmother will give you breakfast."

"Loretta Whitewater?"

You nod.

She beams. "Let me git a head start, okay? I really need this job." Then she turns and leaves the room, her soft shoes making a pattering sound across the tiles. You take up your position near the window for the last time. Sunlight has barely broken the horizon, throwing a shroud of pure gold across the top of far-off Mount Shasta. The window does not open, but soon you will smell the freshness you can see in the air. The parking lot glistens wet beneath street lamps and a few clouds still hang in the sky. Several puffs of smoke in the distance reveal where lightning found its mark. Sacred Mountain is too far away to be seen, but you send up a prayer that fire has not found its mark there.

Urgency sends your legs moving and you walk down the hall toward the nearest stairway. The quiet murmur of voices from the far end lets you know most of the hospital is still asleep. A weary staff takes no notice of your retreat.

Chapter 61

*Who can understand how Creator Yahweh
thunders from his pavilion above the heavens?*
Ghostdancer

Loretta

LORETTA STOOD AT HER EASEL as soft light colored the distant hills with glowing beauty. A coyote let out a long plaintive howl, followed by haunting loon music. Red Dog had already taken up his favorite sleeping position near her feet. She searched the skyline for any sign of smoke or fire and was grateful to see none.

"*Sepkeec'a*," she whispered. "Thank you Jesus."

She was also grateful everyone in the house was still asleep. Moriah would probably sleep till noon, her usual wake-up time. Loretta would certainly not wake her beforehand; the girl had caused enough problems last night, complaining about every part of ranch life. If she didn't like it, why didn't she just leave? Loretta had asked her that very question, but the girl just folded her arms across her chest and glared.

Turning from the beauty of the breaking new day, Loretta faced her blank canvas. Then she opened a tube of alizarin crimson and squeezed it onto her palette. Next came Hansa yellow and ultramarine blue. She piled titanium white on the right side; then she added small dabs of various colors down the front. Mixing was a pleasure and she took her time at it. Then she picked up a palette knife and stared at the canvas.

"Enough of this already!"

With furious strokes, she spread colors in large sweeps, not caring if they made any sense. Soon she was lost in the art of discovery, stepping back often to scrutinize her work. At first it looked like some kind of Picasso, wild slashes of emotion without much order, but after a while it began to take shape, and she could see a lion's face coming out of the shadows. No one else would be able to see it yet, but Loretta took delight in chipping away at the turbulent background. There would be time enough later to bring out what she already knew was there. Finding herself lost in the joy of creating, she prayed for Sayla as she painted.

Though Sayla showed signs of being on drugs, Loretta was convinced it had to either be by accident or coercion. It was hard enough to get the girl to swallow aspirin when she needed it.

Loretta threw another slash of red in the background. Had Jacob given Sayla drugs? Didn't seem possible. Peyote was more his style, and it was next to impossible to slip peyote on an unsuspecting victim. The strong taste and smell of it often caused the participant to vomit uncontrollably. Loretta knew this by experience. On the other hand, it was possible Sayla could have used peyote on purpose. The shaman may have talked her into it. To him it was not a drug, but a useful tool in connecting with the spiritual realm. Loretta knew Sayla was interested in that realm.

She took a step back and examined her canvas. The lion's eyes were just beginning to form in the foreground. It had been years since she and her granddaughter had done anything fun together, yet there was a time when the two of them had been inseparable. She shuddered, remembering the peyote-colored dreams that had made her feel so powerful as a young woman. Such nonsense. Such tragedy. She forced herself to consider the last time she had confronted Jacob. He didn't call himself a shaman back in those days.

"We can't go on like this," she had told him. It was the day after Kadai's mother had died. But Jacob had insisted the death of Kadai's mother had been caused by Loretta's ineptness. According to him, the right chant would have saved her.

"Asking for help would have saved her," Loretta insisted.

Jacob was adamant. "Asking for help would have only interfered. The woman would have still died. Your guilt was in the lack of preparation, nothing else."

Loretta had turned from Jacob and had never spoken to him again . . . until last Thursday. What he had done with the required live chickens was enough to turn her stomach. He had certainly not gotten that little trick from any of their tribal customs.

She filled her palette knife with Alizarin crimson and Hansa yellow and focused on the lion. She knew this face; it was the great Lion of the Tribe of Judah, the ONE she should have been focused on all along. She began to hum. When she finished the first painting, she grabbed another canvas and began a second. *Yaks dwa!* But it sure felt good to be painting again.

Chapter 62

*What is the way to the place
where lightning is dispersed?*
Creator Yahweh

Sayla

I WAKE RAVENOUS with thoughts of yellow-eyed wolves, and me running through a land of deep shadows. Memories of the day before are patchy. Something about the river and the shaman and bees. I swing my legs over the side of the bed and struggle to stand, but dizziness washes over me. I sit back on the mattress. A plate of cookies rests on the nightstand, so I grab one and munch on it.

The cookie begins to revive me, so I eat two more. Then I head to the shower where I let hot water run over me until it turns cold. I dress and head to the kitchen in search of Gran. The kitchen is empty, so I continue to the porch where two things catch my attention—Gran's canvas is no longer empty, and Moriah's Lincoln Continental is parked near the garage. A groan escapes my lips.

Gran turns from her canvas, a paint rag and pallet knife in her hands. "How are you feeling?"

"Fine." I shrug. "At least I was until I saw Moriah's car. What's she doing here?"

Gran wipes her knife on the rag and sets it down. Then she turns to me. "You don't remember?"

"What?"

"Sayla—" Gran starts but changes her mind and grabs me in a big bear hug. When I try to pull away, she tightens her grip. I relax and enjoy the fragrance of her sweet pea lotion, which causes a slide show of memories to play through my mind—my first fish, my first guitar, my first piano lesson, my first dance—Gran was there for every event, either baiting my hook, paying for my lessons, or beading my regalia. Suddenly, I feel really grateful she wasn't in the truck with Grandfather when it crashed. We have lost a lot, but we still have each other.

"I love you Gran."

"Ohhhh Sayla."

The two of us cling to one another. Red Dog rises from his sleep to whimper at our feet. When was the last time I told Gran I loved her? Would I have even picked up a guitar if not for her? She was the first member of my family to hear me sing in public. She told me Creator had given me the gift and I needed to share it. Then she gave me a journal and told me to write my thoughts as songs. Without that encouragement I might not have written a thing.

I open my mouth to tell her how much I appreciate her, but the sound of a sputtering car engine captures our attention. Over her shoulder I see an old Volkswagen van struggling down our driveway. Red Dog runs out to meet it, barking a welcome. Wildly painted flowers and angels cover every inch of the van's body, except for the front that features a huge peace symbol.

The first impression is of shocking pink. The second is of trouble. Smoke billows from the back as the van burps its last breath on the other side of the pasture. Red Dog sticks his tail between his legs and scampers back to us.

"Yaks dwa!"

Kadai jumps from the passenger side and runs for the back of the van. All kinds of things start flying out of the opened driver's door—paintings, an easel, clothes, a couple of bags—

Gran crosses the yard in a near run, Red Dog at her heals. My legs finally start to work when Gran jumps into the water truck and fires up the engine. Red Dog leaps into the seat beside her. I head toward the van and see Ghostdancer and Kenny running from one of our cabins.

"Get out of that thing!" Kenny yells. "She's gonna blow!"

Kadai runs to the front of the van and pulls a woman out the door. She's a small woman with wild red curls sticking out all over her head, but she fights Kadai, so he throws her over his shoulder and gallops toward us. Gran lays on the horn as she barrels down the road. We all jump out of the way. When she stops the truck near the van Kadai sets the redhead on her feet and jumps on the back of the water truck. After undoing the hose he hands it off to me.

Reaching up to take it, I say, "Welcome home."

His hand touches mine, and our eyes lock. Then I begin feeding the hose to Kenny and Ghostdancer as we form a line stretching from the truck toward the van. Fire has already jumped from the van and is burning through the dry grass along the road edge.

The pump on the water truck begins to rattle as water flows through the hose. Ghostdancer is in front. "Hold on!" he yells.

It takes our collective strength to hold the hose as Ghostdancer aims it, but soon water sizzles over the fire turning flames to black smoke. A coughing fit hits me, but I hold on. And just when I think my arms will break from the strain, a woman I've never seen before steps in to help.

"I'm Karen," she says, as she digs in her feet and grabs the hose.

She looks like some kind of older Annie Oakley wearing a jean skirt and flannel shirt. Straw tendrils stick out of her hair. I'm guessing she must have slept in the barn.

"I'm Ghostdancer's friend," she says.

"The one who relays his messages?"

"That's the one. Friend, message service, and cohort."

I throw her a smile. She's prettier than I imagined, especially for an older woman, but she isn't as old as Gran.

The tiny redhead is up front between Ghostdancer and Kenny. The hose sinks low to her shoulder and then back up again, yet she holds on like a trooper. Shouts spring from her mouth, but it is impossible to understand her words over the deafening engine and pump. Then out of nowhere, Link appears. He's dressed in another fancy suit, but he doesn't think twice before he leaps between Ghostdancer and Kenny and lifts the hose from the redhead's shoulders. I hope he has deep pockets full of money, because his suit will be ruined before the morning is over.

A tall woman with beautiful skin the color of midnight and dressed in a sky blue pantsuit with a long flowing yellow scarf joins us. She looks as if she came straight out of Africa. Our escapade is turning into some kind of show. Kenny must be thinking the same thing, because he looks back at me with the biggest grin I have ever seen on his face.

"Gotta love this ranch life!" he shouts.

His face is already blackened with soot, and I notice for the first time his shirt is unbuttoned and he isn't wearing any shoes.

With one final groan, the pump quits and Gran shuts off the engine.

When the smoke starts to clear, the redhead wails, "It's a goner."

The shocking pink van is now nothing more than a charred mess. The redhead turns back to the rest of us looking as if she is ready to cry, and then suddenly she points at us and laughter bubbles from her mouth. The rest of us stare at her for a full minute before Kenny joins her. Then one by one we fall in, each pointing to the other and breaking into chuckles and guffaws, all of us with blackened faces and flakes of soot covering our heads and shoulders. Link records the event on his smart phone.

Too soon, Ghostdancer and Gran start passing out shovels and rakes. The pump has breathed its last, so those of us wearing shoes must put out the hot spots by digging in and dousing them with buckets of water. Those without shoes work on the bucket brigade. Gran fills the buckets from the spigot on the water truck and others pass them along. Kenny starts singing an old folk song about work on a railroad to keep us in sync. His bass voice rings out across the pasture while Red Dog howls along, making everyone laugh and encouraging Kenny to no end.

The sun is high in the sky when we finally get things under control. Link surprises us by retrieving water bottles from the trunk of his car and passing them around. We all spread out, either sitting on the ground or leaning against the water truck. Kadai introduces the redhead as River Williams. "Everything I had was in that van," she moans. "My paintings, my photo albums." She looks down at her dirty nurse's uniform. "And my clothes."

Gran opens her arms, and I am surprised to see River fall into them. She sobs while Gran pats her on the back and Red Dog licks her arm. It brings back memories of the many times Gran has done that very thing with me.

"She lived in her van," Kadai explains.

"So she lost her home as well as her vehicle," I say. "Tough break."

Kenny steps between us and sticks out his hand to Kadai. "Been wanting to meet you."

Kadai shoots me a questioning glance before he takes Kenny's hand.

"He's my agent," I say, "and the one who hired your lawyer."

"And speaking of lawyers," Link says. "It's good to see you out of the hospital." Then he turns to the dark-skinned woman who still manages to look classy while covered with soot. "I would like you to meet Isabel Kennedy. She represents Amnesty International, and she's the one who will keep you out of jail."

She offers Kadai a hand, but changes her mind midstream and gives him a hug instead. Kadai surprises me by accepting Isabel's hug and thanking her for "springing" him.

"You're not quite sprung yet," she says with a wide smile, "but you're at least on the safe side. I don't think they'll be bothering you for a while, but you'll eventually have to make a statement before a judge."

Kadai's head jerks back.

"We'll practice beforehand," she says, "and you can write your response and read it to the judge if you want."

When he turns his eyes on me, I can see the plea in them. "I'll help him write it," I say.

"You can help write it," Isabel agrees, "but Kadai will have to speak for himself."

Behind Isabel I can barely see the top of River's head, scrunched between Gran and Karen. I've heard the story of how Karen lost her home in a fire many years ago. She wasn't as lucky as River. After carrying Karen to safety, her husband went back to retrieve their three-month-old baby. Neither made it out. Karen has been single ever since. I wonder what comforting words she is offering River. I also wonder if the memories still cause pain. And I wonder how long the pain will stay with her and how long my pain will stay with me.

Kadai leans close, "You alright, Little Fire?"

The stubbornness melts right out of me.

Noticing my clenched fists he reaches out and takes one of my hands in both of his. His touch is warm and alive, so different from the Shadow Warrior. He rubs the stiffness out of my hand; then he does the same for the other. "Come," he says. "Let's see what we can salvage for River."

We head for the van and, for the first time since the Coming-Out of Grief Ceremony, we are alone.

Chapter 63

Have the gates of death been shown to you?
Creator Yahweh

Sayla

MOST OF RIVER'S BELONGINGS are either burned or water soaked, but we manage to gather a couple of armloads worth salvaging. We add them to a pile of canvases she managed to throw out before Kadai pulled her from the burning van. She's quite the painter. Colorful flowers and beautiful angels smile up at me as the pile grows bigger. While Kadai searches the van further, I organize her personal items. Then I notice something strange in the soft earth alongside the road.

I holler for Kadai, "Check this out!"

Kadai is quick to join me and we both stare in silence at a single set of goat tracks leading from the van. For a long while, neither of us says a word. I'm thinking of the goat tracks found at Grandfather's crash site. I'm sure Kadai is thinking the same. Then I remember the goat tracks at the river when I was with the shaman. "It's probably just a coincidence," I say. "I've never seen goats this far from the river, but all things are possible." What I don't say is that it is certainly not probable with all the fence lines between the river and where we stand.

Without a word, Kadai returns to the van. At first I think he's ignoring me, but he returns with a shredded rubber belt in his hand. "This is what started the fire," he says. "And no warning lights came on either. I'm betting someone cut the fan belt and clipped the line to the warning light."

My stomach lurches. "Do you think River has any enemies?"

He stares at me for a long while before he says, "I think we should keep this between us for now."

"Don't you think we should notify the authorities?"

His answer comes quick. "No. I'll talk with Ghostdancer."

Kadai is staring at the goat tracks. Cold shivers run down my legs. "You don't think—"

"Best not to think anything at this point," Kadai interrupts. "But it is also good to cover all bases. Strange things have been happening."

Tell me about it, I want to say, but I remain silent, not wanting to tell him about the wolf. Obviously, Kadai thinks a shape-shifter is involved. I think of the shaman, but I toss the thought aside. Turning into a goat wouldn't be his style. There's nothing courageous or honorable in turning into a goat. But who other than the shaman would know River would be bringing Kadai home?

Kadai places his hands on my shoulders. I look up into his dark eyes, feeling strangely comforted and ready to flee at the same time. "Who would want to harm your family?" he asks.

His words cut deep into my heart. For a long while, I've convinced myself my worries are the result of an overactive imagination. To hear Kadai validate my worry is like saying it's true.

"I don't know," I say. "But I would sure like to find out." My thoughts spring to the shaman. I'm sure he can shed light on our problem, and then I remember I have a date with him this very night.

Midnight at the river.

Chapter 64

> My flesh and my heart cry out
> for Creator Yahweh.
> *Ghostdancer*

Kadai

AS YOU AND SAYLA gather River's belongings you have much time to think. Someone timed it so the van would overheat just as you returned to Sacred Mountain Ranch. Did they mean to kill? Or to frighten? Whatever their purpose, they cared little that River was caught in their plan. They did not mind hurting the innocent to gain their goal. And it had to be someone who had overheard your hospital conversation with River and knew you planned a ride home with her.

Someone is out to harm Sayla. You know this to be true. You are not their main goal. You are simply a connection. You try not to think about the goat tracks, but you do not hold much value in coincidence. A single goat out here is more than coincidence. But the other alternative, the existence of a shape-shifter creates a whole new set of problems. Sayla does not know it yet, but someone close to her, someone she trusts, has betrayed her.

Thoughts of betrayal sicken your heart and take you back to Iraq, that desert land that dried your tears. You remember waking in the warm dark of each morning to the sound of a hundred muezzins calling Muslim men and women to prayer.

Above the sounds of blaring horns, the reverberating buzz of American helicopter rotors echoed over the rooftops. You often knelt on those dusty rooftops looking down to spot an enemy, breathing in nauseating exhaust fumes.

You became friends with several Iraqis. Similarities in your customs and your dark skin promoted a sense of bonding. There is good and bad in all. It is important to separate the two. You heard oaths much different from your Native home but very similar in meaning. It is the same in any language, to curse or to bless, the words hold the power of life and death. You respected their customs without taking them on as your own. Natives are good at melding, and you have long been blending in, but your heart still runs with Native blood. And all those months in Iraq you longed for a horse instead of an armored tank.

Perhaps that is why you made friends with the young ones, giving candy and sharing jokes. While doctoring a nine-year-old boy's wound you felt his power stealing your heart.

Afterward, you looked for him every day, ignoring your Special Forces' training to remain detached. Ibrahim reminded you of yourself as a young boy, motherless and seeking courage. His beaming smile belied the fear clutching his chest whenever bombs exploded throughout the city. Would the next one be too close? You entertained thoughts of bringing him home to America, and you vowed to keep him safe.

But you did not keep him safe, and you wonder now, if you will be able to protect the one you love. Are you the warrior you claim to be? Is your heart full of courage to fight this battle to the end? Only time will tell.

Chapter 65

*Call on Creator Yahweh and HE will save you
from any evil thing that comes against you.*
Ghostdancer

Sayla

MORIAH STANDING ON THE PORCH like a queen reminds me of those long ago years when she would wait for me when I returned home. Her arms are crossed over her chest in the same way and the same hate fills her eyes. Whatever has caused her to hate me is still very much alive.

I brush by her, trying to avoid contact, but she grabs my arm. One of River's paintings falls to the floor. Moriah stomps on it with a well-aimed, thousand-dollar boot before I can reach it.

"Clumsy fool," She says as if am the one at fault.

A smirk plays about her mouth as she picks up the ruined painting. Kadai steps between us. He doesn't do anything but look down on Moriah, but I see something akin to fear flicker in her dark eyes. She stares up at Kadai and takes a step back. Kadai takes the painting while Moriah reaches for her throat as if she is having trouble breathing.

River steps to the porch and stares at the ruined canvas. "Ohhh."

Gran places an arm over River's shoulders. "I'm so glad that's not one of your angels. The flowers are nice, but I suspect they will be easier to recreate."

Glassy-eyed, River raises her head. It makes me want to throttle my sister, but Kadai stands between us like an impenetrable wall. It is hard to tell which one of us he is protecting. He reaches over my head and opens the screen door. After Gran and River pass through, he motions for me to do the same. I almost don't. Seems like Moriah and I should have it out right here in a good old-fashioned, hair-pulling brawl.

Karen and Isabel are already in the kitchen pulling eggs and bacon from the fridge.

"Grab the sausage," Gran says, "and turn on the kettle. I've promised this girl my famous fry bread and sausage."

A cheer rises from behind me and I turn to see Kenny still beaming and holding Red Dog in his arms. Gran turns on him. "You," she says, "must get a layer of that grime off before you get your share. Now off with you and that dog."

He looks like a kid who just lost his lunch to some schoolyard bully. Ghostdancer and Kadai sneak up behind him and grab his shoulders, which causes Red Dog to leap to the ground. Off they go with Red Dog slinking past Moriah and then barking madly behind the men. Kenny is about to get the treat of his stay here—an honest-to-goodness Native initiation with a bath in the horse trough.

I run for the door. "Don't forget to take his cigars out of his shirt pocket!"

Kenny will see the fun of his initiation as long as it doesn't involve his precious cigars.

Moriah is still standing on the porch. I'm thinking about revisiting our little argument, but Gran pulls me into the kitchen.

"Mix up the dough," she says.

"What?" I have never mixed fry bread dough in my life, and I'm sure mine won't measure up to hers.

"It's about time you learned. I'll walk you through."

And that's exactly what she does. After we all wash our hands up to our elbows, we pitch in and make a breakfast fit for a chief. Soon spicy sausage and fry bread smells waft through the entire house.

We haul all the food out to two picnic tables in the front yard where Gran orders everyone to sit and asks if anyone would like to lead us in prayer. I'm sitting next to Karen and almost fall off the bench in shock when Link accepts the honor. He's clean now and wearing a pair of Kadai's jeans and a flannel shirt. The jeans are a little big, but they make him look as if he belongs on Sacred Mountain Ranch.

Keeping my eyes open through the prayer, I watch Link's face. Something has changed in him. Strength seems to write itself all over his features. When he ends his prayer, we all dig in, passing butter and honey and homemade huckleberry jam around the tables. I bite into my fry bread, making sure it's okay. It is surprisingly light and delicious. The feeling of accomplishment makes me sit up straighter.

Moriah surprises me by bringing tea. "A peace offering," she says, setting it and my Stevia on the table.

I barely mumble a thank you and watch as she brings out cups of tea for others as well. It is very uncharacteristic for Moriah. Karen accepts her tea and asks if she can share my Stevia. She admits she usually doesn't eat sugar but can't resist Native cooking. She takes a full helping of fry bread and elk sausage, not the dainty serving most women settle for. She confesses she slept in the barn last night. "With the most cuddly horse," she says.

"That's gotta be Duchess," I say. "She's as cuddly as a lap dog."

"She snores quite a bit though," Karen says.

"True," I admit. As many nights as I've slept with that horse, I should know.

Somewhere in the conversation I realize sleeping in the barn would be a good excuse to get away for my meeting with the shaman at midnight. "Tell you what," I say to Karen, "let's trade tonight. You take my bed and I'll sleep in the barn."

"Absolutely not."

"Sorry, I must insist. Can't let you have all the fun. Besides, you'll love my down comforter."

Her fork stops halfway to her mouth. "Down?"

"The best."

"Okay," she concedes. "You have a deal, but only if we trade back tomorrow."

"You staying?"

"Yes," she says. "Long enough to attend your concert. She starts to rise to her feet, grabbing her teacup in the process.

"Let me." I take her cup into the kitchen where Moriah is leaning on the counter.

"Ready for another cup?" she asks.

"Not me." I reach for the bowl containing my Stevia. "This is for Karen."

She snaps my hand away. "I just filled that." She shoves the Stevia bag at me, acting more her usual self. "So what colors are you seeing today?" she asks.

"Colors?"

"How long have you been on mescaline?"

The spoon in my hand freezes over Karen's cup.

"Word is all over town. James called to let me know. Said everyone is talking about how you've turned to drugs. You know how he adores your songs. He's afraid drugs will affect your singing, so he asked me to come down and make sure you stay clean for the concert."

"Bunk!" My retort comes out much stronger than I intend. Suddenly Red Dog appears at my feet. He growls at Moriah even though his tail is tucked between his legs. I reach down and pat his head. He's trying so hard to be brave.

Swinging her hips from side to side, Moriah heads for the door. She turns at the last minute to remind me to put the Stevia bag away when I'm through. She's on the other side of the door before I can respond. I've lost track of how many teaspoons of Stevia I've stirred into Karen's tea, so I pour it out and start over, using the Stevia in the precious filled sugar bowl just to spite my sister.

Chapter 66

> Under the great wings of Creator Yahweh
> you will find sweet refuge.
> *Ghostdancer*

Sayla

BY THE TIME I RETURN to the picnic table, my fry bread is cold. I scrape my plate into the pig barrel, wishing I could do the same thing with some of the people in my life, one person in particular.

Moriah is up to something, but her motive escapes me. She has a fancy house, three children and a nanny, and someone who comes in to clean twice a week. From the looks of her, she probably has her hair and nails done every other day. What could she possibly want?

Too much thinking has caused me to scrape a good-sized hole in my paper plate, so I crumple it and throw it in the garbage. When I turn back around, I am amazed at how much our little gathering looks like some kind of Quaker meeting. The men are sitting at one table, thoroughly bonded and taking turns telling stories, and Red Dog is back at Kenny's feet. I suspect my agent is bribing the dog with some delectable treat.

The women sit around the other table just as thoroughly bonded and telling their own stories, except for Moriah who sits at the end of the table eating a sliced pear with a knife and fork, European style, something I've never seen another Native do.

Kadai appears at my side. "Come with me."

He hands me a shovel and leads me down the driveway, back to the burn site. The two of us search for reoccurring hot spots, working in silence. When a meadowlark offers a song, we stop to listen, each leaning on our shovel handles, me resting my chin and Kadai leaning his arms over the top. A breeze blows across the field and ruffles my hair. The clear day is made all the more special following weeks of smoke. It makes me grateful Kadai is here with me, and I want to apologize for him going to jail because of me. But I say nothing, because I cannot stand the thought that I caused him pain.

Closing my eyes, I will the wind to sweep all the pain away.

"The breath of Creator," Kadai says.

A classic Grandfather line. I wonder if the wind has taken Grandfather up into heaven. He would have liked that. Then a repressed memory returns to me of Grandfather talking about death not long before he died. We were standing outside, leaning on our shovels and helping plant Gran's garden.

"It's okay to be sad for a while after I die," Grandfather said. "I'd hate to think my passing made little difference. But don't mourn, Little Fire. I will be with my Great Chief and Captain where there is true life, waiting for you when your time of crossing comes."

I wonder if Grandfather can see me now. I turn to Kadai. "Heard you had quite an experience in the hospital?"

"Which time?"

I lift my chin. "There was more than one?"

He nods.

"Heard you died."

"That's what they say."

"What do you say?"

He begins shoveling dirt over the last hot spot. We already drowned it with water and covered it with dirt. His action is just a busy thing.

"I was more alive than I've ever been, Little Fire. It's hard to call that dead, but I wasn't in my body."

"An out-of-body experience."

"Something like that, yet more." He stops and turns to me, his eyes glistening. "I saw Creator, Sayla. He called me *sawalineeas*."

"Friend." The word falls off my tongue as a whisper. "How did he say it?"

"*Waqlisi sawalineeas*."

"So Creator speaks Klamath?" I am only half teasing.

Kadai nods and stares out over the field, one of his booted feet on the shovel's blade and both hands over the handle. "I suspect Creator speaks to everyone in their own language."

"And you saw him?"

"No human can see him and live."

"But you said—"

"I saw him, Sayla. For all intents and purposes my body was dead. The doctor and his team had already given up."

Reminding myself this man has never lied to me in his entire life, I realize whatever happened in that hospital room, Kadai believes he saw Creator.

"And get this Sayla." Tears fill Kadai's eyes, something I haven't seen since his return from Iraz. He ignores them and continues. "He touched me. We were both solid, in real bodies, and held onto each other like two brothers who haven't seen each other for a long time."

Kadai pauses and I try to imagine what he has seen. "What did he look like?"

Kadai shakes his head and turns away. A nearby meadowlark trills repeatedly. How close had I come to losing Kadai? The thought shakes me to the core. Does Creator desire to take everyone from me?

Kadai says in a shaky voice, "I didn't want to come back."

The truth hits me hard. If my parents and grandfather had the choice, they would stay where they are. They wouldn't want to come back to me. For some reason the thought makes me lash out. "So why did you?"

Alarm colors Kadai's eyes as he peers into my soul. "I'm sorry, Little Fire."

He offers no other explanation, and I don't expect one. Creator is the only one who can answer the questions plaguing me, but Creator is being incredibly silent. I can't see one good reason for him taking my parents, especially with Moriah causing so much trouble. If he must take somebody, why didn't he take her?

I push my shovel's blade into the earth and stand back. "Did you see my parents?"

Blinking, Kadai opens his mouth, but nothing comes out. This discussion is too painful and getting nowhere. I decide to change the subject. "Moriah's accusing me of taking drugs."

It was the right thing to say. Kadai turns to face me, tears replaced with fire. "She talks out of both sides of her mouth. Says only what will benefit her."

His words startle me. "How will she benefit?"

Kadai lifts his shovel. "I don't know Little Fire, but that's how she works, and if I can figure it out, it will probably explain a lot."

Swinging the shovel over his shoulder, spoon end up, Kadai doesn't miss a beat. "Tell me about the shaman's fire."

My first reaction is to deny I saw anything, but Kadai knows me too well. Dreading it as I do, the moment for confession has come.

Chapter 67

> In frenzied excitement the horse cannot stand still
> when the trumpet sounds.
> *Creator Yahweh*

Kadai

KNOWING THAT BODY LANGUAGE speaks louder than words, you keep your eyes on Sayla while she tries to explain. You have spent a lifetime among horses and understand the nuisances of side-turned eyes and tightening muscles. Sayla's twisting fingers tells you she doesn't want to talk about this subject, but you are already aware of that. What you don't understand is why. Her inability to look you in the face lets you know she isn't telling you the entire story. Hands suddenly looking for pockets, lets you know there is a desperate measure to her fascination with the Shaman.

She speaks of the shaman's fire and how she saw a warrior in the flames, insisting he was alive but unharmed, and of how she believes she could have stepped into the fire and not be burned.

You point toward the ruined car. "Fire always burns. That is the result."

Sayla's fingers clench. "I saw him as clearly as you saw Creator. The fire did not burn him."

Holding your tongue, you pray for patience. She is not ready for your "religious" answers.

Sayla's shoulders relax as she stares into your eyes. "You saw him too. He was wearing hundreds of eagle feathers, the most beautiful headdress I've ever seen."

"He was no dog soldier, Sayla." Though the words are a whisper, you regret them as soon as they leave your mouth, but the claim is too much to leave unchallenged. Charlie Whitewater was a true dog soldier who would have given his life for any of his family or tribal members. This so-called Shadow Warrior means Sayla harm, though she does not see it. Fortunately she seems to not have heard your words.

She looks at the ground and draws circles in the gravel with the toe of her Ryder boot. You know by her actions she is reluctant to tell you more, so you wait, because you do not yet understand what it is about her Shadow Warrior that has drawn her so deeply. The sun beats down hard and thirst constricts your throat. Last night's storm did little to cool the air or dampen the ground. It made an appearance and swept away the smoke but little else. You wonder if this Shadow Warrior is the same for Sayla. Did he simply make an appearance, or is there something more she's withholding?

Still refusing to meet your eyes, she has given you all she will give this day. So you break the silence with your own words. "If the warrior was from our world the fire would have burned him."

Sayla's foot stops its incessant twirling, and her eyes look up at you with such hope that you waver. Hope has been far away for so long that you hate to remove it, but misplaced hope is worse than no hope at all. Or is it? You debate the issue in the shadows of your mind.

"That's exactly what I've been saying." Sayla holds your eyes for the first time. "The Shadow Warrior *is* from another world. He's calling me there. Don't you see? Just like Creator called you there."

"Tread lightly, Little Fire. Don't forget that my heart stopped beating. If there were no doctors in the room I may have never returned."

"You said yourself that you didn't want to."

Your body stiffens. These words are arrows coming back to haunt you. You must find other words that may come zinging back as well. You don't know what to do with your hands as you talk. You have no horse to run them across, no hat to twist, so you pull the shovel off your shoulder and lean on it. "It wasn't the same place, Sayla. Please understand. There are many different worlds."

"So what makes you think this is a bad one?"

You push the shovel blade into the ground; then you hold your hands palm up for her to see the scars.

Her eyes widen at the ugly welts. For a moment you think she finally understands, but then she spins and heads back up the road, her shoulders taut and arms stiff. Watching her, you wonder if you should follow. Why your scars make Sayla angry is an enigma beyond your understanding.

You run your fingers through your hair, realizing that for too long you have let it hang loose. You have paid little attention to your appearance for the past few days while living, as you have been, first in a jail and then a hospital. For the first time since returning home you wonder how Sayla has viewed your appearance. She doesn't seem overjoyed at your return.

A sound rumbles in the ground. You feel it before you hear it. First you think it is a car's engine, but then as the rumble grows louder you suddenly know.

"Sayla!"

She turns and stops; fear written in every curve of her body. War Paint is running hard toward her.

There is no way she can outrun him to safety. Furious with rage, the stallion throws his head down in a charge. A rope trails from his neck, and you realize he has been out here all night. Though you could stop him on a good day, you know this is not one of those days. The rope has undone all the good you worked so hard to achieve.

With wings on your feet, you fly to Sayla, grabbing her and rolling to the ground. Her screams fill the air while you petition Creator to keep those thundering hooves off her body. It is too much to hope that both of you can come through this unscathed.

War Paint never slows. The ground rumbles and shakes beneath you. Ducking your head to your chest, you cover as much of Sayla's body as possible, hoping to take the blows upon your own back.

War Paint is almost upon you, so you roll, keeping Sayla tight in your arms. Dust clogs your lungs.

War Paint's hooves come down in the road, sending a shower of gravel over the two of you. "Keep your eyes closed," you command Sayla. The stallion rears again and again until it seems as if you are in the middle of a storm. The ground shakes and gravel flies, some of it hitting your back as you continue to roll, keeping you and Sayla as one unit. So far, you have been able to dodge the horse's flying hooves, but you cannot keep this up for long. You search your mind for some way to divert the angry beast, but before you can come up with an idea, Ghostdancer shouts, "War Paint!"

His voice is too near. You look up and see that he stands between you and the mad horse.

"No!" You let go of Sayla and rise to push Ghostdancer aside, but it is too late.

His arms are raised over his head, but they do little to stop the hooves that crash down on his skull. Gushing blood immediately covers his face as he falls to the ground.

You stand like a helpless old woman while War Paint turns and thunders across the field.

Chapter 68

Everything under heaven belongs to me.
Creator Yahweh

Sayla

GHOSTDANCER IS NOT A SMALL MAN, but Kadai carries him as if he weighs no more than a child.

A yelp leaves Gran's mouth as she hurries toward us. At the sight of blood she lays a hand on Kadai's arm. "You shouldn't move him."

Kadai ignores her and heads toward the house. The rest of us follow the trail of blood. No one says a word.

The change in River is astounding. Gone is the laughing, ditzy girl, and in her place is a woman in charge. She beats Gran to the house and holds the door open. I run ahead, stopping at the porch sink to get a layer of dirt and blood off me. By the time Kadai carries Ghostdancer inside I'm ready to help.

"Get a clean sheet," River demands.

Kadai lays Ghostdancer on my bed and a crimson flow quickly colors my white comforter. I pull a sheet from my closet.

"Tear it into strips," River says, then she turns to Gran. "What bandages do you have?"

Gran already has her bag in hand. She sets it on my dresser and opens it. She is surprisingly calm, which makes me feel a lot better. She leans close and puts a hand on River's shoulder. "I'll take over from here."

River stares up at Gran. "But—"

I start handing the torn strips to Gran, one by one. She lays the first over Ghostdancer's wound. When blood soaks through she reaches for another. I keep the strips coming, wondering at all the blood.

"Can you hear me Ghostdancer?" Gran's voice is soft and calm.

Ghostdancer's eyes flicker open, and he reaches a hand toward Gran's face. "Kadai—" It looks as if he used his last bit of strength as his hand drops to the bed and his eyes close.

Gran looks up, but Kadai is nowhere in sight. Kenny stands in the door. "I'll get him," he says.

"Get my bag," Gran says to River. "You can help." Then she turns to Karen. "Get the teapot going."

Isabel's hands are folded beneath her chin.

"Are you a praying woman?" Gran asks.

Without hesitation Isabel says, "Yes."

"Then pray. We need all the help we can get."

Isabel leaves the room and Karen turns to follow. She stops at the doorway and looks back, one hand covering her mouth. Gran looks up. "We'll take good care of him. My recipe for Turmeric tea is on the inside of the cupboard. It will help with the pain."

Karen nods and leaves. Link takes her place in the doorway. While Gran works on Ghostdancer's forehead, I notice blood is soaking the pillow. I point it out to her. Carefully reaching behind his head, she moans. Her hand comes out completely covered in blood.

"He needs a hospital," River says.

Link disappears. The poor man probably can't stand the sight of blood.

River lays a hand on Gran's back. "I've been medically trained."

"So have I, young woman." Gran reaches for my cloth strips and moves to the other side of the bed. Gently, she removes the pillow and applies the cloths to a second wound on the back of Ghostdancer's neck. "He should be elevated a bit, but I don't see how to do it with this bed." Gran applies the cloth strips until a good wad covers the wound, then she turns to me. "Pull up a chair and keep pressure on this wound."

I do as instructed, but when I place my hand behind Ghostdancer's head, he's so pale and still, for a moment I'm not sure he's still alive.

Seeing the shock on my face, River says, "The body shuts down like that when traumatized. It's a protection. The wound seems clean."

"Don't see how any bacteria could be left in there after all this blood flow," I say.

River nods, tossing her auburn curls into a frenzy. "That's a good assessment. Let's make sure it stays clean."

Link reappears in the doorway. "Mercy Flights is on the way."

"Whaa—" I begin to say.

"Kadai is cleaning the air strip."

My hand slips from Ghostdancer's neck. "The strip hasn't been used in years."

"Keep pressure, Sayla," Gran demands.

I do as she says and continue to do so even when Kadai steps into the room and freezes. His complexion is nearly as pale as Ghostdancer's, and his mouth is set in a hard grimace. I can't remember seeing such an animal look on his face, though I have heard he was pretty scary when he first returned from Iraq. His hardened face is that of a dangerous man. Capturing his eyes, I shudder. "They're bringing a plane," I say.

He blinks. In that brief second the dangerous man disappears and my *sawalineeas* returns. "I've been running a blade across the strip," he says. Stopping at the door, he looks back at Ghostdancer. Some people might not call it a miracle, but it sure seems so to me, the way Ghostdancer chooses that very moment to open his eyes and fix them on Kadai. He raises a hand and Kadai crosses the room in one stride. They cling to one another in a one-handed grip.

Silent tears fall from Gran's eyes and River doesn't even get after Kadai for getting dirt on the sheets.

Kadai pulls away. "I'll get the runway ready."

When he leaves, Ghostdancer speaks, though his voice is not much more than a whisper. "Where's Karen?"

Gran leans close to hear him. "She's fixing tea."

Weak as he is, Ghostdancer's stubbornness comes to the front. "Trust yourself, Loretta. No white man's medicine."

River leans close. "Mr. Ghostdancer, you've been hurt really bad."

Squinting his eyes, Ghostdancer tries to lift his head. I feel the pressure lift from my hand and a gush of blood spills across the sheet. "Loretta is well-trained," he says.

"Lie still." Gran's voice is soft but firm as she continues to hold pressure on Ghostdancer's forehead. She gently pushes him back to the bed.

Ghostdancer seems to be reading something in River's face. After a long minute he says, "Loretta is a good healer. Trust her."

River nods.

Ghostdancer's eyes close and his breathing slows. It scares me to see him this way, as if he will stop breathing any minute.

Chapter 69

*Through many long winters
I have followed Creator Yahweh's footsteps
in the clean, unbroken snow,
never wavering from the clear laid-out path.*
Ghostdancer

Loretta

A WEEK AGO, Loretta would have given in to River, but not now. She had learned too much about forgiveness and the grace of God. Jesus Yeshua had given her a gift and she needed to use it. Just because Jacob had soiled the office of healer by using his gift for bad things, didn't mean she couldn't undo his wrong by using her gift for good things. She would let River help, but she would also let River have a taste of what it meant to be a Native healer.

She sent Sayla off on an errand.

River took over Sayla's place holding pressure on Ghostdancer's wound. "Where did you learn your medicine?" she asked.

Loretta leaned her elbows on the bed. "Most of it was passed down from my mother and grandmother, the rest was from Ghostdancer and a famous healer named Vincent Windwalker."

River sighed. "I'd give anything to have the history you have."

Her comment made Loretta realize she knew nothing about the girl. River had blown into their lives in the most extraordinary way, and now she sat across from Loretta caring for Ghostdancer as if she had known him all her life. "Why were you living in your car?" Loretta asked.

Before River could respond Sayla returned with a bucket of warm water and traded places with Loretta. Loretta began washing Ghostdancer's face. Though his eyes never opened, a smile formed on his lips.

"I was livin' in my car," River said, "because it was the last piece of my momma I own."

"How was the car a piece of your mother?" Loretta asked.

River smiled. "She drove it everywhere, never lived in it like I do, but she carried all her art from show to show and often slept in it while on the road. She was quite a well-known artist. The paintings on the van were hers."

"Angel Flyer," Loretta said. "I thought I recognized that van.

River raised her eyebrows. "She wasn't from around here."

"No," Loretta agreed. "She was from Arkansas, but she came through the Rogue Valley once and taught a class. I attended. A very nice woman full of energy. I can see how you take after her." Loretta squinted her eyes and examined River. "She must have been up in years when she had you."

River sighed. "Actually, she was my grandma, but since she raised me from the day I was born, I always called her Momma. Never met my birth mother. She never even showed up at my grandmother's funeral."

Sayla shifted her hold on the dressing and focused on River. "How did your grandmother die?"

Loretta could tell Sayla immediately wished she could pull back the words The question was way too personal.

River seemed to take no offense. "Four years ago. Momma had a stroke when we were home alone. Stupid me, didn't even know what was happenin'. If I'd known the signs she would probably still be alive today."

"But you're a nurse," Sayla said.

"Today. Not then. I sold the house to attend school, and I'm not a full-fledged nurse, just an aide, but I know enough to help save lives."

Loretta dried Ghostdancer's face and moved to River's side of the bed to inspect the dressing. "It's clear you know what you're doing. Thanks for stepping in like you did."

Ghostdancer opened his eyes and fixed them on Loretta. He smiled.

"Do you hurt?" Loretta asked.

"Headache."

River shook her head. "No aspirin till the doctor checks him out." She sighed, "And I hate to tell you this but . . . no tea. We need to be careful with liquids in case swelling is happenin' on the inside. Swelling is rather normal under these circumstances."

Loretta opened her mouth to object about the tea, but then she thought of Kadai's mother and how she had wished for help back then. Perhaps it was good to accept River's help. "That's a good observation," she said.

Karen and Isabel peeked into the room. "Can we come in?" Karen asked.

Loretta nodded. "Of course."

Karen leaned over River and whispered in her ear; then they changed places. Isabel put an arm on Sayla's shoulder. "You and River need a break."

"But Gran needs a break more than me," Sayla objected.

Loretta shook her head. "I'm not going anywhere." She pointed to the door. "Go."

Obeying, River and Sayla left the room.

Loretta took over River's place and had Karen wash the sweat from Ghostdancer's face. It did her good to see the woman minister in such a loving way. Clearly the woman was in love, Loretta just hoped Ghostdancer would live long enough to realize the fact.

Chapter 70

*Creator Yahweh broadens the path
beneath our feet.*
Ghostdancer

Sayla

I POUR US EACH A CUP of soothing St. John's Wort tea and River and I sit at the kitchen table, cradling our cups in our hands. Though it is hot outside a chill has seeped into my body, so the hot cup feels good. We have a great view out the window. Kadai is running a tractor blade across the landing strip while Kenny and Link rake up debris. It makes me proud to see them both working as if they are part of the family. Red Dog still follows close to Kenny. It's clear he has adopted Kenny for as long as Moriah is with us. The thought of my sister makes me wonder where she's taken off to.

I turn back to River. "It's good to have Sacred Mountain Ranch filled with people. The three of us have been alone for the last year."

"Yeah," River says, "I know somethin' about loneliness."

"Where did you park your van at night?"

She takes a sip of tea and makes a face. "Boy howdy. This tea smells good, but it don't taste that great."

"Mint gives the good aroma. I don't remember St. John's Wort being this bitter, but it's good for you. Gran says it calms the nerves."

River sets her cup down, clearly not about to take another sip no matter how soothing it is. "About my car," she says. "I park it different places each night. Sometimes at Wally World, sometimes at the hospital, wherever it ain't too conspicuous. Walmart is fun. Lots of characters to watch."

"So you're homeless?"

"No." River shakes her head, making her red curls fly. "Take my home with me. Can have lake front property any time I want. All I need do is move my van."

"Where will you stay now?"

She sets her cup back on the table. "I have no idea."

"You can stay here."

Her eyebrows shoot up. "Here?"

"There's plenty of room. This house has four bedrooms, and we have three cabins across the field."

Before River can digest that fact, the low rumble of a plane shakes the house. Moriah runs out of her bedroom in her bathrobe, "Can't a person get a little sleep around here?"

I can't see how she could sleep through everything that has been happening. Maybe her job at the Casino is harder than I thought, or perhaps she needs a rest from all her running around shopping. Then I remember she sleeps with earplugs and one of those fancy noise machines that sounds like a rain forest.

Suddenly the rumbling of the plane flying overhead makes me think of my parents flying off the road into the Guano Desert. The image is incredibly real. Flames devour the screaming faces of my parents and Grandfather as their truck flies through the air in slow motion. I try to shake off the image, but it will not leave. I stand and my chair crashes to the floor.

Shadows drift from the corners of the room. Moriah's voice drones on, but I don't hear a word. I'm flabbergasted at the glowing red triangles pouring from her mouth.

"You okay, Sayla?" River's voice sounds very far away.

Chapter 71

*Can you raise your voice to the clouds
and cover yourself with a flood of water?*
Creator Yahweh

Loretta

ONE OF THE HARDEST THINGS Loretta had ever done was allowing the paramedics to put Ghostdancer on that plane. They had stormed into the house and strapped Ghostdancer to a gurney to keep his neck stable. Kenny repeatedly assured Loretta that everything would be okay, but that was just words. Her hand kept going to her chest. The vice grips were back, but she had to remain strong for Sayla. The poor girl looked as if she would faint.

Loretta put an arm around her granddaughter as the plane started to take off. Wind from the engine tossed their hair.

At Ghostdancer's unusual request, Kadai had gone in the plane with him. Such a request was seldom honored, but Ghostdancer insisted Kadai was his spiritual advisor and that he needed such at such an hour as this. "It's my Native right," he had said. He had also told Loretta to not come to the hospital. "You can pray best here at the ranch," he had said.

The paramedics had assured Loretta that the women had done their job well, but Ghostdancer would need blood. Loretta insisted Ghostdancer not get blood from a stranger, it just wasn't the Native way. Turned out River and Link had the rare type of blood Ghostdancer needed. River was already in Link's car speeding across Highway 140 to the Rogue Valley Medical Center in Medford. Karen and Isabel had gone too, following Link in Karen's Jeep. Isabel said she needed to make sure Kadai didn't run off before trial date.

Clinging to one another as if they couldn't stand on their own, Loretta and Sayla watched the plane take off. They were still in each other's arms when the plane circled and disappeared over the forest. It flew straight into the sun that was now low in the sky.

"We're alone again," Loretta said, feeling the cut of it more sharply than normal.

"Not quite," Sayla said.

"Moriah," Gran groaned. "How could I have forgotten?"

Sayla pulled away. "I'll take care of the horses. And I'm sleeping out there tonight if you don't mind."

Loretta didn't mind. Moriah hated the barn, so it was a place where Sayla could have a measure of peace. "Could you help me with the room first?" She hoped to buy some time with Sayla. Her granddaughter had been acting a bit strange ever since the plane flew in.

They walked across the meadow, still clinging to one another like two old women. Sayla's feet were dragging as if she had no energy to lift them. Arguing with herself, Loretta thought about Moriah's accusation of drugs. But Sayla had been in full view all day. When could she have taken any drugs? Still, she was showing some of the symptoms Loretta had discovered at one of the clinic meetings—slurred speech, depression, extreme fatigue.

Yaks dwa! Loretta felt all those things at the moment and she hadn't taken any drugs. She stopped when they reached the doorway of Sayla's room. The stink almost made her gag. Without Ghostdancer's living body, the room smelled of spoiled blood.

Snatching up the comforter, Sayla said, "I'll get rid of this."

"It can be washed. Cold water should do the trick."

"Not this much blood."

Watching Sayla ducking out of the room, Loretta had to agree. The sight of all the blood spattered sheets and cloths made her wish she had gone to the hospital with the others, but she could pray here as well as there, and so that's what she did. She prayed while she picked up the sheets and piled the rags. The mattress would have to be replaced and eventually the carpet. The carpet was old and there was hardwood beneath, so it wasn't a great loss. Perhaps Sayla would even hang a few pictures, but she doubted it. Sayla's memories were all out in the sound room. That's where she kept everything that held meaning to her.

Inspiration struck Loretta. She hurried down the hall and retrieved the second painting she had finished this morning. Snatching up a hammer and nails from her stash next to the fireplace, she decided this was a good way to give Sayla a new start.

After hanging the painting, she stood back. The lion took over the focus of the entire room. Stunning in its color and captivating in wild movement, the lion seemed to be running right out of the painting. Loretta clasped her hands and prayed Sayla would understand the lion represented Creator coming after her. "Love is on the move," she said aloud. "And he's coming to get you Sayla!"

Next she retrieved, "Lion of Judah," and hung it above Sayla's headboard. The great lion's head was nearly lost in the slashes of paint covering the canvas, but for those with eyes to see, it was a representation of how the great Lion of Judah is always there, waiting in the shadows of their everyday lives.

Feeling better, Loretta grabbed the pile of sheets and rags and headed outside to dump them in the trash. When she opened the door she heard Red Dog barking and saw blazing fire in the night sky. She dropped the rags and ran for the water hose. "Fire!" she yelled before realizing no one was home to answer her call.

"Jesus," she prayed. "Do you see us here? Could use a little help."

Grabbing the hose she hurried to the fire. She was shocked to see Sayla dancing around the flames. Red Dog chased the girl, barking and nipping at her heels, but the Sayla didn't seem to notice. She must have gone quite mad. Tiny tongues of flame drifted in the breeze. It looked as if tiny candles were floating in the dark. Mesmerized, Loretta stood in a trance, the water pouring at her feet. Her mind couldn't quite decipher what was happening.

Sayla pulled her tee shirt high over her head and threw it into the air as she reached for the flames. No cry escaped her lips when fire met skin.

"What on earth?" Loretta's question was answered as quickly as it was asked. What she had thought were tongues of fire were feathers from Sayla's comforter having ignited and were now floating through the air. Horror gripped Loretta's throat. Hundreds of flaming feathers fell around her granddaughter. She shuddered to think what would happen if the wind kicked up and carried them across the dry grass. With no one to help, she was torn between putting out the fire and saving Sayla. Just one of those flaming feathers could singe her granddaughter's hair or burn her skin.

When Sayla stepped out of her jeans, Loretta did the first thing that came to mind.

Chapter 72

Do you send the lightning bolts on their way?
Creator Yahweh

Sayla

ANGELS DANCE THROUGH THE NIGHT, each with a flaming candle. Shimmering colors float between us. Impossible harmonies stretch endlessly crossing through mystical boundaries into my world. Delight replaces all anxiety. Joy captures my soul. Laughing, I stretch my arms high among those brightly colored hues, hearing the Shadow Warrior singing another song.

Come, come, come away. Come, come, come away with me. Through the night. To a place of unspeakable delight.

The music carries a drumbeat older than time. My feet bounce with the rhythm, as light as if they have taken flight.

Come, come, come away. Come, come, come away through clouds of glory. Let your heart soar free.

Iridescent blues, glowing yellows, reds that speaks of passion and greens that whisper peace. They float around me like fireflies dancing in the breeze, tinkling bells accompanying their song.

Come, come, come away. warrior woman wonderful and bright. Come, come, come away.

A shimmering full-circle rainbow breaks before me and there in the midst of it stands the Shadow Warrior. Bright eagle feathers lift him in flight. Levitating, the Shadow Warrior dances in the flames. The drum beats harder, louder, matching the beat of my heart. Wanting to give myself completely to him, I rip off my shirt and immediately feel the undulating heat kiss my skin. Wild with excitement, my heart joins the thrumming drums, creating its own sweet music.

Passionate fire fills the Shadow Warrior's eyes as he stares at me through the flames. I am his, forever, completely; I want nothing more. The Shadow Warrior twirls, dancing harder, leaping higher, until he looks down on me. Beautiful beyond belief, he stares at me, his feathers aflame but not being consumed.

Come, come, come away. My beautiful warrior woman. Be all that you can be.

His words fall as a warm caress over my nakedness. I see his words color a gold wash over my arms, scintillating my flesh like something otherworldly. Never have I felt so beautiful, so loved. My skin glows lustrous and kaleidoscopic.

Come, come, come away, he calls, but I am too mesmerized by the beauty of my own skin. Swirling in the joy of it, I lift my arms high, beautiful glowing arms of transparent color. I can see right through them as if they are filled with a thousand stars. Reaching down I pull off my jeans wanting my entire body to feel the caress of that strange glowing realm.

Chapter 73

Who can tip over the water jars of the heavens?
Creator Yahweh

Loretta

TURNING THE HOSE ON SAYLA may not have been the right thing to do, but it certainly got results. Stunned, Sayla turned and looked at Loretta before examining her own near naked body. Then she stared at the flames as if she could see something in them that Loretta could not.

"Enough!" Loretta said. "Get out of there!"

Sayla stood in a daze, unmoving. The tee shirt was an arm's throw away, but she made no move toward it. The jeans were at her feet, but Sayla simply stared at her arms and legs.

"Jesus, Yeshua." Loretta whispered. "Give me wisdom."

If there was an overreaching song in her life, it was this one prayer petitioning Creator for wisdom. He had never failed her and He didn't now. For the moment, Sayla was safe, and there was no one to see her nakedness, so Loretta turned the hose to the fire and concentrated on stopping any further disasters. This day had certainly been a day from the devil himself.

At the thought, a germ of an idea formed in Loretta's mind. She thought of Job in the Bible who had faced a day quite similar to her own. One after another, his servants had arrived to tell him of how he had lost his enormous herds of oxen, sheep and camels. Then later the same day, he was told he had lost all of his children. In all these losses Job had remained true in his devotion to Creator. Not so, when Creator allowed Satan to touch Job's body with terrible boils. Though Job never cursed God, he certainly had his questions.

What about Loretta?

She had faced the loss of her beloved husband and one of her children, something no mother should ever have to experience. Now Sacred Mountain Ranch that had been in her family for generations was falling apart, and Moriah, her own granddaughter, was threatening to take it away. Was she being tested like Job? Or were these occurrences simply facts of life, as sure as gravity and the rotation of the earth? Was Jesus Yeshua a God somewhere far off watching from heaven? Or was he close as he claimed to be? Had Creator set his Spirit within her heart?

Strangely, knowing the answers was more a matter of the head than a matter of the heart, unlike what most people thought about Christians living on blind faith. Her faith had eyes and there was plenty to see.

Spraying water over the dying embers, she thought of Job. Having memorized great portions of the book in one of Ghostdancer's tribal Bible studies, she recalled them now. Young Elihu referring to God said, "For God does speak—now one way, now another—though man may not perceive it. In a dream, in a vision of the night, when deep sleep falls on men as they slumber in their beds, he may speak in their ears."

Loretta had always loved those words. Creator speaking through visions and dreams had long been known among the Modoc and Klamath Indians. *Cheelaqsdi* Mountain, the Sacred Mountain of vision quests, was named for that very reason. Her people still visited the Sacred Mountain to seek Creator for visions and dreams. Some went to the dark side to find visions of another kind. Sayla seemed to be exhibiting signs of that kind of dark vision.

Stealing a glance at Sayla, Loretta was pleased to see her granddaughter was fully dressed and stomping out small spot fires where flaming feathers had landed. The time would come when they would talk. Her granddaughter had experienced so much suffering for one so young.

Elihu had also talked of why Creator allowed pain and suffering to enter a person's life. He said, "God does all these things to a man—twice, even three times—to turn back his soul from the pit, that the light of life may shine on him."

The words fell from Elihu's mouth in the same way words fell from the elders' mouths who spoke for the tribe. Loretta had often wondered if Native Americans had descended from this man, Elihu. He had been so aware of Creator and his creation, just like her people still were. He was aware of the spiritual connectedness of all things. Natives believed all things, even inanimate objects held life. Elihu seemed to feel the same way. His language painted pictures as clearly as the elders telling stories around the campfire. The story of Job, itself, was a long poem, set to music for those who had ears to hear.

So where did Loretta fit in all this?

Elihu had ascribed justice to his maker. In the end, Job did the same, but not until he had to brace himself like a man and take an enormous tongue-lashing from Creator. Interesting, though, the tongue-lashing was nothing more than a reminder of Job's smallness and Creator's majestic bigness.

"Where were you?" Creator asked again and again.

"Surely I spoke of things I did not understand," Job responded, "things too wonderful for me to know."

Repentance was the answer for Job, and repentance was also the answer for Loretta. There were things going on here she did not understand. Perhaps it was time for her to listen more and talk less.

Chapter 74

Do you hunt the prey for the lioness?
Creator Yahweh

Sayla

GRAN IS ON THE PHONE when I climb from the tub smelling of honeysuckle. Cinnamon tea adds to the pleasant aroma. After giving no excuse for not helping us with the fire, Moriah has disappeared again, probably holed up in her room. Finally, Gran and I have some precious time to ourselves. Knowing Gran wants to talk, and feeling the need to pick her brain, I pull up a chair to the kitchen table. It's ten o'clock, two more hours until I meet the shaman at the river. After my experience with the shimmering angels, a thundering herd of horses couldn't stop me from meeting the shaman.

Hanging up the phone, Gran examines me. Neither of us says a word; then we both begin talking at the same time.

"I'm sorry—" we both start. Then we each give a little laugh. The mirth of it doesn't reach Gran's eyes, and I know she is worried about me.

"Tell me what happened," Gran says. "Convince me this isn't drugs."

I shake my head. "You know I wouldn't take drugs."

"I *believe* you wouldn't take drugs." She puts emphasis on believe. "But I don't *know* you wouldn't. None of us know what we'll do under trying circumstances until we're actually faced with them."

Gran falls silent and sips her tea. I am thankful for the cinnamon and honey instead of the foul tasting St. John's Wort and I tell her so.

"Foul tasting?"

"It was worse than usual. River couldn't even drink it."

"Hmmm. Something must have gone wrong when Karen followed my recipe."

"Probably." I'm buying time and we both know it, attempting to avoid the real issue.

Gran pierces me with a concerned glare. "You've been keeping your thoughts to yourself. It's time for you to talk to me."

"Okay." I lean back in my chair. "Where should I start?"

"Tell me what happened at the Coming-Out?"

I fidget with my cup. This is going to be more difficult than I thought.

"It can't be that bad, Sayla, I'm your grandmother who loves you."

I shake my head. Will she love me if she knows the *whole* story? Choosing the way of compromise, I decide to tell her *part* of the story. "The shaman threw something into the fire."

"And it made bright sparkles."

"Yes." I say, surprised.

"I'm aware of that little trick."

I stare into my twisting cup. "Didn't seem like a trick to me."

"What did you see?"

I blink. "How did you know?"

Gran sighs and leans back, her tea untouched on the table. "Perhaps I need to tell you a few things first."

I wait.

She leans forward, her eyes bright and pleading. "When I was your age I was just as fascinated by magic."

Magic. It is the perfect word for what I've been experiencing.

Not missing the agreement in my eyes, she shakes her head. "I'm not denying magic is real. In fact, it is so real that Creator talks of it in the Bible as being something that if it were possible would fool the very elect. Pharaoh's magicians did magic, nearly keeping up with the miracles Moses performed, but if you recall, their magic was quite limited. It often got out of hand and they couldn't control it. It was the same way with the false prophets of Elijah's day."

She touches my arm so that I must stop twirling my cup.

"It's still the same today," she says. "From what I hear, the shaman can perform powerful magic, but it often gets away from him."

"In what way?"

"People have died, Sayla."

Shudders skitter across my arms. Gran squeezes my hand, sending the shudders away. "Creator is more powerful than magic. No matter what you've gotten yourself into he can get you out."

"What if I don't want out?"

The truth rings before us. Gran falls back in her chair as if I had slapped her.

I straighten. "You don't understand, Gran. He gives me songs. I feel closer to Creator than I've ever felt before, I feel special and beautiful and good."

"It's all feelings," Gran murmurs. "They pass as quickly as morning dew after sunrise."

"Maybe for you. Perhaps not for me."

Gran's eyes turn to fire. I can easily see the younger woman who had been known for her stubborn wildness. "With every gift comes a price."

"What does that mean?"

"What was your first gift?"

Thinking back, I try to decide whether it was seeing the Shadow Warrior or receiving my first song. "Probably the Shadow Warrior."

"Shadow Warrior?"

I push back my chair and stand. Gran hates it when people pace, but I can't just sit here. Choosing the lesser of two evils, I swing up and sit on the tiled counter, gripping the edge and letting my legs swing. "Okay, I'll tell you. I saw a warrior in the shaman's fire. He was the most beautiful creature I've ever seen, dressed in eagle feathers."

"So that was your first gift?"

"Yes."

"The price of which was Kadai's burned hands."

I stop swinging my legs. "You're putting that on me?"

"Blame and price are not the same things. That is the number one difference between magic that comes from the dark world and a miracle that is born of Creator. Magic from the dark world is a ploy at manipulating the supernatural for your own benefit. It can be done, but it always demands a price. Always. Creator's miracles are a free gift that fills the recipient with wonder and awe and draws them to salvation. He never demands a payment; instead, he paid the price for our blame. He gives miracles as a free gift."

My mouth must be hanging open.

Gran presses on. "And I'm guessing the second gift was the song?"

I nod.

"And the price of that gift was a stay in the mental ward and a lot of trouble for Kadai."

I shake my head. Surely, she can't be right.

"And the next gift?"

"The bees."

"Hmmm. I think you're forgetting the song you received the same day Ghostdancer faced off with the shaman."

The wolf. I almost say it aloud but refrain. Gran has enough imagination without me fueling it, but she is like a hawk narrowing on its prey.

"Have you seen an animal manifestation yet?"

I push off the counter and pace, not caring if it bothers Gran.

"Wolves and bears are most common," Gran continues, "although some see coyotes or birds of prey. And let's talk about those bees, Sayla. If anyone other than Ghostdancer had tried to help they would have been in trouble. What if Kenny or Link had tried to save you?"

That thought never occurred to me.

"And another price of the shaman's magic was Kadai ending up in the hospital."

Stopping my pacing, I clench my hands and turn on Gran. "What does Kadai have to do with this?"

Silence fills the house. I hear nothing but the ticking clock. Gran rises from her chair and places her hands on my shoulders. "Kadai is your true warrior. You can do nothing that won't touch him in some way. It's the same with me. Whatever you do will touch my life. Your mistakes will eat away a piece of my heart. Ghostdancer is in this too, because of his relationship with your Grandfather and the fact we have always looked to him as a respected elder."

It is too much to bear. I already feel bad enough about what happened to Ghostdancer.

Gran swallows. "Nothing touches us unless Creator allows it, but I do want you to be aware of how closely connected we all are and of the price the shaman's gifts will require."

Knowing it will take another piece of her heart, I pull her hands off my shoulders. "I didn't ask for this connectedness you're talking about, and I'm not convinced the shaman's gifts have caused any harm. These things would have happened either way."

Gran holds her ground, not cowering in tears as I expected. "It will do you well to consider these so-called gifts, Sayla. Creator gives gifts that bring pleasure to all involved. Will the words of your songs bring life to your listeners or death?"

With that last statement, Gran turns and leaves the kitchen.

Her words continue to haunt me long after she closes herself in her room. It shocks me to realize I haven't even asked her of

Ghostdancer's condition. She was on the phone when I first entered the kitchen. Why didn't she offer me the information?

Gathering my overnight bag, I decide it was probably some kind of test I had most likely failed. Selfishness must be another result of the shaman's gifts. With bag in hand, I grab a blanket and head for the door, slamming it behind me so Gran will know I have left. I have less than an hour to get to the shaman.

Chapter 75

> Who provides food for the raven
> when its young cry out to God?
> *Creator Yahweh*

Kadai

THICK DARKNESS HAS COVERED the sky by the time the plane lands at Jackson County International Airport. You are thankful it is not a helicopter, but the scene on the ground reminds you of hot nights in Iraq where the wounded were lifted into waiting ambulances. Ghostdancer is the one who is wounded this time and you feel as if you should have done more to protect your friend.

Keeping up with the paramedics is no easy task. They scamper across the tarmac and into the ambulance, nearly locking the door before you have a chance to swing it open and jump in. The screaming siren reminds you of the constant noise of war.

While the ambulance rushes through the streets of Medford you are aware only of the man on the gurney, the man who has been like an uncle to you. He opens his eyes and reaches out a hand; you take it and lay it on your lap, keeping his fingers in yours. Understanding grows in your mind—he hates this as much as you do. As a Vietnam vet he, too, has memories of such places of war and violence. He is more than an uncle, for the horrors of war have grafted you as brothers. Stronger than blood, this allegiance binds you together;

you both serve the same Chief and Captain. You discover strength and peace in the moment, regardless of the screaming siren and beeping monitors.

By the time the ambulance pulls into the hospital bay, you have found the strength to stand by your *sawalineeas*. You are no longer relying on your own prowess for you are not alone. You belong to the brotherhood of all warriors who trust in Creator.

Chapter 76

*Do you count the months
till the doe bears her fawn?*
Creator Yahweh

Sayla

A HALF MOON HANGS in the sky as I make my way to the river. It's creepy being out here by myself. Though I love open meadows beneath a full moon, sliding through brush and trees in the dark makes me feel as if some beast is watching my every step. Thin moonlight casts strange shadows over my path. Yipping coyotes sound from somewhere near Sacred Mountain, and I wonder what poor creature they have hunted down. My senses rise to high alert. Bear and mountain lions have wandered through this area in the past; I hope they will stay clear tonight.

The fresh smell of willows wafts from the river as I near our place of rendezvous. My heart picks up its pace. Yesterday's gifts were more wonderful than I could have imagined. What more does the shaman have to offer? Whatever it is, I am ready, but I also have questions.

Flipping on my flashlight, I strain to see the shaman. When I find no sign of him, I tread softly over the berm leading to the river. When I reach the riverbank, I switch off the flashlight and wait, allowing my eyes to adjust to darkness. Little light filters through the night canopy above. Eerie shivers make me want to turn the flashlight back on, but I force myself to wait, knowing the shaman wouldn't agree with such modern methods.

The forest grows incredibly quiet, empty of chirping cicadas and croaking frogs. Cascading water is the only sound. It is as if all creation is holding its breath in expectation. Rustling leaves catch my attention to the right.

Red Dog bounds out of the bushes. I can't believe he followed. I didn't even hear him behind me. The heat of human skin immediately to my left nearly brings a scream from my throat. Red Dog whimpers and runs back the way he came.

"This way." The shaman's voice sends shivers down my neck.

I can barely make him out as he moves swiftly toward the south, toward Sacred Mountain. I hope he will not take us up on that stark place where coyotes so recently found their dinner. Nevertheless, I follow with the eagerness of a terror-stricken teen entering a haunted house. Who knows what unfathomable mysteries await me?

We don't walk far when the shaman stops and makes fire in his hands. He blows on tender and lets it fall to the ground. A prepared cache of wood crackles into flame. He gives me a red robe to wear and motions for me to sit on a grassy area he has prepared with sage. I fasten the blanket robe with a macaw feather from the shaman. The robe is soft and smells of spice.

He sits next to me wearing very little, exotic and mysterious. Most of his body is smothered with an ash mixture, and he has tied another macaw feather into a topnotch of his hair. The rest of his hair flows free.

His eyes catch mine in the firelight glow. "Did you fast?"

I nod. Though I had forgotten to fast, it is true I haven't eaten anything since breakfast. I figure the bite of fry bread I managed this morning or the sip of tea by Ghostdancer's bed isn't enough to make a difference.

Flames cast an eerie glow over the shaman. Red paint covers the lower half of his face and white covers his forehead and eyes.

A thick black line runs horizontally below his eyes. A row of black dots stretches across his forehead. It makes me think of the time when Kadai was counting coup and, for a moment, I wonder if the shaman is counting coup. Is it possible he and Kadai are in a battle of sorts? But such thoughts make no sense. I've never seen the shaman and Kadai together. If they are at war it certainly couldn't be in this world.

The shaman's eyes are unblinking as he stares back. He looks so much like a Native from ancient times I begin to wonder if I should have worn something more fitting than jeans and a tee shirt. I ask him.

"This time it does not matter, but next time you must wear regalia."

Next time. So, I truly am his *saayoogalla*.

"Tonight I teach you about peyote."

Uh-oh. Here is a line I am not prepared to cross. We have been doing so well without drugs, I wonder if peyote is really necessary.

"Tonight's peyote is a jealous woman," he says. "You do not want to offend her. She is your ticket into the mystical world."

He pulls out a handful of small balls and hands them to me. They look like brown rolls of dirt.

"These buttons may make you throw up," he says, "but the effect will still be the same. Chew them and do as you wish, but you must swallow."

Wanting to be brave so as to impress my *Hahas? Iwgis* and not wanting to offend the jealous woman, I take the offered buttons and drop one in my mouth. The taste is worse than I expected. I gag and nearly throw up. Chewing quickly, I swallow as soon as it feels small enough to go down. The peyote comes back up. I catch the wad in my hands and try again.

The shaman laughs.

His laughter is so unexpected that I stop chewing and stare at him. A big mistake. The wad seems to grow as it sits on my tongue. This time I swallow while holding both hands over my mouth. The shaman pops a button down his own throat and throws me a smile. He didn't even chew. I look at the five buttons in my hand. How will I ever get them down?

The shaman must have understood my dilemma because he hands me a cup filled with foul-smelling liquid. I take the liquid and gulp. Surprisingly, it tastes very much like the tea I drank earlier. It stays down, so I pop another ball in my mouth and chew furiously.

The shaman pops another button. Then he says, "I gathered this jealous woman myself while visiting the Mescalero near the Rio Grande. I did it in the right way, singing songs in the field and praying with tobacco each time I reached down to pick some. Now I will teach you how to do this in a good way."

I manage to chew and swallow the rest of the buttons, but my stomach objects loudly.

The shaman continues his explanation, his voice sounding as wild and ancient as Sacred Mountain. "Women are not often allowed in peyote gatherings, but I am inviting you to a special gathering where two women will be present—you and your sister."

He could knock me over with a feather.

"You are surprised, are you not? Your sister has long been a *saayoogalla* to me. She is the one who has prepared this robe for you in just the right way. Now you have two jealous women to contend with. Are you still willing, *saayoogalla?*"

Bending away from the fire, I vomit violently in the grass.

Instead of being angry, the shaman pats me on the back and tells me not to worry. "Peyote will still give you visions, whether good or bad is up to you." He leans back and wrinkles his nose as if the smell of me is offensive. "Tonight you smell of honeysuckle. Next time you must bathe with yucca. Peyote will be less jealous, and next time, *saayoogalla,* peyote will be a jealous man. You will not want to offend him."

Dizzy now, I try to sit up straight, but my aching stomach makes me double over.

The shaman hands me another cup of liquid. I shake my head.

"This is not the same," he says. "The taste is much sweeter and it will give you better visions."

I accept the cup and drink. It helps the peyote stay down.

"Now *saayoogalla*, we will sing." He pulls out a drum and hands me a rattle.

Together we sing and play. Soon a wonderful sense of elation washes over me.

The shaman smiles. "Go with it *saayoogalla*. You have pleased the jealous woman. She will give you good visions."

While the shaman continues to beat softly on the drum, I fall to the grass and stare at the treetops. Moonlight filters through the branches, raining colorful prisms down upon me. I catch the rainbows in my hands and let them paint my robe. Their heat warms my face. Soon I am caught up into the heavens, lost in a parallel world. I rise to my feet and wait, expecting the gift, but hoping for something more, longing for a night uninterrupted with the Shadow Warrior. A river still runs beside me, the forest is quiet and still, but the shaman and fire are gone.

Hearing the sound of heavy breathing I spin around, but see nothing.

There! Between the trees darting, a shadowy shape I know too well. Slanting yellow eyes stare. When I hear the growl, I turn and run, splashing through water until the waves catch me in their grip. This is not the calm river of Sacred Mountain Ranch; this is a wild, angry river full of danger. The waves pull me under, swiftly moving me downstream. Gasping for air, I gulp one clean breath before being pulled back under. Stone scrapes my legs and arms. Too late, I think of Gran's warning and wonder if my own life will be the price of this most recent gift.

Music breaks through, plaintive and lilting, calling my name from afar. Struggling, I reach air for another gulp then madly try to swim against the current. My paltry strokes are of no use against this wild rushing water. My frigid fingers fail to respond.

"Wherever you are," a voice calls out. "Creator will hear and answer. His arm is not too short."

Recognizing Ghostdancer's voice, I swim harder, keeping my head above water.

"Call on Creator, Sayla!" This time it is Gran's voice." He gives strength to the weary."

This is just a dream isn't it? Some kind of vision or hallucination? Yet it seems so real. I'm soaked and freezing as exhaustion claims my arms and legs.

Then as quick as lightning, a horse splashes through the water. "Grab hold Little Fire!"

I nearly answer Kadai's plea, but the horse is fighting its own battle, its eyes wild in the moonlight. Fear of being crushed by those thrashing hooves sends me plunging beneath the water. It is strangely calm in the depths below, a quiet world of peace. I long to stay in those dark arms, but my empty lungs soon send me gasping for air.

"Remember Creator!" Kadai yells. "Call upon him and be saved!"

Again the river takes me in its powerful grasp and I realize this strength is that of the jealous woman. She roars, angry and demonic. I think of Moriah and her hatred of me. Whether dream or vision, I know not, but this is a dangerous place that demands my very life.

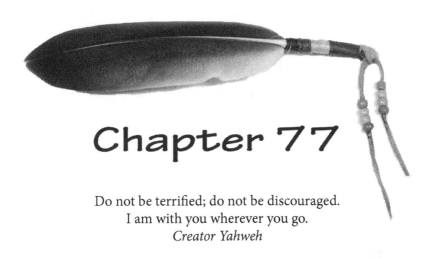

Chapter 77

*Do not be terrified; do not be discouraged.
I am with you wherever you go.*
Creator Yahweh

Kadai

NOTHING ABOUT THIS NIGHT is usual, in fact, your life for the past few days has had very little to do with such a description. Pacing in the bowels of Rogue Valley Medical Center you watch as River and Link talk with an admitting nurse.

None of you with Native blood—Grandmother, Sayla or yourself—have the type of blood Ghostdancer needs, only the white lawyer and a white nurse. Creator has a sense of humor. River is bouncing off the walls for the sheer joy of being able to give her blood to Ghostdancer. She says it makes them blood siblings, the next best thing to being Native. River has no idea what she is talking about, ignorant of the prejudice you've faced your entire life. Growing up Native has a mystic appeal to her that is unrealistic, but you see her heart and acknowledge the goodness residing there. She means well.

Link keeps reminding River this is a serious matter involving needles and Ghostdancer's life, but you see the smile on his face. He, too, is pleased to be able to help. These people are servants, thinking more of other lives than their own. You are humbled by the genuineness of their love. Urgency requires that River and Link sign waivers absolving the hospital of any possible suits if one or both of them come down with HIV or something worse. Both sign the waivers without hesitation, and a nurse leads them through the double doors where Ghostdancer and a skillful staff await.

Kenny is somewhere off in a business office, offering his own money to pay for whatever services might run above what the veteran's affairs will pay. He wants nothing but the best care for Ghostdancer. His generosity astounds you. Karen is a mass of nerves, twisting her hands and crossing and uncrossing her legs. Isabel sits next to her, both women talking quietly in a corner where lamplight reveals the stress lining their faces. You feel the need for a quiet place to pray.

When you step through the electronic door, a blast of humid air filled with exhaust fumes hits you in the face. A lighted parking lot separates you from the endless array of stars you know are up there somewhere but you cannot see. The low rumble of car engines overrides all other sounds until you hear splashing water from somewhere nearby. You discover a small fountain set in stone with not one living thing around it. This will not do. You head back inside.

Following an instinctive path reaching for the heavens, your feet move fast, nearly running up the stairs. On the third floor, you discover an empty waiting room, dimly lit and quiet.

Standing at yet another window, you look out on a night skyline that is too bright. Glass spreads across a twenty-foot span of curved wall. From your vantage point, you see only a few stars dotting the heavens. A strange glow hovers over the town as if it cannot breathe on its own but is dependent on some kind of behemoth machine. You recognize this machine, similar yet different from that of Baghdad. Different sounds, different smells, but the same sense of being disconnected from Creator—a mass of humanity, tumbled together with deaf ears and tongues too quick to speak.

You pull a cushioned chair from the wall and move it in front of the window. Sitting with your head in your hands you pray, but the cushion feels foreign. You long for earth or wood. Murmuring voices and the distant patter of feet are too distracting. With no one to see, you slip to the floor, pushing off the chair and falling face first across the carpet.

At last you enter Creator's presence, but you find no peace in this place. He lifts you in a vision to the heat of battle. You are mounted on a steed that is wild with fright and swimming through turbulent water. Your love is near, you can smell her sweet scent, but the stink of wolves is cloying and strong. Keeping an eye out for your enemy, you call for Sayla.

An answering gasp and bursting of water capture your attention. Guiding your steed you reach out a hand. "Grab hold, Little Fire!"

Flashing moonlight reveals her alarm-filled eyes. Plunging beneath the torrent, she disappears. The river is a mass of swirling death; the chords of the grave coil around the one you love. You try to guide your steed, but it has caught the stink of wolves and fights your every move. Slitted yellow eyes line the riverbanks. The horse goes mad with terror.

Sayla slips further away, caught in the raging current. Unable to move your mount you cry out to your love, "Remember Creator. Call upon him and be saved."

You turn and face the wolves.

Chapter 78

> Awake every morning full aware
> of Creator Yahweh's unfailing love.
> *Ghostdancer*

Sayla

I KNOW NOW I will die.

Sadness grips my heart. I do not want to die, even to join Grandfather and my parents. I think of Kadai and Gran and know I have much to live for. With a sudden flash of realization, I *know* I am not ready to meet the Creator who gave me breath in the first place. I have wasted my life, thinking fame and stability were what I needed, so I wouldn't be just another Indian.

If what Ghostdancer says is true, Creator made me Native, and HE delights in my songs as I dance before him. What I really need is to be part of Creator's story, to open myself to love, to celebrate my uniqueness. The fact I am Native is part of that. But it is too late. I will die, though I'm not ready to hear the judgment of my life or to be separated from those who offer me love.

I barely notice the water swirling around me. The cuts on my arms and legs mean little. I must soon take a breath that will be my drowning.

"Hang on Little Fire."

Hallucination takes over, probably from lack of air. It sounds as if Ghostdancer is right next to me, speaking in my ear. When I open my eyes, he is there! Smiling at me. "Don't weep for me. I go to the land of the living."

I wonder at his words. Don't weep for him? Shouldn't he be weeping for me?

"Choose Creator, Little Fire. Be the reflection you were meant to be."

Ghostdancer disappears, and deep yearning fills my soul. A reflection? As the moon reflects the sun? But I think he means more than that. *Saayoogalla.* I am to be Creator's apprentice. It is not the jealous woman who has hold of me this night. It is someone bigger and more powerful who will not share my love with another. Creator is more jealous than the jealous woman.

I must die, for I have wronged him, and there is no time to make things right.

Yet before I take my last breath, I cry again, *"Sat'waa Yi?is!"* a weak cry that melts in my heart. But this time my thought is directed upward, to Ghostdancer's Yahwah, the Creator I now know is real, the ONE who made all things and in whom all things dwell. I must choose, and in this moment before I take my last breath, I choose Creator, hoping with all that is within me that the grace of which Ghostdancer often talks is enough.

"Blaydal'knii! Moo ?am ni stinta God above all, I love you very much. Please forgive me."

The river swirls around me in a whirlpool, but I am no longer able to hold back. My mouth opens to gulp the liquid that will fill my lungs. I close my eyes, ready for death. But death does not come to me this night.

Thunder shouts from heaven and strong hands grab my shoulders. They draw me from the river and lift me into windswept skies. I gasp and breathe in a fragrance so sweet it nearly stings my lungs. The sun, blazing and brilliant, shines around me; its warmth reaches to my core. Then a breath, like warm summer wind, washes peace over my soul.

This breath, sweet with the scent of everything wild, blows over me in waves of knowledge. I know as I have never before known. Thoughts, rich with meaning, whirl by in a cataclysmic slideshow of history and invention. They flip through my mind, as if I have been alive from the beginning of time. Music, wild and soaring, meets my ears and I know I am hearing angel song at the moment the earth was born. Beneath it all beats a drum with a strong, sure cadence. A Native drum, precisely in tune with Creator's heartbeat.

At once I am caught up in that heartbeat, floating free in a sea of thought. But all these thoughts are Creator's thoughts of me. Beginning before my birth, when I was formed in the secret place, they stretch beyond measure, vast and precious, into infinity. Every choice I ever made, every choice I might have made, all spread out as if I had walked those myriad paths. Thoughts beyond measure. They outnumber the grains of sand on every shore in existence.

Laughter pours from me in endless waves of joy. The sound of it joins with angel song at creation's beginning so long ago. I see small hands, helping her Gran, making cookies for Grandfather and Kadai. A young woman, bathed in moonlight, dancing her prayers alongside her childhood friend. A grown woman, receiving her first song and giving thanks to her ancestors.

Suddenly, more knowledge fills my mind, and this time I raise my hands to my ears in a useless effort to block it out. Evil. Lies that poured from my mouth not so long ago. Each piece of knowledge a memory long suppressed. Did I really say those words? Did I really think those thoughts? There is nothing good in me. Nothing at all.

Then, when I think I can take no more, when my heart screams in tormented agony, another knowledge replaces the first.

Creator loves me.

This time I sink to my knees, on a ground I know not where, bowing my head and raising my arms, palms up, in submission. This knowledge of love washes over me in pure, cleansing waves, one long caress that satisfies every desire from eternity past. Creator saw me, knew my every word before it was on my tongue—the violence and evil lurking just below the surface, every offensive way and every anxious thought, every wrong choice—he saw it all. Yet, *he loves me.*

I bask in the pure rightness of the moment, suspended beyond time and space.

Chapter 79

> Close your eyes in sleep
> with the sweet name of Yeshua
> trembling from your lips.
> *Ghostdancer*

Kadai

THE WOLVES VANISH as suddenly as they appeared. Several moments pass before you realize someone is calling your name. Someone who has laid a small hand on your back while you remain prostrate on the floor. The sound of her sobs shoots fear into your bones. *Ghostdancer.*

"He's askin' for you." River says.

You jump to your feet and fly down the hallway. The elevator will take too long, so you skim down the stairs three at a time and burst through the door, nearly knocking over an unsuspecting aid.

Link is the first to see you, his expression one of shock when he sees the fire in your eyes. He hurries to the nurse's station, blocking her path as you push through the double doors leading to Ghostdancer's cubicle set aside for those who need special care. Karen stands over Ghostdancer, holding his hands in hers. When she sees you enter, she leans down and kisses him on the forehead, and then turns and leaves the room, pulling the curtains closed behind her. The heavy cloth does not hide the sound of her weeping as she moves down the hallway.

"Come," Ghostdancer says. "Hear what I have to say."

His words are soft but hold much strength for someone who is dying, spoken with the surety of a man in charge. You do not move. Your feet are planted like a taproot that refuses to let go. All you see is a broken body of a man, small and insignificant, when you know a heart of a great warrior beats inside.

Ghostdancer smiles. "Yahweh is not surprised by this moment. My days were numbered before I ever came to be. You know this to be true, Kadai."

The pain in your gut nearly doubles you over.

"Come closer," Ghostdancer says. "I have words to speak to you."

Like a puppet on a string, with no feeling or thought, you obey, dropping into a chair near his bedside.

Ghostdancer's arm comes up, and his warm hand falls on your shoulder. "This heart has been weak for a long time. You know that, Kadai. You know I have wanted to go."

You close your eyes and shake your head, unable to think of the loss of this great mentor and friend. Then you hear his voice rise in song.

"I wanna go where the blind can see—"

You flinch. He is singing a song called "Ghostdance." It is one he claimed for himself years ago, written by a Mohican singer and artist who walks the Jesus Way, fully Native and fully Christian.

Bill Miller's words through Ghostdancer's mouth are too intimate, too real, the pain of Ghostdancer's leaving too great.

"I am a mighty warrior. And I'm finally going home."

As if reading your mind Ghostdancer says, "You are stronger than you think, Kadai."

With great effort you raise your head and look into Ghostdancer's shining eyes. There is no fear in those eyes, no sign the man has walked in great sorrow. Instead you see expectation and a bit of worry that has nothing to do with himself and everything to do with you.

"I name you War *Wach* for the war horse you are."

No, you think, but then yearning for his blessing rises in you, thirsty and strong.

Ghostdancer squeezes your shoulder. "But you must remember the war horse is not the one leading in battle, it is the rider who calls the moves. My being here was called by Yahweh. He is calling me home, and I am more than ready to go. We are only the carriers of his command."

You are afraid his words are true, but still you do not want him to go, this great mentor who has always walked beside you, who led you through those long dark months when you chose the alcohol way.

"I have some words to say to you," Ghostdancer says, "and you must share their meaning with Loretta and Little Fire." He swallows, and you sit a little straighter, as a warrior should.

"Sayla will soon choose the right way and you must help her walk in it. The enemy will try to sift her like wheat."

Your thrumming heart tells you Ghostdancer's words are true, that your battle has just begun.

"Now here are my words I want you to remember." Ghostdancer's eyes pierce into your soul as new energy seems to blossom in his body. "Listen carefully, Kadai, who is now War *Wach*."

You tune out the hospital sounds and lean close. These are the last words of a great elder, speaking Creator's truth.

"If one lives long enough, as this old man has, one will see the shifting shadows that darken Yahweh's smile. You have seen those shadows when you walked the sorrow way. Those shadows are never put there by Yahweh, but by our own evil desires. White men call it sin.

"The white man's word has lost its meaning. It conjures an image of a prankster or mischievous child, but sin is much deeper than that. We forget sin originates from the Beast and the Beast is out to rob, kill, and destroy. We also forget sin is a wall that separates us from Yahweh. To separate one's self from our Creator is to deny the very essence of life. That is the mistake Jacob made in choosing the gift of magic over the Giver Himself. Make sure Loretta knows this, and keep it in your heart and place it in Sayla's."

Ghostdancer lets go of your shoulder and falls back to the bed. "Now I am tired, Kadai who is now War *Wach. Pleya gi.* Be blessed." He sinks into his pillow, exhausted and broken, but then a smile breaks out on his face. "But soon," he says, "I will dance." A chuckle erupts from his throat.

Your eyes close as you picture your mentor, this great warrior of the spiritual realm, dancing before his Creator. And just as suddenly, you are caught up on the other side.

A Native drum beats a tune older than the earth, but then you realize it is not a drum; it is the heartbeat of Creator, thrumming across a vast expanse of sky. The sweet fragrance of something like roses fills the air. You breathe it in and become drunk with joy. Laughter pours from your throat.

Both you and Ghostdancer are dressed in the finest regalia, white and shining like the sun and trimmed with row after row of soft eagle feathers. The bells on your feet match perfectly with Creator's heartbeat as you pump them up and down. You duck and swoop and wave your arms in a dance that is as much a part of you as the blood pumping through your veins. Joyous whoops lift from Ghostdancer's mouth, and then from your own. You spread your arms wide, and in this realm of endless possibilities, you suddenly take flight.

Weightless and free Ghostdancer soars beside you, his eyes full of wonder. The two of you sweep in and out, caught up in the very breath of Creator.

Then your eyes open and you are back in the physical realm, sitting beside a broken old man. The crossing back was as smooth as taking a breath.

Ghostdancer's voice is weak, but his eyes shine like fire. They are not the eyes of a broken old man as he makes his request. "Speak a blessing over me, Kadai who is now War *Wach*. Send me on to the land of the true living. My work in the shadowlands is finished. Like Elisha with Elijah, you will receive a double portion of Creator's spirit."

Long moments pass before you can speak the blessing, but when you do, it is as if Ghostdancer's pronouncement over you comes true. A new boldness floods across your limbs as you stand and sing a blessing over the most important man in your life. The blessing is for his ears alone.

Chapter 80

> My ears had heard of Creator Yahweh
> but now the eyes of my heart
> look on his glorious face!
> *Ghostdancer*

Sayla

I WAKE, LYING FLAT on my back before the shaman's fire, an eagle feather across my chest. Creator is still with me, but the shaman is gone. Clasping my fingers around the feather and closing my eyes, I bask in the feeling of being completely and totally loved.

The most amazing feeling has captured me, more than a feeling really, an awareness of something . . . someone . . . totally other. He is bigger, brighter, more beautiful, more numinous. He is both in me and I am in him, untouchable, yet touching me. The breath of his caress brushes my face. I breathe in the sweet scent of him. I swim in the water of him. I want nothing more than this great mystery made known.

Bathed in his light yet comforted beneath his shadow, calmed by his nearness yet terrified at his presence. More terrified that he will leave, that he will take my breath away, my every reason for existence, my hope, my joy, my tomorrows. Yet even as the thought surfaces, warm assurance replaces all fear, and I discover some of the knowledge flooding over me in the vision is still with me.

I had heard of Creator, but had not known the truth of him. No one could know the full truth. Truth is as much a part of his being as soul and spirit are a part of mine. Truth is this person, this being who transcends every thought.

Pulsating with life, he is the word spoken, quickened in every beating heart. He is wisdom shouting in the street, love weeping in the night, an underlying refrain resonating inside every living soul. I want to sing for the joy of such knowledge, to add my voice to thousands upon thousands of grateful creatures extolling his work through song.

Padding feet move through the forest, and I open my eyes. The wolves are back, but a clap of thunder shouts through the night. "Listen," I whisper. "Creator thunders in marvelous ways. He does great things beyond our understanding."

The words fall from me like a song set to music. Like warm honey over fry bread, the taste of them is sweet and satisfying.

"Listen," I say, louder this time. "This is the voice of the one who laid the earth's foundations and shut the sea behind doors. He gave orders to the morning and journeyed to the springs of the sea. He follows the recesses of the deep and walks in the way of the abode of light."

I fall silent, listening for his voice. The sound of padded feet recedes, moving away from me. Then, out of the silence Creator's voice comes, thundering from heaven like fire, splitting the heavens with lightning and pouring forth a flood of water.

I laugh and open my mouth to catch the fresh taste of rain, letting it slide down my throat, clean and sweet.

Chapter 81

Beware of turning to evil.
Ghostdancer

Jacob Wiseman

THE JEALOUS WOMAN has turned on me. I felt my strength lessening soon after Sayla plunged into the river. She has clouded my vision so I cannot discern the path back to my own body. I run in the form I know best, an innocuous goat that can climb to high places.

I climb now in the heat of the night, running toward the dark side of Sacred Mountain. I must gather new power before brother moon finds its way across the sky.

Worry does not plague me. This has happened before. But never have I been so close to the mountain in order to recharge. This battle is still mine. Ghostdancer's strength is lessening, and he has not seen the true nature behind his injuries. His need is not for healing done by human hands, but no one recognizes this fact. And so he will die without using that precious power available. It is his own fault for turning his back on so many of our traditions.

My one worry is regarding whatever happened to Sayla this night. She has received power of which my spirit guide failed to warn me. There is still time to grab her back, but I must act with expediency before she gains strength to fight the siren song.

I crown the top of Sacred Mountain with the wolves howling behind me. I drop to the other side into darkness and sit in silence waiting for strength to return.

Chapter 82

*Creator Yahweh's throne was established long ago;
HE is from all eternity.*
Ghostdancer

Loretta
August 31, 2014
Sunday morning

GHOSTDANCER'S VOICE was barely more than a whisper as he gave Loretta instructions over the phone. The call had come at three in the morning and had woken her from a deep sleep. He kept her so busy writing things down that she didn't have much time to think about the fact he was dying. By the time they got around to saying "good-bye," his imminent death didn't seem real. But it was real enough for Loretta to drop to her knees and remain that way until more word came.

The second call came at seven, after the sun had just risen over Sacred Mountain. It seemed fitting Ghostdancer's spirit slipped into a coma with the rising sun, and what a glorious rising it was! Golden light poured over Sacred Mountain, washing the treetops and sweeping across open fields. Horses and antelope all stopped and looked upward. A light breeze caressed Loretta's face as she sat upon a blanket in the front yard and watched.

She believed that even in the coma, Ghostdancer was already with his beloved Yahweh, dancing and singing his prayers as never before. A bit of jealousy struck Loretta. She would love to be dancing like a young girl again, but her time would come.

She thought about Sayla. How would the poor girl take this news of Ghostdancer's imminent death? The doctors held little hope for his survival. Sayla had returned home changed last night, leaving the shaman behind and clinging to new faith in Creator. The change in Sayla was like the difference between a fog shrouded in funereal fog and the morning sunrise after wind has swept the skies clean. But would her faith remain in the face of more sorrow?

Ghostdancer's last words hit her hard in the stomach. "You have everything you need *sawalineeas*. Yahweh has equipped you."

She struggled to rise from the hard ground, not feeling equipped for much of anything other than a rocking chair. She returned to the porch where another blank canvas awaited. It seemed fitting to start a painting in Ghostdancer's honor, so she picked up a wide brush and slapped strokes of blue and yellow across the white surface. She was painting another lion . . . *Warrior King* . . . the One who breaks back through the veil of death and fights our battles for us.

A song drifted from the open window of the living room where Sayla played the piano one of Charlie's Irish relatives had brought out west in a horse-drawn wagon. Loretta thought of how shocked the woman would be to discover Native blood in her offspring. Charlie had shown Loretta the journals that talked of savages. That was the very word his grandmother had used, *savages*.

If truth were told, Loretta suspected a savage lived in every human heart. Given the right conditions, that savage could jump to the front in a moment's time. Hadn't history proved that to be true? She had lived through the assassination of President Kennedy; she had shook hands with him when he had visited the Rogue Valley on his campaign trail. A white man had taken his life. Another white man had taken the life of Martin Luther King Jr. not many years after. And then an Arab man had sent a bullet through the heart of Bobbie Kennedy.

Savages.

And what about crimes of passion or our feelings regarding such crimes? How often had Loretta thought she would have done the same thing given the same situation?

Hence the saying, ". . . until you've walked a mile in my moccasins . . ."

Loretta always felt as if she could solve the world's problems while she was painting. Secret thoughts she would never tell a soul waxed eloquent in the chambers of her mind. No, she decided, no one knew what they would do under any given circumstance until they were faced with it. They could talk lofty and large about how they "would never." But "never" often presented itself at the most surprising times.

Stepping back to inspect the painting, Loretta knew all of her philosophizing was just buying time before she would have to tell Sayla the news of Ghostdancer's coma and expected death. Yet, as she viewed the painting, she felt Ghostdancer's approval. "Warrior King" was the one they all needed. Creator, Jesus, Yeshua—Yahweh as Ghostdancer called him—returning to make all things right. That day would come and Loretta hoped it would be soon.

Soon enough for this old woman, she thought. It wouldn't be long before she would see her Creator face-to-face.

Loretta would dedicate this painting to Ghostdancer during Friday's concert. It was the only time they could honor him, since he insisted on no ceremony after his death. So they would honor him while he was still alive and they would pray to Creator for complete healing this side of glory. Kadai was told that in the event of Ghostdancer's death, he was to take his ashes up *Cheelasqui* Mountain and let the wind carry them across the land.

Applying the initials of her signature to the canvas, she called the painting done. After untwisting the screws that held it to the easel, she removed her latest lion and carried it toward the barn. There she would let it dry in the loft until her chosen time of unveiling. It was easy to hide things in the barn loft because it was full of old trunks and an enormous collection of regalia from several generations of Whitewaters. Red Dog rose from his sleeping spot in the sun and followed her.

As soon as Loretta neared the barn Red Dog commenced barking. Goosebumps crawled up and down her arms when Red Dog refused to enter the barn with her. She thought she caught a faint whiff of skunk and hoped that was what had Red Dog in such a dither. Climbing the ladder leading to the loft, she took care with each step. All they needed was for one more person to end up in the hospital.

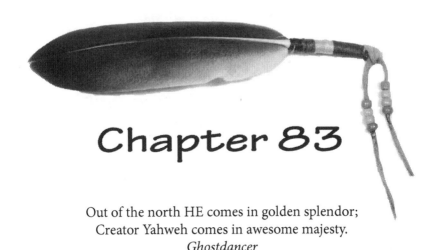

Chapter 83

*Out of the north HE comes in golden splendor;
Creator Yahweh comes in awesome majesty.*
Ghostdancer

Sayla

I CAN'T REMEMBER having so much fun writing songs. One after another the words fall from my mouth and the tunes from my fingers. One strange thing about the morning is that I am still seeing colors; each note drifting up in a separate emblem and hue. A's are red diamonds, C's yellow triangles; B's float up in circles the color of overripe peaches. They rise strong and fade in puffs, floating through the air like bubbles. I try not to think about what might be causing them. I feel no other effects of having been drugged. Perhaps the colors are another of Creator's gifts.

It is still difficult for me to believe I accepted the shaman's drugs so easily. Not just peyote, but also the second cup of whatever strange potion he concocted. I, who was determined never to touch the stuff, accepted it with little coercion.

The nightmare of my body being tossed by the raging river is still a frightening sensation, but it is far surpassed by the memory of meeting Creator. My gratefulness flows through the piano keys.

It will take the rest of my life to describe the ecstasy of knowing HIS love.

Creator is my high tower, to him will I run. He is a fortress tall and strong. Creator is a solid rock on which my feet can stand. And when my world is shaking. I run to him.

I know something about shaking, trembling worlds. I have tasted the bile of deep loss and walked the sorrow way. But now I also know of the sure existence of a strong high tower that offers shelter, and for the first time since the accident, I can think of the death of my parents and grandfather. Instead of seeing their broken bodies scattered across the desert, I picture them with beautiful bodies that will never again be broken, dancing with Creator in a place called Heaven that isn't so very far away, an unseen place as far as my human eyes are concerned, but more real and lasting than the world in which I currently live. Spiritual worlds, I have discovered, are as close as a breath and easily crossed given the right circumstances.

Creator is a shelter from the storm. He is a shade from the heat. Creator is a river that will never run dry. I drink and am completely satisfied.

When was the last time I could say I was satisfied?

Writing new songs satisfied for a brief time, but expectations of false power soon drove me to the shaman. I still wonder about the Shadow Warrior, whether or not he was truly from the evil one, but I am convinced his power, as great as it is, cannot satisfy my deepest longings as Creator can.

When my world is shaking, I know I've lost my way. I run to him and always find him near.

Creator lives and rules in all worlds and his Holy Spirit is able to touch and know every creature at each and every moment. Spirit is not limited to time and space. Creator alone knows my frame. Before I uttered one word, He knew it completely. How can I not trust him?

He spreads his wings about me, and shields me in his hands. He leads me into promised lands.

The truth of the words make me want to run out the door and dance beneath the heavens until he appears once more. Desire is strong in my soul. Then suddenly, my fingers stop playing.

Something is wrong.

Chapter 84

*When Creator Yahweh's voice resounds
HE holds nothing back.*
Ghostdancer

Loretta

LORRETTA HAD JUST CLIMBED off the ladder and taken no more than two steps when an armful of hay caught her full in the face. The painting flew into the air, landing on the floor below the ladder behind her. To keep from tumbling backward after it, she pushed hard ahead, grabbing at whatever was there. Her hands found skin, and she was startled to look up into the face of her neighbor's son, James. The two of them went down on the soft hay of the loft.

"*Yaks dwa!* What are you doing here?"

Instead of answering, James shoved Loretta to the side and jumped to his feet. His dark eyes were full of menace as he stood over her. He had the crazed look of a treed cougar.

Loretta froze, sending up silent prayers to Jesus Yeshua, the best thing to do when faced with a frightened predator.

She thought of her self-defense training taken so long ago. What was it? Twenty years? Thirty? Three moves and then three more. She couldn't remember six moves, but she did remember being thrown to the floor during the last class. The instructor had dressed in a fully padded suit with a face guard. While the students sparred with one another, he attacked each of them in turn when they least expected it.

Loretta's biggest fear was realized when she ended up on the floor. With her self-defense teacher standing over her she had not panicked, and she didn't panic now.

James pulled out a knife and took a step forward.

Remaining on her back, knees bent, Loretta kept him in full view. When he lunged, she caught his chest with the bottoms of her feet and used her knees like a spring. She caught the look of complete surprise in his wide eyes as she thrust her legs upward. James went flying over the edge of the loft landing, but what she didn't expect is that he would pull her over with him. James landed with a hard thud on the floor one story below and Loretta landed on top of him. The jolt took her breath away. Her first thought was that she might join Ghostdancer in that great dance in the sky. The next moment she found her fingers clinging to fur and her eyes staring into the yellow eyes of a wolf. Her world went black.

Chapter 85

Creator Yahweh reigns in majesty.
He is the Great Chief and Captain of our souls!
Ghostdancer

Sayla

I PUSH BACK the piano bench and rise. Searching through the house, I find no sign of Gran, so I move to the porch. There I discover the source of my unease. Red Dog is out by the barn, barking up a storm. My head feels light as I move across the porch and scatter a flock of turkeys. Red Dog is running in circles. He doesn't even stop to greet me when I near the barn, but his abrupt silence when I reach him is more eerie than the noise before.

Alert, I stop and tune to the slightest change in sound. Clucking chickens, murmuring turkeys, the mooing of cows all seem normal, but something sends a chill across my shoulders. Gran is in trouble, I know it by the fear that grips my heart and steals Red Dog's tongue. He is laying on the ground next to me, his head on his front paws and his ears turned back.

I take a step forward.

Red Dog whimpers.

Straining my eyes to search the shadows, I look for something Red Dog can see that I cannot. The smell hits me first, strong and feral like rotting meat, and then I begin to make out the shape of a four-footed animal. When slanted yellow eyes open and stare at me, I nearly scream.

The wolf of my nightmares stands before me as real as the horses that graze in the meadow behind. It opens its mouth in a bloody snarl.

The purr of Link's Lexus meets my ears, but I force myself not to turn around. Keeping my eyes on the wolf, my feet apart, knees slightly bent, I brace myself for its charge. Wolves never travel alone in my dreams, but I see no sign of companions. Blood drips down its chin and colors its fur a dark red.

My breath stops. *Gran.*

The Lexus squeals to a stop behind me and I hear thundering hooves heading my way.

Be still.

I feel Creator's strength though I am standing on trembling legs. Still keeping my eyes on the wolf, I see Link in my peripheral vision. He bursts from the driver's seat, gun drawn and ready to fire. The wolf snarls and slinks to the right, keeping the fence between itself and Link. Then the sound of pounding hooves captures my full attention. I turn my head in time to see War Paint barreling across the road in front of the Lexus. Kadai grabs for the rope that hangs from the stallion's neck. With one smooth move I have seen him do a thousand times before, he swings to the horse's back and drives War Paint toward the wolf.

The wolf runs, darting beneath the rungs of the corral and nearly straight into Link. A shot rings out, and the wolf yelps but keeps moving. Kadai turns War Paint in the tightest circle I've ever seen, or perhaps it is War Paint turning Kadai, for the two have melded so entirely that one mind is the same as the other. War Paint wears no bridle or bit, he simply reads his master's heart. I turn and run into the darkened barn.

A crumpled form lies on the ground. "Gran!"

Link is right behind me

"No!" I cry.

Link pulls me to his chest and places himself between me and the bloody mess on the ground. "It's not your Gran."

Gran's voice drifts from the far corner. "I'm okay Sayla."

My heart melts with relief, even though Gran's shaky voice belies her words. I push Link away and meet Gran as she crawls from behind a stack of hay bales. We grab each other in a firm hug and look at the body on the ground. The wolf's fur, once shiny and black is now drenched in blood, its yellow eyes open and sightless, forever frozen in terror. Gran sinks to the ground in a faint. A scream leaves my mouth as I try to break her fall.

She is covered in blood.

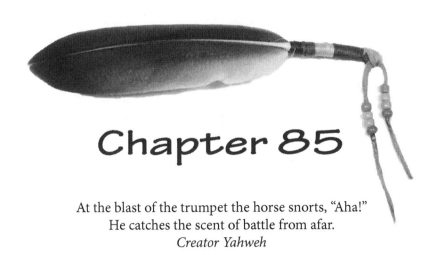

Chapter 85

At the blast of the trumpet the horse snorts, "Aha!"
He catches the scent of battle from afar.
Creator Yahweh

Kadai

WAR PAINT STORMS across the meadow forever keeping the wounded wolf in his sight. His mind and yours are one, but he cannot run through brush that the wolf can easily slink beneath. Skirting the thick growth you wait on the other side, watching to see where the wolf will reappear. It is no surprise the mad animal is headed to the dark side of Sacred Mountain.

There! It darts off before you can catch him. You spur your mount ahead feeling the mixture of excitement and dread.

You cannot deny the thrill of the wild horse responding to your will; it is the first he has done so. His withers quicken to your slightest move. The wind on your face is another pleasure for which you are thankful; you could have so easily been in a jail cell instead of running free with this magnificent horse. If it weren't for the dread of what you will discover and a broken heart over Ghostdancer being in a coma, you could bask in the thrill.

When the wolf crosses the top of *Cheelaqsdi* and heads down the dark side, you slow. War Paint's ears perk, as do yours. If the wolf's companions are waiting for an opportune moment, this dark side is where they will attack. The patch of brush ahead where the wolf has disappeared is thick and dark. Peering into its depths, you see movement and are not surprised to find yellow eyes staring back. A low growl rumbles across the mountain. Then a black shape rises from the earth, flapping and squawking. An enormous raven flies straight for you.

War Paint rears. If it weren't for the rope still tied around his neck you would be on the ground, but your purchase on his back and your gripping fingers hold true. He drops to his feet, panting deep breaths, his thrumming heart matching yours.

You turn and watch the raven's flight. It cuts a crooked path through the sky and dips and flaps as if gravity's pull is too strong. You continue to watch until it turns into a speck in heaven's vast expanse and disappears. Too late you realize your mistake in watching the raven. A hoard of wolves now completely surrounds you. War Paint gives a mighty roar and bolts, dropping you to the ground in a heap. Without even a second of warning, you are caught up to the shadowlands in the midst of heavy battle.

As weak as Delilah's Samson without his hair, you crawl through thick ooze that pulls you down. A hundred hands clutch at your body, clawing, grasping, tearing flesh. Your closed eyes struggle to open but something holds them tight, like pennies of death taping your eyelids shut. Yet, still you fight to move forward to reach the one you love. Though you struggle to shout a warning, your voice remains mute. The stink of wolves hungry for blood fills your lungs till you nearly pass out from the stench. Onward you crawl, climbing ever upward, reaching for another handhold toward your love. Just one more breath and you will reach her, one more handhold to save her life. But one enemy becomes two and two becomes twenty and still she is far away, lost in a place where you cannot touch her.

Where is the double portion of Creator's Spirit Ghostdancer promised? Despair is your sister, sadness your brother, hopeless the parents who bore you. They scream in your ears and taunt you with jibes, some honest and some lies, but none with the scent of life.

Onward you crawl till your palms are raw, torn, and scarred from exertion. How could these hands caress the one you love; their ugliness appalls you. Misery beckons, depression is a smothering blanket; annihilation reaches out long arms. *You have no right; she has chosen another.* The voices continue to taunt and tempt you to slide back to the ooze from which you were born.

Upward you claw with the faintest of breath and the weakest of feeble knees. *You cannot make it, man born of flesh, and even if you do, she will not have you. There is nothing beautiful in you.* Darkness and death are twin companions chained to your wrists and legs.

Chapter 87

> Proclaim the love of Creator Yahweh every morning
> and praise his faithfulness when the stars
> track their way across the heavens.
> *Ghostdancer*

Sayla

RIVER AND ISABEL watch me like a couple of hawks as they prepare a small lunch of tea and sandwiches. They are worried, because they know my loss is more than I can bear. The men are busy cleaning the barn, promising it will be as good as new. I don't even ask what they plan to do with the wolf's body.

I cannot believe Ghostdancer is in a coma. How can that be? River explained that just before dropping into the coma, Ghostdancer had waved his arm and told everyone to return to Sacred Mountain Ranch where they could do some good. They had all obeyed, except for Karen.

My thoughts turn to Kadai who still hasn't returned after taking off after the wolf. "Be with him, Creator," I whisper. And then I think of Gran who is caught in a deep sleep and I worry she will die, though River tells me Gran will be okay.

River puts a hand on my arm as I sit at the table. "She's just in shock. She'll come out of it. None of that blood was hers."

Remembering the blood makes my teeth grind. The smell of it was utterly nauseating and there was so much of it. I force myself to think of something else.

"I don't understand about Ghostdancer," I say. "Why would Creator take him?"

River pulls out a chair and sits next to me. "Remember when Kadai saw God in the hospital?"

"How can I forget?"

"Right." River smiles, her whole face showing delight. "He saw God!"

"Yeah." I say again. "So?'

"So?" River pulls back and examines me. "He didn't want to come back. Remember?"

And suddenly I do remember, and I also remember the thought was not comforting. But now, I know a bit more about Creator and the thought brings a little comfort. In fact, the more I think about Ghostdancer and Grandfather and my parents dancing together with no worries or pain or sickness, I feel a bit jealous. "So, why don't we all go right now?" I ask.

River's laughter pours over the kitchen.

Isabel stops buttering the bread. "Why do you laugh, River?" She points the knife at me. "I agree with Sayla. If it's so wonderful up there, then why don't we all just go, be done with it here. That doesn't seem like any way to live."

River stands and takes the knife from Isabel. "God knows the exact number of our days." She waves the knife in the air, making her point. "We have a real purpose in this world. It's my goal when I reach heaven I'll hear the words, 'Well done, good and faithful servant.' I wanna be known as a woman who did everythin' her Lord wanted her to do."

Isabel snatches the knife back from River and slaps butter on another slice of bread. "So who's to say when the job is finished?"

"God of course," River says. "I ain't claimin' to know everythin'. But I do know Ghostdancer is ready to go and when he does he ain't gonna be yearnin' for no return trip. Of that I can assure you." She holds out her arm for us to see the Band-Aid that's still in place. "And I outta know."

We stare at her arm.

"I'm now Ghostdancer's blood sister."

I laugh, but the laughter catches in my throat. My world is becoming a lonely place and getting lonelier by the minute. I don't know where Kadai has ended up, and I can't go looking for him with Gran still in shock.

River sits back down and puts her hands on my shoulders. "Am I Native enough now?" she whispers. "Can you accept my friendship?"

I pull back, but not too far. I want her to see the sincerity in my eyes. "River," I say. "Please. Accept my apology. I always thought it was the whites who didn't accept us Natives, but here I've been pulling from you simply because of your skin color. What a silly girl I am. Of course, I accept you as my *sawalineeas*.

River's eyes dance with delight. "Good. Then let's finish makin' our meal."

River puts the water on to boil while I pull out the basket of tea. Isabel opens the cupboard and brings out a bag of Stevia. "That's not necessary," I say. "The sugar bowl is full of Stevia."

"Sugar bowl?" River looks at me over the top of her granny glasses. She looks absolutely adorable in them, but insists on only wearing them when she truly wants to see something. Says the world is a much better place most of the time when it's all blurry like an abstract painting.

"Top cupboard on the right," I say.

"Ah ha!"

I jump at River's exclamation and drop the basket, scattering little bags of tea to the floor. I let them lay there. "What?"

River and Isabel exchange looks, then both women start talking at once.

"We think—"

"Karen thinks—"

They stop, then Isabel waves for River to take the lead while River does the same to her. My patience is wearing thin. "In case neither of you have considered, this has been a trying day."

"Drugs." Says River.

My mouth falls open.

"Karen was seeing strange colors," says Isabel.

"Me too," says River, "but not nearly bad as Karen. She was out of it most of the way to Rogue Valley."

I start to say something but Isabel interrupts.

"First we thought it was the tea, but that didn't make sense, because I drank the tea but never had any symptoms. You and Karen were the only ones who used Stevia."

I stare at the bag.

"The bowl," says River. "That's how I figured it out. I used your spoon to remove my teabag. That's also why my reaction was small, just enough to see pretty pictures, might even try to paint 'em someday." She gives a little giggle. "I'm hopin' it's peyote. Don't all Natives use peyote?"

Still unable to speak, I shake my head and pick up the sugar bowl. I remove the lid and sniff. Finally the words come. "Peyote smells terrible. This has no smell."

River licks her finger and sticks it in the bowl. When she puts her finger to her tongue, her eyes widen. "Mescaline."

I think of how James brought me sugared tea the morning he visited with his mother, the same morning I saw the wolf. Something else occurs to me.

"Moriah," I say.

"What?" River sets the basket of tea on the counter.

"Moriah filled the sugar bowl."

The three of us stare at each other. It's a horrible thought. Could one's sister do such a thing?

Chapter 88

*The righteous will grow
like mighty trees planted in sacred soil.
Ghostdancer*

**Sayla
September 1, 2014
Monday morning**

THE SHADOWS BEGIN SHIFTING somewhere after midnight. Though I merely guess the time, it seems fitting, the hour of fading fairy-tale princesses and lost glass slippers, everything beautiful falling apart. Everyone is asleep but me, and Kadai has not returned. I'm worried sick about him, not to mention that my own sister may be a murderer. I've been in the barn for a while now, brushing Duchess in the glow of lamplight and hoping to see Kadai return safe and sound. When Duchess' fur is as soft as goose down, I close her stall and sit on an old milk stool where I try to figure out Moriah's goal.

It's clear Moriah is the shaman's jealous *saayoogalla*. She will not stop until she alone holds his full admiration. Though I chose to walk away from the shaman, he will not easily let me go. But something else is at stake here as well, and that is what eludes me. Moriah has always been about money. She desires position and fame above all else and those things require money, but for the life of me I can't think of anything Gran or I own that she would want. Sure. Sacred Mountain Ranch would bring a good chunk of change, but it's been in the Whitewater family for so long that I doubt she would be able to talk the Tribal Council into letting her sell it, and she would have to get rid of Gran and me in the process.

Before I can come up with a satisfying answer, I notice the shifting shadows and sit up in full alert.

"Saaaaaaaaylaaaaaaaaaaaaa."

This is the moment I have been dreading. Is Creator's power truly enough to keep me from succumbing to the siren song? Duchess nickers, but it is a far-a-way sound, and I feel myself sinking into the shadowlands.

"No!" I shout.

Immediately, I'm back in the barn, leaving the shadowlands before the sirens can sink their claws in me, but the Shadow Warrior still stands in lamplight, more beautiful than ever. His eyes bore into my soul, inviting me to dive into their depths. I blink. And in that blink I catch a glimpse of a creature so grotesque it makes me gasp. The vision leaves so fast I think I must have imagined it.

"Saaaaaaaaylaaaaaaaaaaaaa."

A strange wind blows through the Shadow Warrior's flowing hair. Perhaps I only imagined the grotesque creature. But when the wind hits my face, it carries the smell of sulfur. I nearly gag at the stink of it. Doubling over, I hold my stomach while staring at the Shadow Warrior's feet. Ugly cloven goat's feet stand beneath all that colorful finery.

I want to run but, instead, I straighten, and though my voice is weak, I speak with authority. "You no longer have a hold on me."

"Saaaaaaaaylaaaaaaaaaaaaa."

Shivers run up and down my legs with familiar longing. My voice comes out shaky. "I-I do not belong to you."

A beautiful glow radiates from the Shadow Warrior as he reaches out to me, and the music of his hornpipes nearly sends me into a trance. But then I look back down at those cloven feet. The smell of burning animal hair meets my nostrils as I stare at the blackened hooves. I remember the goat tracks that caused Grandfather's and my parent's deaths, and I remember the goat tracks by River's burned van.

Louder now, I say, "I belong to Jesus Yeshua, the Creator of all things seen and unseen."

"Saaaaaaaaylaaaaaaaaaaaaaa."

Weakness overtakes my knees and I nearly stumble to the floor. Catching myself, I straighten and stand, shouting two words, "Be gone!"

Flames climb the warrior's regalia.

"Be gone in the name of Christ!"

Not seeming to notice the flames, the Shadow Warrior calls my name. "Saaaaaaaaylaaaaaaaaaaaaaa."

For a moment, I waver, as the Shadow Warrior's hand reaches out for me. I nearly reach back. "Leave" I whisper. "I belong to Creator Yeshua."

A horrible scream rips through the night. Once again, the grotesque creature replaces the beautiful warrior. All air leaves my lungs as I watch the creature's face melt in great globs of rotting flesh. In a puff of nauseating smoke, it finally disappears.

I stand shaking in lantern light, feeling strong in spite of my physical weakness. Creator has given me both the knowledge to see the ugly reality behind the appearance of beauty and the power to withstand the evil one. The battle was Creator's all along. My Shadow Warrior was nothing more than a demon conjured up by the Shaman. I suspect the wolves were conjured up as well, because no body of a wolf lies on the barn floor now. No blood. Nothing. The Shaman's mistake was in thinking he could control the demon without it controlling him. But I suspect something else is going on here as well. James and Moriah have probably been doing some conjuring of their own. Good little apprentices that they are. I shudder to think how close I came to joining them.

Duchess nickers, and a noise in the loft grabs my attention. Probably a mouse or some other night critter, but something compels me to investigate. When I reach the top rung, a hand grabs mine and pulls me forward.

A yelp leaves my lips, but the hand does not let go.

"Tell me where they are."

My sister's grip is surprisingly strong. I struggle to wrench away, but she holds fast. Her nails draw blood in the soft flesh of my arm.

"I have no idea what you're talking about," I say truthfully.

Her slap hits me hard in the face. "Don't play stupid with me."

"Okay." I wipe blood from my mouth. "Let me go and I'll take you to them."

She laughs, throwing her head back but not loosening her grip. "You never were good at lying Sayla. Tell me where the journals are."

I try to think of some reason why she would be interested in the journals. Most are impossible to read, being mere symbols on leather.

"Last I saw the journals," I say, "they were beneath my mattress." Of course, I don't say anything about Gran removing them to who knows where.

Her nails dig into my wrists. "I checked every part of your room, and I saw no sign of them." Her voice is a hiss.

I'm not sure which surprises me more, that she searched my room or that she is so angry about the journals being gone. "Why—" I start, but her breath washes over my face with the stink of liquor.

"You're no better than our parents," she says. Then she spits in my face.

I reel at both the spit and the vehemence of her words. Hate fills every syllable. "Moriah," I say, but she is inconsolable.

"Grandfather was just as bad," she says. "He would never tell me what he did with the journal that told of the gold story."

"Gold story? Surely you don't believe that old tale?"

She turns fiery eyes on me. "It's not an old tale, Sayla. I've seen some of the gold."

My mouth drops open and, for a moment, I forget the danger I'm in. The story has been told for years of three Indians who took over a dead prospector's claim somewhere on the other side of Sacred Mountain and mined a fortune in gold. Then the prospectors hid the gold, and the only time anyone ever saw any sign of it was when one of the three culprits ventured to the other side of the Cascades and tried to buy something in the town of Prospect. All three died mysterious deaths and that was the end of the story . . . or . . . at least I thought it was the end. Is it possible the story is true and that one of my relatives knew the hiding place? Worse yet, is Moriah capable of murder?

I think of the broken fan belt and my heart plummets. "What does the shaman have to gain with gold?"

"Hmmph. Jacob could care less about gold. He just wants the right to Sacred Mountain. Wants you off the land."

Sickness grabs my stomach. Could Moriah and the shaman have been behind the deaths of my parents and Grandfather? To keep myself from erupting into a fit of anger, and remembering that Gran says we're supposed to love our enemies, I whisper, "Creator's love endures forever."

Rage colors Moriah's face.

I speak the words again, a tiny bit louder. "Creator Yeshua's love endures forever."

Moriah screams in agony, pulling her hand from mine.

"His love endures forever," I say as calm and clear as if I'm talking to Kadai on a moonlit night.

Moriah slaps me hard across the face and I fall to the floor. After I struggle to my feet, I stare in shock. In place of my sister, a snarling wolf now stands before me, trembling in its rage.

"No matter how far you go," I begin Ghostdancer's words. "Whether the sun hangs high in the sky or deep blackness hides the light—"

A howl rips through the night.

"No matter who you hurt, or who has been hurt because of you—"

The wolf crouches, but I feel no fear. "Not one drop of Creator Yeshua's blood will ever be lessened."

Eyes wild with fury, the wolf springs.

Chapter 89

*Hope in Yeshua
and walk the Jesus Way.
Ghostdancer*

Sayla

THE IMPACT NEVER COMES. The wolf appears to leap right through me as harmless and empty as a breath of air. I feel a tingling of energy and nothing more. Tongues of flame eat at the wolf's fur as it disappears through the barn doors. Did Moriah actually turn into a wolf? Or was the wolf a demon in disguise as Moriah, conjured by the Shaman or Moriah herself? I don't have long to think about it.

Immediately, I am transported to the open meadow below Sacred Mountain, naked and bloodied as if I have fought a thousand battles. A full moon stands in a cloudless sky bathing my battered skin in light, but I feel no shame, as I am being reborn. The breath of Creator falls over me in cleansing waves. I bask in the healing flow, holding my arms open for more. When I am at last shining and clean, I stand. A soft Native blanket falls over me, clothing my nakedness and warming my soul, healing every broken part.

I pull the blanket close and smell the sweet scent of wild roses; then I notice two nighthawks flying across an open sky—nighthawks being a symbol of healing. Love fills my heart till I am afraid I will burst at the strength of it. I fall to my face in reverence.

"*Child,*" a voice whispers, "*receive the joy I have for you.*"

I am immediately caught up to the heavens where I am completely known and where I know everything. Thoughts too deep, too wonderful, swirl through my brain, a movie spinning at impossible speeds, with me capturing every nuance. Beauty, truth, love—all with new definitions and countless examples. Exquisite aromas, delectable tastes, unbelievable colors, mountain vistas, desert sand, cascading waterfalls, roaring oceans—until it all comes together in joyous laughter so strong it threatens to undo me. When I think I can take no more, a warm mantle of peace covers me, and I'm back in the meadow still clothed with the nighthawk robe.

I open my eyes to see Kadai's bowed head. The most exquisite beauty paints his features with peace. How could I have not known till now that I love him?

War Paint stands behind him, his proud head bowed in obedience. He is no longer a wild, bucking bronco. Perhaps we have all been tamed on this moonlit night. Creator's grace is enough for both human and beast.

I touch Kadai's hand, and he looks at me, but before we can say a word an eagle feather floats between us, glowing white and carrying the scent of sage and cedar. When it brushes against the fingers of my open palm, I see Grandfather's beading. I know Creator has given this gift, that he has given me all the eagle feathers. He has been here through the worst of my pain, through every confused moment, through the times I questioned truth, through all my mistakes and unbelief.

I close my fingers around the feather.

Five eagle feathers now—five for the Hebrew number of Creator's grace.

In this moment I know life for the first time.

For life is not measured by the breaths we breathe while attempting to satisfy our own desires. Neither is it measured by the number of riches or fame we attain. Life is measured by the unexpected moments when we are aware of Creator's presence, when magic and miracles meet to take our breath away. This is the true essence of life.

Hands joined together, Kadai and I follow a path of moonlight back to the house.

There will be difficult days ahead; my questions may not all be answered, but my faith is now based on real evidence instead of relying on someone else's belief. I know Creator is with me at all times, even in the darkest places.

Beside me, Kadai begins to sing, his voice a caress that warms my soul.

"The heavens declare the glory of Creator, day after day they pour forth speech. There is no tongue or language where their voice is not heard."

As if in answer, one clap of thunder shouts through the cloudless sky.

Chapter 90

The righteous will bear fruit in old age.
Ghostdancer

Loretta
September 5, 2014
Friday evening, Sayla's concert

STANDING WITH AN ARM over River's shoulders, Loretta listened to Sayla sing and watched Kadai dance. Both did so with passion, their faces alight with joy though both had known deep sorrow and still swam in rushing waters of pain.

They had all endured a sad week of dark discovery and loss. It was painful to learn that Jacob was probably the cause of the crash that took their loved ones. The plan was for Moriah to take over Sacred Mountain Ranch so Jacob could own *Cheelaqsdi* Mountain, as if anyone could own the sacred mountain. White people owned mountains, not Natives. Jacob and James were both missing—the cause of many rumors she was sure would last for many years.

At first, she was convinced the wolf that died in the barn was James. That's why she had fallen into a coma. But lately she was more inclined to believe Sayla was right in thinking the same demon that appeared as a wolf had also appeared as James. Truth was, James was probably off somewhere licking his wounds, and Loretta doubted he would be doing that as a wolf.

That Moriah was culpable in Jacob's act was the most painful of discoveries, but Loretta shouldn't have been surprised. After all, the very first murder in the Bible was between the world's first siblings. She shook her head and mumbled, "Why do we think we're any different?"

"What did you say?" River asked.

Loretta squeezed River's shoulder and removed her arm. "Just mumbling."

The answer seemed to satisfy River, so Loretta turned back to watch Kadai. He was absolutely mesmerizing in his regalia. She felt hypnotized as she watched him swirl and spin while her thoughts returned to the events of the last few days.

It was still difficult for her to think of how far Moriah had fallen. Money was certainly the root of all evil in the girl's case. She was now home, denying any wrongdoing, but Loretta knew the girl would live with many painful accusations in the dark recesses of her own mind. Loretta hoped one day Moriah would repent and come to belief, otherwise she faced the worst judgment—the second death—the judgment of Creator. But Loretta knew Moriah would no longer bother Sayla, because Loretta had told her the journal was ruined.

To prove her point, she had handed over the ruined journal, watching Moriah's expression change from disbelief to rage. It didn't even bother Loretta that she had told a lie of omission by not informing Moriah she had copied every page of the journal and given it to Ghostdancer before ruining the original. Now, with Ghostdancer in a coma, it was unlikely any of them would ever find the journals.

Looking at the thousands of people attending the concert, Loretta was struggling with her own disbelief. She had never dreamed so many would come. Her heart was alight with joy and pride. Sayla's voice rang across the valley proclaiming the great love of Creator.

Creator is my high tower. To him will I run. He is a fortress tall and strong.

Kadai swirled in a mass of color, lost in the worship of Creator, the ONE he adored. Gran's brothers Henry and Cobby were dancing beside him. All, including Sayla, had finally come out of grief through Creator's magic—the miracle of changed lives.

Rivers's life was certainly changed. She had agreed to stay on with Loretta, helping with the horses and other chores between shifts at the hospital. Loretta was amazed at how the girl had poured out her grief and then risen as though from ashes to start again.

Link seemed amazed as well and appeared to have more than a cursory eye on the young woman. Perhaps River and Link could get Kenny more excited about Sayla's new choice in songs. Sayla now believed Creator had given her all the songs through the entire Shadow Warrior ordeal and, with a few tweaks; she turned them all back toward praise of her Maker. Said she didn't care so much about becoming famous; she had to sing what was on her heart. But from the looks of tonight's crowd, what was on her heart was also a crowd pleaser.

Kenny must have caught on to that fact, because Red Dog followed at his feet as the agent passed out cigars and pointed at Sayla. He was as proud as a father with his firstborn child and was giving out gifts in the Native way. Who would have thought? Rumors had it that he wanted to move to Sacred Mountain Ranch and help Kadai run it for Loretta. He was already talking about ways to make money and planning to bring back the rodeo and Indian relay races. Loretta wasn't sure what to think about it all.

Kenny was also funding an art event to help Isabel and Amnesty International. He had offered River a full-time job in the capacity of art director, and she was considering accepting it. Meanwhile, Link had surprised them all by offering Amnesty International his services free and buying a small motor home for River. Loretta suspected the lawyer didn't want to let the energetic girl roam too far from his sight. River already had plans to paint the motor home with colorful pictures. She had already started with a beautiful painting of *Cheelaqsdi* at sunrise.

Looking down at River, Loretta understood why Link didn't want to let the girl out of his sight. Ghostdancer hadn't wanted to let Karen too far out of his sight either. She was still at the hospital, praying for a miracle that would bring Ghostdancer back. If he did pull through, his decision regarding Karen would not be rash. All things would work out in Creator's perfect timing.

River looked up. "Is it time?"

Loretta's heart skipped, thinking her friend had read her mind; then she realized River was asking about getting the sweat lodge ready. Loretta and Sayla would share a private Coming-Out of Grief Ceremony. And they would do it in the sweat lodge that Ghostdancer had built. Had he known it would come to this... that Sayla would finally be ready?

"Yes," Loretta said. "It is time."

She looked up at Sacred Mountain glowing silver in the moonlight; then she thought of the words Ghostdancer had once said to her. Yes, she thought, if one lives long enough they will see the shifting shadows that darken Yahweh's smile. But they may also see the light of life that sprouts out of those dark places.

"Creator," she whispered. "If it's not too selfish for an old woman to ask. Would you please return Ghostdancer to us?" Then she had a strange thought and continued her prayer. "And if there are any lingering curses on Ghostdancer, I ask that you break them right now in the name of Jesus Yeshua!"

Immediately she felt as if something had loosened in the spiritual world. She knew Ghostdancer wouldn't like for her to pray him back, but he would just have to get over it. She wasn't quite ready to let him go. And even though the doctors didn't give much hope, there was always hope when Jesus Yeshua was involved. And he was very involved with his creation. She could already feel something shifting.

She smiled at River.

"You're thinkin' about Ghostdancer, ain't you?" River asked.

The young girl was very perceptive.

"Yes," Loretta admitted. "And I'm thinking we need to keep praying. Between that hippy blood you gave him and Creator's amazing grace, there may yet be hope."

River laughed. "Wouldn't that be somethin'?"

They turned and left together to the far-off sound of coyote song and Sayla's music ringing across the pasture. Loretta's heart nearly exploded with the joy of it.

Creator is a river that will never run dry. I drink and am completely satisfied.

Chapter 91

*There is no dark place, no deep shadow
that Creator Yahweh's light cannot fill.
Ghostdancer*

Ghostdancer

"NO MATTER HOW FAR YOU GO, dear reader, no matter how deep the wrong. Whether the sun hangs high in the sky or deep blackness hides the light. Whether your heart is hard as cold winter ice or soft as a newborn lamb. Whether you run with horses or walk with shadows. No matter who you hurt, or who has been hurt because of you, remember . . . not one drop of Creator's blood will ever be lessened.

He spilled his life for you and his arms are always open. One word from you and he will make the shadows fly away."

Pleya gi.

ACKNOWLEDGMENTS

Shaman's Fire was years in the making. The story was in me, along with sequels, but I wasn't ready to write it the way it should be until many people came into my life and mentored me either in writing, spiritual growth, or in Native culture.

THANK YOU!

My Creator Redeemer, my Lord, my Great Chief and Captain to whom I am forever grateful. What a blessing to be a part of Your amazing Story! I am humbled by your love for me.

My husband, The Cat Man, for living these stories with me and holding me together through the rough times. I wouldn't be able to do any of this without you. Your love carries me through.

Diana Shadley for answering "the call" and being a wonderful "chief" in this project. Your direction and encouragement took this vision much higher than I first dreamed.

Calvin "Buttons" "Ghostdancer" and Diana Shadley, Cobby Shadley, and Don and Mary Gentry. Thanks Cobby for taking me and The Cat Man on "tour" up *Cheelaqsdi*. Thanks Mary for letting me walk the land and "dream." Thanks for sharing your stories. Thanks for wonderful meals around your table. Thanks for sharing your hearts and home. My life is so much richer because of your sweet embrace.

Laura Ellen Picard Grabner and Papa Ray Grabner for opening your home and hearts to me.

The following people were special mentors to me on this writing journey: Dr. Rick Booye of Trail Christian Fellowship; Stuart McCallister of Ravi Zacharias International Ministries; Robert Liparulo; Steve Barclift; Bill Watkins; Don Richardson; and Heidi Mitchell.

ACKNOWLEDGMENTS

The following people shared Native culture with me in very special ways: Adam of First Youth Nations; Arrows of Faith; Aaron Gentry; Micayla and Elissa Peacock; Coby Tran; Lana Gentry; Arwin (AWOL) and Stilez and Tiarah Head; Pastor John (Starbucks); Jerry and Marlene; Wiconi International and Casey and Laura Church; Julian and Lupe and Azusa Medel; Joseph and Martha Manzo; Pastor Richard: Ralph Medina (Screaming Eagle); Pastor Dave Gomez; Grand Chief Lynda Prince; Jonathan Maracle; Jerry and Leslie Chapman; Dr. Randy and Edith Woodley; Bill Gowey; Mary Bennet (Dancing Dove); Dr. Suuqiina; Nigeil Bigpond; and Robert Soto. You have all blessed me with your dancing, singing, drumming, and beautiful worship and have enriched my life through sharing your Native culture. Thank you all for being true to the unique person Creator called you to be.

I had many early readers over three drafts of this book. It's been so long I am sorry to say that I have forgotten who some of you are! BUT I so appreciate each and every one of you. If you are not listed here and were an early reader, get hold of me and I'll give you a free, signed copy. Here are the ones I remember: Phil Lemons; Patti Iverson; Larry Schumacher; Heather Kelly; Charles Sutherland; Jackee Randall; Gina Bates; and Barb Haley. Also thanks to my writer friends who helped me along the journey: John Wiuff; Lynn Leissler; Jinny Sherman; Kristen Parr; Garret Miller; Nathan Bailey; Marlene Bagnull; Lori Benton; Lonnie Hull DuPont; Bonnie Leon; Susan Warren; Kathy Tyers; and James L. Rubart.

Pastor Joe and the congregation of Mountain View Church for allowing the cowboys and Indians to gather in your church. Thank you for your heart for Native Youth.

Becky Hyde for sharing your story at Journey to Healing at Klamath Falls and for being a good "listener."

Marjorie Vawter and Linda Brittan for editing this book.

Stella Quilala for taking our "Restoring the Heart" card with you and placing it in the Western Wall on your trip to Israel. What a blessing you are.

ACKNOWLEDGMENTS

The incredibly talented Jeff Bates for cramming us into your busy schedule and coming up with something wonderful for our book trailer. Thank you Gina Bates for being an early reader.

Robert Kruse for his amazing cover art!

Bill Miller for your beautiful songs! I wrote this entire book listening to *The Best of Bill Miller*. "Listen to Me" became Sayla's song. Thank you for allowing us to use your music and words and thanks for sharing your beautiful gift.

First Youth Nations: Henry and Sandy Mena and Chelsea and Ezme Clement. We are proud to donate a portion of the proceeds from this book to your ministry.

GHOSTDANCE
By Bill Miller

I wanna go where the blind can see
I wanna go where the lame will walk
I wanna see the sick ones clean
Where the deaf can hear and the silent talk

Where are you going, to a ghostdance in the snow?
I am a mighty warrior and I'm finally coming home

I wanna go where the dead are raised
Where the mountain lion lays down with the lamb
I wanna stand where God is praised
I wanna ride across the plains to the promised land

Where are we going, to a ghostdance in the snow?
I am a mighty warrior and I'm finally coming home

Where I'm going don't need to raise your voice
No starvation have plenty to eat
No guns no wars, no hateful noise
Just a victory dance, we'll never taste defeat
Where there's nothin' done or said that can't be forgiven
Every step you take is on sacred ground

Walk away from death to the land of the living
Where all the lost tribes are finally found

Where are you going, to the ghostdance in the snow?
I am a mighty warrior and I'm finally coming home

LISTEN TO ME (Sayla's Song)
By Mill Miller

If I took away your shelter, put you on the street
If I took away your table and chairs and threw away your meat
Stole away your wife and child, see how lonesome you would be
Is that what it would take for you to listen to me?

If I took away your legs, you could never walk
If I took away your words, you could never talk
Blinded your eyes, you could never see
Locked you up in shackles, you were no longer free
Is that what it would take for you to listen to me?

(chorus)
Listen to me, I am the thunder you refuse to hear
I am the rock you can't hide under, you have nothing more to fear
This is a time for healing, the scars upon the land
My child, listen to me

If I gave you a blanket, you could be warm
If I gave you a roof to stay under,
would that save you from the storm?
Gave you all the money you could ever spend
Do you think that means your troubles, they would finally end?
Is that what it would take for you to listen to me?

(chorus)

I give you the seed, dig your roots deep in the land
Here's a blade to turn the soil, grow somethin' in the sand
I give you all my blessings, my blood runs through your veins
I will stand beside you, even when it rains
My child, just listen to me

(chorus)

*In Bill's original version "child" is "son."
It is change to "child" here to fit Sayla.

Laura Ellen Picard Grabner

INTERESTING FACTS

The boarding school experience of Loretta Whitewater is completely taken from the true account of what happened to my dear friend Laura Grabner. I have since talked with other Natives who experienced similar "reeducation." I was shocked to discover that these things happened in my lifetime.

The facts regarding the Klamath Tribes dispersement are completely true. The more I learn about how they were made to "sell" their land, the more I am shocked and saddened.

War Paint is patterned after the real-life horse of the same name owned by Ora Summers, Great Uncle of Mary Gentry. Ora later sold War Paint to the Christensen Brothers Rodeo Contractors. As part of the Christensen Brothers string, War Paint was voted the PRCA Bucking Horse of the Year in each of the first three years the honor was bestowed. War Paint, who retired in 1964 after mistreating cowboys for 14 years, was stuffed and mounted after his death in 1976 and placed at the entrance to the Pendleton Round-Up and Happy Canyon Hall of Fame.

The photos of Indian rodeo riders in Loretta's house are actual photos hanging on the walls of Don and Mary Gentry's ranch. Family members were amazing horsemen in their day. Wish I could have been there to see it.

The paintings Gran creates in this book are actual paintings of mine that will soon be offered as prints for sale. I have found great delight in depicting Creator Yahweh's heart through the analogy of the lion.

Today, Klamath Falls is a lot kinder to their Native population, but when I lived there in the seventies prejudice ran high. Sad to say,

FACTS

some of that still lives on and, in some ways, the water wars have made it even worse. However, when whites and Natives get together and actually listen to one another amazing healing and restoration takes place. It is my hope that this story will help promote some of that listening and healing.

ABOUT THE AUTHORS

SANDY CATHCART is an award-winning writer, photographer, and artist. She has traveled extensively, fishing the Sea of Ohotsk in Far East Russia, sailing over Lake Baikal in Siberia, cycling the backroads of China, rowing across the rivers of Vietnam, swimming in Israel's Dead Sea and the Gulf of Mexico, trekking across Peru and Haiti, and hiking across Lantau Island.

Sandy grew up on stories of her Cherokee great grandmother who was a healer in the Red Rock, Arkansas area. Because of these stories and her involvement with Native Americans, she believes in restoration and transformation through giving worth to a people who offer valuable ways of worshiping Creator, the God of the Bible. She has spent the last two years traveling with and documenting the journey of her many Native friends who walk The Jesus Way. She is honored to be called their "scribe."

She and her husband, The Cat Man, just completed nearly two decades as cook and guide for 4E Guide and Supply, a wilderness outfitter in the High Cascades of Oregon. With The Cat Man, she rafts rivers in tahitis, hunts deer and elk, skis cross-country and downhill, canoes marshlands, tracks antelope across the desert, fishes rivers and lakes, sailboards and water skis, climbs mountains, hikes on a daily basis, and just about anything else there is to do in the outdoors.

Sandy writes about Creator and everything wild.

AUTHORS

PASTOR DIANA SHADLEY is affiliated with the Kahnawake Band of Mohawk, First Nations, Quebec, Canada. She became reservation connected when she married Calvin "Buttons" Shadley (Ghostdancer Shadley), a member of the Wasco and Klamath Tribes. They became ministers along with Calvin's extended family as a ministry team. They offered love, support and encouragement to natives, veterans, elders, and homeless people wherever they went. As she walked the Jesus way, as fully Christian and fully native, Diana submitted herself to the teaching of Calvin's mother and respected elder, Laura Grabner. Now, Diana teaches as a widow and elder who is received with honor and respect as a valuable part of the family ministry team.

Diana's message is of how the Creator loves His children and desires to bring His forgiveness, love, reconciliation, and restoration to the wounded warriors who have suffered at the hands of an oppressor. This message is delivered in respect to Native culture with honor and dignity. It teaches and encourages worship of the Creator (Jesus) the way He created each individual, incorporating language, dance, instruments, songs and storytelling.

Made in the USA
Middletown, DE
27 July 2024

58031220R00205